"DESIREE," HE MURMURED. "I LOVE YOU."

With his eyes on hers, he began to unbuckle his belt. She snatched up a paperweight and heaved it as she dashed to the door. It grazed the side of his head.

It was a nightmare, she thought. But dreams didn't hurt. She heard her blouse rip even as she struggled.

"You promised. You promised," he said over and over. He could feel her skin now, soft and hot, just as he'd imagined. Nothing was going to stop him.

The passion was exploding in his head, but not the way he'd wanted. Her screaming was tearing into him, spoiling it. "Stop it!" But she wouldn't stop screaming. She scratched, but the pain only inflamed his need, and fury. She'd lied. This wasn't the way it was supposed to be. She was a liar and a whore, and still he wanted her.

Flinging a hand out, she shoved, knocking over the table. The phone fell on the floor beside her head.

And he took the cord and wrapped it around her throat, pulling hard until the screaming stopped. . . .

Bantam Books by Nora Roberts

Nora Roberts

Brazen Virtue

BANTAM BOOKS

BRAZEN VIRTUE

A Bantam Book

PUBLISHING HISTORY
Bantam paperback edition published May 1988
Bantam hardcover edition / June 2001
Bantam mass market reissue / December 2002

Library of Congress Catalog Card Number: 00-52939

ISBN: 0-553-27283-7

Published simultaneously in the United States and Canada

Bantam Books are published by Bantam Books, a division of Random House,
Inc. Its trademark, consisting of the words "Bantam Books" and the portrayal
of a rooster, is Registered in U.S. Patent and Trademark Office and in other
countries. Marca Registrada. Bantam Books, 1540 Broadway, New York, New
York 10036.

To Amy Berkower
with gratitude and affection

Prologue

"AND WHAT WOULD YOU like me to do to you?" the woman who called herself Desiree asked. She had a voice like rose petals. Soft and sweet. She did her job well, very well, and customers asked for her over and over again. She was talking to one of her repeaters now, and she knew his preferences. "I'd love to," she murmured. "Just close your eyes, close your eyes and relax. I want you to forget all about the office, and your wife, and your business partner. It's just you and me."

When he spoke to her, she answered with a low laugh. "Yes, you know I will. Don't I always? Just close your eyes, and listen. The room's quiet and lit by candles. Dozens of white, scented candles. Can you smell them?" She gave another low, teasing laugh. "That's right. White. The bed's white too, big and round and white. You're lying on it, naked and ready. Are you ready, Mr. Drake?"

She rolled her eyes. It killed her that the guy wanted her to call him mister. But it took all kinds. "I've just come out of the shower. My hair's wet, and there are little beads of water all over my body. There's a drop clinging to my nipple. It slides off and onto you as I kneel on the bed. Feel it? Yes, yes, that's right, it's cool, cool, and you're so hot." She fought back a yawn. Mr. Drake was already breathing like a steam engine. Thank God he was so easily satisfied. "Oh, I want you. I can't keep my hands off you. I want to touch you, to taste you. Yes, yes, it drives me crazy when you do that. Oh, Mr. Drake, you're the best. The very best."

For the next few minutes she just listened to his demands and delights. Listening was the biggest part of her job. He was right on the edge now, and she glanced at her watch, grateful. Not only was his time almost up, but he was her last customer of the evening. Dropping her voice to a whisper, she helped him go over the top.

"Yes, Mr. Drake, it was wonderful. You're wonderful. No, I'm not working tomorrow. Friday? Yes, I'll look forward to it. Good night, Mr. Drake."

She listened for the click, then hung up the phone. Desiree became Kathleen. Ten-fifty-five, she thought with a sigh. She was off at eleven, so there should be no more calls that night. She had papers to grade, and a pop quiz to make up for her students for tomorrow. As she rose, she glanced at the phone. She'd made two hundred tonight, thanks to AT&T and Fantasy, Incorporated. With a laugh, she picked up her coffee cup. It was a hell of a lot better than selling magazines.

Only miles away, another man clung to the phone receiver. His hand was damp. The room smelled of sex, but he was alone. In his mind Desiree had been there. Desiree with her white, wet body and her cool, soothing voice.

Desiree.

With his heart still pumping fast, he stretched out on his bed.

Desiree.

He had to meet her. And soon.

Chapter 1

THE PLANE BANKED OVER the Lincoln Memorial. Grace had her briefcase open on her lap. There were a dozen things to be packed away, but she stared out the window, pleased to see the ground rushing up toward her. There was nothing, as far as she was concerned, that was quite the same as flying.

The plane was late. She knew that because the man across from her in seat 3B kept complaining about it. Grace was tempted to reach across the aisle and pat his hand, to assure him that ten minutes in the scheme of things really didn't matter so much. But he didn't look as though he would appreciate the sentiment.

Kathleen would be complaining too, she thought. Not out loud or anything, Grace mused as she smiled and settled back for the landing. Kathleen might have been just as irritated as 3B, but she would never have been rude enough to mumble and moan.

If Grace knew her sister, and she did, Kathleen would have left home over an hour before, making certain to take into consideration the unpredictability of Washington traffic. Grace had heard the note in Kathleen's voice betraying her annoyance with Grace that she'd chosen a flight that would arrive at six-fifteen, the height of rush hour. With twenty minutes to spare, Kathleen would have parked her car in the short-term lot, rolled up the windows, locked the doors, and made her way, without being tempted by the shops, to the gate. She would never have gotten lost or mixed the numbers up in her mind.

Kathleen was always early. Grace was always late. That was nothing new.

Still she hoped, really hoped, there could be some common ground between them now. Sisters they were, but they had rarely understood each other.

The plane bumped to earth and Grace began tossing whatever came to hand into her briefcase. Lipstick tumbled in with matchbooks, pens with tweezers. That was something else a woman as organized as Kathleen would never understand. A place for everything. Grace agreed in principle, but her place never seemed to be the same from one time to the next.

More than once, Grace had wondered how they could be sisters. She was careless, scatterbrained, and successful. Kathleen was organized, practical, and struggling. Yet they had come from the same parents, had been raised in the same small brick house in the suburbs of D.C., and had gone to the same schools.

The nuns had never been able to teach Grace anything about organizing a notebook, but even as far back as sixth grade at St. Michael's, they had been fascinated by her skill at spinning a tale.

When the plane was at the gate, Grace waited while the passengers who were in a hurry to deplane clogged the aisle. She knew Kathleen would probably be pacing, certain that her absentminded sister had missed a flight again, but she needed a minute. She wanted to remember the love, not the arguments.

As Grace had predicted, Kathleen was waiting at the gate. She watched the passengers file off and felt another flash of impatience. Grace always traveled first-class, but she wasn't among the first people off the plane. She wasn't among the first fifty. Probably chatting with the flight crew, Kathleen thought, and tried to ignore a quick stab of envy.

Grace had never had to try to make friends. People were simply drawn to her. Two years after graduation and Grace, who had skimmed through school on charm, had been rising in her career. A lifetime later and Kathleen, the honor student, was spinning her wheels in the same high school they had graduated from. She sat on the other side of the desk now, but little else had changed.

Announcements for incoming and outgoing planes droned on. There were gate changes and delays, but still no Grace. Just as Kathleen had decided to check at the desk, she saw her sister walk through the gate. Envy faded. Irritation vanished. It was next to impossible to be annoyed with Grace when faced with her.

Why was it she always looked as though she'd just stepped off a merry-go-round? Her hair, the same dark sable as Kathleen's, was cut to the chin and looked forever windswept around her face. Her body was long and lean, again like Kathleen's, but where Kathleen always felt sturdy, Grace looked like a willow, ready to bend whichever way the breeze beckoned. Now she looked rumpled, a hip-length sweater riding over leggings, sunglasses falling down her nose, and her hands full of bags and briefcases. Kathleen was still dressed in the skirt and jacket that had gotten her through her history classes. Grace wore high-top jogging shoes in canary yellow to match her sweater.

"Kath!" The moment she saw her sister, Grace set everything down without giving a thought to blocking the flow of passengers behind her. She hugged as she did everything, with full enthusiasm. "I'm so glad to see you. You look wonderful. New perfume." She took a big sniff. "I like it."

"Lady, you want to move?"

Still hugging Kathleen, Grace smiled at the harassed businessman behind her. "Go right ahead and step over them." He did, grumbling. "Have a nice flight." She forgot him as she forgot most inconveniences. "So how do I look?" she demanded. "Do you like the hair? I hope so, I just spent a fortune on publicity shots."

"Did you brush it first?"

Grace lifted a hand to it. "Probably."

"It suits you," Kathleen decided. "Come on, we'll have a riot in here if we don't move your things. What's this?" She hefted one of the cases.

"Maxwell." Grace began to gather bags. "Portable computer. We've been having the most marvelous affair."

"I thought this was a vacation." She managed to keep the edge out of her voice. The computer was one more physical example of Grace's success. And her own failure.

"It is. But I have to do something with myself while you're in school. If the plane had been another ten minutes late I would have finished a chapter." She glanced at her watch, noticed it had stopped again, then forgot it. "Really, Kath, this is the most marvelous murder."

"Luggage?" Kathleen interrupted, knowing Grace would launch into the tale without any encouragement.

"My trunk should be delivered to your place by tomorrow."

The trunk was another of what Kathleen considered her sister's deliberate eccentricities. "Grace, when are you going to start using suitcases like normal people?"

They passed baggage claim, where people stood three deep, ready to trample each other at the first sign of familiar Samsonite. When hell freezes over, Grace thought, but only smiled. "You really do look great. How are you feeling?"

"Fine." Then because it was her sister, Kathleen relaxed. "Better, really."

"You're better off without the sonofabitch," Grace said as they passed through the automatic doors. "I hate to say it because I know you really loved him, but it's true." There was a stiff northern breeze to make people forget it was spring. The sound of incoming and outgoing planes hammered overhead. Grace stepped off the curb toward the parking lot without looking right or left. "The only real joy he brought to your life was Kevin. Where is my nephew, anyway? I was hoping you'd bring him."

The little slice of pain came and went. When Kathleen made up her mind about something, she also made up her heart. "He's with his father. We agreed that it would be best if he stayed with Jonathan through the school year."

"What?" Grace stopped in the middle of the street. A horn blasted and was ignored. "Kathleen, you can't be serious. Kevin's just six. He needs to be with you. Jonathan probably has him watching *MacNeil-Lehrer* instead of *Sesame Street.*"

"The decision is made. We agreed it would be best for everyone involved."

Grace knew that expression. It meant Kathleen had closed up and wouldn't open again until she was damn good and ready. "Okay." Grace fell into step beside her as they crossed to the parking lot. Automatically, she altered her rhythm. Kathleen always rushed. Grace meandered. "You know you can talk to me whenever you want."

"I know." Kathleen paused beside a secondhand Toyota. A year before she'd been driving a Mercedes. But that was the least of what she'd lost. "I didn't mean to snap at you, Grace. It's just that I need to put it aside for a while. I've almost got my life back in order."

Grace set her bags in the rear and said nothing. She knew the car was secondhand and a long step down from what Kathleen had been accustomed to but was much more worried about the edge in her sister's voice than the change of status. She wanted to comfort but knew that Kathleen considered sympathy the first cousin of pity. "Have you talked to Mom and Dad?"

"Last week. They're fine." Kathleen slid in, then strapped on her seat belt. "You'd think Phoenix was paradise."

"As long as they're happy." Grace sat back and for the first time took in her surroundings. National Airport. She'd taken her first flight out of there, eight, no, dear Lord, almost ten years before. And had been scared right down to her toenails. She almost wished she could experience that same fresh and innocent feeling again.

Getting jaded, Gracie? she wondered. Too many flights. Too many cities. Too many people. Now she was back, only a few miles from the home where she'd grown up, and seated beside her sister. Yet she felt no sense of homecoming.

"What made you come back to Washington, Kath?"

"I wanted to get out of California. And this was familiar."

But didn't you want to stay near your son? Didn't you need to? It wasn't the time to ask, but she had to fight the words back. "And teaching at Our Lady of Hope. Familiar again, but it must be strange."

"I like it really. I suppose I need the discipline of classes." She drove out of the parking lot with studied precision. Tucked into the flap of the sun visor were the parking stub for the short-term lot and three singles. Grace noted she still counted her change.

"And the house, do you like it?"

"The rent's reasonable and it's only a fifteen-minute drive to school."

Grace bit back a sigh. Couldn't Kathleen ever feel strongly about anything. "Are you seeing anyone?"

"No." But she smiled a little as she merged with traffic. "I'm not interested in sex."

Grace's brow rose. "Everyone's interested in sex. Why do you think Jackie Collins always makes the best-seller list? In any case, I was speaking more of companionship."

"There's no one I want to be with right now." Then she laid a hand on top of Grace's, which was as much as she had ever been able to give to anyone except her husband and son. "Except you. I really am glad you came."

As always, Grace responded to warmth when warmth was given. "I'd have come sooner if you'd let me."

"You were in the middle of a tour."

"Tours can be canceled." Her shoulders moved restlessly. She'd never considered herself temperamental or arrogant, but she would have been both if it would have helped Kathleen. "Anyway, the tour's over and I'm here. Washington in the spring." She rolled the window down though the April wind still had the bite of March. "How about the cherry blossoms?"

"They got hit with a late frost."

"Nothing changes." Did they still have so little to say to each other? Grace let the radio fill the gap as they drove. How could two people grow up together, live together, fight together, and still be strangers? Each time she hoped it would be different. Each time it was the same.

As they crossed the Fourteenth Street Bridge, she remembered the room she and Kathleen had shared throughout childhood. Neat as a pin on one side, tumbled and messy on the other. That had been only one bone of contention. There had been the games that Grace had invented, which had frustrated more than amused her sister. What were the rules? Learning the rules had always been Kathleen's first priority. And when there weren't any, or they were too flexible, she simply hadn't been able to grasp the game itself.

Always rules, Kath, Grace thought as she rode in

silence beside her sister. School, church, life. No wonder she was always confused when the rules changed. Now they'd changed on her again.

Did you quit marriage, Kathy, the way you used to quit the game when the rules didn't suit you? Did you come back to where we started so you could wipe out the time in between and restart, on your own terms? That was Kathleen's style, Grace thought, and hoped for her sister's sake it worked.

The only thing that surprised her was the street on which Kathleen had chosen to live. An efficiency apartment with up-to-date appliances and twenty-four-hour maintenance would have been more Kathleen's style than this tired, slightly run-down neighborhood of big trees and old houses.

Kathleen's was one of the smallest homes on the block, and though Grace was sure her sister had done nothing to the little patch of grass other than trim it, some bulbs were beginning to push their way through along the walk that had been carefully swept.

As she stood beside the car, Grace let her gaze roam up and down the street. There were bikes and aging station wagons and little fresh paint. Used, worn, lived in, the neighborhood was either on the edge of a renaissance or ready to slide slowly into old age. She liked it, liked the feel of it.

It was precisely what she would have chosen if she had decided to move back. And if she'd had to choose a house . . . it would be the one next door, Grace decided on the spot. It was in definite need of help. One of the windows was boarded up and some shingles were missing from the roof, but someone had planted azaleas. The dirt was still fresh and patted into mounds at their base, and they were small, only a foot or so high. But the little buds were almost ready to burst open. Looking at them, she hoped she'd be able to stay long enough to see them flower.

"Oh, Kath, what a wonderful spot."

"It's a long way from Palm Springs." She said it without bitterness as she started to unload her sister's things.

"No, honey, I mean it. It's a real home." She did mean it. With her writer's eye and imagination she could already see it.

"I wanted to be able to give Kevin something when—when he comes."

"He'll love it." She spoke with the confidence she carried like a flag. "This is definitely a skateboard sidewalk. And the trees." There was one across the street that looked as though it had been struck by lightning and never recovered, but Grace passed over it without breaking rhythm. "Kath, looking at this makes me wonder what the hell I'm doing in upper Manhattan."

"Getting rich and famous." Again it was said without bitterness as she passed bags to Grace.

For the second time Grace's gaze drifted to the house next door. "I wouldn't mind having a couple of azaleas as well." She linked arms with Kathleen. "Well, show me the rest."

The interior wasn't as much of a surprise. Kathleen preferred things neat and orderly. The furniture was sturdy, dust-free, and tasteful. Just like Kathleen, Grace thought with a twinge of regret. Still, she liked the hodgepodge of small rooms that seemed to tumble into each other.

Kathleen had turned one into an office. The desk still shone with newness. She'd taken nothing with her, Grace thought. Not even her son. Though she found it odd that Kathleen should indulge in a phone on the desk and another a few feet away beside a chair, she didn't comment. Knowing Kathleen, the reason would make perfect sense.

"Spaghetti sauce." The scent led Grace unerringly into the kitchen. If anyone had asked her to name her favorite pastimes, eating would have topped the list.

The kitchen was as spotless as the rest of the house. If

Grace made bets, she'd wager there wasn't a crumb to be found in the toaster. Leftovers woud be neatly sealed and labeled in the refrigerator and glasses would be arranged according to size in the cupboards. That was Kathleen's way, and Kathleen hadn't changed a whit in thirty years.

Grace hoped she'd remembered to wipe her feet as she crossed the aging linoleum. Lifting the lid off a slow cooker, she breathed in, long and deep. "I'd say you haven't lost your touch."

"It came back to me." Even after years of cooks and servants. "Hungry?" Then, for the first time, her smile seemed genuine and relaxed. "Why do I ask?"

"Wait, I've got something."

As her sister dashed back into the hall, Kathleen turned to the window. Why was she suddenly aware of how empty the house had been now that Grace was in it? What magic did her sister have that filled a room, a house, an arena? And what in God's name was she going to do when she was alone again?

"Valpolicella," Grace announced as she came back into the room. "As you can see, I was counting on Italian." When Kathleen turned from the window, the tears were just starting. "Oh, honey." With the bottle still in her hand, Grace rushed forward.

"Gracie, I miss him so much. Sometimes I think I could die."

"I know you do. Oh, baby, I know. I'm so sorry." She stroked the hair Kathleen brushed firmly back. "Let me help, Kathleen. Tell me what I can do."

"There's nothing." The effort cost more than she would have admitted, but she stopped the tears. "I'd better make the salad."

"Hold on." With one hand on her sister's arm, Grace led her to the small kitchen table. "Sit. I mean it, Kathleen."

Though she was older by a year, Kathleen bowed

before authority. That was something else that had become a habit. "I really don't want to talk about it, Grace."

"I guess that's too bad then. Corkscrew?"

"Top drawer left of the sink."

"Glasses?"

"Second shelf, cabinet next to the refrigerator."

Grace opened the bottle. Though the sky was darkening, she didn't bother with the kitchen light. After setting a glass in front of Kathleen, she filled it to just below the rim. "Drink. It's damn good stuff." She found an empty Kraft mayonnaise jar, just where her mother would have kept them, and removed the lid for an ashtray. She knew how much Kathleen disapproved of smoking and had been determined to be on her best behavior. Like most of Grace's vows to herself, this one was easily broken. She lit a cigarette, poured her own wine, and then took a seat. "Talk to me, Kathy. I'll only badger you until you do."

She would, too. Kathleen had known that before she'd agreed to let her come. Perhaps that was why she had agreed. "I didn't want the separation. And you don't have to say I'm stupid to want to hang on to a man who doesn't want me, because I already know."

"I don't think you're stupid." Grace blew out smoke a bit guiltily because she had thought just that, more than once. "You love Jonathan and Kevin. They were yours and you want to keep them."

"I guess that sums it up." She took a second, longer sip of wine. Grace was right again. It was good stuff. It was hard to admit, hateful to admit, but she needed to talk to someone. She wanted that someone to be Grace because, no matter what their differences, Grace would be unquestioningly on her side. "It came to a point where I had to agree to separate." She still couldn't form the word *divorce*. "Jonathan . . . abused me."

"What do you mean?" Her low, slightly husky voice

had barbs in it. "Did he hit you?" She was half out of her chair, ready to hop the next flight to the coast.

"There are other kinds of abuse," Kathleen said wearily. "He humiliated me. There were other women, plenty of them. Oh, he was very discreet. I doubt if even his broker knew, but he made sure I did. Just to rub my nose in it."

"I'm sorry." Grace sat down again. She knew Kathleen would have preferred a sock on the jaw to infidelity. When she thought it over, Grace had to admit she and her sister agreed—on that, at least.

"You never liked him."

"No, and I'm not sorry." Grace flicked an ash into the lid of the empty mayonnaise jar.

"I guess there's no point in it now. In any case, when I agreed to separate, Jonathan made it clear it was going to be on his terms. He would file, the terms would be no-fault. Just like a fender bender. Eight years of my life over, and no one to blame."

"Kath, you know you didn't have to accept his terms. If he'd been unfaithful, you had a recourse."

"How could I prove it?" This time there was bitterness, hot and sharp. She'd waited a long time to set it free. "You have to understand what kind of world it is out there, Grace. Jonathan Breezewood the third is a man above reproach. He's a lawyer, for God's sake, a partner in the family firm that could represent the devil against God Almighty and come away with a settlement. Even if anyone had known or suspected, they wouldn't have helped me. They were friends with Jonathan's wife. Mrs. Jonathan Breezewood III. That's been my identity for eight years." And next to Kevin, that was the most difficult to lose. "Not one of them would give a hang about Kathleen McCabe. It was my mistake. I devoted myself to being Mrs. Breezewood. I had to be the perfect wife, the perfect hostess, the perfect mother and homemaker. And I became boring. When I bored him enough, he wanted to be rid of me."

"Goddamn it, Kathleen, must you always be your own worst critic?" Grace stabbed out her cigarette and reached for her wine. "He's at fault, for Chrissake, not you. You gave him exactly what he said he wanted. You gave up your career, your family, your home, and centered your life on him. Now you're going to give up again, and toss Kevin into the bargain."

"I'm not giving Kevin up."

"You told me—"

"I didn't argue with Jonathan, I couldn't. I was afraid of what he'd do."

Very carefully, Grace set down her wine again. "Afraid of what he'd do to you, or to Kevin?"

"Not to Kevin," she said quickly. "Whatever Jonathan is or has done, he'd never do anything to harm Kevin. He really adores him. And despite the fact that he was a bad husband, he's a wonderful father."

"All right." But Grace would reserve judgment on that. "You were afraid of what he'd do to you then. Physically?"

"Jonathan rarely loses his temper. He keeps it under tight control because it's very violent. Once, when Kevin was just a baby, I gave him a pet, a kitten." Kathleen picked her way carefully through the story, knowing Grace always could take crumbs and make a whole cake. "They were playing and the kitten scratched Kevin. Jonathan was so outraged when he saw the marks on Kevin's face that he threw the kitten off the balcony. From the third floor."

"I always said he was a prince," Grace mumbled and took another sip.

"Then there was the assistant gardener. The man had dug up one of the rosebushes by mistake. It was just a misunderstanding, he didn't speak very much English. Jonathan fired him on the spot, and they argued. Before it was over, Jonathan had beaten the man so badly he had to be hospitalized."

"Good God."

"Jonathan paid the bill, of course."

"Of course," Grace agreed, but sarcasm was wasted.

"He paid him off to keep it out of the papers. It was just a rosebush. I don't know what he would do if I tried to transplant Kevin."

"Kath, honey, you're his mother. You have rights. I'm sure there are some excellent lawyers in Washington. We'll go see some, find out what can be done."

"I've already hired one." Because her mouth was dry, Kathleen sipped again. The wine made the words come easier. "And I've hired a detective. It isn't going to be easy, and I've already been told it could take a great deal of time and money, but it's a chance."

"I'm proud of you." Grace linked hands with her sister. The sun had almost set and the room was in shadows. Grace's eyes, as gray as the light, heated. "Honey, Jonathan Breezewood the third is in for a surprise when he runs into the McCabes. I've got some connections out on the coast."

"No, Grace, I have to keep this quiet. Nobody is to know, not even Mom and Dad. I just can't take the chance."

She considered the Breezewoods a moment. Old families, old, wealthy families, had long tentacles. "All right, that's probably best. I can still help. Lawyers and detectives cost money. I've got more than I need."

For the second time, Kathleen's eyes filled. This time she managed to clear them again. She knew Grace had money and didn't want to resent the fact that she'd earned it. But she did. Oh God, she did. "I have to do this myself."

"This isn't the time for pride. You can't fight a battle like this on a teacher's salary. Just because you were an idiot and let Jonathan sweep you out without a penny isn't any reason to refuse money from me."

"I didn't want anything from Jonathan. I came out of the marriage with exactly what I went into it with. Three thousand dollars."

"We won't get into women's rights and the fact that you earned something after eight years of marriage." Grace was an activist if and when it suited her. "The point is I'm your sister, and I want to help."

"Not with money. Maybe it is pride, but I have to do this myself. I'm moonlighting."

"What—selling Tupperware? Tutoring kids on the Battle of New Orleans? Hooking?"

With the first good laugh she'd had in weeks, Kathleen poured more wine for both of them. "That's right."

"You're selling Tupperware?" Grace considered it a moment. "Do they still have those little cereal bowls with the lids?"

"I have no idea. I'm not selling Tupperware." She took a long drink. "I'm hooking."

As Kathleen got up to turn on the overhead light, Grace picked up her own glass. It was a rare thing for Kathleen to make a joke, so she wasn't sure whether to laugh or not. She decided against it. "I thought you said you weren't interested in sex."

"Not for myself, at least not at the moment. I make a dollar a minute for a seven-minute call, ten dollars for the call if it's a repeater. Most of mine are. I average twenty calls a night, three days a week, plus twenty-five to thirty on weekends. That comes out to roughly nine hundred dollars a week."

"Jesus." Her first thought was that her sister had a hell of a lot more energy than she'd suspected. Her second was that the whole thing was a huge joke to get her to mind her own business.

In the harsh fluorescent light, Grace stared at her sister. There was nothing in Kathleen's eyes to indicate she was joking. But Grace recognized that self-satisfied look. It was the same one she'd worn when she'd been twelve and Kathleen had sold five more boxes of Girl Scout cookies than Grace had.

"Jesus," she said again and lit another cigarette.

"No lecture on morality, Gracie?"

"No." Grace lifted her wine and swallowed hard. She wasn't quite sure where she stood on the subject morally, not yet. "It's going to sink in in a minute. You're serious?"

"Perfectly."

Of course. Kathleen was always serious. Twenty a night, she thought again, then shook that image away. "No lecture on morality, but you're about to get one on common sense. Good God, Kathleen, do you know what kind of creeps and maniacs there are out there? Even I know, and I haven't had a date that wasn't business oriented in almost six months. And it's not only a matter of getting pregnant, it's a matter of catching something you won't be able to bounce on your knee in nine months. It's stupid, Kathleen, stupid and dangerous. And you're going to stop right now or I'll—"

"Tell Mom?" Kathleen suggested.

"This isn't a joke." Grace shifted uncomfortably because that had been precisely what had been on the tip of her tongue. "If you won't think of yourself, think of Kevin. If Jonathan gets wind of this you haven't a prayer of getting him back."

"I am thinking of Kevin. He's all I do think about now. Drink your wine, Grace, and listen. You always were prone to spin out a story without having all the facts."

"It's fact enough that my sister is moonlighting as a call girl, if an amazingly resilient one."

"That's exactly it. A call girl. I'm selling my voice, Grace, not my body."

"A couple of glasses of wine and my brain fogs right up. Why don't you spell it out for me, Kathleen?"

"I work for Fantasy, Incorporated. It's a small store-front operation that specializes in phone services."

"Phone services?" she repeated as she blew out smoke. "Phone services?" This time both eyebrows rose. "Are you talking about phone sex?"

"Talking about sex is the closest I've come in a year."

"A year?" Grace had to swallow that first. "I'd offer my sympathies, but at the moment I'm too fascinated. You mean you're doing what they advertise in the back of men's magazines?"

"Since when did you start reading men's magazines?"

"Research. And you're saying you make almost a thousand a week talking to men over the phone?"

"I've always had a good voice."

"Yeah." Grace sat back to take it in. In all of her life she couldn't remember Kathleen doing one single unconventional thing. She'd even waited until marriage to sleep with Jonathan. Grace knew because she'd asked. Both of them. Then it struck her not only how out of character it was but how funny. "Sister Mary Francis said you had the best speaking voice in the eighth grade. I wonder what the poor old dear would say if she knew her best student was a phone whore."

"I'm not particularly fond of that term, Grace."

"Oh come on, it has a nice ring." She chuckled into her wine. "Sorry. Well, tell me how it works."

She should have known Grace would see the lighter side of it. With Grace you rarely got recriminations. The muscles in Kathleen's shoulders unknotted as she drank again. "The men call Fantasy's office, if they're repeaters they might ask for a specific woman. If they're new, they're asked to list their preferences so they can be set up with someone suitable."

"What sort of preferences?"

Kathleen knew Grace had a tendency to interview. Three glasses of wine kept her from being annoyed. "Some men like to do most of the talking, about what they'd do to the woman, what they're doing to themselves. Others like the woman to talk, just sort of walk them through, you know. They want her to describe herself, what she's wearing, the room. Some of them want to talk about S and M or bondage. I don't take those calls."

Grace struggled to take it all seriously. "You only talk straight sex."

For the first time in months, Kathleen felt pleasantly relaxed. "That's right. And I'm good at it. I'm very popular."

"Congratulations."

"Anyway, the men call, they leave their phone number and the number of a major credit card. The office makes sure the card's good, then contacts one of us. If I agree to take the call, I phone the man back on the telephone Fantasy had installed here, but that's billed directly to the office address."

"Of course. And then?"

"Then we talk."

"Then you talk," Grace murmured. "That's why you have the extra phone in your office."

"You always notice the little things." Kathleen realized, with no small satisfaction, that she was well on her way to getting drunk. It felt good to have a buzz in her head, the weight off her shoulders, and her sister across the table.

"Kath, what's to keep these guys from finding out your name and address? One of them might decide he doesn't just want to talk anymore."

She shook her head as she carefully wiped the slight ring from the glass off the table. "Fantasy's employees' files are strictly confidential. The callers are never, under any circumstances, given our number. Most of us use false names too. I'm Desiree."

"Desiree," Grace repeated with some respect.

"I'm five-two, blond, and have a body that won't quit."

"No shit?" Though she held her liquor better, Grace had eaten nothing that day but a Milky Way on the way to the airport. The idea of Kathleen having an alter ego not only seemed plausible but logical. "Congratulations again. But, Kath, say one of the people at Fantasy decided he wanted closer employer/employee relations?"

"You're writing a book again," Kathleen said dismissively.

"Maybe, but—"

"Grace, it's perfectly safe. This is a simple business arrangement. All I do is talk, the men get their money's worth, I'm paid well, and Fantasy gets its cut. Everyone's happy."

"Sounds logical." Grace swirled her wine and tried to push away any doubts. "And trendy. The new wave of sex as we rush toward the nineties. You can't get AIDS from a phone call."

"Medically sound. Why are you laughing?"

"Just getting a picture." Grace wiped the back of her hand across her mouth. " 'Afraid of commitment, tired of the singles scene? Call Fantasy, Incorporated, talk to Desiree, Delilah, or DeeDee. Orgasms guaranteed or your money back. Major credit cards accepted.' Christ, I should be writing ad copy."

"I have never considered it a joke."

"You never considered enough in life a joke," Grace said, not unkindly. "Listen, the next time you're working, can I sit in?"

"No."

Grace shrugged off the refusal. "Well, let's talk about it later. When do we eat?"

When she slipped into bed that night in Kathleen's guest room, full of pasta and wine, Grace felt an ease about her sister she hadn't felt since they'd been children. She didn't know the last time she and Kathleen had sat up late, drinking and talking, like friends. It was hard to admit that they never had.

Kathleen was finally doing something unusual, and standing up for herself while she was about it. As long as it didn't bring her sister any trouble, Grace was thrilled. Kathleen was taking charge of her life. And she was going to be just fine.

*H*E LISTENED FOR THREE hours that night, waiting for her. Desiree never came. There were other women, of course, with exotic names and sexy voices, but they weren't Desiree. Curled up in bed, he tried to get himself off by imagining her voice, but it wasn't enough. So he lay, frustrated and sweaty, wondering when he would work up the nerve to go to her.

Soon, he thought. She'd be so happy to see him. She'd take him to her, undress him just the way she described. And let him touch her. Wherever he wanted. It had to be soon.

In the shadowy moonlight he rose and went back to his computer. He wanted to see it again before he went to sleep. The terminal came on with a quiet hum. His fingers, thin but competent, tapped out a series of numbers. In seconds the address came up on the screen. Desiree's address.

Soon.

Chapter 2

GRACE HEARD THE LOW, droning buzz and blamed it on the wine. She didn't groan or grumble about the hangover. She'd been taught that every sin, venial or mortal, required penance. It was one of the few aspects of her early Catholic training she carried with her into adulthood.

The sun was up and strong enough to filter through the gauzy curtains at the windows. In defense, she buried her face in the pillow. She managed to block out the light, but not the buzzing. She was awake, and hating it.

Thinking of aspirin and coffee, she pushed herself up in bed. It was then she realized the buzzing wasn't inside her head, but outside the house. She rummaged through one of her bags and came up with a ratty terry-cloth robe. In her closet at home was a silk one, a gift from a former lover. Grace had fond memories of the lover, but preferred the terry-cloth robe. Still groggy, she stumbled to the window and pushed the curtain aside.

It was a beautiful day, cool and smelling just faintly of spring and turned earth. There was a sagging chain-link fence separating her sister's yard from the yard next door.

Tangled and pitiful against it was a forsythia bush. It was struggling to bloom, and Grace thought its tiny yellow flowers looked brave and daring. It hadn't occurred to her until then how tired she was of hothouse flowers and perfect petals. On a huge yawn, she looked beyond it.

She saw him then, in the backyard of the house next door. Long narrow boards were braced on sawhorses. With the kind of easy competence she admired, he measured and marked and cut through. Intrigued, Grace shoved the window up to get a better look. The morning air was chill, but she leaned into it, pleased that it cleared her head. Like the forsythia, he was something to see.

Paul Bunyan, she thought, and grinned. The man had to be six-four if he was an inch and built along the lines of a fullback. Even with the distance she could see the power of his muscles moving under his jacket. He had a mane of red hair and a full beard—not a trimmed little affectation, but the real thing. She could just see his mouth move in its cushion in time to the country music that jingled out of a portable radio.

When the buzzing stopped, she was smiling down at him, her elbows resting on the sill. "Hi," she called. Her smile widened as he turned and looked up. She'd noticed that his body had braced as he'd turned, not so much in surprise, she thought, but in readiness. "I like your house."

Ed relaxed as he saw the woman in the window. He'd put in over sixty hours that week, and had killed a man. The sight of a pretty woman smiling at him from a second-story window did a lot to soothe his worn nerves. "Thanks."

"You fixing it up?"

"Bit by bit." He shaded his eyes against the sun and studied her. She wasn't his neighbor. Though he and Kathleen Breezewood hadn't exchanged more than a dozen words, he knew her by sight. But there was something familiar in the grinning face and tousled hair. "You visiting?"

"Yes, Kathy's my sister. I guess she's gone already. She teaches."

"Oh." He'd learned more about his neighbor in two seconds than he had in two months. Her nickname was Kathy, she had a sister, and she was a teacher. Ed hefted another board onto the horses. "Staying long?"

"I'm not sure." She leaned out a bit farther so the breeze ruffled her hair. It was a small indulgence the pace and convenience of New York had denied her. "Did you plant the azaleas out front?"

"Yeah. Last week."

"They're terrific. I think I'll put some in for Kath." She smiled again. "See you." She pulled her head inside and was gone.

For a minute longer Ed stared at the empty window. She'd left it open, he noted, and the temperature had yet to climb to sixty. He took out his carpenter's pencil to mark the wood. He knew that face. It was both a matter of business and personality that he never forgot one. It would come to him.

Inside, Grace pulled on a pair of sweats. Her hair was still damp from the shower, but she wasn't in the mood to fuss with blow dryers and styling brushes. There was coffee to be drunk, a paper to be read, and a murder to be solved. By her calculations, she could put Maxwell to work and have enough carved out to be satisfied before Kathleen returned from Our Lady of Hope.

Downstairs, she put on the coffee, then checked out the contents of the refrigerator. The best bet was the spaghetti left over from the night before. Grace bypassed eggs and pulled out the neat plastic container. It took her a minute to realize that her sister's kitchen wasn't civilized enough to have a microwave. Taking this in stride, she tossed the top into the sink and dug in. She'd eat it cold. Chewing, she spotted the note on the kitchen table. Kathleen always left notes.

Help yourself to whatever's in the kitchen. Grace smiled and forked more cold spaghetti into her mouth. *Don't worry about dinner, I'll pick up a couple steaks.* And that, she thought, was Kathleen's polite way of telling her not to mess up the kitchen. *Parent conference this afternoon. I'll be home by five-thirty. Don't use the phone in my office.*

Grace wrinkled her nose as she stuffed the note into her pocket. It would take time, and some pressure, but she was determined to learn more of her sister's moonlighting adventures. And there was the matter of finding out the name of her sister's lawyer. Kathleen's objections and pride aside, Grace wanted to speak to him personally. If she did so carefully enough, her sister's ego wouldn't be bruised. In any case, sometimes you had to overlook a couple of bruises and shoot for the goal. Until she had Kevin back, Kathleen would never be able to put her life in order. That scum Breezewood had no right using Kevin as a weapon against Kathleen.

He'd always been an operator, she thought. Jonathan Breezewood the third was a cold and calculating manipulator who used family position and monied politics to get his way. But not this time. It might take some maneuvering, but Grace would find a way to set things right.

She turned the heat off under the coffeepot just as someone knocked on the front door.

Her trunk, she decided, and snatched up the carton of spaghetti as she started down the hall. An extra ten bucks should convince the delivery man to haul it upstairs. She had a persuasive smile ready as she opened the door.

"G. B. McCabe, right?" Ed stood on the stoop with a hardback copy of *Murder in Style*. He'd nearly sawed a finger off when he'd put the name together with the face.

"That's right." She glanced at the picture on the back cover. Her hair had been styled and crimped, and the photographer had used stark black and white to make her look mysterious. "You've got a good eye. I barely recognize myself from that picture."

Now that he was here, he hadn't the least idea what to do with himself. This kind of thing always happened, he knew, whenever he acted on impulse. Especially with a woman. "I like your stuff. I guess I've read most of it."

"Only most of it?" Grace stuck the fork back in the spaghetti as she smiled at him. "Don't you know that writers have huge and fragile egos? You're supposed to say you've read every word I've ever written and adored them all."

He relaxed a little because her smile demanded he do so. "How about 'you tell a hell of a story'?"

"That'll do."

"When I realized who you were, I guess I just wanted to come over and make sure I was right."

"Well, you win the prize. Come on in."

"Thanks." He shifted the book to his other hand and felt like an idiot. "But I don't want to bother you."

Grace gave him a long, solemn look. He was even more impressive up close than he'd been from the window. And his eyes were blue, a dark, interesting blue. "You mean you don't want me to sign that?"

"Well, yes, but—"

"Come in then." She took his arm and pulled him inside. "The coffee's hot."

"I don't drink it."

"Don't drink coffee? How do you stay alive?" Then she smiled and gestured with her fork. "Come on back anyway, there's probably something you can drink. So you like mysteries?"

He liked the way she walked, slowly, carelessly, as though she could change her mind about direction at any moment. "I guess you could say mysteries are my life."

"Mine too." In the kitchen, she opened the refrigerator again. "No beer," she murmured and decided to remedy that at the first opportunity. "No sodas, either. Christ, Kathy. There's juice. It looks like orange."

"Fine."

"I've got some spaghetti here. Want to share?"

"No, thanks. Is that your breakfast?"

"Mmmm." She poured his juice, gesturing casually to a chair as she went to the stove to pour her coffee. "Have you lived next door long?"

He was tempted to mention nutrition but managed to control himself. "Just a couple of months."

"It must be great, fixing it up the way you want." She took another bite of the pasta. "Is that what you are, a carpenter? You have the hands for it."

He found himself pleasantly relieved that she hadn't asked him if he played ball. "No. I'm a cop."

"You're kidding. Really?" She shoved her carton aside and leaned forward. It was her eyes that made her beautiful, he decided on the spot. They were so alive, so full of fascination. "I'm crazy about cops. Some of my best characters are cops, even the bad ones."

"I know." He had to smile. "You've got a feel for police work. It shows in the way you plot a book. Everything works on logic and deduction."

"All my logic goes into writing." She picked up her coffee, then remembered she'd forgotten the cream. Rather than get up, she drank it black. "What kind of cop are you—uniform, undercover?"

"Homicide."

"Kismet." She laughed and squeezed his hand. "I can't believe it, I come to visit my sister and plop right down beside a homicide detective. Are you working on anything right now?"

"Actually, we just wrapped something up yesterday."

A rough one, she decided. There'd been something about the way he'd said it, the faintest change of tone. Though her curiosity was piqued, it was controlled by compassion. "I've got a hell of a murder working right now. A series of murders, actually. I've got . . ." She trailed off. Ed saw her eyes darken. She sat back and propped her bare feet on an empty chair. "I can change the location," she began slowly. "Set it right here in D.C. That's better. It would work. What do you think?"

"Well, I—"

"Maybe I could come down to the station sometime. You could show me around." Already taking her thought processes to the next stage, she thrust her hand into the pocket of her robe for a cigarette. "That's allowed, isn't it?"

"I could probably work it out."

"Terrific. Look, have you got a wife or a lover or anything?"

He stared at her as she lit the cigarette and blew out smoke. "Not right now," he said cautiously.

"Then maybe you'd have a couple of hours now and again in the evening for me."

He picked up his juice and took a long swallow. "A couple of hours," he repeated. "Now and again?"

"Yeah. I wouldn't expect you to give me all your free time, just squeeze me in when you're in the mood."

"When I'm in the mood," he murmured. Her robe dipped down to the floor but was parted at the knee to reveal her legs, pale from winter and smooth as marble. Maybe miracles did still happen.

"You could be kind of my expert consultant, you know? I mean, who'd know murder investigations in D.C. better than a D.C. homicide detective?"

Consultant. A little flustered by his own thoughts, he switched his mind off her legs. "Right." He let out a long breath, then laughed. "You roll right along, don't you, Miss McCabe?"

"It's Grace, and I'm pushy, but I won't pout very long if you say no."

He wondered as he looked at her if there was a man

alive who could have said no to those eyes. Then again, his partner Ben always told him he was a sucker. "I've got a couple hours, now and then."

"Thanks. Listen, how about dinner tomorrow? By that time Kath will be thrilled to be rid of me for a while. We could talk murder. I'm buying."

"I'd like that." He rose, feeling as though he'd just taken a fast, unexpected ride. "I'd better get back to work."

"Let me sign your book." After a quick search, she found a pen on a magnetic holder by the phone. "I don't know your name."

"It's Ed. Ed Jackson."

"Hi, Ed." She scrawled on the title page, then unconsciously slipped the pen into her pocket. "See you tomorrow, about seven?"

"Okay." She had freckles, he noticed. A half dozen of them sprinkled over the bridge of her nose. And her wrists were slim and frail. He shifted the book again. "Thanks for the autograph."

Grace let him out the back door. He smelled good, she thought, like wood shavings and soap. Then, rubbing her hands together, she went upstairs to plug in Maxwell.

She worked throughout the day, skipping lunch in favor of the candy bar she found in her coat pocket. Whenever she surfaced from the world she was creating into the one around her, she could hear the hammering and sawing from the house next door. She'd set up her workstation by the window because she liked looking at that house and imagining what was going on inside.

Once she noticed a car pull up in the driveway next door. A rangy, dark-haired man got out and sauntered up the walk, entering the house without knocking. Grace speculated on him for a moment, then dove back into her plot. The next time she bothered to look, two hours had passed and the car was gone.

She arched her back, then, digging her last cigarette

out of the pack, read over a few paragraphs. "Good work, Maxwell," she declared. Pushing a series of buttons, she shut him down for the day. Because her thoughts drifted to her sister, Grace got up to tidy the bed.

Her trunk stood in the middle of the room. The delivery man had indeed carried it upstairs for her, and with the least encouragement from her would have unpacked it as well. She glanced at it, considered, then opted to deal with the chaos inside it later. Instead she went downstairs, found a top-forty station on the radio, and filled the house with the latest from ZZ Top.

Kathleen found her in the living room, sprawled on the sofa with a magazine and a glass of wine. She had to fight back a surge of impatience. She'd just spent the day battling to push something into the minds of a hundred and thirty teenagers. The parent consultation had gotten her nowhere, and her car had begun to make ominous noises on the way home. And here was her sister, with nothing but time on her hands and money in the bank.

With the bag of groceries in her arm, she walked over to the radio and switched it off. Grace glanced up, focused, and smiled. "Hi. I didn't hear you come in."

"I'm not surprised. You had the radio up all the way."

"Sorry." Grace remembered to put the magazine back on the table rather than let it slide to the floor. "Rough day?"

"Some of us have them." She turned and walked toward the kitchen.

Grace swung her feet to the floor, then sat for a minute with her head in her hands. After taking a few deep breaths, she rose and followed her sister into the kitchen. "I went ahead and beefed up the salad from last night. It's still the best thing I cook."

"Fine." Kathleen was already lining a broiling pan with foil.

"Want some wine?"

"No, I'm working tonight."

"On the phone?"

"That's right. On the phone." She slapped the meat onto the broiler.

"Hey, Kath, I was asking, not criticizing." When she got no response, Grace reached for the wine and topped off her glass. "Actually, it crossed my mind that I might be able to use what you're doing as an angle in a book."

"You don't change, do you?" Kathleen whirled around. In her eyes, the fury was hot and pulsing. "Nothing's ever private where you're concerned."

"For heaven's sake, Kathy, I didn't mean I'd use your name or even your situation, just the idea, that's all. It was simply a thought."

"Everything's grist for the mill, your mill. Maybe you'd like to use my divorce while you're at it."

"I've never used you," Grace said quietly.

"You use everyone—friends, lovers, family. Oh, you sympathize with their pain and problems on the outside, but inside you're ticking away, figuring how to make it work for you. Can't you be told anything, see anything without thinking how you can use it in a book?"

Grace opened her mouth to deny, to protest, then closed it again on a sigh. The truth, no matter how unattractive, was better faced. "No, I guess not. I'm sorry."

"Then drop it, all right?" Kathleen's voice was abruptly calm again. "I don't want to argue tonight."

"Neither do I." Making the effort, she started fresh. "I was thinking I might rent a car while I'm here, play tourist a little. And if I was mobile, I could do the shopping and save you some time."

"Fine." Kathleen switched the broiler on, shifting her body enough so that Grace couldn't see her hand wasn't steady. "There's a Hertz place on the way to school. I could drop you off in the morning."

"Okay." Now what, Grace asked herself as she sipped her wine. "Oh, I met the guy next door this morning."

"I'm sure you did." Her voice was taut as she slid the meat under the flame. She was surprised Grace hadn't made friends with everyone in the entire neighborhood by now.

Grace sipped her wine and worked on her temper. It was usually she who lost it first, she remembered. This time she wouldn't. "He's very nice. Turns out to be a cop. We're having dinner tomorrow."

"Isn't that lovely." Kathleen slammed a pot on the stove and added water. "You work fast, Gracie, as usual."

Grace took another slow sip, then set her glass carefully on the counter. "I think I'll go for a walk."

"I'm sorry." With her eyes closed, Kathleen leaned against the stove. "I didn't mean that, I didn't mean to snap at you."

"All right." She wasn't always quick to forgive, but she only had one sister. "Why don't you sit down? You're tired."

"No, I'm on call tonight. I want to get this done before the phone starts ringing."

"I'll do it. You can supervise." She took her sister's arm and nudged her into a chair. "What goes in the pan?"

"There's a package in the bag." Kathleen dug in her purse, pulled out a bottle, and shook out two pills.

Grace dipped in the grocery bag and took out an envelope. "Noodles in garlic sauce. Handy." She ripped it open and dumped it in without reading the directions. "I'd just as soon you didn't jump down my throat again, but do you want to talk about it?"

"No, it was just a long day." She dry-swallowed the pills. "I've got papers to grade."

"Well, I won't be able to do you any good there. I could take the phone calls for you."

Kathleen managed a smile. "No, thanks."

Grace took out the salad bowl and set it on the table. "Maybe I could just take notes."

"No. If you don't stir those noodles, they'll stick."

"Oh." Willing to oblige, Grace turned to them. In the silence, she heard the meat begin to sizzle. "Easter's next week. Don't you get a few days off?"

"Five, counting the weekend."

"Why don't we take a quick trip, join the madness in Fort Lauderdale, get some sun?"

"I can't afford it."

"My treat, Kath. Come on, it'd be fun. Remember the spring of our senior year when we begged and pleaded with Mom and Dad to let us go?"

"You begged and pleaded," Kathleen reminded her.

"Whatever, we went. For three days we partied, got sunburned, and met dozens of guys. Remember that one, Joe or Jack, who tried to climb in the window of our motel room?"

"After you told him I was hot for his body."

"Well, you were. Poor guy nearly killed himself." With a laugh, she stabbed a noodle and wondered if it was done. "God, we were so young, and so stupid. What the hell, Kath, we've still got it together enough to have a few college guys leer at us."

"Drinking sprees and college boys don't interest me. Besides, I've arranged to be on call all weekend. Switch the noodles down to warm, Grace, and turn the meat over."

She obeyed and said nothing as she heard Kathleen setting the table. It wasn't the drinking or the men, Grace thought. She'd just wanted to recapture something of the sisterhood they'd shared. "You're working too hard."

"I'm not in your position, Grace. I can't afford to lie on the couch and read magazines all afternoon."

Grace picked up her wine again. And bit her tongue. There were days she sat in front of a screen for twelve hours, nights she worked until three. On a book tour she was on all day and half the night until she had only enough energy to crawl into bed and fall into a stuporous sleep. She might consider herself lucky, she might still be astonished at the amount of money that rolled in from royalty checks, but she earned it. It was a constant source of annoyance that her sister never understood that.

"I'm on vacation." She tried to say it lightly, but the edge was there.

"I'm not."

"Fine. If you don't want to go away, would you mind if I did some puttering around in the yard?"

"I don't care." Kathleen rubbed her temple. The headaches never seemed to fade completely any longer. "Actually I'd appreciate it. I haven't given it much thought. We had a beautiful garden in California. Do you remember?"

"Sure." Grace had always thought it too orderly and formal, like Jonathan. Like Kathleen. She hated the little stab of bitterness she felt and pushed it aside. "We could go for some pansies, and what were those things Mom always loved? Morning glories."

"All right." But her mind was on other things. "Grace, the meat's going to burn."

Later, Kathleen closed herself in her office. Grace could hear the phone ring, the Fantasy phone, as she'd decided to term it. She counted ten calls before she went upstairs. Too restless to sleep, she turned on her computer. But she wasn't thinking of work or of the murders she created.

The contented feeling that had been with her the night before and most of the day was gone. Kathleen wasn't all right. Her mood swings were too quick and too sharp. It had been on the tip of her tongue to mention therapy, but she'd been too aware of what the reaction would have been. Kathleen would have given her one of those hard, closed-in looks, and the discussion would have ended.

Grace had mentioned Kevin only once. Kathleen had told her she didn't want to discuss him or Jonathan. She knew her sister well enough to realize that Kathleen was regretting her visit. What was worse, Grace was regretting it herself. Kathleen always managed to point out the worst aspects of her, aspects that under other circumstances Grace herself managed to brush over.

But she'd come to help. Somehow, despite both of them, she was going to. But it would take some time, she told herself for comfort, resting her chin on her arm. She could see lights in the windows next door.

She couldn't hear the phone ring now with the office door closed and her own pulled to. She wondered how many more calls her sister would take that night. How many more men would she satisfy without ever having seen their faces? Did she grade papers between calls? It should have been funny. She wished it were funny, but she couldn't stop seeing the tension on Kathleen's face as she'd pushed her food around her plate.

There was nothing she could do, Grace told herself as she scrubbed her hands over her eyes. Kathleen was determined to handle things her way.

$\mathcal{I}$T WAS WONDERFUL TO hear her voice again, to hear her make promises and give that quick, husky laugh. She was wearing black this time, something thin and filmy that a man could tear away on a whim. She'd like that, he thought. She'd like it if he were there with her, ripping off her clothes.

The man she was talking to barely spoke at all. He was glad. If he closed his eyes, he could imagine she was talking to him. And only him. He'd been listening to her for hours, call after call. After a while, the words no longer mattered. Just her voice, the warm, teasing voice that poured through his earphones and into his head. From somewhere in the house a television was playing, but he didn't hear it. He only heard Desiree.

She wanted him.

In his mind he sometimes heard her say his name.

Jerald. She would say it with that half laugh she often had in her voice. When he went to her, she would open up her arms and say it again, slowly, breathlessly. Jerald.

They would make love in all the ways she described.

He would be the man to finally satisfy her. He would be the man she wanted above all others. It would be his name she said over and over again, on a whisper, on a moan, on a scream.

Jerald, Jerald, Jerald.

He shuddered, then lay back, spent, in the swivel chair in front of his computer.

He was eighteen years old and had made love to women only in his dreams. Tonight his dreams were only of Desiree.

And he was mad.

Chapter 3

So where are you going?"

Because Ed had won the toss, he was behind the wheel. He and his partner, Ben Paris, had just spent the better part of the day in court. It wasn't enough to catch the bad guys, you had to spend hours testifying against them.

"What?"

"I said where are you going?" Ben had an oversize bag of M&M's and was eating steadily. "With the writer."

"I don't know." He downshifted at a stop sign, hesitated, then cleared the intersection.

"You didn't come to a complete stop." Ben crunched into the candy. "The deal was if you drove you'd obey all traffic signals."

"Nobody was coming. Do you think I should wear a tie?"

"How do I know if you don't know where you're going? Besides, you look ridiculous in a tie. Like a bull with a bell around his neck."

"Thanks, partner."

"Ed, the light's changing. The light—shit." He tossed

the candy into his pocket as Ed cruised through. "So, how long's the famous novelist going to be in town?"

"I don't know."

"What do you mean you don't know? You talked to her, didn't you?"

"I didn't ask. I didn't figure it was my business."

"Women like you to ask." Ben worked the imaginary brake with his foot as Ed squealed around a corner. "She writes good stuff. Got some grit to it. I guess you remember I was the one who turned you on to her books."

"You want me to name the first kid after you?"

With a chuckle Ben punched in the car lighter. "So does she look like the picture on the book, or what?"

"Better." Ed grinned but rolled down the window as Ben lit a cigarette. "She's got big gray eyes. And she smiles a lot. Got a great smile."

"Doesn't take you long to get hip-deep, does it?"

Ed shifted uncomfortably and kept his eyes on the road. "I don't know what you mean."

"I've seen it happen before." Ben relaxed his brake foot as Ed dropped behind a slow-moving sedan. "Some little number with big eyes and a great smile flutters her lashes and you're gone. You've got no resistance when it comes to women, pal."

"Studies show that men married less than six months develop an annoying tendency to give advice."

"*Redbook*?"

"*Cosmopolitan*."

"I bet. Anyway, when I'm right, I'm right." The only person he knew better than himself was Ed Jackson. Ben would have been the first to admit he didn't even know his wife as intimately. He didn't need a magnifying glass to recognize the first stages of infatuation. "Why don't you bring her over for a drink or something? Tess and I can check her out."

"I'll do my own checking, thanks."

"Back up, partner. You know, now that I'm a married man, I take a very objective view of women."

Ed grinned through his beard. "Bullshit."

"Truth, absolute truth." Ben swung an arm over the back of the seat. "Tell you what, I can call Tess and we can arrange to go with you tonight. Just to protect you from yourself."

"Thanks, but I want to try to struggle through this on my own."

"Have you told her you only eat nuts and berries?"

Ed gave him a mild look as he took the next turn.

"It might influence the choice of restaurant." Ben flipped his cigarette out the window, but his grin faded when Ed pulled into a parking lot. "Oh no, not the hardware store. Not again."

"I need to pick up some hinges."

"Sure, that's what you always say. You've been a pain in the ass since you bought that house, Jackson."

As they got out of the car, Ed flipped him a quarter. "Go across to the 7-Eleven and get a cup of coffee. I won't be long."

"You got ten minutes. It's bad enough I have to spend the morning in court having to outmaneuver Torcelli's P.D., but now I have to put up with Harry Homeowner."

"You told me to buy a house."

"That's beside the point. And I can't get coffee for a quarter."

"Show your badge, maybe they'll give you a discount."

Grumbling, Ben jogged across the street. If he had to cool his heels while his partner pored over nuts and bolts, he might as well do it with coffee and a Danish.

The little convenience store was almost empty. It would be a couple of hours yet before the rush-hour crowd stopped in for a loaf of bread or a Big Gulp for the road. The cashier was reading a paperback but glanced up and smiled as he walked by. Objectively, he decided she had a nice bust.

In the back of the store by the hot plates and microwave, he poured himself a large coffee, then grabbed the pot of hot water and poured a cup for Ed, who always had a tea bag in his pocket.

There'd been a time he'd been certain Ed had made a huge mistake in buying that wreck of a house. But the truth was, watching it come together little by little had set him to thinking. Maybe he and Tess should start looking for a house. Nothing with holes in the ceiling or rats in the attic like Ed's, but a place with a real yard. A place where you could have a grill and barbecue steaks in the summer. A place where you could raise kids, he thought, then told himself to slow down. It must be marriage that made you think about next year as often as you thought about tomorrow.

Downing coffee as he went, Ben walked to the cashier. He barely had time to swear when he was shoved and the coffee splashed down his shirt.

"Dammit!" he shouted, immediately going silent and still as he saw the knife trembling in the hand of a kid of about seventeen.

"The money." The kid poked the knife at Ben as he gestured to the cashier. "All of it. Now."

"Great," Ben muttered and glanced at the woman behind the counter, who was pale and frozen to the spot. "Listen, kid, they don't keep diddly in those cash registers."

"The money. I said give me the fucking money!" The boy's voice rose and broke. A thin trail of spittle flew out as he spoke; it was tinted with blood from the lip he'd been biting. He needed a fix and he needed it bad. "You'd better move your ass right now, you stupid bitch, or I'll carve my initials into your forehead."

The woman took another look at the knife and sprang into action. She grabbed the tray out of the drawer and dumped it on the counter. Loose change bounced out and hit the floor.

"Your wallet," he said to Ben as he began to stuff bills and silver into his pockets. It was his first robbery. He'd had no idea it could be so easy. But his heart was still jammed into his throat and his armpits were dripping. "Take it out slow and toss it on the counter."

"Okay. Take it easy." He considered reaching inside his jacket for his weapon. The kid was sweating like a pig and had as much terror in his eyes as the woman behind the counter. Instead, Ben reached for his wallet with two fingers. He held it up, watching the kid's eyes follow it. Then he tossed it an inch short of the counter. The minute the kid looked down, he moved.

He knocked the knife away easily. The grip was slippery with sweat. It was then that the woman behind the counter started to scream, one keening wail after the next as she continued to stand rooted. And the kid fought like a wounded bear. Ben locked his arms around the kid's waist from the rear, but even as he planted his feet, they were going over onto a display table. It cracked, going down with them. Ho-Ho's and Chiclets scattered. The boy screamed and swore, flopping like a fish as he groped for the knife. Ben's elbow cracked against the frozen-food cabinet hard enough to have stars dancing in his head. Beneath him, the boy was rail thin and soaked now from a nervous bladder. Ben did what seemed easiest: He sat on him.

"You're busted, friend." Pulling out his shield, he stuck it in front of the boy's face. "And the way you're shaking it's the best thing that could've happened to you." The boy was already weeping as Ben took out his cuffs. Annoyed and out of breath, he looked up at the cashier. "You want to call the cops, sweetie?"

Ed came out of the hardware store with a bag of hinges, a half-dozen brass handles, and four ceramic pulls. The pulls were a real find, as they'd pick up the color in the tile he'd chosen for the upstairs bath. His next project. Since the car was empty, he glanced across the street and saw the black and white. With a sigh, he set the bag carefully in the car and sauntered over to find his partner. He took one look at Ben's shirt, then at the kid sobbing and shaking in the back of the patrol car.

"See you got your coffee."

"Yeah. On the house, you bastard." Ben nodded to the uniform, then with his hands stuffed in his pockets started back across the street. "Now I've got a frigging report to fill out. And look at this shirt." He held it away from his skin where it had plastered, cold and sticky. "What the hell am I supposed to do about these coffee stains?"

"Spray 'N Wash."

I WAS NEARLY SIX when Ed pulled into his driveway. He'd hung around the station, dawdled at his desk, and scrounged for busywork. The simple fact was, he was nervous. He liked women well enough, without pretending to understand them. The job itself put certain limits on his social life, but when he dated, he was usually drawn to the easygoing and none-too-bright. He'd never had his partner's flare for gathering females in droves or juggling them like a circus act. Nor had he ever experienced Ben's sudden and total commitment to one woman.

Ed preferred women who didn't move too fast or push too many buttons. It was true he liked long and stimulating conversations, but he rarely dated a woman who could give him one. And he never analyzed why.

He admired G. B. McCabe's brain. He just wasn't sure how he'd deal with Grace McCabe on a social level. He wasn't used to a woman asking him out and setting the time and place. He was more accustomed to pampering and guiding—and would have been appalled and insulted if anyone had accused him of chauvinism.

He'd been a staunch supporter of the ERA but that was politics. Though he'd worked with Ben for years, he wouldn't have blinked twice at a female partner. But that was business.

His mother had worked as long as he could remember, while raising three sons and a daughter. There had been no father, and as the oldest, Ed had taken over as head of the house before he'd reached his teens. He was used to a woman earning a living, just as he was used to managing her paycheck and making the major decisions for her.

In the back of his mind had always been the thought that when he married, his wife wouldn't have to work. He'd take care of her, the way his father had never taken care of his mother. The way Ed had always wanted to take care of her.

One day, when his house was finished, the walls painted and the garden planted, he'd find the right woman and bring her home. And take care of her.

As he changed, he glanced out the window to the house next door. Grace had left her curtains open and her light on. Even as he thought about giving her a gentle hint about privacy when he saw her, she slammed into the room. Though he could only see her from the hips up, he was sure she kicked something. Then she began to pace.

*W*HAT WAS SHE GOING to do? Grace dragged both hands through her hair as if she could pull out the answers. Her sister was in trouble, bigger trouble than she'd ever imagined. And she was helpless.

She shouldn't have lost her temper, she told herself. Shouting at Kathleen was the equivalent of reading *War and Peace* in the dark. All you got was a headache and no understanding. Something had to be done. Dropping down on the bed, she rested her head against her knees. How long had it been going on? she wondered. Since the divorce? She'd gotten no answers out of Kathleen, so Grace jumped to the conclusion that this too was Jonathan's fault.

But what was she going to do about it? Kathleen was furious with her now and wouldn't listen. Grace knew about drugs—had seen too often what they could do to people. She'd comforted some who'd been struggling on the road back and had distanced herself from others who'd been racing toward destruction. She'd broken off a relationship because of drugs and had pushed the man totally out of her life.

But this was her sister. She pressed her fingers to her eyes and tried to think.

Valium. Three bottles of it from three different doctors. And for all she knew, Kathleen could have more stashed at school, in her car, God knew where.

She hadn't been snooping, not the way Kathleen had accused her of. She'd needed a damn pencil and had known that Kathleen would have kept one in the drawer beside her bed. She'd found the pencil all right. Freshly sharpened. And the three bottles of pills.

"You don't know what it's like to have nerves," Kathleen had raged at her. "You don't know what it's like to have real problems. Everything you've ever touched has turned out exactly the way you wanted it. I've lost my husband, I've lost my son. How dare you lecture me about anything I do to stop the pain?"

She hadn't had the right words, only anger and recriminations. Face up to it, goddamn it. For once in your life, face up to it. Why hadn't she said I'll help you. I'm here for you. That's what she'd meant. She could go back down now and plead, grovel, scream, and get only one reaction. The wall was up. She'd faced that same wall before. When Kathleen had broken up with a longtime boyfriend, when Grace had gotten the lead in the class play.

Family. You didn't turn away when it was family. On a sigh, Grace went downstairs to try again.

Kathleen was in her office with the door shut. Promising herself she'd stay calm, Grace knocked. "Kath." There was no answer, but at least the door wasn't locked. Grace pushed it open. "Kath, I'm sorry."

Kathleen finished checking a tenth-grade paper before she looked up. "You don't have to apologize."

"Okay." So she was calm again, Grace thought. Whether it was from the pills or that her temper had cooled, she couldn't be sure. "Look, I thought I'd run next door and tell Ed we'd make it another night. Then we could talk."

"There's nothing more to talk about." Kathleen put the graded paper on one pile and picked up a new paper from another stack. She was deadly calm now. The pills had given her that. "And I'm on call tonight. Go have a good time."

"Kathy, I'm worried about you. I love you."

"I love you, too." She meant it, she only wished she were capable of showing just how much she meant it. "And there's nothing for you to worry about. I know what I'm doing."

"I know you're under a lot of pressure, terrible pressure. I want to help."

"I appreciate it." Kathleen marked an answer wrong and wondered why her students couldn't pay more attention. No one seemed to pay enough attention. "I'm handling it. I told you I'm glad you're here, and I am. I'm also happy to have you stay as long as you like—and as long as you don't interfere."

"Honey, valium addiction can be very dangerous. I don't want to see you hurt."

"I'm not addicted." Kathleen gave the paper a C minus. "As soon as I have Kevin back and my life's in order, I won't need pills." She smiled and picked up another paper. "Stop worrying, Gracie. I'm a big girl now." When her phone rang, she got up from her desk and moved to the chair. "Yes?" Kathleen picked up a pencil. "Yes, I'll take him. Give me the number." She wrote it down, then pushed down the disconnect button. "Good night, Grace. I'll leave the porch light on for you."

Because her sister was already dialing the number, Grace backed out of the office. She grabbed her coat from the hall closet where Kathleen had hung it, then rushed outside.

The bite of early April made her think again of Florida. She might still persuade Kathleen to go. Or perhaps to the Caribbean or Mexico. Anywhere warm and relaxed. And once she had her out of town, away from the worst of the pressure, they could really talk. If that failed, Grace had memorized the names of the three doctors that appeared on the labels of the bottles of pills. She'd go to them.

Still struggling into her coat, she knocked at Ed's door.

"I know I'm early," she said as soon as he'd opened it. "I hope you don't mind. I thought we could have a drink first. Can I come in?"

"Sure." He stepped back, understanding she didn't want an answer to any question but the last. "You okay?"

"It shows?" With a half laugh she brushed her tumbled hair away from her face. "I had a fight with my sister, that's all. We've never been able to go more than a week without words. Usually my fault."

"Fights are usually two people's fault."

"Not when they're with me." It would be too easy to open up and let it pour. He had the kind of eyes that spoke of comfort and understanding. But this was family business. Deliberately she turned to look at the house. "This is wonderful."

Grace looked beyond the peeling wallpaper and stacks of lumber to the size and scope of the room. She saw the height of the ceiling rather than the chipped plaster, and the beauty of the old hardwood floor beneath the stains and scratches.

"I haven't gotten to this room yet." But in his mind's eye, he'd already seen it finished. "The kitchen was my first priority."

"It's always mine." She smiled and held out a hand. "Well, are you going to show me?"

"Sure, if you want." It was strange, but usually he felt as though he swallowed up a woman's hand. Hers was small and slim, but it held firmly in his. She glanced at the staircase as they passed.

"Once you strip that wood, you're going to have something really special. I love these old houses with all these rooms stacked on top of each other. It's funny, because my condo in New York is practically one huge room, and I'm very comfortable there, but . . . oh, this is terrific."

He'd torn out, scraped, steamed, and rebuilt. The kitchen was the result of nearly two months of work. As far as Grace was concerned, whatever astronomical amount of time he'd put into it was worth every moment. The counters were a dark rose, a color she wouldn't have expected a man to appreciate. He'd painted the cabinets in a mint green for contrast. The appliances were stark white and straight out of the forties. There was a brick hearth and oven that had been lovingly restored. There must have been old linoleum to scrape up, but now the floor was oak.

"Nineteen-forty-five, the war's over, and living in America couldn't be better. I love it. Where did you find this stove?"

It was strange how right she looked there, with her hair frizzed and flyaway and her coat padded at the shoulders. "I, ah, there's an antique store in Georgetown. There was hell to pay to get parts."

"It's terrific. Really terrific." She could relax here, she thought, as she leaned against the sink. It was white porcelain and reminded her of home and simpler times. There were little peat pots in the window with green sprigs already poking through. "What are you growing here?"

"Some herbs."

"Herbs? Like rosemary and stuff?"

"And stuff. When I get a chance I want to clear a little spot in the yard."

Glancing out the window, she saw where he'd been working the day before. It was appealing to her to imagine a little herb garden springing up, though she didn't know thyme from oregano. Herbs in the window, candles on the table. It would be a happy house, not stilted and tense like the one next door. She shook off the mood with a sigh.

"You're an ambitious man, Ed."

"Why?"

She smiled and turned back to him. "No dishwasher. Come on." She offered her hand again. "I'll buy you a drink."

KATHLEEN SAT IN HER chair, her eyes closed, the phone tucked between her shoulder and her ear. This one wanted to do most of the talking. All she was required to do was make approving noises. Nice work if you can get it, she thought, and brushed a tear from her lashes.

She shouldn't let Grace get to her this way. She knew exactly what she was doing, and if she needed a little help to keep from losing her mind, then she was entitled to it.

"No, that's wonderful. No, I don't want you to stop."

She bit off a sigh and wished she'd remembered to fix herself a pot of coffee. Grace had thrown her off. Kathleen shifted the phone and checked her watch. He had two minutes coming. Sometimes it was incredible how long two minutes could be.

She glanced up once, thinking she'd heard a noise, then gave her attention back to her client. Maybe she would let Grace take her to Florida for a weekend. It might be good for her to get away, get some sun. And stop thinking for a few days. The trouble was that when Grace was around she never stopped thinking about her own faults and failures. It had always been that way, and Kathleen accepted that it always would be. Still, she shouldn't have snapped at Grace, she told herself as she rubbed at her temple. But that was done now and she had work to do.

Jerald's heart was beating like a trip-hammer. He could hear her, murmuring, sighing. That low laugh washed over his skin. His palms were like ice. He wondered how it would feel to warm them against her.

She was going to be so happy to see him. He dragged the back of his hand over his mouth as he moved closer. He wanted to surprise her. It had taken him two hours and three lines of coke, but he'd finally worked up the courage to come to her.

He'd dreamed about her the night before. She'd asked him to come, pleaded with him. Desiree. She wanted to be his first.

The hall was dim, but he could see the light under the door of her office. And he could hear her voice coming through. Beckoning. Teasing.

He had to stop for a minute, rest his palm against the wall. Just to catch his breath. Sex with her would be wilder than any high he'd pumped or snorted into his body. Sex with her would be the ultimate, the pinnacle. And when they'd finished, she'd tell him he was the best.

She'd stopped talking now. He heard her moving around. Getting ready for him. Slowly, almost faint from excitement, he pushed the door open.

And there she was.

He shook his head. She was different, different from the woman of his fantasies. She was dark, not blond, and she wasn't wearing filmy black or lacy white, but a plain skirt and blouse. In his confusion, he simply stood in the doorway and stared.

When the shadow fell across her desk, Kathleen glanced up, half expecting Grace. Her first reaction wasn't fear. The boy who stared back at her might have been one of her students. She stood, as she might have stood to lecture.

"How did you get in here? Who are you?"

It wasn't the face, but it was the voice. Everything else faded but the voice. Jerald stepped closer, smiling. "You don't have to pretend, Desiree. I told you I'd come."

When he stepped into the light, she tasted fear. One didn't have to have experience with madness to recognize it. "I don't understand what you're talking about." He'd called her Desiree, but that wasn't possible. No one knew. No one could know. She groped on the desk for a weapon as she gauged the distance to the door. "You'll have to leave or I'll call the police."

But still he smiled. "I've been listening for weeks and weeks. Then last night you told me I could come. I'm here now. For you."

"You're crazy, I never spoke to you." She had to stay calm, very calm. "You've made a mistake, now I want you to leave."

That was the voice. He'd have recognized it among thousands. Millions. "Every night, I listened for you every night." He was hard, uncomfortably hard, and his mouth was dry as stone. He'd been wrong, she was blond, blond and beautiful. It must have been a trick of the light before, or her own magic. "Desiree," he murmured. "I love you." With his eyes on hers, he began to unbuckle his belt. Kathleen snatched up her paperweight and heaved it as she dashed to the door. It grazed the side of his head.

"You promised." He had her now, thin wiry arms clamped around her. His breathing came in gasps as he pressed his face close to hers. "You promised you'd give me all those things you talk about. And I want them. I want more than talk now, Desiree."

It was a nightmare, she thought. Desiree was make-believe, and so was this. A dream, that was all. But dreams didn't hurt. She heard her blouse rip even as she struggled. His hands were all over her, no matter how she fought and kicked. When she sunk her teeth into his shoulder, he yelped, but dragged her to the floor, ripping at her skirt.

"You promised. You promised," he said over and over. He could feel her skin now, soft and hot, just as he'd imagined. Nothing was going to stop him.

When she felt him push inside her, she started to scream.

"Stop it." The passion was exploding in his head, but not the way he'd wanted. Her screaming was tearing into him, spoiling it. It couldn't be spoiled. He'd waited too long, wanted too long. "I said stop it!" He thrust harder, wanting the magnificence of all her promises. But she wouldn't stop screaming. She scratched, but the pain only inflamed his need, and fury. She'd lied. This wasn't the way it was supposed to be. She was a liar and a whore, and still he wanted her.

Flinging a hand out, she shoved, knocking over the table. The phone fell on the floor beside her head.

And he took the cord and wrapped it around her throat, pulling hard until the screaming stopped.

So your partner's married to a psychiatrist." Grace rolled down the window as she lit a cigarette. The dinner had relaxed her. Ed had relaxed her, she corrected. He was so easy to talk to and had such a sweet, funny way of looking at life.

"They met on a case we were working on a few months ago." Ed reminded himself to come to a complete stop at the intersection. After all, Grace wasn't Ben. She wasn't like anyone else. "You'd probably be interested since it was a serial killer."

"Really?" She never questioned her fascination with murder. "I get it, the shrink was called in to do a psychiatric profile."

"You got it."

"Is she any good?"

"The best."

Grace nodded, thinking of Kathleen. "I'd like to talk to her. Maybe we could have a dinner party or something. Kathleen doesn't socialize enough."

"You're worried about her."

Grace let out a little sigh as they turned a corner. "I'm sorry. I didn't want to spoil your evening, but I guess I wasn't the best company."

"I wasn't complaining."

"That's because you're too polite." When he pulled into the drive, she leaned over and kissed his cheek. "Why don't you come in for coffee—no, you don't drink coffee, it's tea. I'll brew you some tea and make it up to you."

She was already out of the car before he could get out and open the door for her. "You don't have to make anything up to me."

"I'd like the company. Kath's probably in bed by now and I'll just stew." She dug in her bag for her key. "And we can talk about when you're going to give me that tour of the station. Damn, I know it's in here somewhere. I'd have an easier time if Kath had remembered to leave the porch light on. Here." She unlocked the door, then dropped the keys carelessly into her pocket. "Why don't you sit in the living room and turn on the stereo or something while I get the tea?"

She shed her coat as she walked, tossing it negligently at a chair. Ed picked it up as it slid to the floor and folded it. It smelled like her, he thought. Then, telling himself he was foolish, he laid it over the back of the chair. He crossed to a window to study the trim work. It was a habit he'd gotten into since he'd bought his house. Running a finger along it, he tried to imagine it at his own window.

He heard Grace call her sister's name, like a question, then call it again and again and again.

He found her kneeling beside her sister's body, pulling at it, shouting at it. When he gathered her up, she tore at him like a tiger.

"Let me go. Goddamn it, let me go. It's Kathy."

"Go in the other room, Grace."

"No. It's Kathy. Oh God, let me go. She needs me."

"Do it." With his hands firm at her shoulders, he shielded her from the body with his own and gave her two hard shakes. "Go in the other room now. I'll take care of her."

"But I need—"

"I want you to listen to me." He kept his gaze hard into her eyes, recognizing shock. But he couldn't cosset or soothe or tuck a nice warm blanket around her. "Go in the other room. Call 911. Can you do that?"

"Yes." She nodded and stumbled back. "Yes, of course. 911." He watched her run out, then turned back to the body.

Number 911 wasn't going to help Kathleen Breezewood. Ed crouched down beside her and became a cop.

Chapter 4

IT WAS LIKE A scene out of one of her books. After the murder came the police. Some of them would be weary, some tight-lipped, some cynical. It depended on the mood of the story. Sometimes it depended on the personality of the victim. It depended, always, on her imagination.

The action could take place in an alley or in a drawing room. Atmosphere was always an intricate part of any scene. In the book she was writing, she'd plotted out a murder in the Secretary of State's library. She'd enjoyed the prospect of bringing in Secret Service, politics, and espionage as well as police.

That would be a matter of poison and drinking out of the wrong glass. Murder was always more interesting when it was a bit confusing. She was delighted with her plot line so far because she hadn't quite made up her mind who the murderer was. It had always fascinated her to figure it out and surprise herself.

The bad guy always tripped up in the end.

Grace sat on the sofa, silent and staring. For some reason, she couldn't get beyond that thought. The self-defense mechanism of the mind had turned hysteria into numbing shock so that even her shudders seemed to be pulsing through someone else's body. A good murder had more punch if the victim left someone behind to be stunned or devastated. It was almost a foolproof device to draw the reader in if done right. She'd always had a talent for painting emotions: grief, fury, heartache. Once she understood her characters, she could feel them too. For hours and days at a time, she could work, feeding off the emotions, reveling in them, delighting in both the light and the dark sides of human nature. Then she could switch them off as carelessly as she switched off her machine, and go on with her own life.

It was only a story, after all, and justice would win out in the final chapter.

She recognized the professions of the men who came and went through her sister's house—the coroner, the forensic team, the police photographer.

Once, she'd used a police photographer as the protagonist in a novel, painting the stark and gritty details of death with a kind of relish. She knew the procedure, had depicted it again and again without a blink or a shudder. The sights and smells of murder weren't strangers, not to her imagination. Even now, she almost believed if she squeezed her eyes tight they would all fade and reassemble into characters she could control, characters that were only real in her mind, characters that could be created or destroyed by the press of a button.

But not her sister. Not Kathy.

She'd change the plot, Grace told herself as she brought her legs up to curl under her. She'd do rewrites, delete the murder scene, restructure the characters. She'd change it all until everything worked out exactly as she wanted. All she had to do was concentrate. She closed her eyes and, wrapping her arms tight over her breasts, struggled to make it all play.

"She didn't go easy," Ben murmured as he watched the coroner examine the body of Kathleen McCabe Breezewood. "I think we're going to find that some of the blood belongs to him. We may get some prints off the phone cord."

"How long?" Ed noted down the details in his book while he fought to keep his mind off Grace. He couldn't afford to think of her now. He could miss something, something vital, if he thought of the way she was sitting in the other room like a broken doll.

The coroner tapped a fist against his chest. The chili and onions he'd had for dinner kept coming back on him. "No more than two hours, probably less." He took a look at his watch. "At this point, I'd put the time between nine and eleven. Should be able to hone it when I get her in." He signaled to two men. Even as he rose, the body was being transferred into a thick black plastic bag. Very tidy. Very final.

"Yeah, thanks." Ben lit a cigarette as he studied the chalk outline on the rug. "From the looks of the room, he surprised her in here. Back door was forced. Didn't take much, so I'm not surprised if she didn't hear."

"It's a quiet neighborhood," Ed murmured. "You don't even have to lock your car."

"It's harder when it hits close to home, I know." Ben waited, but received no response. "We're going to have to talk to the sister."

"Yeah." Ed tucked his notebook back into his pocket. "You guys want to give me a couple of minutes before you carry that out?" He nodded to the coroner as he started out. He hadn't been able to prevent Grace from finding the body, but he could prevent her from being a part of what happened now.

He found her where he'd left her, sitting huddled on the sofa. Her eyes were closed so that he thought, hoped, she was asleep. Then she was looking up at him. Her eyes were huge and completely dry. He recognized the dull sheen of shock too well.

"I can't make it play." Her voice was steady, but so quiet it barely carried beyond her lips. "I keep trying to restructure the scene. I came back early. I didn't go out at all. Kath decided to tag along for the evening. Nothing works."

"Grace, let's go to the kitchen. We'll have that tea and talk."

She accepted the hand he held out but didn't rise. "Nothing works because it's too late to change it."

"I'm sorry, Grace. Why don't you come with me now?"

"They haven't taken her away yet, have they? I should see her, before—"

"Not now."

"I have to wait until they take her. I know I can't go with her, but I have to wait until they take her. She's my sister." She rose then, but only to go to the hall and wait.

"Let her be," Ben advised when Ed started forward. "She needs this."

Ed thrust his own hands into his pockets. "Nobody needs this."

He'd seen others say good-bye to someone they loved this way. Even after all the scenes, all the victims, all the investigations, he couldn't feel *nothing*. But he'd taught himself to feel as little as possible.

Grace stood, hands cold and clasped, as they carried Kathleen out. She didn't weep. She dug deep for feeling, but found nothing. She wanted the grief, needed it, but it seemed to have crept off into some corner and curled into itself, leaving her empty. When Ed's hand fell on her shoulder, she didn't jerk or shiver, but took a long breath.

"You have to ask me questions now?"

"If you're up to it."

"Yes." She cleared her throat. Her voice should be stronger. She'd always been the strong one. "I'll make the tea."

In the kitchen, she set the kettle on, then fussed with cups and saucers. "Kath always keeps everything so neat. All I have to do is remember where my mother kept things, and . . ." She trailed off. Her mother. She'd have to call and tell her parents.

I'm sorry, Mom, I'm so sorry. I wasn't here. I couldn't stop it.

Not now, she told herself as she fumbled with tea bags. She couldn't think of it now. "I don't imagine you want sugar."

"No." Ed shifted uncomfortably and wished she'd sit down. Her movements were steady enough, but there wasn't a breath of color in her face. There hadn't been since he'd found her bent over her sister's body.

"How about you? You're Detective Paris, aren't you? Ed's partner?"

"Ben." He put his hand on the back of a chair to pull it from the table. "I'll take two teaspoons of sugar." Like Ed, he noted her lack of color, but he also recognized her determination to see this through. She wasn't so much fragile as brittle, he thought, like a piece of glass that would snap rather than shatter.

As she set the cups on the table, she glanced at the back door. "He came in through here, didn't he?"

"That's the way it looks." Ben took out his own pad and set it next to his saucer. She was holding off the grief, and as a cop, he had to take advantage of it. "I'm sorry we have to go into this."

"It doesn't matter." She lifted her tea and sipped. She felt the heat of the liquid in her mouth but tasted nothing. "There isn't anything I can tell you, really. Kath was in her office when I left. She was going to work. That was, I don't know, six-thirty. When we got back, I thought she'd gone to bed. She hadn't left the porch light on." Details, she thought as she fought back another brush with hysteria. The police needed details, just as any good novel did. "I started to go into the kitchen and I noticed her door, her office door, was open and the light was on. So I went in." She picked up her tea again and carefully shut her mind to what happened next.

Since Ed had been there, Ben didn't have to push. They all knew what had happened next. So he'd go back. "Was she seeing anyone?"

"No." Grace relaxed a little. They would talk about other things, logical things, and not the impossible scene beyond the office door. "She'd just gone through a nasty divorce and wasn't over it. She worked, she didn't socialize. Kathy's mind was fixed on making enough money to go to court and win back custody of her son."

Kevin. Dear God, Kevin. Grace picked up her cup in both hands and drank again.

"Her husband was Jonathan Breezewood the third, of Palm Springs. Old money, old lineage, nasty temper." Her eyes hardened as she looked at the back door again. "Maybe, just maybe you'll find he took a trip east."

"Do you have any reason to think the ex-husband would want to murder your sister?"

She looked up at Ed then. "They didn't part amicably. He'd been cheating on her for years and she'd hired a lawyer and a detective. He might have found out. Breezewood is the kind of name that doesn't tolerate any grime attached to it."

"Do you know if he ever threatened your sister?" Ben sampled the tea even as he thought longingly of the coffeepot.

"Not that she told me, but she was frightened of him. She didn't initially fight for Kevin because of his temper and the power his family wields. She told me he'd put one of the gardeners in the hospital once because of an argument over a rosebush."

"Grace." Ed laid a hand over hers. "Have you noticed

anyone around the neighborhood who made you uneasy? Has anyone come to the door, delivering, soliciting?"

"No. Well, there was the man who delivered my trunk, but he was harmless. I was alone with him in the house for fifteen or twenty minutes."

"What was the company's name?" Ben asked.

"I don't know . . ." She rubbed the bridge of her nose between her thumb and forefinger. Details always came easily to her, but thinking now was like fighting through a fog. "Quik and Easy. No 'c' in quick. The guy's name was, um, Jimbo. Yeah, Jimbo. He had it stitched over the pocket of his shirt. Sounded like Oklahoma."

"Your sister was a teacher?" Ben prompted.

"That's right."

"Any problems with the other staff?"

"Most of them are nuns. You have a hard time arguing with nuns."

"Yeah. How about the students?"

"She didn't tell me anything. The fact is, she never did." It was that thought that had her stomach churning again. "The first night I came into town, we talked, had a little too much wine. That's when she told me about Jonathan. But since then, and for most of our lives, she closed off. I can tell you that Kathleen didn't make enemies, and she didn't make friends either, not close ones. For the past few years, her life has been wrapped up in her family. She hasn't been back in D.C. long enough to make any ties, to meet anyone who would want—who could do this to her. It was Jonathan, or it was a stranger."

Ben said nothing for a moment. Whoever had broken in hadn't come to rob, but to rape. There was a feel to a robbery attempt, a feel to a rape. Every room but the office was as neat as a pin. There was a smell of violation in this house.

"Grace." Ed had already come to the same conclusion as his partner, but had taken it one step further. Whoever had broken in had come for the woman he'd gotten, or for the one sitting next to him. "Is there anyone who has a grudge against you?" At her blank look, he continued. "Is there anyone you've been involved with recently who might want to hurt you?"

"No. I haven't had time to get involved enough for that." But just the question was sufficient to start the panic. Had she been the cause? Was she the reason? "I've just come off a tour. I don't know anyone who would do this. Not anyone."

Ben picked up the next stage. "Who knew you were here?"

"My editor, publisher, publicist. Anyone who wanted to. I've just done twelve cities with plenty of PR. If anyone had wanted to get to me, they could have done so a dozen times, in hotel rooms, on the subway, in my own apartment. It's Kathleen who's dead. I wasn't even here." She took a moment to calm down. "He raped her, didn't he?" Then she shook her head before Ed could answer. "No, no, I don't want to focus on that right now. I can't really focus on anything." She got up and found a small bottle of brandy in the cupboard beside the window. Taking a tumbler, she poured it half full. "Is there more?"

Ed wanted to take her hand, to stroke her hair and tell her not to think anymore. But he was a cop with a job to do.

"Grace, do you know why your sister had two phone lines in her office?"

"Yes." Grace took a quick slug of the brandy, waited for the punch, then took another. "There's no way to keep this confidential, is there?"

"We'll do what we can."

"Kathleen would hate the publicity." With the tumbler cupped in her hands, she sat again. "She always wanted her privacy. Look, I don't think the extra phone line really applies to all of this."

"We need everything." Ed waited until she drank again. "It's not going to hurt her now."

"No." The brandy wasn't helping, she realized, but she couldn't think of a medicine for her sickness, and the brandy seemed the best she could come up with. "I told you she'd hired a lawyer and so forth. She needed a good one to fight Jonathan, and good lawyers aren't easily had on a teacher's salary. She wouldn't take money from me. Kathy had a lot of pride, and to be frank, she always resented— never mind." She took a long breath. The brandy had headed straight for her stomach and was turning it over. Regardless, she drank again. "The other line was for business. She was moonlighting. For a company called Fantasy, Incorporated."

Ben cocked a brow as he wrote it down. "Fantasy calls?"

"That's a PG way of putting it." On a sigh, Grace rubbed the heels of her hands under her eyes. "Phone sex. I thought she was being pretty innovative, even wondered how I could work it into a plot." Her stomach turned over again, so she reached for a cigarette. When she fumbled with the lighter, Ben took it, flicked it, then set it beside the tumbler of brandy. "Thanks."

"Just take it slow," he advised.

"I'm all right. She was making a lot of money, and it seemed harmless. None of the callers had her name or number, because everything was put through from the main office, then she called the john—I guess that's the word for it. She called him back collect."

"Did she ever mention anyone who got a little too enthusiastic?"

"No. And I'm sure she would have. She told me about the job the first night I got here. If anything, she seemed to be a little amused by it, and a bit bored. Even if someone had wanted more personal contact, they wouldn't have been able to find her. Like I said, she didn't even use her own name. Oh, and Kath told me she didn't talk anything but straight sex." Grace spread her palm on the table. They'd sat at this very spot that first night, while the sun went down. "No bondage, no S and M, no violence. She was very picky about who she'd talk to. Anyone who wanted something, well, unconventional had to go elsewhere."

"She never met anyone she talked to?" Ed asked.

It wasn't a fact she could prove, but one she was sure of. "No, absolutely not. It was a job she took just as professionally as her teaching. She didn't date, she didn't go to parties. Her life was the school and this house. You lived next door to her," she said to Ed. "Did you ever see anyone come here? Did you ever see her stay out past nine in the evening?"

"No."

"We'll need to check on the information you've given us," Ben began as he rose. "If you remember anything, just call."

"Yes, I know. Thanks. Will they call me when—when I can take her?"

"We'll try to make it soon." Ben glanced at his partner again. He knew, better than most, how frustrating it was to mix murder and emotion, just as he knew that Ed would have to work out his involvement in his own way and time. "I'll file the report. Why don't you tie things up here?"

"Yeah." He nodded to his partner as he rose to take the cups to the sink.

"He's a nice man," Grace said after Ben had left. "Is he a good cop?"

"One of the best."

She pressed her lips together, wanting, needing to accept his word. "I know it's late, but would you mind not going yet? I have to call my parents."

"Sure." He stuck his hands in his pockets because she still looked too delicate to touch. They'd only begun to be friends, and now he was a cop again. A badge and a gun had a way of putting a lot of distance between him and a "civilian."

"I don't know what to say to them. I don't know how I can say anything."

"I can call them for you."

Grace drew hard on her cigarette because she wanted to agree. "Someone's always taking care of the ugly things for me. I guess this is one time I have to do it myself. If something like this can be easier, it'll be easier for them to hear it from me."

"I can wait in the other room."

"I'd appreciate it."

Grace watched him walk out, then braced herself to make the call.

Ed paced the living room. He was tempted to go back to the murder scene and sift through everything but held back. He didn't want to chance Grace walking in on him. She didn't need that, he thought, to see it all, to remember it all. Violent death was his business, but he'd never grown completely immune to the ripples it caused.

One life was over, and often dozens of others were affected. It was his job to look at it logically, to check out the details, the obvious and the elusive ones, until he compiled enough evidence for an arrest. It was the compilation that was the most satisfying aspect of police work for him. Ben was instinct and intensity; Ed was method. A case was built, layer by logical layer, fact by detailed fact. Emotions had to be controlled—or better, avoided altogether. It was a fine line he'd learned to walk, the line between involvement and calculation. If a cop stepped over the edge on either side, he was useless.

His mother hadn't wanted him to be a cop. She'd wanted him to join his uncle in the construction business. You've got good hands, she'd told him. You've got a strong back. You'd make union wage. Even now, years later, she was still waiting for him to turn in his badge for a hard hat.

He had never been able to explain to her why he couldn't, why he was in for the duration. It wasn't the excitement. Stakeouts, cold coffee or, as in his case, tepid tea, and reports in triplicate weren't exciting. And he certainly wasn't in it for the pay.

It was the feeling. Not the feeling when you shouldered on your gun. Never the feeling when you were forced to draw it. It was the feeling you took to bed with you at night, sometimes, only sometimes, that made you realize you'd done something right. If he were in a philosophical mood, he would talk of the law as the finest and most important invention of mankind. But in the gut, he knew it was more elemental than that.

You were the good guy. Maybe, just maybe, it was that simple.

Then there were times like this, times when you ended your day by looking down at a body and knew you had to be a part of finding the one who'd caused it . . . and bringing him in. You enforced the law and depended on the courts to remember the heart of it.

Justice. It was Ben who talked of justice. Ed pared it down to right and wrong.

"Thanks for waiting."

He turned to see Grace standing in the doorway. If possible, she was more pale. Her eyes were dark and huge, her hair disheveled as if she had dragged her hands through it again and again.

"You okay?"

"I guess I just realized that no matter what happens in my life, no matter what, I'll never have to do anything more painful than what I just did." She pulled a cigarette out of a crumpled pack and lit it. "My parents are getting the first flight out in the morning. I lied and told them I'd called a priest. It was important to them."

"You can call one tomorrow."

"Jonathan needs to be contacted."

"That'll be taken care of."

She nodded. Her hands were beginning to shake again. Grace took a long drag from her cigarette as she struggled to keep them steady. "I—I don't know who to call about arrangements. The funeral. I know Kath would want something subdued." She felt the hitch in her chest and filled her lungs with smoke. "We'll have to have a Mass. My parents will need that. Faith cushions despair. I think I wrote that once." She took a pull on the cigarette again until the tip was a hard red ball. "I want to have as much taken care of as possible before they come. I have to call the school."

He recognized the signs of emotions thawing. Her movements were jerky, her voice wavering between taut and trembling. "Tomorrow, Grace. Why don't you sit down?"

"I was angry with her when I left, when I came next door. I was upset with her, frustrated. The hell with it, I thought. The hell with her." She took another shaky drag. "I keep thinking if I'd just been able to get through, if I'd just been willing to push hard enough and stay to have it out with her, then—"

"It's a mistake, it's always a mistake to take on things that you don't have any control over." He reached for her arm, but she moved aside, shaking her head.

"I could have had control. Don't you understand? Nobody manipulates like I do. It was just with Kath that I couldn't find the right buttons. We were always edgy around each other. I didn't even know enough about her life to name six people she had contact with. If I did, I might know. Oh, I'd ask." Grace gave a quick, breathless laugh. "Kath would put me off and I wouldn't push. It was easier that way. Just tonight I found out she was an addict—prescription drugs."

She hadn't told them that, Grace realized. She hadn't intended to tell the police that. Letting out a shaky breath, she realized she wasn't talking to a cop anymore but to Ed, the guy next door. It was too late to back up; even though he said nothing, it was too late to back up and remember he wasn't just a nice man with kind eyes.

"There were three goddamn bottles of valium in the drawer of her bedside table. I found out and we fought, then when I couldn't get through, I just left. It was easier." She crushed out her cigarette with quick, violent taps, then immediately reached for another. "She was in trouble, she was hurting, and it was easier to walk away."

"Grace." Ed moved over to take the cigarette from her. "It's usually easier to blame yourself too."

She stared at him for a minute. Her hands went to her face as the dam burst. "Oh God, she must have been so scared. She was all alone, no one to help her. Ed, why? Dear God, why would anyone do this to her? I can't fix it. I just can't fix it."

He put his arms around her and held gently. Even when her fingers curled into his shirt and dug in, he held gently. Without speaking, he stroked her back.

"I loved her. I really loved her. When I got here, I was so glad to see her, and for a little while it seemed we might get close. After all these years. Now she's gone, like this, and I can't change it. My mother. Oh God, Ed, my mother. I can't bear it."

He did the only thing that seemed right. Lifting her into his arms, he carried her to the sofa to rock and soothe. He knew little about comforting women, about the right words to use or the right tone. He knew a lot about death and the shock and disbelief that followed it, but she wasn't just another stranger to question or offer polite sympathy to. She was a woman who had called to him from an open window on a spring morning. He knew her scent and the sound of her voice and the way the slight movement of her lips brought out small dimples. Now she was weeping against his shoulder.

"I don't want her to be gone," she managed to say. "I can't stand thinking about what happened to her—about what's happening now."

"Don't. It doesn't do any good." He held her tighter, just a little tighter. "You shouldn't stay here tonight. I can take you next door."

"No, if my parents call . . . I can't." She pressed her face hard against his shoulder. She couldn't think. As long as the tears kept coming she couldn't think. And there was so much to be done. But the shock was taking its toll in exhaustion and she couldn't sort it out. "Could you stay? Please, I don't want to be alone. Could you stay?"

"Sure. Try to relax. I won't go anywhere."

HE LAY IN BED with his heart hammering and screams still echoing in his head. The fleshy part of his arm was still throbbing where she'd torn at it. He'd wrapped it to keep blood off the sheets. His mother was fussy about her linens. But the steady ache was a reminder. A souvenir.

My God, he'd never known it would be like that. His body, his mind, maybe even his soul if there was such a thing, had risen so high, stretched so tight. Every other device he'd used, the alcohol, the drugs, the fasting, none of them had even come close to that kind of rough-edged pleasure.

He'd felt sick. He'd felt strong. He'd felt invincible.

Was it the sex, or was it the killing?

Laughing a little, he shifted on his sweat-damp sheet. How could he know, when it had been a first for both? Perhaps it had been that fascinating combination of the two. In any case, he'd have to find out.

For one cold, brief moment, he considered going downstairs and murdering one of the servants in her sleep.

When the idea didn't stir his blood, he discounted it just as coldly, just as quietly. He needed to wait a few days, to think it through logically. In any case, it wouldn't excite him to kill someone who meant as little to him as a servant.

But Desiree.

Turning again, he began to weep. He hadn't meant to hurt her. He'd wanted to love her, to show her how much he had to give. But she'd kept screaming, and her screams had driven him mad, driven him to a passion he'd been unaware existed. It had been beautiful. He wondered if she'd felt that wild, rising flood just before she'd died. He hoped so. He'd wanted to give her the best.

Now she was gone. Though she'd died by his hands, and he'd unexpectedly derived pleasure from it, he could mourn for her. He'd no longer hear her voice, arousing, teasing, promising.

He had to find another. Even the thought of it had his muscles trembling. Another voice that spoke only to him. Surely such glory wasn't meant for only once in a lifetime. He would find Desiree again, no matter what she called herself.

Rolling over, he watched the first pale light of dawn seep through his window. He'd find her.

Chapter 5

GRACE AWOKE AT FIRST light. There was no buffer of disorientation, no momentary lull of confusion. Her sister was dead, and that one bleak fact hammered in her head as she pushed herself up and struggled to cope with it.

Kathleen was gone, and she couldn't change it. Anymore than she'd ever been able to change the flaws in their relationship. It was harder to face that now, in the daylight, when the first burst of grief had dulled to a dry kind of ache.

They'd been sisters, but never friends. The truth was she hadn't even known Kathleen, not in the way Grace could claim to know at least a dozen other people. She'd never been privy to her sister's dreams and hopes, failures and despair. They had never shared giddy secrets or tiny miseries. And she'd never pushed, not really, not hard enough to crack the barrier.

Now she'd never know. Grace rested her face in her hands for a moment, just to gather strength. She'd never have the opportunity to find out if the gap could be bridged. There was only one thing for her to do now: to handle the details that death callously left scattered for the living to sweep up.

She pushed aside the blanket Ed had spread over her sometime during the night. She'd have to thank him. He'd certainly gone above and beyond the call of duty to stay with her until she'd been able to sleep. Now she needed a gallon of coffee so that she could pick up the phone and make the necessary calls.

She didn't want to stop in front of her sister's office. She wanted to walk straight by without a glance. But she stopped, felt compelled to stop. The door would be locked, she knew. The police seal was already stretched across it, but her writer's imagination made it too easy for her to see beyond the wood. She could remember now what even through shock her mind had absorbed. The overturned table, the shower of papers, the broken paperweight, and the phone, the phone upended on the floor.

And her sister. Bruised, bloody, half-naked. In the end, she hadn't even been allowed her dignity.

Kathleen was a case now, a file, a headline for the curious to scan over coffee and during car pools. It didn't help to realize that if Kathleen had been a stranger, Grace would have read the headline while downing coffee too. Her feet propped on the table, she would have absorbed each tiny detail. Then she'd have clipped the story and filed it for possible reference.

Murder had always fascinated her. After all, she made her living from it.

Turning away, she walked down the hall. Details, she would fill her time with details until she had the strength to face emotions. For once in her life she'd be practical. That was the least she could do.

She hadn't expected to find Ed in the kitchen. For a man of his size, he moved quietly. It was odd, the moment of awkwardness she felt. She couldn't remember feeling awkward with anyone before.

He'd stayed, not just until she'd slept, but through the night. He'd stayed with her. It might have been his basic kindness that caused the awkwardness. She stood in the doorway and wondered how you thanked someone for being decent.

His sleeves were rolled up, his feet bare as he stood in front of the stove stirring something that smelled distressingly like oatmeal. Over that, gratefully, Grace caught the scent of coffee.

"Hi."

He turned and in one quick glance noted that she was rumpled and hollow-eyed but sturdier than the night before. "Hi. I thought you might be able to sleep a couple more hours."

"I've got a lot to do today. I didn't expect you to be here."

Ed reached for a mug and poured her coffee. He hadn't expected to be there either, but he hadn't been able to leave. "You asked me to stay."

"I know." Why did she feel like crying again? Grace had to swallow, then take a couple of steadying breaths. "I'm sorry. You probably didn't get any sleep."

"I caught a few hours in the chair. Cops can sleep anywhere." Because she hadn't moved, he crossed to her and offered the coffee. "Sorry, I make lousy coffee."

"This morning I could drink motor oil." She took the cup, then his hand before he could turn away. "You're a nice man, Ed. I don't know what I'd have done without you last night."

Because he was never sure he had the right words, he simply squeezed her hand. "Why don't you sit down? You could use something to eat."

"I don't think—" She jolted and slopped coffee over her hand when the phone rang.

"Sit down. I'll get it."

Ed nudged her into a chair before picking up the wall

receiver. He listened for a moment, glanced back at Grace, then turned the burner off under the pan. "Ms. McCabe has no comment at this time." After he hung up, Ed began to spoon oatmeal into a bowl.

"It doesn't take them long, does it?"

"No. Grace, you're bound to have calls all day. The press knows you're Kathleen's sister and that you're here."

"Mystery writer discovers sister's body." Grace nodded, preparing herself. "Yes, it would make an interesting lead story." She stared at the phone. "I can handle the press, Ed."

"It might be better if you moved into a hotel for a few days."

"No." She shook her head. She hadn't thought about it, but her mind was instantly made up. "I need to stay here. Don't worry, I understand reporters." She managed to smile before he could argue. "You don't want me to eat that, do you?"

"Yeah." He set the bowl in front of her, then handed her a spoon. "You're going to need more than cold spaghetti."

Leaning over, she sniffed. "Smells like first grade." Since she felt she owed him, Grace dipped in. "Do I have to come down and sign a statement?"

"When you're ready. Since I was here, it simplifies things."

She nodded and managed to swallow the first spoonful. It didn't taste like her mother's. He'd done something to it, honey, brown sugar, something. But oatmeal was oatmeal. Grace switched to her coffee.

"Ed, will you give me an honest answer?"

"If I can."

"Do you think, I mean going on your professional judgment, do you think that whoever . . . whoever did this chose this house randomly?"

He'd already been through the room again the night

before, as soon as he'd been certain Grace was really asleep. There'd been little of value there, but a new electronic typewriter had been untouched, and he remembered seeing a small gold locket that would have hocked for fifty or sixty around Kathleen's neck before they'd put her body into the plastic bag. He could give Grace a comfortable lie, or the truth. It was her eyes that decided him. She already knew the truth.

"No."

Nodding, Grace stared into her coffee. "I have to call Our Lady of Hope. I'm hoping the Mother Superior can recommend a priest and a church. How soon do you think they'll let me have Kathleen?"

"I'll make some calls." He wanted to do more but only covered her hand with his, the gesture clumsy, he thought. "I'd like to help you."

She looked down at his hand. Both of hers could fit easily into it. There was strength there, the kind that could defend without smothering. She looked at his face. The strength was there too. Dependable. The thought made her lips curve a little. There was so little in life you could truly depend on.

"I know." She lifted a hand to his cheek. "And you have already. The next steps I have to take myself."

He didn't want to leave her. As far as he could remember, he'd never felt this way about a woman before. Because he did, he decided it was best to leave right away. "I'll write down the number of the station. Call me when you're ready to come down."

"Okay. Thanks for everything. I mean it."

"We've arranged for pass-bys, but I'd feel better if you didn't stay here alone."

She'd lived on her own too long to consider herself vulnerable. "My parents'll be here soon."

He scrawled down a number on a napkin before he rose. "I'll be around."

Grace waited until the door closed behind him, then stood to go to the phone.

Nobody saw anything, nobody heard anything." Ben leaned against the side of his car and drew out a cigarette. They'd been doing a house-to-house all morning with the same result. Nothing. Now he took a moment to study the neighborhood with its tired houses and postage-stamp yards.

Where were the busybodies? he wondered. Where were the people who stood by the windows peering through openings in the drapes at all the comings and goings? He'd grown up in a neighborhood not so different from this. And, as he remembered, if a new lamp was delivered, news of it ran up and down the street before the proud owners could plug it in. Apparently Kathleen Breezewood's life had been so bland that no one had been interested.

"According to this, Breezewood never had any visitors, almost invariably arrived home between four-thirty and six. She kept obsessively to herself. Last night, everything was quiet. Except 634's dog, who went on a barking spree about nine-thirty. That fits if the guy parked a block over and cut through their yard. Wouldn't hurt to check the next street over and see if anyone noticed a strange car or a guy on foot." He glanced at his partner to see Ed staring steadily down the street. The curtains were still closed at the Breezewood house. It looked empty, but Grace was inside. "Ed?"

"Yeah?"

"You want to take a break while I check out the next place?"

"I just hate to think about her in there by herself."

"So go keep her company." Ben flipped his cigarette into the street. "I can handle this."

He hesitated and had nearly made up his mind to

check on her when a cab drove by. It slowed, then stopped three doors down. Together they watched a man and a woman get out on opposite sides. As the man paid off the driver and grabbed a single bag, the woman started up the walk. Even with the distance Ed could see the resemblance to Grace, the build, the coloring. Then Grace herself was running out of the house. The woman's sobs carried as Grace folded her into her arms.

"Daddy." Ed saw her reach out and clasp hands so that the three of them stood and, for a moment, grieved in public.

"It's rough," Ben murmured.

"Come on." Turning away, Ed stuffed his hands in his pockets. "Maybe we'll get lucky."

He knocked on the door himself, resisting the urge to turn back and look at Grace. Watching her now was an intrusion. In his business he had to do enough of that with strangers.

"Lowenstein's checking out the ex," Ben put in. "She should have something for us when we get back."

"Yeah." Ed rubbed a hand over the back of his neck. Sleeping in the chair had left it stiff. "It's hard for me to buy the guy flying here, sneaking in the back door, and doing his wife."

"Stranger things've happened. Remember th—" He broke off as the door opened a crack. He had a glimpse of a mop of white hair and a gnarled hand studded with cheap glass rings. "Police officers, ma'am." He held up his badge. "Would you mind answering a few questions?"

"Come in, come in. I've been expecting you." The voice cracked with age and excitement. "Move back now, Boris, Lillian. Yes, we have company. Come in, come in," she repeated a bit testily as she bent, bones popping, and scooped up a fat slug of a cat. "There, Esmerelda, don't be afraid. They're policemen. You can sit down, sit right down." The woman wound her way through cats—Ben counted five of them—into a dusty little room with lace curtains and wilting doilies. "Yes, I told Esmerelda only this morning that we should expect some company. Sit, sit, sit." She waved a hand at a sofa alive with cat hair. "It's about that woman, of course, that poor woman down the street."

"Yes, ma'am." Ed stifled a sneeze as he sat on the edge of the cushions. An orange cat crouched at his feet and hissed.

"Behave yourself, Bruno." The woman smiled and re-arranged the symphony of wrinkles on her face. "Now isn't this cozy? I'm Mrs. Kleppinger. Ida Kleppinger, but you probably know that." With some ceremony, she fit a pair of glasses on her nose, squinted, and focused. "Why, you're the young man two doors down. Bought the Fowler place, didn't you? Terrible people. Didn't like cats, you know. Always complaining about their trash being strewn about. Well, I told them if they'd just put the lids on tight my babies would never dream of bothering with their nasty garbage. They're not savages, you know. My babies, I mean. Glad to see them gone, indeed yes. Aren't we, Esmerelda?"

"Yes, ma'am." Ed cleared his throat and tried not to breathe too deeply. It was more than apparent that litter boxes were placed liberally through the house. "We'd like to ask you some questions."

"About that poor Mrs. Breezewood, yes, yes. We heard it on the radio just this morning, didn't we, darlings? I don't own a television machine. I've always believed they make you sterile. Strangled her, did he?"

"We wondered if you noticed anything last night." Ben tried not to jolt when a cat leapt into his lap and dug in, dangerously close to his crotch.

"Boris likes you. Isn't that nice?" The old woman sat back and stroked her cat. "We were meditating last night. I'd gone back to the eighteenth century. I was one of the queen's handmaidens, you know. Such a trying time."

"Uh-huh." Enough was enough. Ben stood and struggled to detach the cat from his leg. "Well, we appreciate your time."

"Not at all. Of course, I wasn't surprised to hear about all of this. Been expecting it."

Ed, who'd been more than concerned that Boris would let loose on his shoes, looked back at her. "Have you?"

"Oh, absolutely. The poor dear never had a chance. Past sins catch up with you."

"Past sins?" Interested again, Ben hesitated. "Did you know Mrs. Breezewood well?"

"Intimately. We survived Vicksburg together. A dreadful battle. Why, I can still hear the cannon fire. But her aura . . ," Mrs. Kleppinger gave a sad shake of the head. "Doomed, I'm afraid. She was murdered by a group of Yankee raiders."

"Ma'am, we're more interested in what happened to Mrs. Breezewood last night." Ed's patience, usually generous, was running thin.

"Well, of course you are." Her glasses slipped down her nose so that she stared myopically over them. "Such a sad woman. Repressed, sexually, I'm sure. I thought she might be happy when her sister came to visit, but it didn't seem so. I can see her leave for work each morning while I'm watering my gardenias. Tense. The woman was tense, bundle of nerves, just as I remember from Vicksburg. Then there was the car that followed her one morning."

Ben sat back down, cats or not. "What car?"

"Oh, a dark one, one of those rich cars, so big and quiet. I wouldn't have thought a thing of it, but as I was watering my gardenias, one has to be so careful with gardenias. Fragile things. Anyway, as I was watering, I watched the car drive down the street behind Mrs. Breezewood's, and I got such palpitations." The woman waved her hand in front of her face as if to cool it. The glass on her fingers was too dull to sparkle in the light. "My heart just pounded and skipped until I had to sit right down. Just like

Vicksburg—and the Revolution, of course. All I could think was poor Lucilla—that was her name before, you know. Lucilla Greensborough. Poor Lucilla, it's going to happen again. Nothing I could do, of course," she explained as she went back to stroking her cat. "Fate is fate after all."

"Could you see who was driving the car?"

"Oh my goodness no. My eyes aren't what they were."

"Did you notice the license plate?"

"My dear, I can hardly see an elephant in the yard next door." She pushed her glasses straight again, and surprised her eyes into focusing. "I have my feelings, sensations. That car gave me a bad feeling. Death. Oh yes, I wasn't surprised at all to hear the news on the radio this morning."

"Mrs. Kleppinger, do you remember which day you noticed the car?"

"Time means nothing. It's all a cycle. Death is quite a natural event, and very temporary. She'll be back, and perhaps finally, she'll be happy."

*B*EN CLOSED THE FRONT door behind him and breathed in hard and deep. "Christ, what a smell." Cautious, he pressed a hand to his upper thigh. "I thought that little bastard had drawn blood. Probably didn't have shots either." As he walked to the car he tried vainly to brush off clinging cat hair. "What did you make of her?"

"She's lost a few bricks since Vicksburg. She might have seen a car." Glancing back, he noted that several windows of her house would afford a clear enough view of the street. "Which may or may not have been following Breezewood's. Either way, it doesn't mean shit."

"You've got my vote." Ben took the driver's seat. "You want to stop in for a minute?" he asked with a nod toward the house down the street. "Or head back in?"

"Let's go back. She probably needs time with her parents."

GRACE HAD PLIED HER mother with spiked tea. She'd held her father's hand. She'd wept again until she simply had no energy for more. Because they had needed it, Grace had lied. In her version, Kathleen had been well on the way to establishing a new life. There was no mention of pills or controlled bitterness. Grace was aware, if Kathleen hadn't been, that their parents had had great hopes for their elder daughter.

They had always considered Kathleen the stable one, the reliable one, while being able to smile and think of Grace as amusing. They'd enjoyed Grace's creativity without being able to understand it. Kathleen, with her conventional marriage, her handsome husband and son, was easily understood.

True, the divorce had shaken them, but they were parents, loving ones, and had been able to shift their beliefs enough to accept, while harboring the hope that in time their daughter would be reconciled with her family.

Now they had to accept that it would never be. They had to face that their older daughter, the one they'd pinned their first hopes on, was dead. It was enough, Grace had decided. It was more than enough.

So she didn't mention the mood swings, the valium, or the resentment she'd discovered had been eating her sister from the inside out.

"She was happy here, Gracie?" Louise McCabe sat huddled beside her husband and tore a Kleenex into small pieces.

"Yes, Mom." Grace wasn't sure how many times she'd answered that question in the last hour, but continued to soothe. She'd never seen her mother look helpless. Throughout her life, Louise McCabe had been dominant, making decisions, executing them. And her father had always been there. He'd been the one to slip an extra five dollars into a waiting hand, or to clean up after the dog had had an accident on the rug.

Looking at him now, she suddenly realized for the very first time that he'd aged. His hair was thinner than it had been when she'd been a girl. He was tanned from the hours he spent out-of-doors. His face was fuller. He was a man in the prime of his life, she thought, healthy, vigorous, but just now his shoulders were slumped, and the liveliness that had always been there was gone from his eyes.

She wanted to hold these two people who had somehow made everything come out right for her. She wanted to turn back the clock for all of them so that they were young again, living in a pretty suburban home with a scruffy dog.

"We wanted her to come to Phoenix for a while," Louise continued, dabbing at her eyes with the ragged remains of the tissue. "Mitch talked to her. She always listened to her dad. But not this time. We were so happy when you came to visit her. All the trouble she's been having. Poor little Kevin." She squeezed her eyes shut. "Poor, poor little Kevin."

"When can we see her, Gracie?"

Grace squeezed her father's hand, watching intently as he spoke. He looked around the room, trying, Grace believed, to absorb what was left of his older daughter. There was so little here, a few books, a pot of silk flowers. She held on to him, hoping he didn't see how cold the room was.

"Tonight maybe. I asked Father Donaldson to come by this afternoon. He's from the old parish. Why don't you come upstairs now, Mom, so you'll be rested when he comes? You'll feel better when you talk to him."

"Grace is right, Lou." And he'd seen. Like Grace, he had an eye for detail. The only spot of life in the room was the jacket Grace had negligently tossed over a chair. He wanted to weep for that more than anything else, but couldn't explain it. "Let me take you up."

She leaned heavily against her husband, a slim woman with dark hair and a strong back. As she watched them go, Grace realized that in grief they had shifted her to the head of the family. She could only hope that she had the strength to pull it off.

Her mind was dull from weeping, cluttered with the arrangements she'd already made and those yet to be settled. She knew when the grief ebbed, her parents would have the comfort of their faith. For Grace, it was the first time she'd been slapped down with the knowledge that life wasn't always a game to be played with a grin and a clever brain. Optimism wasn't always a shield against the worst of it, and acceptance wasn't always enough.

She'd never had a full-power emotional blow before, not personally or professionally. She'd never considered that she'd led a charmed life and had never had patience with people who complained about what fate had handed them. People made their own luck. Hit a rough spot, coast for a while, then find the best way out, she'd always thought.

When she'd decided to write, she'd sat down and done it. It was true she had natural talent and a fluid imagination and willingness to work, but she'd also had an innate determination that if she wanted something badly enough, she'd get it. There'd been no starving in a garret or creative suffering. There'd been no angst or agony of the artist. She'd taken her savings and had moved to New York. A part-time job had paid the rent while she drove through her first novel in a wild and breathless ninety days.

When she'd decided to fall in love, she'd done so with the same sort of verve and energy. There'd been no regrets, no hesitation. She'd fed on the emotion as long as it had lasted, and when it was over, she'd moved on without tears or recriminations.

She was nearly thirty and had never had her heart

broken or her dreams smashed. Shaken a time or two, perhaps, but she'd always managed to right herself and forge ahead. Now, for the first time in the whirlwind of her life, she'd hit a wall that couldn't be climbed over or breached. Her sister's death wasn't something she could change by shifting into neutral. Her sister's murder wasn't something she could accept as one of life's little twists.

She found she wanted to scream, to throw something, to rage. Her hands shook as she lifted the cups from the table. If she'd been alone, she'd have given in to it. More, she'd have wallowed in the release of it. Instead she steadied herself. Her parents needed her. For the first time, they needed her. And she wouldn't let them down.

She put the cups down at the sound of the doorbell and went to answer it. If Father Donaldson had come early she'd go over the funeral arrangements with him. But when she opened the door, it wasn't to a priest but to Jonathan Breezewood the third.

"Grace." He nodded at her but didn't offer his hand. "May I come in?"

She had to struggle against the urge to slam the door in his face. He hadn't cared about Kathleen when she was alive, why should he care about her dead? Saying nothing, she stepped back.

"I came the moment I was informed."

"There's coffee in the kitchen." She turned her back on him and started down the hall. Because he put his hand on her shoulder, more, because she didn't want to show him a weakness, she stopped in front of Kathleen's office.

"Here?"

"Yes." She looked at him long enough to see something move across his face. Grief, disgust, regret. She was too tired to care. "You didn't bring Kevin."

"No." He continued to stare at the door. "No, I thought it best that he stay with my parents."

Because she was forced to agree, she said nothing. He

was a child, too young to face funerals or the sounds of mourning.

"My parents are upstairs resting."

"Are they all right?"

"No." She moved again, compelled to distance herself from the locked door. "I wasn't sure you'd come, Jonathan."

"Kathleen was my wife, the mother of my son."

"Yes. But apparently that wasn't enough to insure your fidelity."

He studied her with calm eyes. He was undoubtedly a beautiful man, clear-cut features, thick, California-blond hair, a hard, well-kept body. But it was the eyes Grace had always found so unattractive. Calm, always calm, just edging toward cold.

"No, it wasn't. I'm sure Kathleen told you her version of our marriage. It hardly seems appropriate now for me to tell you mine. I came here to ask you to tell me what happened."

"Kathleen was murdered." Holding herself together, Grace poured coffee. She'd lived on nothing else all day. "Raped and strangled in her office last night."

Jonathan accepted the cup, then slowly lowered into a kitchen chair. "Were you here when—when it happened?"

"No, I was out. I came back a little after eleven and found her."

"I see." Whatever he felt, if anything, wasn't apparent in the two brief words. "The police, do they have any idea who did this?"

"Not at the moment. You're free to talk to them, I'm sure. Detectives Jackson and Paris are handling it."

He nodded again. With his connections, he could have copies of the police reports in an hour without having to deal directly with detectives. "Have you set a time for the funeral?"

"The day after tomorrow. Eleven o'clock. There will be a Mass at St. Michael's, the church we used to belong to.

There'll be a viewing tomorrow night because it's important to my parents. At Pumphrey's. The address is in the book."

"I'd be glad to help with any of the details, or expenses."

"No."

"All right then." He rose without having tasted his coffee. "I'm staying at the Hotel Washington if you need to contact me."

"I won't."

He lifted a brow at the venom in her voice. As sisters, he'd never seen the least resemblance between Kathleen and Grace. "You never could stand the sight of me, could you, Grace?"

"Barely. It hardly matters how you and I feel about each other at this point. I would like to say one thing." She dug the last cigarette out of her pack and lit it without a tremor. Loathing brought out a strength she could only be grateful for. "Kevin is my nephew. I'll expect to be able to see him whenever I'm in California."

"Naturally."

"And my parents." She pressed her lips together a moment. "Kevin is all they have left of Kathleen. They're going to need regular contact."

"It goes without saying. I've always felt my relationship with your parents was reasonable."

"You consider yourself a reasonable man?" The bitterness slipped out, surprising her. Just for an instant, she'd sounded like Kathleen. "Did you think it reasonable to take Kevin away from his mother?"

He said nothing at first. Though his face was bland, she could almost hear the workings of his mind. When he spoke, it was brief and without expression. "Yes. I'll let myself out."

She cursed him. Swinging around to lean on the counter, she cursed him until she was empty.

◆ ◆ ◆

ED PUSHED HIS FACE into a sink filled with cold water and held his breath. Five seconds, then ten, and he could feel the fatigue draining. A ten-hour day wasn't unusual. A ten-hour day on two hours' sleep wasn't unusual. But the worry was. He was discovering that it sapped energy more completely than a fifth of gin.

What was he supposed to tell her? He lifted his head so that water ran down his beard. They didn't have the first lead. Not a glimmer. She was smart enough to know that if the trail cooled during the first twenty-four hours, it got dead cold fast.

They had a batty old woman who may or may not have seen a car that may or may not have followed her sister's car sometime or other. They had a barking dog. Kathleen Breezewood had no close friends or associates, no one closer than Grace herself. If she was telling everything she knew, the trail led to suspect unknown. Someone who had seen Kathleen on her way to work, at the market, in the yard. The city had its share of violence, provoked and otherwise. At this point, it looked as though she had simply been one more random victim.

They'd questioned a couple of rejects that morning. Two parolees whose lawyers had bargained them back on the streets after separate assaults on women. Gathering evidence and making a clean arrest didn't mean a conviction, just as the law didn't mean justice. They hadn't had enough to hold either one of them, and though Ed knew that sooner or later they'd probably rape some other woman, they hadn't done Kathleen Breezewood.

It wasn't good enough. He grabbed a towel from a closet. The lattice doors he'd chosen for it were tilted against a wall downstairs, waiting for sanding. He'd planned to work on them tonight for an hour or two so they'd be ready for hanging on his day off. Somehow he didn't think working with his hands would make his mind easy this time.

He buried his face in the towel and thought about calling her. To say what? He'd made certain she'd been notified that the body would be released to her in the morning. The medical examiner's report had been on his desk when he'd checked into the station at six.

It wasn't any use giving her the details. Sexual assault, death by strangulation. Death between 9:00 and 10:00 P.M. Coffee and valium in the system and little else. Blood type O positive. Which meant that the perp's blood type was A positive. Kathleen hadn't let him get away clean.

She'd taken some skin and some hair with the blood, so they knew he was white. And he was young, under thirty.

They'd even lifted a couple of partial prints off the phone cord, which made Ed figure the killer had either been stupid or the murder unpremeditated. But prints only worked if they could be matched. So far, the computer hadn't come up with anything.

If they brought him down, they had enough circumstantial evidence to bring him to trial. Maybe enough to convict him. If they brought him down.

It wasn't enough.

He tossed the towel over the lip of the sink. Was he edgy because the murder had been committed in the house next to his? Because he knew the victim? Because he'd begun to have a few entertaining fantasies that involved the victim's sister?

With a half laugh, Ed dragged his damp hair away from his face and started downstairs. No, he didn't think his feelings for Grace, whatever they were, had anything to do with the fact that instinct told him there was something nastier about this than was already apparent.

Maybe it was close, but he'd lost people who had been a great deal closer to him than Kathleen Breezewood.

People he'd worked with, people whose families were familiar to him. Their deaths had left him feeling angry and frustrated, but not edgy.

Dammit, he'd feel better if she were out of that house.

He walked to the kitchen. He was more comfortable in the room he'd redesigned and rebuilt with his own hands. With his mind on other things, he pulled over a basket of fruit to chop for a salad. He worked briskly, as a man who'd been fending for himself, and fending well, for most of his life.

A great many of the men he knew satisfied themselves by settling for a can or a frozen dinner eaten over the sink. To Ed that was the most depressing act of single life. The microwave had made it even more so. You could buy a complete meal in a box, zap it for five minutes, and eat it without using a pan or a plate. Neat, convenient, and lonely.

He often ate alone, with only a book for company, but he did more than watch his cholesterol and carbohydrates. It was all a matter of attitude, he'd decided long ago. Real plates and a table made the difference between a solitary meal and a lonely one.

He dropped some carrots and celery into his juicer and let them whirl through. The knock at his back door surprised him. Ben used the back way occasionally, but he never knocked. Partners and spouses developed similiar intimacies. Ed switched off the machine, then grabbed a dishcloth for his hands before answering.

"Hi." Grace gave him a quick smile but kept her hands in her pockets. "I saw the light, so I hopped over the fence."

"Come on in."

"I hope you don't mind. Neighbors can be a pain." She stepped into the kitchen and felt solid and safe for the first time in hours. She'd told herself she'd come to ask the questions that had to be asked, but knew she'd come just as much for comfort. "I'm messing up your dinner. Listen, I'll run along."

"Sit down, Grace."

She nodded, grateful, and promised herself she wouldn't weep or rage. "My parents went to church. I didn't realize how I'd feel about being alone over there." She sat, moving her hands from her lap to the table, then back to her lap. "I want to thank you for pushing through the paperwork or whatever. I'm not sure my parents could get through another day without, well, seeing Kath." She shifted her hands to the table again. "Don't let me hold up your dinner, okay?"

He realized he could stay happy for several hours just looking at her. When he caught himself staring, he started to fuss with the salad. "Are you hungry?"

She shook her head and nearly managed to smile again. "We ate before. I figured the only way to get my parents to eat was to set the example. It's funny how something like this will have you switching roles. What's that?" She glanced at the glass Ed set on the table.

"It's carrot juice. Want some?"

"You drink carrots?" It was a small thing, but enough to pull out what passed for a laugh. "Got a beer?"

"Sure." He pulled one out of the fridge, remembered a glass, then put both down in front of her. When he dug an ashtray out of a kitchen drawer, she shot him a look of profound gratitude.

"You're a pal, Ed."

"Yeah. You need any help tomorrow?"

"I think we'll manage." Grace ignored the glass and drank straight from the bottle. "I'm sorry, but I have to ask you if you found out anything."

"No. We're still in the preliminary stages, Grace. It takes time."

Though she nodded, she knew as well as he that time

was the enemy. "Jonathan's in town. Will you question him?"

"Yes."

"I mean you." She took out a cigarette as he sat across from her. "I'm sure you've got a lot of good cops in your department, but can you do it?"

"All right."

"He's hiding something, Ed." When he said nothing, she picked up her beer again. It would do her no good to become hysterical, to make the accusations that had been simmering in her brain all day. Ed might have been kind and sympathetic, but he wouldn't take anything she said in the heat of emotion seriously.

And the truth was, she wanted to believe Jonathan had been responsible. That would be easy, that would be tangible. It was so much more difficult to hate a stranger.

"Look, I know I'm not functioning at top level. And I know that I'm starting off biased against Jonathan." She took a steadying breath. Her voice was calm and reasonable. She didn't hear, as Ed did, the light trace of desperation around the edges. "But he's hiding something. It's not just instinct, Ed. You're a trained observer, I'm an innate one. I was born cataloging people. I can't help it."

"Whenever you're too close to something, the vision blurs, Grace."

Her hackles rose, prompted by the strain of the last twenty-four hours. She felt her temper slip and barely managed to catch it. "All right. That's why I'm asking you to talk to him. You'll see for yourself. Then you can tell me."

Ed ate his salad slowly. The longer this went on, he thought, the harder it was going to be. "Grace, I can't tell you about the investigation, not specifics, not any more than the department decides to release to the press."

"I'm not a goddamn reporter, I'm her sister. If Jonathan had anything to do with what happened to Kathleen, don't I have a right to know?"

"Maybe." His eyes were on hers, very calm and suddenly distant. "But I don't have the right to tell you anything until it's official."

"I see." Very slowly, and with a precision she possessed only when she deliberately controlled her temper, Grace tapped out her cigarette. "My sister was raped and murdered. I found her body. I'm the only one left to comfort my parents. But the cop says the investigation's confidential." She rose, knowing she was on the edge of another crying jag.

"Grace—"

"No, don't give me any platitudes, I'll hate you for it." She willed herself to calm down again as she studied him. "You have a sister, Ed?"

"Yeah."

"Think about it," she said as she reached the back door. "And let me know how much departmental procedure would mean to you if you were putting her in the ground."

When the door shut, Ed pushed aside his plate, then picked up her beer. He finished it off in two long swallows.

Chapter 6

*J*ERALD WASN'T SURE WHY he sent flowers to her funeral. In part it was because he felt it necessary to acknowledge the odd and unique role she'd played in his life. He thought too that if he acknowledged it, he would be able to close the chapter, stop dreaming about her.

He was already searching for another, listening hour after hour for that one voice that could bring him the rush and thrill. He never doubted that he'd find it, that he would recognize it with one phrase, one word. The voice would bring him the woman, and the woman would bring him the glory.

Patience was important, timing was vital, but he wasn't sure how long he could wait. The experience had been so special, so unique. To experience it again would be, well, perhaps like dying.

He was losing sleep. Even his mother had noticed it, and she rarely noticed anything between her committees and her cocktails. Of course she'd accepted his excuse about studying late and had tutted and patted his cheek and told him not to work so hard. She was such a fool. Still, he didn't resent her. Her preoccupations had always provided him with the space he needed for his own diversions. In return, he'd given her the illusion of the ideal son. He didn't play loud music or go to wild parties. Such things were childish anyway.

He might have considered school a waste of time, but he maintained good, even excellent, grades. The simplest way to keep people from bothering you was to give them what they wanted. Or to make them think you were doing so.

He was fastidious, even fussy, about his room and his personal hygiene. In that way it was accepted that the servants would stay out of his personal space. His mother considered it a mild, even endearing, eccentricity. And it insured that no one would find his cache of drugs.

More important, no servant, no family, no friend ever touched his computer.

He had a natural aptitude for machines. They were so much better, so much cleaner than people. He'd been fifteen when he'd tapped into his mother's personal checking account. It had been so easy to take what he needed, and so much more rewarding than asking for it. He'd tapped into other accounts, but he'd soon tired of the money.

It was then he'd discovered the phone, and how exciting it could be to listen to other people. Like a ghost. The Fantasy line had been an accident at first. But soon it was all he cared about.

He couldn't stop, not until he'd found the next, not until he'd found the voice that could soothe the pounding in his head. But he had to be careful.

He knew his mother was a fool, but his father . . . if his father noticed anything, there'd be questions. Thinking of it, Jerald took a pill, then two. Though he preferred amphetamines to barbiturates, he wanted to sleep that night, and dreamlessly. He knew just how clever his father was.

He'd put his talent to use for years in court before he'd

made the almost seamless switch to politics. From Congress to the Senate, Charlton P. Hayden had earned a reputation for power and intelligence. His image was that of a wealthy, privileged man who understood the needs of the masses, who fought for lost causes and won. A paragon, without a shadow to smear his reputation. No, his father had always been a very careful man, a very dedicated man, a very clever man.

Jerald had no doubt that when election year was over, when the votes were tallied and the last of the confetti swept up, his father would be the youngest and most glamorous resident of the Oval Office since Kennedy.

Charlton P. Hayden wouldn't be pleased to learn that his only son, his heir apparent, had strangled one woman and was waiting for the opportunity to do so again.

But Jerald knew himself to be very clever. No one would ever know that the son of the front-running candidate for president of the United States had a taste for murder. He knew if he could hide it from his father, he could hide it from anyone.

So he sent the flowers, and he sat late at night in the dark, waiting for the right voice and the right words.

THANK YOU FOR COMING, Sister." Grace knew it was foolish to feel odd about shaking a nun's hand. It was simply that she couldn't help remembering how many times her knuckles had been whacked by one with a ruler. And she couldn't quite get used to the fact that they didn't wear habits anymore. The nun who had introduced herself as Sister Alice wore a small silver crucifix with her conservative black suit and low-heeled pumps. But there was no wimple and robe.

"All our prayers are with you and your family, Miss McCabe. In the few months I knew Kathleen, I came to respect her dedication and skill as a teacher."

Respect. The word came again as it had, in cold comfort, for an hour. No one spoke of affection or of friendship. "Thank you, Sister."

There were several members of the faculty as well as a handful of students in the church. Without them, the pews would have been all but empty. She'd had no one, Grace thought as she stationed herself in the rear, no one who hadn't come out of a sense of duty or compassion.

There were flowers. She looked at the baskets and wreaths in the nave. She wondered why she seemed to be the only one who found the colors obscene under the circumstances. Most were from California. A bunch of gladioluses and a formal card were apparently enough from the people who had once been a part of Kathleen's life. Or of Mrs. Jonathan Breezewood's life.

Grace hated the smell of them, just as she hated the glossy white casket she'd refused to approach. She hated the music that flowed quietly down the aisle and knew she'd never be able to hear an organ again without thinking of death.

These were the trappings the dead expected from the living. Or was it that the living expected them from the dead? She wasn't sure of anything except that when her time came, there would be no ceremonies, no dirges, no friends and relatives staring teary-eyed down at what was left of her.

"Grace."

She turned, hoping nothing showed on her face. "Jonathan. You came."

"Of course." Unlike Grace, he looked down the aisle at the white casket and his former wife.

"Still image-conscious, I see."

He noted the heads that turned at Grace's statement but merely glanced at his watch. "I'm afraid I can only stay for the service. I have an appointment to speak with a

Detective Jackson in an hour. Then I have to get to the airport."

"It's good of you to fit your wife's funeral into your schedule. Doesn't it bother you, Jonathan, to be such a hypocrite? Kathleen meant nothing, less than nothing to you."

"I don't think this is the appropriate time or place for this discussion."

"You're wrong." She took his arm before he could pass her. "There'll never be a better time or place."

"If you push, Grace, you'll hear things you'd prefer not to."

"I haven't begun to push. It makes me sick to see you here, playing the grieving husband after what you put her through."

It was the murmurs that made up his mind. The murmurs, and the almost guilty glances over the shoulder. Clamping his hand to Grace's arm, he drew her outside. "I prefer to keep family discussions private."

"We aren't family."

"No, and it would be foolish to pretend there's ever been any affection between us. You've never bothered to disguise your contempt for me."

"I don't believe in veneers, especially over feelings. Kathleen should never have married you."

"On that we agree completely. Kathleen should never have married anyone. She was a barely adequate mother and a poor excuse for a wife."

"How dare you? How dare you stand here, now, and speak that way? You humiliated her, you flaunted your affairs in her face."

"Better if I had had them behind her back?" With a half laugh, he looked beyond her to an elm that had been planted when the church's cornerstone had been laid. "Do you think she cared? You're more of a fool than I believed you to be."

"She loved you." Her voice was furious now. Because it

hurt, hurt more than she'd ever conceived of to stand here on the steps where she'd stood so often before with her sister. In the May Procession in frilly white dresses, on Easter Sunday in yellow bonnets and Mary Janes. They'd walked up and down those same steps so many times together as children, and now she stood alone. The organ music came low and mournful through the cracks of the doors. "You and Kevin were her whole life."

"You're very much mistaken, Grace. I'll tell you about your sister. She cared about no one. She had no passion, no capability for it. Not just physical, but emotional passion. She never turned a hair over my affairs, as long as they were discreet, as long as they didn't interfere with the one thing she really prized. Being a Breezewood."

"Stop it."

"No, you'll listen now." He caught her before she could run back into the church. "It wasn't just sex she was ambivalent about, it was anything that didn't fit into her plans. She'd wanted a son, a Breezewood, and once she had Kevin, she considered her duty ended. He was a symbol more than a child to her."

It hit home, too close to where her own thoughts had drifted over the years. And it made her ashamed. "That's not true. She loved Kevin."

"As much as she was capable. You tell me, Grace, did you ever see one spontaneous act of affection from her, to yourself, to your parents?"

"Kathy wasn't demonstrative. That doesn't mean she didn't feel."

"She was cold." Grace jerked her head back as if she'd been slapped. It wasn't a surprise to hear it; it was a surprise to realize she'd harbored the same secret opinion all of her life. "And the worst of it is, I don't think she could help it. For most of our marriage we went our own ways because it was convenient for both of us."

It made her worse than ashamed. It made her sick.

Because she'd known it, she'd seen it, but she'd refused to believe it. She saw the way he smoothed his hair when the light breeze disturbed it. It was the casual gesture of a man who preferred no imperfections. Kathleen might have been at fault, but she hadn't been alone.

"Then it stopped being convenient for you."

"That's correct. When I asked her for a divorce she showed the first emotion I'd seen from her in years. She refused, she threatened, even pleaded. But it wasn't me she was afraid of losing, it was the position she'd grown comfortable in. When she saw I was resolute, she left. She refused a settlement of any kind. She'd been gone three months before she contacted me and asked for Kevin. For three months she hadn't seen or spoken to her son."

"She was suffering."

"Perhaps she was. I no longer cared. I told her she was not going to uproot Kevin, but that we would make arrangements for her to have him for a time during his school vacation."

"She was going to fight you for him. She was afraid of you and your family, but she was going to fight for Kevin."

"I'm aware of that."

"You knew," Grace said slowly. "You knew what she was doing?"

"I knew she'd hired a lawyer and a detective."

"And what would you have done to keep her from winning custody?"

"Whatever became necessary." Again, he glanced at his watch. "It appears we're holding up the service."

He opened the door to the vestibule and stepped inside.

BEN PULLED A GLAZED doughnut out of a white paper bag as he stopped at a red light. It had warmed enough to have the windows at half mast so that the tunes from the easy listening station on the radio of the car beside him drifted over his own choice of B. B. King.

"How can anybody listen to that crap?" He glanced over, saw the car was a Volvo, and rolled his eyes. "I figure it's a Soviet conspiracy. They've taken over the airwaves, filled them with inane orchestrated pap, and are going to keep playing it until the minds of average Americans turn to Jell-O. Meanwhile, waiting for us to fall over in a Manilow coma, they're listening to the Stones." He took another bite of doughnut before turning King up another notch. "And we're worried about midrange missiles in Europe."

"You ought to write the Pentagon," Ed suggested.

"Too late." Ben drove through the intersection and turned right at the next corner. "Probably already piping in Carpenters ballads. They're mellowing us out, Ed, mellowing us out and just waiting for us to mold."

When his partner didn't comment, Ben switched the radio down again. If he wasn't going to be able to take Ed's mind off it, he might as well shoot straight on.

"The funeral's today, isn't it?"

"Yeah."

"When we finish this, you could take a couple hours of personal time."

"She's not going to want to see me unless there's something I can tell her."

"Maybe we'll have something." Ben began checking numbers on the narrow side street. "When's she going back to New York?"

"I don't know." And he'd done his best not to think of it. "A day or two, I guess."

"You serious about the writer?"

"I haven't had time to think about it."

Ben swung the car over to the curb. "Better think fast." He looked beyond Ed to the tiny little shop nestled in the middle of a half-dozen others. It might have been a trendy boutique once, or a craft shop. Now it was Fantasy, Incorporated.

"Doesn't look like a den of iniquity."

"You'd know about that." Absently, Ben licked glaze from his thumb. "For a business that's chugging along at a steady profit, they don't seem to be putting much into their image."

"I watch *Miami Vice*." Ed waited until two cars passed before opening his door to step out on the street.

"I wouldn't guess they'd get many social visits from clients."

Inside, the office was the size of an average bedroom, with no frills. The walls were painted white and the carpet was industrial grade. There were a couple of mismatched chairs that might have been picked up at a yard sale. Space was at a premium because the pair of desks stretched nearly wall-to-wall. Ben recognized them as Army issue, sturdy and unimpressive. But the computer was top of the line.

Behind one of the monitors, a woman stopped tapping keys as they entered. Her fall of brown hair was pulled back from a round, pretty face. Her suit jacket was draped behind her chair. Over a white silk blouse she wore a trio of gold chains. With a half smile for both men, she rose.

"Hello. May I help you?"

"We'd like to talk to the owner." Ben pulled out his badge. "Police business."

She held out a hand for Ben's identification, studied it, then handed it back. "I'm the owner. What can I do for you?"

Ben pocketed his badge again. He wasn't sure what he'd been expecting, but it hadn't been a tidy young woman who looked as though she'd just come from planning a field trip for Brownies. "We'd like to talk to you about one of your employees, Miss . . ."

"Mrs. Cawfield. Eileen Cawfield. This is about Kathleen Breezewood, isn't it?"

"Yes, ma'am."

"Sit down, please, Detective Paris." She glanced at Ed. "Jackson."

"Please, sit down. Can I get you some coffee?"

"No, thanks," Ed answered before Ben could accept. "You know Kathleen Breezewood was murdered."

"I read it in the paper. Horrible." She sat behind the desk again and folded her hands on a neat pink blotter. "I only met her once, when she came in to interview, but I feel very close to all my employees. She was popular. In fact Desiree—I'm sorry, I'm afraid we get into the habit of thinking of them as their alter egos—Kathleen was one of my most popular. She had such a soothing voice. That's very important in this business."

"Did Kathleen complain about any of her callers?" Ed flipped over a page in his notebook. "Did anyone make her uneasy, threaten her?"

"No. Kathleen was very particular about the kind of calls she would take. She was a very conservative woman, and we respected that. We have one or two who handle the more . . . unusual fantasies. Excuse me," she said as her phone rang.

"Fantasy, Incorporated." With the efficiency of a veteran receptionist, she had a pen in hand. "Yes, of course. I'll be happy to see if Louisa's available. I'll need the number of a major credit card. Yes? And the expiration date. Now the number where you can be reached. If Louisa isn't available, do you have another preference? Yes, I'll see to it. Thank you."

After hanging up the phone, Eileen sent Ben and Ed an apologetic smile. "I'll just be another minute. He's a regular so it simplifies things." She pushed a few buttons on her keyboard, then picked up her phone again. "Louisa? Yes, it's Eileen. I'm fine, thanks. Mr. Dunnigan would like to talk to you. Yes, the usual number. You have it? That's it.

You're welcome. 'Bye now." After replacing the receiver, she folded her hands again. "Sorry for the interruption."

"You get many like that?" Ben asked. "Callbacks, regulars?"

"Oh yes. There are a lot of lonely people, sexually frustrated people. In today's climate, there are more who prefer the safety and anonymity of a phone call over the risks of singles' bars." She settled back and crossed her legs under the desk. "We're all aware of the rise in sexually transmitted diseases. The life-styles of the sixties and seventies have had to alter greatly in the latter half of the eighties. Fantasy calls are just one alternative."

"Yeah." Ed imagined she could take that routine on Donahue with some success. In fact, he didn't disagree with her but was simply more interested in murder than in philosophy or mores. "Did Kathleen have a lot of regulars?"

"As I said, she was popular. Several clients have called for her in the last couple of days. They've been very disappointed when I told them she was no longer with us."

"Has anyone not called her who should have?"

Eileen paused to think this through, then again turned to her computer and put it to work. "No. I'm aware you'd have to question anyone connected with Kathleen. But you see, the men who call here only know of Desiree. She was a voice, faceless, or we'll say with whatever face they chose for her. We're very careful here, for legal reasons as well as professional ones. The women have no last names, they aren't permitted to give out their private home telephone numbers to any of the clients or to see them, ever. Anonymity is part of the illusion as well as part of the protection. None of the clients has any way to contact a woman except through the office telephone numbers."

"Who has access to your files?"

"Myself, my husband, and his sister. This is a family business," she explained as the phone began to ring again.

"My sister-in-law is working her way through college and mans the phones in the evenings. One minute."

She handled the next call with the same routine. Ed glanced at his watch. Twelve-fifteen. Obviously phone sex was a popular lunchtime activity. Then he wondered if the funeral was over and Grace was home alone.

"I'm sorry," she said again. "Before you ask, our files are confidential. None of us discusses our clients or employees with outsiders. It's business, gentlemen, but not the kind we chat about over cocktails. We're very careful to keep things legitimate and well within the law. Our women aren't whores. They don't sell their bodies, but conversation. Our employees are screened, carefully screened, and if they break any of our rules, they're fired. We're aware that there are some businesses similar to ours where a young boy can call and charge the conversation to his parents' phone bill. I happen to think that's irresponsible and sad. We serve adults only, and our terms are explained in full up front, before any charge is made."

"We're Homicide, not Vice, Mrs. Cawfield," Ben told her. "In any case, we've already checked out your business and you're within your rights. At the moment, we're only interested in Kathleen Breezewood. It might help us if we had a list of her clients."

"I can't do that. My client list is confidential for obvious reasons, Detective Paris."

"And murder isn't confidential, Mrs. Cawfield, for obvious reasons."

"I understand your position. You'll have to understand mine."

"We can get a warrant," Ed reminded her. "It'll just take time."

"You'll need a warrant, Detective Jackson. Until you have one, I'm obliged to protect my clients. I'll tell you again, none of them could have located her unless they had access to this machine and broke the code to the program."

"We'll have to talk to your husband and sister-in-law."

"Of course. Short of breaking client confidentiality, we want to cooperate in every way."

"Mrs. Cawfield, do you know where your husband was on the night of April tenth?" Ed gave her a mild look as he held his pencil over his pad. Ben saw her fingers tighten quickly.

"I suppose you have to ask that, but I find it tasteless."

"Yeah." Ben crossed his legs. "Murder doesn't have such a sweet taste either."

Eileen moistened her lips. "Allen plays softball. He had a game on the night of the tenth. He pitched all nine innings; I was there. It was over about nine, maybe a bit before. Afterward, we went out for pizza with several other couples. We got home a little after eleven."

"If we find we need names, you can provide them?"

"Of course. I'm sorry, very sorry about Kathleen, but my business isn't involved in her murder. Now, if you'll excuse me, I've got to take this call."

"Thanks for your time." Ed pushed the door open and waited for Ben to join him on the sidewalk. "If she's playing it straight, and I think she is, none of the clients would have gotten Kathleen's location through the main office."

"Maybe Kathleen broke the rules." He pulled out a cigarette. "Gave out her address, her real name. Maybe she met one of the guys and he followed her back, decided he wanted more than talk."

"Maybe." But it was hard for him to think of his former neighbor as a woman who broke the rules. "I wonder what Tess would say about the possibility of a man who uses a MasterCard to charge sex talk committing rape and murder."

"She's not in this one, Ed."

"Just a thought." Because he recognized the tone in his partner's voice, he let it ride. Ben had already had to deal with his wife being involved in a homicide investigation.

"You know, it's more likely that someone busted in, came across her, and lost it."

"But it doesn't feel right."

"No," Ed agreed as he pulled open the car door. "It doesn't feel right."

"We're going to have to talk to Grace again."

"I know."

*H*E HAD TO LISTEN again. It had been too long. As soon as his last class was over, he came home to lock himself in his room. He'd wanted to ditch school altogether that day, but knew his father would be involved if he was reported. So he'd sat through all of his classes, a quiet, bright, well-behaved boy who spoke in a clear voice. The fact was, he blended in so well none of his teachers would have noticed him if he wasn't the son of a potential president.

Jerald didn't like to be obtrusive. He didn't like people to look at him because if they looked too long they might see some of his secrets.

It was rare that he took the chance of tapping into Fantasy's line during the day. He liked the dark better; he could imagine so much better in the dark. But since Desiree, he'd been obsessed. He put on his headphones and cued his terminal. Sitting back, he waited for the right voice.

He knew Eileen's. It didn't interest him. Too businesslike. The other one, the one who worked at night, wasn't right either. Too young, too prim. Neither of them ever made any promises.

He closed his eyes and waited. Somehow he was sure, absolutely sure, that he would find the right one soon.

When he did, her name was Roxanne.

Chapter 7

*H*YACINTHS. GRACE SAT ON the steps in front of her sister's house and stared at the pink and white hyacinths that had opened, thankful their scent was too light to carry. She'd had enough of the fragrance of flowers that day. The hyacinths looked different, too—sturdy and hopeful beside the cracking concrete. They didn't remind her of white caskets and weeping.

She couldn't sit with her parents any longer. Though she hated herself for it, she had left them huddled together over their endless cups of tea and escaped, needing the air, the sun, the solitude. She had to stop grieving, even if only for an hour.

Occasionally a car passed, so she watched. A few children in the neighborhood were taking advantage of the warming weather and lengthening days to ride bikes or skateboards over the uneven sidewalk. Their calls to each other were the calls of the summer that was just around the corner. Now and then one would stare over at the house with the round, avid eyes of the curious. The word was out, Grace thought, and cautious parents had warned their sons and daughters to stay clear. If the house remained empty long, those kids would be daring each other to go as far as the porch to touch the forbidden. The very brave might race to the windows and peek in.

The haunted house. The Murder House. And the children's palms would sweat, their hearts thunder as they ran away again to report their derring-do to their less courageous friends. She'd have done exactly the same as a child.

Murder was so fascinating, so irresistible.

Already, Grace knew, Kathleen's murder would have been discussed in the quiet little houses up and down the street. New locks would have been bought and installed. Windows and doors would be checked with extra care. Then a few weeks would pass, and with the buffer of time, people would forget. After all, it hadn't happened to them.

But she wouldn't forget. Grace rubbed her fingers under her eyes. She couldn't forget.

When she recognized Ed's car pulling up, she drew a deep breath. She hadn't realized she'd been waiting for him but had no trouble admitting it now. She rose and cut across the grass, arriving at his car just as he stepped out.

"You put in long hours, Detective."

"Goes with the territory." He jingled his keys before he popped the trunk. All that was left of her makeup were a few swipes of mascara. "You all right?"

"So far." She glanced back toward the house. Her mother had just switched on the kitchen light. "I'm taking my parents to the airport in the morning. It doesn't help them or me for them to stay here, so I convinced them to go. They're propping each other up." She ran her hands along the hips of her slacks, then finding nothing better to do with them, stuck them in her pockets. "You know, I never realized how married they were, how really married, until the last couple of days."

"At times like this it helps to have someone."

"I think they're going to be all right. They've . . . they've accepted it."

"What about you?"

Grace glanced up at him, then away again. The answer was in her eyes. Acceptance was still a long way off. "They're going home for a few days, then flying out to the coast to see Kevin, my sister's son."

"You going with them?"

"No. I thought about it, but—not now. I don't know, the funeral seemed to steady them."

"And you?"

"I hated it. The first thing I'm going to do when I get back to New York is check into cremations." She pulled both hands through her hair. "Christ, that sounds sick."

"No, it doesn't. Funerals force you to face the fact of dying. That's their purpose, isn't it?"

"I've been trying to figure out the purpose all day. I think I prefer the way the Vikings did it. Out to sea in a burning boat. Now *that's* a send-off. I don't like thinking of her in a box." Catching herself, she turned back to him. It was better, far better, to think of the children playing across the street and the flowers just opening. "Sorry. I came out here to stop dwelling on it. I told my parents I was going for a walk. I didn't get very far."

"You want to walk?"

Grace shook her head and touched his arm. Decent. She'd been on the mark when she'd tagged that one-word description to him. "You are a nice man. I want to apologize for dumping on you the other night."

"It's okay. You had a point." A mother called for her children from a porch across the street and bargaining ensued for an extra fifteen minutes.

"I'm not sorry for what I said, but for the way I said it. I go for long stretches of time without having much contact with people, then when I do I always end up being pushy." She turned to watch the children again. She could remember playing like that, running fast to beat sundown. She and Kathleen together on a street not so very different from this one. "So, are we still friends?"

"Sure." He took the hand she offered and held it.

That was exactly what she'd needed. Until the contact had been made, she hadn't realized it. "Does that mean we can have dinner or something before I go back?"

He didn't release her hand but curled his fingers around hers. "When are you leaving?"

"I'm not sure. There are a lot of loose ends. Probably next week." Without thinking, just going with the urge, she lifted their joined hands to her cheek. It felt good, the contact. She knew she needed it as much as she needed long spells of time by herself. Right now she didn't want to think of solitude. "You ever get to New York?"

"Not so far. You're getting cold," he murmured as his knuckles grazed over her skin. "You shouldn't have come out without a jacket."

She smiled as she released his hand. His lingered a few seconds more on her cheek. Grace had always moved on instinct, accepted the scrapes along with the pleasures. Before he could drop his hand, she slipped her arms around him. "Do you mind? I need something to show me I'm still alive."

She lifted her face and closed her mouth quietly over his.

Solid. That was the first thought that ran through her mind. This was solid, this was tangible. His mouth was warm against hers, and giving. He didn't push or grope or try to impress with smooth technique. He simply kissed her back. The cushion of his beard brought comfort. The sudden tightening of his fingers on her skin brought excitement. How wonderful it was to discover she could still need and appreciate both. She was alive, all right. And it felt wonderful.

She'd taken him by surprise, but he found his footing

quickly enough. He'd wanted to hold her like this, let his hands wander through her hair. Dusk fell with a chill around them so he drew her closer, warming her. He felt his pulse pick up rhythm and race as her body softened against his.

She drew away slowly, a bit stunned by her own reaction. He let her go, though the wildly romantic image of sweeping her into his arms and into his house hadn't faded.

"Thanks," she managed.

"Anytime."

She laughed, surprised that she was nervous, delighted that she'd been moved. "I'd better let you get going. I know you work at night. The lights," she explained when he lifted a brow.

"I've been putting the bathroom together. I'm almost down to the wallpaper."

She glanced in his trunk and saw four five-gallon buckets of paste. "Must be some bathroom."

"Paste was on sale."

"My mother would love you," she said, smiling. "I'd better go in, I don't want them to worry. I'll see you later."

"Tomorrow. I'll fix you dinner."

"Okay." She started back across the lawn, then stopped and looked over her shoulder. "Hold the carrot juice."

*R*OXANNE HAD BEEN BORN Mary. She'd always harbored a hint of resentment for her parents' lack of imagination. If she'd been given a more exotic name, a more sophisticated, more frivolous name, she'd also wondered, would she have become a different person?

Mary Grice was twenty-eight, single, and seventy-five pounds overweight. She'd started to run to fat as an adolescent and easily blamed that on her parents as well. Fat genes, her mother was wont to say, and with some truth.

The full truth was, however, that the Grices, as a family, had enjoyed a long-standing love affair with food. Eating was a religious experience, and the Grices—Moma, Popa, and Mary—a devoted congregation.

Mary had grown up in a house where the pantry and refrigerator overflowed with chips and dips and cans of chocolate syrup. She'd learned to take the erector set of bread and meat and cheese and build a sandwich of gastronomic wonder, then wash it all down with a quart of chocolate milk and still have room for a box of Ho-Ho's.

Her skin had revolted during her teens and had resembled one of the bubbly pizzas she was so fond of, so that now, nearing thirty, she still bore the pits and scars. She'd gotten into the habit of plastering her skin with heavy pancake foundation, and in the warm weather, when her sweat glands opened, her makeup cracked and ran like the face of a melting rubber doll.

She'd gone through high school and college without a date. Her personality had been such that she hadn't even been able to attain the position of friend and confidante. Food had again come to the rescue. Whenever her feelings were hurt or her sex drive hummed, Mary would stuff a double cheeseburger or a plate of fudge brownies into her mouth.

She'd lost sight of her neck at twenty. It had simply vanished in a riot of flabby folds. She wore her hair long and straight, clipped back with a barrette. There were too many mirrors in the beauty parlor. She did, occasionally, go with a whim and dye it herself, a siren red, a raven black, and once, a flashy Harlow blond. Each change had made her feel like a different person. Anyone would do, as long as she wasn't herself.

When her doctor warned her about her rising blood pressure and the strain on her heart, she fixed her scale so that she weighed in ten pounds lighter. She'd enjoyed that illusion so much she'd soon put on another ten and had considered herself back to normal.

Then she invented Roxanne.

Roxanne was sultry. Roxanne was, God bless her, a tramp. Roxanne was a size four. Roxanne could turn an iceberg into a mass of steam, as long as the iceberg was male. No inhibitions, no pretensions, and no morals; that was Roxanne.

Roxanne liked sex, anytime, anywhere, anyhow. If a man wanted to talk sex, the hard, fast, and dirty kind, Roxanne was his girl.

Mary had gone to Fantasy on a whim. She didn't need the extra money. She'd gotten a lot of studying done over plates of roast beef and Cheez Whiz in college. She'd majored in economics and now worked for one of the top brokerage houses in the country. To most of her clients, she was just a voice over the phone. And that's what had triggered the idea.

Perhaps it had been one of nature's little jokes to gift her with a beautiful voice. It was soft and sweetly pitched. It had a tendency to grow breathy when she became excited, so that it projected the image of a small, delicate woman of breeding. The thought of using it to do more than sell tax-exempt bonds and mutual-fund shares had been too tempting to resist.

Mary considered herself a phone whore. She was aware that Eileen thought of the business as a social service, but Mary liked the very idea of being a whore. She was in the business of sex for hire, and her pistols were hot and smoking. Every frustration, every desire, every sweat-soaked dream she'd ever had could be eased by a seven-minute conversation.

In her mind she'd been to bed with every man she'd ever spoken to. In reality she'd never had sex. The conversations she had with faceless men were the release valves to the pressure cooker of her own desires. She fulfilled the fantasies of her clients for a buck a minute, and got more than her own money's worth.

By day, she watched the stock index, sold T-bills, and bought commodities futures. At night, she traded her full-figured suit for her best Frederick's of Hollywood and became Roxanne.

And she loved it.

Mary, or Roxanne, was one of the few employees of Fantasy, Incorporated who took calls seven nights a week. If one of the other women found a man too intense, or his tastes too odd, Roxanne was more than willing to take up the slack. The money she made went to red silk lingerie, vanilla incense, and food. Especially food. Between calls, Mary could wolf down a jumbo tin of potato chips with a pint of garlic and sour cream dip.

She knew Lawrence's voice and his preferences very well. Though he wasn't one of her kinkier clients, he enjoyed being surprised occasionally with images of leather and handcuffs. He'd been honest with her about his appearance. No one would lie about an overbite and astigmatism. She talked to him three times a week. One three-minute quickie and two seven-minute regulars. He was an accountant, so besides sex, they had a professional rapport.

Roxanne had candles flickering all over her bedroom. Red ones. She liked to set the mood for herself as she sprawled over her queen-size bed with a two-liter bottle of Classic Coke. She'd splurged on satin pillows and had propped herself up against them. As she spoke, she wound the phone cord around her fingers.

"You know I love to talk to you, Lawrence. I get excited just thinking about hearing your voice. I'm wearing a new nightgown. It's red. You can see right through it." She laughed and snuggled against the pillows. At that moment, she was a hundred-and-five-pound waif with legs that wouldn't quit. "You're so naughty, Lawrence. If that's what you want me to do, I'm doing it right now, and pretending it's you. All right, just listen. Listen and I'll tell you everything."

HE KNEW HE WAS rushing it, but dammit, he had to see if it could happen again. Roxanne sounded so beautiful. As soon as he'd heard her voice, he'd known. The flesh on his arms had puckered up and the ache between his legs had come on hard and fast.

She had to be the next one. She was waiting for him. Not teasing, not promising like Desiree. This was the next level. Roxanne spoke of things his imagination hadn't ever conjured up. She wanted him to hurt her. How could he resist?

But he had to be careful.

This neighborhood wasn't as quiet as the other one. Traffic rushed up and down the street and pedestrians streamed along the sidewalk. Maybe it was better this way. He might be seen, recognized. That added its own edge.

Her apartment building faced Wisconsin Avenue. Jerald had parked two blocks away. During the walk, he'd forced himself to move slowly, not so much out of caution but out of the desire to take in everything about the night. There were clouds and a light wind. His face stayed cool, but inside the pockets of his school jacket, his hands were hot and wet. He closed his fingers over the rope he'd taken from the utility room. Roxanne would appreciate that he'd remembered what she liked, and how she liked it.

He was supposed to be at the library doing research on a report on World War II. He'd written the report a week before, but his mother wouldn't know the difference. She'd flown to Michigan to beat the campaign drums on the trail with his father.

When school was out, he'd be expected to join them for the hot, frantic summer months of politicking. He hadn't yet decided how to avoid that, but he didn't doubt he would. There were six weeks to go before graduation.

Fucking prissy prep school, he thought without much heat. Once he was in college, he would be his own man. He wouldn't have to make excuses about libraries or club meetings or movies to get out for a couple of hours at night.

When his father won the election, there would be the Secret Service to deal with. Jerald looked forward to outwitting them. Bunch of robots in suits and ties.

Stepping into the shrubbery, he took out a tube of cocaine. He snorted it quickly and felt his mind crystallize into a pinpoint of thought.

Roxanne.

Smiling, he skirted around the back of the apartment building. He didn't bother to look around, but carefully cut through the glass of her living room window. No one could stop him now. He was too powerful. And Roxanne was waiting.

He nicked himself on the glass as he reached in to turn the lock, but merely sucked on the wound as he drew up the pane. It was dark inside, and his heart was beginning to hammer a bit too fast. Jerald hitched himself up and in. He didn't bother to close the window behind him.

She would be waiting for him, waiting for him to hurt her, to make her sweat and scream. She would be waiting for him to take her to the ultimate climax.

She didn't hear him. She had already taken Lawrence over the top and was on the edge of an orgasm herself.

He saw her, sprawled on satin pillows, skin damp and glistening in candlelight. Closing his eyes, he listened to the voice. When he opened them again, she wasn't a barrellike woman with flabs of fat, but a long, leggy redhead. Smiling, he walked to the side of the bed.

"It's time, Roxanne."

Her eyes flew open. Caught in the mists of her own

fantasy, she stared at him. Her ample breasts were heaving. "Who are you?"

"You know me." He was still smiling as he straddled her.

"What do you want? What are you doing here?"

"I'm here to give you everything you've been asking for. And more." Lifting both hands, he tore the thin material from her breasts.

She squealed and shoved at him. The receiver fell on the mattress as she scrambled for the edge of the bed. "Lawrence, Lawrence, there's a man in my room. Call the police. Call someone."

"You're going to like it, Roxanne."

She was three times his size, but awkward. She struck out again, bruising his chest, but he didn't even feel the blow. She was screaming at him now, in real terror. Her heart, too weak to support the burden of her body, began to hammer and skip. Her face turned beet red when he hit her.

"You're going to like it," he told her again when she fell back against the pillows. In reflex, she threw up her hands to protect her face from another blow. "You're never going to experience anything like this ever again."

"Don't hurt me." Tears squeezed out of her eyes and ran lines through her makeup. Her breath began to rattle as he jerked her hands toward the bedspread and bound them with rope.

"This is the way you like it. I remember. I heard you say." He plunged into her, grinning like a maniac. "I want you to like it, Roxanne. I want it to be the best."

She was crying loudly, big, shuddering sobs that shook her body and brought him a dizzying kind of pleasure as he rocked on her. He felt it build, climb, soar. And knew it was time.

Smiling down at her, his eyes half-closed, he wrapped the phone cord around her neck and pulled.

♦ ♦ ♦

*E*D GROPED FOR THE phone on the first ring and came fully awake by the second. Across the room, David Letterman was entertaining his late-night audience. Ed flexed the arm that had fallen asleep, focused on the television screen, and cleared his throat.

"Yeah. Jackson."

"Put your pants on, partner. We've got a body."

"Where?"

"On Wisconsin Avenue. I'll pick you up." Ben listened a minute. "If you had a woman, you wouldn't fall asleep watching Letterman."

Ed hung up on him and went into the bathroom to soak his head in cold water.

Fifteen minutes later, he was sitting in the passenger seat of Ben's car. "I knew it was too good to be true." Ben bit off the end of a Hershey bar. "It's been a week since we got a call in the middle of the night."

"Who called it in?"

"Couple of uniforms. They got a call that there was trouble, first-floor apartment, woman living alone. Checked it out and found some glass broken and a window open. When they went in, they found her. She won't be living alone anymore."

"Robbery?"

"Don't know. They didn't give me any more. Cop that called it in was a rookie. Desk said he was busy trying to hold down his coffee break. Look, before I forget, Tess says you've been ignoring her. Why don't you come by for a drink or something? Bring the writer."

Ed cast Ben a mild look. "Does Tess want to see me or the writer?"

"Both." Ben grinned and swallowed the last of the chocolate. "You know she's crazy about you. If I hadn't been so much better-looking than you, you might have had a shot. This is it. Looks like these guys want to make sure everybody in the neighborhood knows there's a body around."

He pulled over to the curb behind two black and whites. The lights turned and blinked on the roofs while the car radios sent out bursts of noise. Ben nodded to the first uniform as he stepped onto the sidewalk.

"Apartment 101, sir. Apparently the perpetrator broke in through a living room window. Victim was in bed. First officers on the scene are inside."

"Forensics?"

"On their way, sir."

Ben judged the uniform to be twenty-two at the most. They were getting younger every year. With Ed right behind him he walked into the building and into 101. Two cops stood in the living room, one of them popping a piece of gum, the other sweating.

"Detectives Jackson and Paris," Ed said mildly. "Get some air."

"Yes, sir."

"You remember your first one?" Ben asked Ed as they moved toward the bedroom.

"Yeah. As soon as I was off duty I got drunk." Ed didn't pose the question to Ben. He was already aware that the first body his partner had faced had been that of his own brother.

They stepped into the bedroom, looked at Mary, then at each other. "Shit," was all Ben said.

"Looks like we've got another serial killer on our hands. Captain's going to be pissed."

*E*D WAS RIGHT.

At eight o'clock the following morning, both detectives were in Captain Harris's office. Their superior sat at his desk studying their reports from behind new and detested reading glasses. The diet he was on had taken off five pounds and soured his disposition. He drummed the fingers of one hand monotonously against the desk.

Ben leaned against the wall, wishing he'd had the time and the energy to make love to his wife that morning. Ed sat, legs stretched out, as he dipped a tea bag into a cup of hot water.

"The forensic report's not in," Harris said at length. "But I don't think we're going to find any surprises."

"The guy nicked himself coming through the window." Ed sipped at his tea. "I think the blood's going to match what was found at the Breezewood homicide."

"We kept the rape and the murder weapon out of the press," Ben continued. "So a copycat's a long shot. There wasn't as much of a struggle this time. Either he was smarter, or she was too scared to resist. She wasn't a small woman, but he managed to bind her hands without so much as upsetting the glass on the nightstand."

"From the papers we found, she was a stockbroker. We're going to check that out this morning and see if we can find a link." As he downed his tea, Ed noted that Ben was lighting his third cigarette of the morning. "A woman called the disturbance in to the desk. Didn't leave her name."

"Lowenstein and Renockie can check out the neighbors." Harris took out two grapefruit pills, scowled at them, then downed them with the tepid water on his desk. "Until information proves differently, we're looking for one man. Let's get this wrapped up before it gets out of hand. Paris, your wife was a lot of help last year. She have any thoughts on this?"

"No." Ben blew out smoke and left it at that.

Harris drank the rest of his water as his stomach growled. The press was already salivating and he hadn't had a decent meal in a month. "I want updated reports by four."

"Easy for him to say," Ben muttered as he closed

Harris's door behind him. "You know, he was enough of a pain before he went on this diet."

"Despite popular belief, being fat does not make you jolly. Excess weight is a strain on the body, making a person uncomfortable and usually marking his disposition. Fad dieting accents the discomfort. Proper nutrition, exercise, and sleep make you happy."

"Shit."

"That helps too."

"Drinks are on me." Lowenstein stepped between them and swung her arms around their waists.

"You had to wait until I got married to be friendly."

"My husband got a raise. Three thousand a year, and baby, we're going to Mexico the minute the kids are out of school."

"How about a loan until payday?" Ed asked her.

"Not a chance. Forensic report came in. Phil and I are going to do the door-to-door. Maybe I can squeeze in some shopping on my lunch hour. I haven't had a bikini in three years."

"Please, you'll get me excited." Ben let her go to pick up the file on his desk.

"Eat your heart out, Paris. In six weeks, I'm going south of the border to drink margaritas and eat fajitas."

"Don't forget the tetracycline." Ed sat on the corner of Ben's desk.

"I've got a cast-iron stomach. Come on, Renockie, let's get moving."

Ben flipped open the file. "How do you think Lowenstein'll look in a bikini?"

"Excellent. What have we got?"

"Blood on the broken glass was A positive. And look at this. Fingerprints on the window sash." He pulled out the Breezewood file. "What would you say?"

"I'd say we've got a match."

"Yeah, we've got a match." Ben set the files side by side. "Now all we have to do is find him."

GRACE TOSSED HER PURSE onto the sofa, then dropped down beside it. She couldn't remember ever being so tired before, not after a fourteen-hour writing marathon, not after an all-night party, not after a twelve-city tour.

From the moment she'd called her parents in Phoenix until she'd put them on the plane home, she'd used every scrap of her energy to keep them going. Thank God they had each other, because she simply had nothing left.

She wanted to go home, back to New York, back to the noise and the frantic pace. She wanted to pack her trunk, close up the house, and catch a flight. But that would be like closing the door on Kathleen. There were still a hundred details to handle. The insurance, the landlord, the bank, all the personal items Kathleen had left behind.

She could pack most of them up and give them to the church, but there were bound to be things she should send to Kevin or her parents. Kathleen's things. No, she didn't think she was quite ready to go through her sister's clothes and jewelry.

So she'd start with the paperwork, beginning with the funeral and working her way back. There were all those cards. Her mother would probably like to have them, to put them away in some little box. Perhaps that would be the easiest place to start. Most of the names would be unfamiliar. Once she'd broken the ice, she could face the more personal of her sister's affairs.

First she was going to wire her system with coffee.

Grace took a pot up to her room. She glanced almost wistfully at her computer. It had been days since she'd turned it on. If she fell behind deadline, which was becoming more and more likely, her editor would be sympathetic. She'd already received half a dozen calls from New York offering help and condolences. It almost made up for the picture in the paper that morning of her at Kathleen's funeral.

AWARD-WINNING WRITER'S SISTER BURIED
G. B. MCCABE ATTENDS FUNERAL OF
BRUTALLY MURDERED SISTER

She hadn't bothered with the text.

The headlines didn't matter, she reminded herself. She'd expected them. Sensationalism was part of the game. And it had been a game to her, up until a few nights ago.

Grace finished off one cup of coffee and poured another before she reached for the manila envelope. It was crammed with cards. She was tempted just to ship them off to her mother. Instead, she sat on the bed and began to go through them. Some of them might require a personal note in response. Better that she do it now than have her mother face it later.

There was one from all the students at Kathleen's school. As she studied it, Grace considered donating money for a scholarship in Kathleen's name. She set the card aside until she could discuss the idea with her lawyer.

She recognized a few names from California, the rich and powerful families that Kathleen had known. Let Jonathan handle any response there, she decided, and dumped them into a pile.

One from an old neighbor made her eyes tear again. They'd lived next door to Mrs. Bracklemen for fifteen years. She'd been old then, or had seemed so to Grace. There had always been cookies baking in the oven or snatches of material that could be made into a puppet. Grace set this card aside as well.

She picked up the next card. She stared at it, rubbed her fingers over her eyes, then stared again. This wasn't right. It was a florist's card with the words IN MEMORIAM printed opposite a spray of red roses. Handwritten in the center was the sentiment:

Desiree, I'll never forget.

Even as she stared, the card slipped out of her fingers and fell faceup on the floor at her feet.

Desiree. The word seem to grow until it spread over the entire card.

"I'm Desiree," Kathleen had said so casually that first night. *I'm Desiree.*

"Oh, God." Grace began to shake as she stared down at the card. "Oh, dear God."

JERALD SAT THROUGH HIS English Literature class as his teacher droned on and on about the subtleties and symbolism of *Macbeth*. Jerald had always liked the play. He'd read it several times and didn't need Mr. Brenner to explain it to him. It was about murder and madness. And, of course, power.

He'd grown up with power. His father was the most powerful man in the world. And Jerald knew all about murder and madness.

Mr. Brenner would have a heart attack if he stood up and explained to him just how it felt to cut off a life. If he explained the sounds it made, or the look on someone's face as the life drained out of it. The eyes. The eyes were the most incredible.

He'd decided he liked killing, in much the same way George Lowell, who sat beside him, liked baseball. It was, in a way, the ultimate sport. So far, he was batting a thousand.

True, Roxanne hadn't meant as much to him as Desiree. He'd enjoyed that one-second flash where orgasm and death had mixed, but Desiree . . . Desiree had meant a great deal more.

If only it could be like that again. If only he could have her back. It wouldn't be fair if he didn't experience again that great rush of love and release.

It had been the anticipation, Jerald decided. Like Macbeth with Duncan, he'd had the buildup, the terror, and the destiny. Roxanne had been more of an experiment. The way in chemistry you tried to reconstruct to prove a theory.

He needed to do it again. Another experiment. Another chance at perfection. His father would understand that. His father never settled for less than perfection. And he was, after all, his father's son.

Addiction came easily to Jerald, and murdering was just one more vice. But the next time, he'd get to know the woman a bit better. He wanted to feel that bond with her.

Mr. Brenner lectured about Lady Macbeth's madness. Jerald rubbed a hand over his chest and wondered how he'd bruised it.

Chapter 8

GRACE HAD BEEN TO police stations before. She'd always found them fascinating. Small town, big city, north or south, they had a certain feel, a certain controlled chaos.

This one was no different. The floor was a dull linoleum with more than a few ripples and bubbles. The walls were either beige or a white that had turned. Posters were tacked up here and there. Crime stoppers, with a number and a plug for good citizenship. Hot lines for drugs, suicide, wife and child abuse. HAVE YOU SEEN THIS CHILD? The venetian blinds needed dusting and there was an OUT OF ORDER sign on a candy machine.

In the Homicide Division, plainclothes cops were huddled over phones or hunched over typewriters. Someone was burrowing into a dented refrigerator. She could smell coffee, and what she thought might have been tuna fish.

"Can I help you?"

When she jerked at the sound of the voice, she realized how close her nerves were to snapping. The cop was young, midtwenties, with dark hair and a dimple in the middle of his chin. Grace forced her fingers to relax on the clasp of her purse.

"I need to see Detective Jackson."

"He's not in." It had taken him a minute to recognize her. He wasn't much of a reader, but he'd seen her picture in the morning paper. "Miss McCabe?"

"Yes?"

"You can wait if you like, or I can check and see if the captain's available."

Captain? She didn't know the captain, or this young cop with the dimple in his chin. She wanted Ed. "I'd rather wait."

Since he was already balancing two soft drinks and a fat file, he nodded to a chair in the corner. Grace sat, closed her hands over her purse, and waited.

She saw a woman walk in. Blond and beautifully dressed in a rose silk suit, she didn't look like a person who had business with Homicide. A professional woman, or a politician's young wife, Grace decided, although she hadn't the energy to go further, as she usually did, and attach an imaginary history to the unknown face. She looked away again toward the hall.

"Hey, Tess," the young cop called from his desk. "It's about time we got some class in here."

She smiled and walked over to stand beside him. "Ben's not here?"

"Out playing detective."

"I had an hour and thought he might be able to swing an early lunch."

"Will I do?"

"Sorry. My husband's a jealous cop who carries a gun. Just tell him I stopped by."

"You coming in on this? Going to give us a psychiatric on our killer?"

She hesitated. It was something she'd considered, something she'd even mentioned casually to Ben. His grim negative and her own caseload had made it easy to back down. "I don't think so. Tell Ben I'll pick up some Chinese and be home by six. Six-thirty," she amended.

"Some guys get all the breaks."

"Tell him that, too." She started out, then spotted Grace. Tess recognized her from book jackets and newspaper photos. She recognized, too, the look of strain and grief on her face. As a doctor she found it almost impossible to walk away. Crossing the room, she waited until Grace glanced up. "Miss McCabe?"

Not a fan, Grace thought. Not here, not now. Tess saw the withdrawal and offered her hand.

"I'm Tess. Tess Paris, Ben's wife."

"Oh. Hello."

"Are you waiting for Ed?"

"Yes."

"Looks like we're both out of luck. Want some coffee?"

Grace hesitated, started to refuse. Then a weeping woman was half carried into the room.

"My son's a good boy. He's a good boy. He was just defending himself. You can't keep him here."

Grace watched as the woman was helped into a chair while a female detective leaned over her and talked steadily. There was blood on both of them. "Yes," Grace said quickly, then, "I'd like that."

Tess stood and walked quickly into the hall. She drew change out of her wallet and pushed it into a machine. "Cream?"

"No, black."

"Good choice. The cream usually sprays all over the floor." She passed the first cup to Grace. Putting herself in the position of a sounding board was part of her profession. It was also part of her personality. Tess noticed the slight tremor in Grace's fingers and knew she couldn't turn away. "Do you want to walk outside? It's a nice day."

"All right."

Tess led the way out, then leaned against the banister. It pleased her to remember that she'd met Ben for the first time in this spot, in the rain. "Washington's at its best in the spring. Are you staying long?"

"I don't know." The sun was bright, almost too bright. She hadn't noticed it on the drive over. "I'm having a hard time making decisions."

"That's not unusual. After a loss, most of us float for a while. When you're ready, things will click back into place."

"Is it usual to feel guilt?"

"About what?"

"About not stopping it."

Tess sipped her coffee and watched a scatter of daffodils wave in the breeze. "Could you have?"

"I don't know." Grace thought about the card she carried in her purse. "I just don't know." With a half laugh, she lowered herself onto the steps. "This sounds like a session. All we need's a couch."

"Sometimes it helps to talk to someone who isn't involved."

Grace turned her head, shielding her eyes with her hand. "Ed said you were beautiful."

Tess smiled. "Ed's a sweet man."

"Yes, he is, isn't he?" Grace turned back to clasp her hand over her purse again. "You know, I've always been able to take things as they come. I'm even better at making them come out the way I like. I hate this. I hate being confused, I hate not being able to decide whether to turn left or right. I don't even feel like the same person anymore."

"Strong people often have a more difficult time with grief and loss." Tess recognized the squeal of brakes and glanced over toward the parking lot, thinking that Ed must be driving. "If you're in town for a while and need to talk, let me know."

"Thanks." She put down her coffee cup and rose

slowly. As she watched Ed approach, her palms grew damp and she rubbed them against her jeans.

"Grace."

"I need to show you something."

Ben slipped his hand over Tess's and started inside.

"No, please, wait a minute." Grace let out a long breath and opened her purse. "I found this when I was going through the sympathy and florists' cards this morning." She took out the plain white envelope she'd slipped the card into and handed it to Ed.

He drew it out, turning it so Ben could read it as he did. "Does this mean something to you, Grace?"

"Yes." She closed her purse, wondering why she felt nauseated. She hadn't eaten. "That was the name Kathy was using for Fantasy. Kathleen was Desiree. That was her cover, you see. Her cover so no one would know who or where she was. But someone did. And he killed her."

"Come inside, Grace."

"I have to sit down."

Tess nudged Ed aside and pushed Grace's head between her knees. "I'll bring her inside in a minute," she said over her shoulder.

"Come on." Ben pushed the door open and laid a hand on Ed's shoulder. "We'd better get this to the captain. Tess'll take care of her," he added when Ed didn't move.

"Take some deep breaths," Tess murmured as she massaged Grace's shoulders. With her free hand, she monitored her pulse.

"Dammit, I'm sick of this." Grace fought back the weakness inch by inch.

"Then you'd better start eating instead of living off coffee, and you'd better start getting some rest. Otherwise, this is going to keep happening."

Grace kept her head down but turned it until her eyes met Tess's. She saw sympathy there and understanding, mixed with cool common sense. It was the exact combination she needed. "Right." She was still pale when she sat up, but her pulse was stronger. "The bastard killed my sister. No matter how long it takes, I'm going to see him pay for it." She pushed her hair back with both hands as she took one long breath. "I think things just clicked back into place."

"Are you ready to go in?"

Grace nodded and rose. "I'm ready."

In short order, Grace found herself seated in Captain Harris's office. Very slowly, and with a coherence she'd just found again, she related the story of Kathleen's involvement with Fantasy.

"I was concerned at first with her talking to some creep who might give her trouble. But she explained the system, how no one but the main office had her number. And how she didn't even use her own name. Desiree. She told me that was the name she was using for the calls. I didn't even remember it until I saw the card. No one but the people she worked for, and the people she talked to, knew her by that name."

Ben took out his lighter and passed it from hand to hand. He hadn't liked the way Tess had looked at him before she'd gone back to her office. She was going to give him grief over this. "Is it possible your sister told someone else about her moonlighting, about the name?"

"I have to say no." She accepted the cigarette Ben passed her. "Kathy was very private. If she'd had a close friend, maybe. But she didn't." She drew deep, then exhaled.

"She told you," Ed reminded her.

"Yes, she told me." Grace paused a moment. She had to keep her mind clear. "When I think it through, I believe the only reason she told me was because she felt a little shaky herself. It was probably an impulse, and one I know she regretted. I pressed her for details a couple of times and she wouldn't say word one. It was her business, hers alone.

Kath was very firm on what was her business." The wheels were beginning to turn again. She closed her eyes and concentrated. "Jonathan. He could have known."

"The ex-husband?" Harris asked.

"Yes, when I talked to him at the funeral, he admitted that he knew Kathy had hired a lawyer and a detective. If he knew that much, it's likely he knew the rest. I asked him what he would have done to keep Kath from getting custody of Kevin, and he told me he'd have done whatever became necessary."

"Grace." Ed passed her a Styrofoam cup of tea. "Breezewood was in California the night your sister was murdered."

"Men like Jonathan don't kill. They hire other people to do it. He hated her. He had a motive."

"We've already talked to him." Ed took the cigarette that had burned down between her fingers and crushed it out. "He was very cooperative."

"I'm sure he was."

"He admitted he'd hired an agency to keep tabs on your sister." Ed saw her eyes darken and went on. "To watch her, Grace. He knew about her plans for a custody suit."

"Then why did you let him go back to California?"

"We didn't have any reason to hold him."

"My sister's dead. Dammit, my sister's dead."

"We have no proof that your former brother-in-law had any part in your sister's murder." Harris, his hands clasped together, leaned forward on his desk. "And there is nothing whatever to tie him to the second murder."

"Second murder?" Forcing herself to take slow, even breaths, she turned to Ed. "There was another?"

"Last night."

She wasn't going to let the weakness take over again. Deliberately, she sipped the tea Ed had given her. It was important to keep her voice calm, even reasonable. The time for hysterics was past. "The same? The same as Kathy?"

"Yes. We need a link, Grace. Did you know a Mary Grice?"

She paused. Her memory was excellent. "No. Do you think Kath knew her?"

"The name wasn't in your sister's address book," Ben told her.

"Then it's unlikely. Kathy was very organized about such things. About everything."

"Captain." The young cop stuck his head in the door. "We got some tax information on Mary Grice." He glanced at Grace before handing the printout to Harris. "It lists her employers for last year."

Harris scanned the report and honed in on one name. Grace pulled out another cigarette. The wheels were indeed working again. "She worked for Fantasy, too, didn't she? That's the link." She flicked on her lighter and felt stronger than she had in days. "That's the only thing that plays."

Harris's eyes narrowed as he studied her. "This investigation is confidential, Miss McCabe."

"Do you think I'd go to the press?" She blew out a stream of smoke as she rose. "You couldn't be more wrong, Captain. The only thing that interests me is seeing my sister's murderer pay. Excuse me."

Ed caught up with her as she reached the hall. "Where are you going?"

"To talk to whoever owns or runs Fantasy, Incorporated."

"No, you're not."

She stopped long enough to level a hard look at him. "Don't tell me what I'm going to do." She turned away, then was more surprised than annoyed to find herself whirled around and shoved into an empty office. "I bet you could clear the backfield single-handed."

"Sit down, Grace."

She didn't, but crushed out her cigarette in an empty cup. "You know something I've noticed? I'm just catching onto it, though it's been happening for some time. You give orders, Jackson. I don't take them." She was calm, almost too calm, but it felt right. "Now, you're bigger than I am, but I swear to God, if you don't get out of my way, I'll mow you down."

He didn't doubt it, but now wasn't the time to put it to the test. "This is police business."

"This is my business. My sister. And I've finally found something I can do besides staring at the ceiling and asking myself why."

Her voice had wavered, then strengthened again. He was absolutely sure if he offered comfort she'd slap it aside. "There are rules, Grace. You don't have to like them, but they're there."

"Fuck the rules."

"Fine, then maybe today we'll find another woman dead, and tomorrow one more." Because he saw that one point had hit home, he pressed. "You write a hell of a detective novel, but this is real. Ben and I are going to do our job, and you're going home. I can slap a restraining order on you." He paused as her eyes challenged him, half-amused, half-furious. "Or I can put you in protective custody. You'd like that."

"Bastard."

The single word might have been furious, but Ed knew he'd gotten his way. "Go home, get some sleep. Better yet, go to my place." Reaching in his pocket, he drew out his keys. "If you don't take care of yourself, you're going to keel over again. That's not going to do anybody a hell of a lot of good."

"I'm not going to sit around and do nothing."

"No, you're going to eat, you're going to sleep, and you're going to wait for me to get back. If there's anything I can tell you, I will."

In reflex, she caught the keys he tossed to her. "What if he kills someone else?"

That was a question he'd been asking himself since two A.M. "We'll get him, Grace."

She nodded because she'd always believed right won out over wrong. "When you do, I want to see him. Face-to-face."

"We'll talk about it. You want someone to drive you home?"

"I'm still capable of driving a car." She opened her purse and dropped his keys inside. "I'll wait, Jackson, but I'm not a patient woman."

As she started to move by him he caught her chin in his hand. There was color in her face again, the first real color he'd seen in days. Somehow, it didn't reassure him. "Get some sleep," he muttered before he swung the door open for her.

*W*HEN THEY WALKED THROUGH the door into Fantasy's cramped office, Eileen was on the phone. She looked up, unsurprised, then finished giving her operator instructions. Even when Ben tossed a warrant on her desk, she didn't miss a beat. Her call finished, she picked it up and read it carefully.

"This seems to be in order."

"You lost another employee last night, Mrs. Cawfield."

She looked up at him, then back down at the warrant. "I know."

"Then you also know that you're the link. Your business is the only connection between Mary and Kathleen."

"I know that's the way it looks." She picked up the warrant again to run it between her fingers. "But I can't believe it's true. Look, I told you before, this isn't a dial-a-porn operation. I run a clean and organized business." There was a flash of panic as she looked up again. Ed noted it, though her voice remained calm and reasonable. "I majored in business management at Smith. My husband's a lawyer. We're not backstreet people. We provide a service. Conversation. If I thought I was responsible, somehow responsible for the deaths of two women . . ."

"Mrs. Cawfield, there's only one person responsible. That's the man who killed them." She shot Ed a look of gratitude, and he pressed his advantage. "A woman called in a disturbance at Mary Grice's place last night. It wasn't a neighbor, Mrs. Cawfield."

"No. Could I have one of those?" she asked when Ben pulled out a cigarette. "I quit two years ago." She smiled a little as he lit it for her. "Or my husband thinks I did. He's into health, you know? Prolonging your life, improving your lifestyle. I can't tell you how much I've grown to detest alfalfa sprouts."

"The call, Eileen," Ben prompted.

She drew on the cigarette, then sent out smoke in a quick, nervous puff. "There was a client on the phone with Mary when—when she was attacked. He heard her scream, and what he thought were sounds of a struggle. In any case, he called back here. My sister-in-law didn't know what to do, so she called me. The minute she explained things to me, I phoned it in." The phone rang beside her, but she ignored it. "You see, the client couldn't have called this in to the police. He wouldn't have known where to tell them to go, or who to tell them was in trouble. That's part of the protection."

"We need the name of the client, Mrs. Cawfield."

She nodded at Ed, then neatly tapped out her cigarette. "I need to ask you to be as discreet as possible. It's not just a matter of my losing business, which I'm bound to do. It's more that I feel I'm betraying client confidentiality."

Ben glanced at her phone as it started to ring again. "Those things get shot to hell when there's murder involved."

Without a word, Eileen turned to her computer. "It's top of the line," she explained when the printer began to hum. "I wanted the best equipment." She picked up the phone and handled the next call. As she hung up, she swiveled in her chair and detached the printout. She handed it to Ed.

"The gentleman who was talking to Mary last night was Lawrence Markowitz. I don't have an address, of course, just a phone number and his American Express."

"We'll take care of it," Ed told her.

"I hope so. I hope you take care of it very soon."

As they walked out, the phone rang again.

*I*T DIDN'T TAKE LONG to run down Lawrence K. Markowitz.

He was a thirty-seven-year-old CPA, divorced, self-employed. He worked out of his home in Potomac, Maryland.

"Jesus, look at these houses." Ben slowed down to a crawl and craned his head out of the car window. "You know what places go for around here? Four, five hundred thousand. These people have gardeners who make more than we do."

Ed bit into a sunflower seed. "I like my place better. More character."

"More character?" Ben snorted as he pulled his head back into the car. "The taxes on that place over there are more than your mortgage."

"The monetary value of a house doesn't make it a home."

"Yeah, you ought to stitch up a sampler. Look at that place. Must be forty, fifty thousand square feet."

Ed looked but was unimpressed with the size; the architecture was too modern for his taste. "I didn't think you were interested in real estate."

"I'm not. Well, I wasn't." Ben drove by a hedge of azaleas in a pale, dusty pink. "I figure Doc and I'll want a place sooner or later. She could handle this," he murmured. "I couldn't. They probably have an ordinance about color coordinating your garbage. Doctors, lawyers, and accountants." And senators' granddaughters, he thought, thinking of the understated elegance of his wife.

"And no crabgrass."

"I like crabgrass. Here we are." He stopped the car in front of a two-story H-shaped house with French doors. "Tax sheltering must pay real good."

"Accountants are like cops," Ed said as he tucked away his bag of seeds. "You're always going to need them."

Ben pulled up in the sloping driveway and yanked on the parking brake. He'd have preferred to stick a couple of rocks behind the back tires, just in case, but there didn't seem to be any available. There were three doors to choose from. They decided to take the front. It was opened by a middle-aged woman in a gray dress and white apron.

"We'd like to see Mr. Markowitz, please." Ed held up his badge. "Police business."

"Mr. Markowitz is in his office. I'll show you the way."

The foyer opened up into a wide room done in black and white. Ed discounted the decor as too stark, but found the skylights interesting. He'd have to price some. They turned right, into a bar of the H. Here there were globe lamps and leather sling chairs and a woman seated at an ebony desk.

"Miss Bass, these gentlemen are here to see Mr. Markowitz."

"Do you have an appointment?" The woman behind the desk looked harassed enough. Her hair stood out in every direction as if she had raked and tugged and pulled on it with her fingers. Now she stuck a pencil behind her ear and began to search through the papers on her desk for her date book. The phone beside her rang steadily. "I'm sorry, Mr. Markowitz is very busy. It's not possible for him to see new clients."

Ben took out his badge and held it under her nose.

"Oh." She cleared her throat and unearthed her intercom. "I'll see if he's available. Mr. Markowitz—" Both Ben and Ed could hear the cranky static that followed the interruption. "I'm sorry, Mr. Markowitz. Yes, sir, but there are two men here. No, sir, I haven't run the Berlin account yet. Mr. Markowitz—Mr. Markowitz, they're policemen." She said the last in an undertone, as if it were a secret. "Yes, sir, I'm sure. No, sir. All right."

She blew her bangs out of her eyes. "Mr. Markowitz will see you now. Right through that door." Her duty done, she yanked up the phone. "Lawrence Markowitz and Associates."

If he had any associates, they weren't to be seen. Markowitz was alone in his office, a skinny, balding man with big teeth and thick glasses. His desk was black, like his secretary's, but half again as large. Files were heaped on it, along with two phones, at least a dozen sharpened pencils, and a pair of calculators. Tape streamed onto the floor. There was a watercooler in the corner. Hanging in front of the window was a bird cage with a big green parakeet in it.

"Mr. Markowitz." Both detectives showed their identification.

"Yes, what can I do for you?" He ran his palm over what was left of his hair and licked his lips. He hadn't lied to Roxanne about the overbite. "I'm afraid I'm swamped at the moment. You know what today is, don't you? April fourteenth. Everybody waits until the last minute, then they want a miracle. All I ask for is a little consideration, a little organization. I can't file extensions for everyone, you know. Rabbits, they want you to pull rabbits out of your hat."

"Yes, sir," Ben began, then it hit him. "April fourteenth?"

"I filed last month," Ed said mildly.

"You would."

"I'm sorry, gentlemen, but these new tax laws have everyone in an uproar. If I work for the next twenty-four hours straight, I might just finish before deadline." Markowitz's fingers hovered nervously over his calculator.

"Fuck the IRS," the parakeet chirped from his perch.

"Yeah." Ben ran his own fingers through his hair and tried not to dwell on it. "Mr. Markowitz, we're not here about taxes. What do you charge, anyway?"

"We're here about Mary Grice," Ed put in. "You knew her as Roxanne."

Markowitz hit the clear button in reflex, then grabbed a pencil. "I'm afraid I don't know what you're talking about."

"Mr. Markowitz, Mary Grice was murdered last night." Ed waited a beat, but saw the accountant had found time to read the morning paper. "We have reason to believe you were talking to her on the phone at the time of the attack."

"I don't know anyone by that name."

"You knew Roxanne," Ben added.

Markowitz's already pale skin took on a hint of green. "I don't understand what Roxanne has to do with Mary Grice."

"They were the same woman," Ben said and watched Markowitz swallow hard.

He'd known. Somehow he'd known as soon as he scanned the morning headlines. But that hadn't made it real. Two cops in his office in the middle of the day made it very real. And very personal. "I have some of the biggest accounts in the metropolitan area. Several of my clients are in the Congress, the Senate. I can't afford any trouble."

"We could subpoena you," Ed told him. "If you cooperate, we may be able to keep things quiet."

"It's the pressure." Markowitz took off his glasses to

rub his eyes. He looked blind and helpless without them. "For months your life revolves around 1099s and Keoghs. You can't imagine it. Nobody wants to pay, you know. You can hardly blame them. Most of my clients have incomes in the high six figures. They don't want to give thirty-five percent or more to the government. They want me to find a way out for them."

"That's tough," Ben said and decided to try one of the sling chairs. "We're not concerned with your reasons for using Fantasy's services, Mr. Markowitz. We'd like you to tell us exactly what happened last night while you were talking to Mary."

"Roxanne," Markowitz corrected. "I feel better thinking of her as Roxanne. She had a wonderful voice, and she was so . . . well, adventurous. I don't have much time for women since my divorce. But that's water under the bridge. Anyway, I developed such an exciting rapport with Roxanne. Three times a week. I could talk to her and come back and face Schedule Cs."

"Last night, Mr. Markowitz," Ed prompted.

"Yes, last night. Well, we hadn't been talking very long. I was just getting into it. You know, relaxing." He took out a handkerchief and mopped his face. "All of a sudden, she was talking to someone else. Like there was someone in the room. She said something like 'Who are you?' or 'What are you doing here?' At first I thought she was still talking to me, so I said something back, a joke or something. Then she screamed. I almost dropped the phone. She said, 'Lawrence, Lawrence, help me. Call the police, call somebody.'" He began to cough as if repeating the words irritated his throat. "I was talking back to her. It was so unexpected. I think I told her to calm down. Then I heard another voice."

"A man's voice?" Ed continued to write in his notebook.

"Yes, I think. Another voice anyway. He said, I think he said, 'You're going to like this.' He called her by name."

"Roxanne?" Ben asked.

"Yes, that's right. I heard him say Roxanne, and I heard—" Now he covered his face with the cloth and waited a moment. "You have to understand, I'm really a very ordinary man. I keep the excitement and complications in my life to a minimum. I have low blood sugar."

Ed gave him a sympathetic nod. "Just tell us what you heard."

"I heard such terrible noises. Breathing and banging. She wasn't screaming anymore, just making some gasping, gurgling sounds. I hung up. I didn't know what to do, so I hung up."

He lowered the cloth again, and his face was gray. "I thought maybe it was a put-on. I tried to tell myself it was, but I kept hearing noises. I kept hearing Roxanne crying and begging him not to hurt her. And I heard the other voice say that she wanted him to hurt her, that she was never going to experience anything like this again. I think, I think he said that he'd heard her say she wanted to be hurt. I'm not sure about that. It was all so garbled. Excuse me."

He got up to go to the watercooler. He filled a paper cup as air bubbled up to the top. After he'd gulped it down, he filled the cup again. "I didn't know what to do, I just sat there thinking. I tried to go back to work, to forget about it. Like I said before, I kept thinking it was probably just a joke. But it didn't sound like a joke." He drained the second cup of water. "The longer I sat there, the harder it was to believe it was just a joke. So I ended up calling Fantasy. I told the girl there that Roxanne was in trouble. I thought maybe someone was killing her. I hung up again, and I—I went back to work. What else could I do?" His gaze darted back and forth between Ed and Ben, never landing on either of them. "I kept thinking Roxanne would call back and tell me everything was okay. That she'd just been kidding. But she didn't call back."

"Was there anything about the voice—the other voice you heard—that made it distinctive?" As he wrote, Ed glanced up and watched Markowitz sweat. "An accent, a tone, a way of phrasing?"

"No, it was just a voice. I could hardly hear it over Roxanne's. Look, I don't even know what she looked like. I don't want to know. Let's be honest about this, she was nothing more to me than, well, a clerk at the supermarket. She was just somebody I called a few times a week so I could forget about work." Distancing himself that far eased his mind. He was an ordinary man, he reminded himself, even honest. To a point. Nobody wanted their accountants to treat honesty like a religion. "I think she probably had a boyfriend who was jealous. That's what I think."

"Did she use a name?" Ben asked.

"No. Just mine. She just called out my name. Please, there's nothing more I can tell you. I did everything I could. I didn't have to call in, you know," he added, his tone altering with the beginnings of self-righteousness. "I didn't have to get involved."

"We appreciate your cooperation." Ben pulled himself out of the chair. "You're going to have to come in and sign a statement."

"Detective, if I so much as move out of this chair until midnight tomorrow, I could be responsible for a dozen fines."

"File early," the parakeet advised. "Cover your ass."

"Come down the morning of the sixteenth. Ask for me or Detective Paris. We'll do our best to keep your name out of it."

"Thank you. You can use this door." He gestured to

the side door, then pulled his calculator forward. As far as he was concerned, he'd done his duty, and more.

"Is it too late to file an extension?" Ben asked as he started out.

"It's never too late." Markowitz began to push buttons.

Chapter 9

GRACE WASN'T SURE WHY she'd taken Ed's advice and waited in his house. Maybe because it was easier for her to think there, without her sister's things around her. She needed to keep busy. Her mind always worked better when her hands were occupied. So she made herself at home while she thought through her options.

It still seemed best to her to talk personally to the manager of Fantasy. Interviewing was one thing Grace excelled at. With a little prodding, a little pushing, she might be able to get her hands on a client list. Then she'd work down it, name by name. If her sister's killer was on it, she'd find him.

Then what?

Then she'd play it by ear. That was the way she wrote. That was the way she lived. Both had been a success so far.

Revenge was part of the motivation. She'd never felt the emotion before, but found it a satisfying one. It strengthened. To follow through meant staying in Washington. She could work here as well as anywhere. And New York would still be there when she was finished.

If she left now, it would be like leaving a book undone and handing it to an editor. No one was going to write the last chapter but G. B. McCabe.

It couldn't be that hard. Grace had always felt that police work took good timing, tenacity, and thoroughness. And a pinch of luck. That's what writing took as well. Anyone who had plotted out and solved as many murders as she had should be able to corner one killer.

She needed the client list, the police reports, and time to think. All she had to do was get around the very sturdy frame of Detective Ed Jackson.

Even as she was working out her strategy, she heard the front door open. He wouldn't be easy to con, she thought as she checked her face in his bathroom mirror. And harder yet because she liked him. Rubbing a smudge off her nose, she started downstairs.

"So you're home." She paused at the bottom of the steps and smiled at him. "How was your day?"

"Okay." He shifted a bag of groceries to his other arm. She was wearing the same snug jeans and baggy sweater she'd had on that morning, but now they were streaked with white. "What the hell have you been doing?"

"Wallpapering your bathroom." She moved to him and took the bag. "It looks great. You've got an eye for color."

"You wallpapered my bathroom?"

"Don't look stricken. I didn't mess it up. The wallpaper, that is. The bathroom's a wreck. I figured it was only fair you clean it up." She gave him an easy smile. "You had half a roll left over."

"Yeah. Ah, Grace, I appreciate it, but wallpapering takes a certain skill." He should know, he'd been reading up on it for a week.

"You pop a line, you measure, you slap on the paste and go for it. You had a couple of how-to books hanging around." She poked into the bag but didn't see anything exciting. "Go on up and take a look. By the way, I ate the rest of your strawberries."

"That's okay." He was too busy calculating just how much the wallpaper and paste had cost him.

"Oh, and mineral water's okay, but you could use some sodas."

He started upstairs, half-afraid to look. "I don't drink them."

"I do, but I had a beer instead. Oh, I almost forgot, your mother called."

He paused halfway up. "She did?"

"Yeah. She's a nice lady. And she was just delighted when I answered. I hope you don't mind, I didn't want to disappoint her, so I said we were lovers and that we were thinking about making it official before the baby comes."

Because she was smiling up at him in a way that left him uncertain whether she was stringing him along, he simply shook his head. "Thanks. Thanks a lot, Grace."

"Anytime. Your sister's got a new boyfriend. He's a lawyer. A corporate lawyer. He owns his own house and has a time-sharing condo in a place called Ocean City. It looks promising."

"Jesus," was all he managed.

"And your mother's blood pressure is one-twenty over eighty. Want me to fix you a drink?"

"Yeah, you do that."

She was humming when she walked into the kitchen. Ed really was adorable. She pulled a bottle of white wine out of the bag. He also had taste, she decided as she read the label. Then she took out what appeared to be a clump of asparagus. She sniffed it, then wrinkled her nose. Taste, yes, but she wasn't at all sure what kind.

She found cauliflower, scallions, and snow peas. The only thing that managed to make her feel relieved was a bag of seedless grapes. Grace didn't hesitate before diving in.

"It looks great."

She swallowed a grape and turned to see him in the doorway.

"The bathroom. It looks great."

"I'm very handy." She held up the asparagus. "What do you do with this?"

"I cook it."

She set it down again. "I was afraid of that. I didn't ask what you wanted to drink."

"I'll get it. Did you rest?"

"I'm feeling fine." She watched him pull a bottle of apple juice out of the refrigerator. It made her lips purse. "I've been doing a lot of thinking while wallpapering your bathroom and chatting with your mother."

"What kind of thinking?" He poured a tumbler of apple juice, then reached in a cabinet and pulled out a bottle of vodka. He poured two shots into the juice.

"That's a hell of a way to get your vitamin A."

"Want one?"

"I'll pass. Anyway, I've been thinking that I should take over Kathy's lease for a while. Stick around."

Ed set his glass down. He wanted her to stay, just as the cop in him knew she'd be better off gone. "Why?"

"I still have lawyers and insurance to deal with." Which she could do just as easily from New York. And he knew it. She could tell from his expression that he saw right through her. She'd been foolish to try to circle him. In any case, she didn't find it easy to be dishonest with him. That was odd in itself. Grace never minded shading the truth. "All right, that's not it. I can't leave here without knowing everything. Kathy and I weren't close. It's never been easy for me to admit that, but it's true. Staying here, trying to find who did this to her, is something I have to do for both of us. I can't put this behind me, Ed, not completely behind me until I have all the answers."

He wished, for both their sakes, that he didn't understand. "Finding your sister's killer isn't your job, it's mine."

"Your job, yes. For me it's a need. Can you understand that?"

"It isn't a matter of what I understand, but what I know."

She crumpled the empty grocery bag before he could take it from her and fold it for storage. "Which is?"

"Civilians can't be involved in investigations, Grace. They screw things up. And they get hurt."

She touched her tongue to her top lip as she stepped toward him. "Which bothers you the most?"

She had incredible eyes. The kind a man could stare into for hours. They were looking into his now, waiting, questioning. Half-fascinated, half-wary, he ran his thumb along her cheekbone. "I don't know." Then, because he needed to, because her lips had curved just a little, he lowered his mouth to hers.

She tasted exactly the way he wanted her to. She felt, as he spread his fingers over her face, exactly the way he wanted her to. It was foolish, he knew. She was New York, bright lights, and fast parties. He was small town, and he never knew when he'd have blood on his hands again. But she felt just right.

Her eyes opened slowly when their lips parted. She let out a long breath before she smiled. "You know, you make a big impression whenever you do that. Maybe you could make it more of a habit." Pressing against him, she nibbled her way to his mouth. When she felt his hands move to her hips, then tense, she sighed. It had been a long time, much too long, since she'd been tempted to let herself go. She wound her arms around his neck and felt, with great satisfaction, his heart thud along with hers. "Are you going to take me to bed, or what?"

He burrowed his lips into her neck, wanting more. It would be easy, so easy, to pick her up, to take her to his bed and just let it happen. As it had happened before. Something told him that with her it shouldn't be easy. With her it shouldn't be a casual tumble onto the sheets without a thought to tomorrow. He pressed his lips to her brow before he released her.

"I'm going to feed you."

"Oh." Grace took a step back. She didn't often offer herself to a man. It took more than a sexual pull, it took affection and a feeling of trust. And to the best of her recollection, she'd never been rejected. "You sure?"

"Yeah."

"Fine." Turning around, she picked up the cauliflower. It might give her momentary satisfaction to throw it at him, but she decided against it. "If you're not attracted, then—"

It was the second time he'd whirled her around. This time she discovered that colliding with his chest was something like ramming into a stone wall. She might have sworn at him if he hadn't already occupied her mouth.

This time he wasn't gentle. It didn't surprise her to feel the licks of passion or the underlying knots of tension. It made her happy. Then, in seconds, she felt nothing but his mouth, his hands, and her own explosive response.

He wanted her so much he'd have found it exciting to take her there, as they stood in the kitchen. But he wanted more than excitement. He wanted more than the flash of the moment. And he needed time to figure out just what it was he did want.

"You think I'm unattracted to you?"

Grace went from her toes to the flat of her feet on a quick whoosh of breath. "I could be wrong." She cleared her throat, then rubbed her fingertip over her lips as they vibrated from his. "Am I still standing up?"

"Looks like it."

"Good. Okay. After we open a window and get rid of some of the heat in here, what are you going to feed me?"

He smiled and touched her hair. "Stuffed artichoke bottoms Bordelaise."

"Uh-huh," she said after a long pause. "You're not making that up, are you?"

"It only takes about a half hour."

"Can't wait." As he began to gather ingredients, she took a chair. "Ed?"

"Yeah."

"Are you planning on maybe having a long-term relationship?"

He glanced over his shoulder as he rinsed vegetables under a cold spray. "I've been giving it some thought."

"Well, if it works out, I'd like to make a deal. Any night we have artichokes, we have pizza the next."

"Whole-wheat crust."

She got up to find a corkscrew. "We'll talk about it."

BEN SHIFTED IN THE passenger's seat and watched for the light to turn. Beside him, Tess drummed her fingers against the wheel. She knew she was right, but the problem was, she no longer had just her own feelings to consider.

"I could have driven in alone," she began. "You're not going to have a car."

"Ed'll drop me off."

The light switched to green. Tess moved along with the sluggish morning traffic. "I'm sorry you're upset about this. Try to understand, it isn't something I'm doing on impulse."

Annoyed, he turned the radio to another station. "I didn't have any say about your involvement in the other case. Apparently I don't have much say this time around either."

"You know that's not true. What you feel means a lot."

"Then drop me off and go to your office. Leave this alone."

She was silent for a full thirty seconds. "All right."

"All right?" He stopped as he was about to punch in the car lighter. "Just like that?"

"Yes." She tightened a loose pin in her hair with a casual gesture, then made the turn to the station.

"No argument?"

"We argued last night. There's no need to go into it again." Tess swung into the parking lot and pulled up. "I'll see you tonight." Leaning over, she kissed him.

He caught her chin in his hand before she drew away. "You're using that reverse psychology shit on me, aren't you?"

Her eyes, violet and clear, smiled at him. "Absolutely not."

"I hate it when you do that." He flopped back on the seat to rub his hands over his face. "You know how I feel about you being involved with this part of my life."

"You know how I feel about being excluded from any part of your life. Ben . . ."

She lifted her hand to brush at his hair. A year ago she hadn't even known him. Now he was the focal point of her life. Her husband, the father of the child she was just beginning to suspect she was carrying. But she was still a doctor. She'd sworn an oath. And she couldn't forget the way Grace's fingers had trembled on a cup of coffee.

"I may be able to help, to let you understand his mind. I did it before."

"And I almost lost you before."

"This isn't the same. I'm not involved in the same way at all. Ben, do you think he'll kill again? Ben." She took his hand before he could draw away. "Do you think he'll kill again?"

"Yeah. The odds favor it."

"Saving lives. Isn't that still what it's all about? For both of us?"

He stared at the bricks of the station house. There was tradition there. His tradition. It shouldn't have anything to do with her. "I like it better when you do it in your cozy little office uptown."

"And I like it better when you're sitting behind a desk grumbling about paperwork. But it can't be that way every time. Not for you, and not for me. I helped once before. I feel very strongly that I can help this time. He's not an ordinary man. Even from the little you've told me I'm sure of it. He's very sick."

His hackles came up instantly. "You're not going to start bleeding for this one too."

"What I'm going to do is help you find him. After that, we'll see."

"I can't stop you." But her hand was still caught in his, and he knew he could. "I won't stop you," he amended, "but I want you to think about your own caseload, the clinic, your private patients."

"I know my capacity."

"Yeah." It seemed endless to him. "If you start lagging, I'll tell your grandfather on you. He'll straighten your ass out, sister."

"I'm forewarned." She drew him to her again. "I love you, Ben."

"Yeah? How about a demonstration?" Her lips curved against his, then softened. Ed stuck his head in the window.

"Don't you two know any of the side streets around here?"

"Kiss off, Jackson."

Tess nuzzled her cheek against Ben's. "Good morning, Ed."

"Tess. We don't usually see you around here twice in one week."

"You'll probably be seeing her more than that." Ben pushed open his door. "Doc's coming in with us on this one."

"Is that right?" It wasn't difficult to sense the discord. He knew them both too well. "Welcome aboard."

"Always happy to lend a hand to a couple of civil servants." She slipped her arm through Ed's as they walked. "How is Grace doing?"

"Holding up. She's decided to stay in town until this is wrapped."

"I see. That's good."

"It is?"

"She strikes me as the type who doesn't do well when things happen around her. She does better when she has a hand in. One of the worst parts of grief is helplessness. If you can get through that, you cope." She waited until he pulled open the door. "Besides, if she went back to New York, how would you make a play for her?"

Ben strolled in behind his wife. "Doc's got your number, Jackson. Nice-looking lady," he said as he jingled the change in his pocket. "Brains, looks, and money." He swung his arm over Tess's shoulder. "Glad to see you're following my example."

"Tess only fell for you because she has a soft spot for disordered minds." He turned into Homicide, grateful that the business at hand would change the subject.

They settled in the conference room. Tess spread the files of both victims out in front of her. There were photos, the autopsies, and the reports prepared by her husband. There had been more violence here than in the other case she had worked on with the department—if murder could be judged in degrees of violence. The common ground was as clear to her as it was to the investigating officers, but she saw something else, something darker.

Patiently, she read over Eileen Cawfield's statement and the notes from the interview with Markowitz. She studied Ed's official report of the events on the night of Kathleen Breezewood's death.

Ben never liked seeing her this way, handling and studying the bits and pieces of the grittier side of his world. It had been difficult enough to accept her work when she was tucked behind a desk in an uptown office. Logically he knew he couldn't shield her, but he was edgy just having her in the department.

She ran a pretty, manicured finger down the medical examiner's report. His stomach tightened.

"It's interesting that both murders occurred at the same time of night."

Harris rubbed a hand over his stomach. It seemed emptier every day. "We can agree on the possibility that that's part of his pattern." He broke off a tiny end of a raisin bun that was rapidly going stale. He'd managed to convince himself that if he took calories in small doses, they didn't really count. "I haven't had the chance to tell you how much the department appreciates your assistance here, Dr. Court."

"I'm sure the department will appreciate it more if I can help." She took her reading glasses off for a moment to rub her eyes. "I think at this point in the investigation, we can agree that we're dealing with someone with a capacity for explosive violence, and that the violence is certainly sexually oriented."

"Rape usually is," Ben put in.

"Rape is not a sexual crime, but a violent one. The fact that the victims were murdered after the assault isn't unusual. A rapist assaults for a number of reasons: frustration, low self-esteem, a poor opinion of women, anger. Anger is almost always a factor. In the cases where the rapist knows his victim, there is also a need to dominate, to express male superiority and strength, to have what he might believe he deserves, what he thinks has been offered. Often the rapist feels as though his victim is resisting or refusing only to add excitement, and that she actually wants to be taken in a violent way."

She put her glasses on again as she sat back. "The violence in both cases was confined to one room, where the victim was found. The same weapon was used, the phone cord. In all probability the telephone is his link with each woman. Through the phone, they promised him something. He came to collect, not through the front door, but by breaking in. To surprise them, perhaps, to add to the arousal. I tend to believe that the first murder was an impulse, a reflex. Kathleen Breezewood fought him, she hurt him, physically, mentally. She wasn't the woman he'd imagined her to be. Or, in his mind, the woman she'd promised to be. He had a relationship with her. He sent flowers to her funeral, or to Desiree's. She was Desiree to him. It's essential to remember he never knew Kathleen Breezewood, only Desiree. He never saw her, even in death, as the person she was, but as the image he'd created."

"Then how the hell did he find her?" Ben demanded, not so much of Tess as of himself. "How did he take a voice over the phone and zero in on a house, a woman. The right woman?"

"I wish I could help you." She didn't reach for his hand as she would have if they'd been alone. Here, she knew, there would always be a certain amount of distance between them. "I can only tell you that in my opinion, this man is very clever. He is, in his way, logical. He follows a pattern, step by step."

"And his first step is to choose a voice," Ed murmured. "And create the woman."

"I'd say that's close to the mark. He has a very strong capacity for fantasy. What he imagines, he believes. He left fingerprints at both murder scenes, but not because he's careless. Because he believes himself to be very clever, to be invulnerable to the realities since he's living in a world of his own creation. He lives out his fantasies, and very likely those he believes his victims have."

"Am I hearing that he rapes and kills women because he thinks they like it?" Ben pulled out a cigarette. Tess watched him light it, recognizing the edge in his voice.

"In simple terms, yes. According to Markowitz's

recollection of what he heard on the phone during the second attack, the man said, 'You know you want me to hurt you.' Rapists often rationalize this way. He bound Mary Grice's hands, but not Kathleen's. I think that's important. From the reports, Kathleen Breezewood offered a more conservative, a more straightforward sexual fantasy than Mary Grice. Bondage and sadism were often included in Mary's conversations. The killer gave her what he thought she preferred. And he killed her, in all probability, because he'd discovered a dark and psychotic pleasure from the first bonding of sex and death. It's highly possible he believes his victims received the same pleasure. Kathleen was an impulse, Mary a reconstruction." She turned to Ben now. He may not have approved, but he was listening. "What do you think about the time of the murders?"

"What should I think?"

She smiled at him. He was the one who always accused her of answering a question with a question. "They both occurred fairly early in the evening, a pattern of sorts. It makes me wonder if perhaps he's married, or lives with someone who expects him to be home by a certain time."

Ben studied the end of his cigarette. "Maybe he just likes to turn in early."

"Maybe."

"Tess." Ed dunked a tea bag in a cup of hot water. "It's generally accepted that a voyeur or a crank caller doesn't go any further. What makes this guy different?"

"He's not a watcher. He participates. These women have spoken with him. There's not the same distance, actual or emotional, as there is with someone who uses binoculars to spy into an apartment across the street or peep into a window. There's not the same kind of anonymity as a random call. He knows these women. Not Kathleen and Mary, but Desiree and Roxanne. I once had a patient who was involved in a date rape."

"Unfortunately, the victim's viewpoint doesn't apply, Dr. Court," Harris put in.

"I treated the rapist, not the victim." Tess took off her glasses to run the stem through her fingers. "He didn't force sex on this girl only for himself. He initiated, persisted, then insisted because he thought she expected it of him. He'd convinced himself that his date wanted him to take the responsibility, and that if he backed off, she'd have thought him weak. Unmanly. In forcing her, he not only received sexual release, but a sense of power. He'd called the shots. In my opinion, the man you're looking for enjoys that same sense of power. He kills these women not so they can't identify him, but because murder is the ultimate power. It's likely he comes from a background where he wasn't able to wield power, where the authority figures in his life were, or are, very strong. He's been sexually repressed, now he's experimenting."

She opened the folders again. "His victims were very different types of women, not only in the personalities of their alter egos, but physically. That could have been a coincidence, of course, but it's more likely it was deliberate. The only things these women had in common were sex and the phone. He used both against them in the most violent and most final of ways. His next choice will probably be someone with a totally different style."

"I'd prefer it if we didn't have the opportunity to test that particular theory out." Harris snuck another corner from the raisin bun. "Could he stop? Stop cold?"

"I don't think so." Tess closed the folders again and set them on his desk. "There's no remorse here, no anguish. The message of the florist card wasn't 'I'm sorry' or 'Forgive me,' but 'I won't forget.' His movements are carefully planned out. He's not grabbing a woman off the street and dragging her into an alley or a car. Again, you must understand, he knows them, or believes he knows them, and he's taking what he feels he deserves. He's very much a product of today's society, where you can pick up the phone and order anything. From pizza to pornography, you only have to push a button and it becomes yours, something you're entitled to. You have a mixture here of the convenience of technology and sociopathic tendencies. It's all very logical to him."

"Excuse me." Lowenstein popped her head in the door. "We've just finished the cross-checks on the credit cards." At Harris's nod, she handed the printouts to Ed. "Not one match."

"None?" Ben stood to look over Ed's shoulder.

"Zero. We looked for matches in the numbers, in the names, addresses, possible aliases or dupes. Nothing."

"Different styles," Ed murmured and he began to think it through.

"So, we're back to square one." Ben took the sheets Ed passed him.

"Maybe not. We tracked down the flowers. It was a phone order to Bloom Town. MasterCard number belongs to a Patrick R. Morgan. Here's the address."

"He show up on either of these?" Ed asked, still studying the printouts.

"Nope. We're still checking the other lists."

"Let's go pay him a visit." Ben checked his watch. "You got a work address?"

"Yeah, Capitol Hill. Morgan's a congressman."

THE REPRESENTATIVE COULD BE found at home that day in his refurbished Georgetown town house. The woman who answered the door looked sour and impatient and carried a mountain of file folders. "Yes?" was all she said.

"We'd like to see Congressman Morgan." Ed had already looked beyond her and zeroed in on the mahogany paneling in the hall. The real stuff.

"I'm sorry, the congressman isn't available. If you'd like an appointment, call his office."

Ben dug out his shield. "Police business, ma'am."

"I don't care if you're God Himself," she said with hardly a glance at his ID. "He's not available. Try his office, next week."

To prevent her from shutting the door in their faces, Ed simply put a shoulder into the opening. "I'm afraid we'll have to insist. We can talk to him here, or down at head-quarters." Ed caught the look in her eyes and was certain, despite his size, that she intended to muscle him aside.

"Margaret, what in hell's going on?" The question was followed by a series of sneezes before Congressman Morgan appeared at the door. He was a small-statured, dark-haired man approaching fifty. Just now he was pale, red-eyed, and wrapped in a bathrobe.

"These men insist on seeing you, sir, and I told them—"

"All right, Margaret." In spite of his red eyes, Morgan managed a wide, political smile. "I'm sorry, gentlemen, as you can see I'm a bit under the weather."

"Our apologies, Congressman." Ben held up his shield again. "But it's important."

"I see. Well, come in then. But I'll warn you to keep your distance. I'm probably still contagious."

He led them down the hall and into a sitting room done in blues and grays and accented with framed sketches of the city. "Margaret, stop scowling at the police officers and go deal with those files."

"Relapse," she predicted, but dutifully disappeared.

"Secretaries are worse than wives. Have a seat, gentlemen. You'll excuse me if I stretch out here." He settled himself on the couch with an angora throw over his knees. "Flu," he explained as he reached for a tissue. "Healthy as a horse all winter, then as soon as the flowers start blooming, I get hit with this."

Cautious, Ed took a chair a good three feet away. "People take better care of themselves in the winter." He noted the teapot and the pitcher of juice. At least he was taking fluids. "We'll try not to take up much of your time."

"Always make it my business to cooperate with the police. We're on the same side, after all." Morgan sneezed heartily into a tissue.

"Bless you," Ed offered.

"Thanks. So what can I do for you?"

"Are you acquainted with a business called Fantasy, Incorporated?" Ben asked the question casually as he crossed his legs, but his eyes never left Morgan's face.

"Fantasy? No," he decided after a moment's thought. "It doesn't ring a bell." He made the pun with seeming innocence as he adjusted his pillow. "Should it?"

"Telephone sex." Ed thought briefly of the germs skittering around in the air. Being a cop had its hazards.

"Ah." Morgan grimaced a bit, then settled back. "Certainly a subject for debate. Still, that's more a matter for the FCC and the courts than a congressman. At least at the moment."

"Did you know a Kathleen Breezewood, Congressman Morgan?"

"Breezewood, Breezewood." Morgan's lip poked out as he studied Ben. "The name's not familiar."

"Desiree?"

"No." He smiled again. "That's not a name a man forgets."

Ed took out his pad and opened it as if he were checking some fact. "If you didn't know Mrs. Breezewood, why did you send flowers to her funeral?"

"Did I?" Morgan looked mildly baffled. "Well, she certainly wasn't someone of close acquaintance, but flowers are sent for any number of reasons. Political mostly. My secretary handles that sort of thing. Margaret!" He bellowed the name, then fell into a quick fit of coughing.

"Overdoing," she muttered as she scurried into the room. "Drink your tea and stop shouting."

He did just that, meekly, Ed thought. "Margaret, do I know a Kathleen Breezewood?"

"Do you mean the woman who was murdered a few days ago?"

The flush that the coughing had brought on faded from Morgan's face. He turned to Ed. "Do I?"

"Yes, sir."

"Did we send flowers, Margaret?"

"Why should we?" She fussed with his lap robe. "You didn't know her."

"Flowers were sent to her funeral that were ordered from Bloom Town Florists with your credit card number. MasterCard." Ed glanced down at his book again and rattled off the number.

"Is that mine?" Morgan asked his secretary.

"Yes, but I didn't order any flowers. We have an account with Lorimar Florists in any case. Don't use Bloom Town. Haven't ordered flowers in two weeks. Last ones went to Parson's wife when she had her baby." She gave Ben a stubborn look. "It's in the log."

"Get the log, please, Margaret." Morgan waited for her to leave. "Gentlemen, I can see this business is more serious than I suspected, but I'm afraid I'm lost."

"Kathleen Breezewood was murdered on the evening of April tenth." Ed waited until Morgan had sneezed into another tissue. "Can you tell us where you were between eight and eleven?"

"April tenth." Morgan rubbed his fingers over his eyes. "That would have been the night of the fundraiser at the Shoreham. Election year, you know. I was just coming down with this miserable flu, and I remember I dragged my feet about going. My wife was put out with me. We were there from seven until, oh, just after ten, I believe.

Came straight home. I had a breakfast meeting the next morning."

"Nothing in the log about flowers since the Parson baby." Smug, Margaret walked back in and handed the oversize book to Ben. "It's my business to know where and when to send flowers."

"Congressman Morgan," Ed began, "who else has access to your credit card?"

"Margaret, of course. And my wife, though she has her own."

"Children?"

Morgan stiffened at that, but he answered. "My children have no need for credit cards. My daughter is only fifteen. My son's a senior at St. James's Preparatory Academy. Both receive an allowance and large purchases have to be approved. Obviously the clerk at the florist made a mistake when noting down the number."

"Possibly," Ed murmured. But he doubted the clerk had misunderstood the name as well. "It would help if you could tell us where your son was on the night of the tenth."

"I resent this." Flu aside, Morgan sat up straight.

"Congressman, we have two murders." Ben shut the log. "We're not in the position to walk on eggshells here."

"You realize, of course, I have to answer nothing. However, to close the subject, I'll cooperate."

"We appreciate it," Ben said mildly. "About your son?"

"He had a date." Morgan reached for the juice and poured a tumblerful. "He's seeing Senator Fielding's daughter, Julia. I believe they went to the Kennedy Center that evening. Michael was home by eleven. School night."

"And last night?" Ben asked.

"Last night Michael was home all evening. We played chess until sometime after ten."

Ed noted down both alibis. "Would anyone else on your staff have access to your card number?"

"No." Both his patience and his need to cooperate had

reached an end. "Quite simply, someone made a mistake. Now if you'll excuse me, I can't tell you any more."

"We appreciate the time." Ed rose, tucking his notebook away. He'd already decided to dose himself with extra vitamin C when he got back to the station. "If you think of any other reason the flowers might have been charged to your account, let us know."

Margaret was more than happy to see them out. When the door closed behind them with a resounding thud, Ben stuck his hands in his pockets. "My gut tells me the guy's on the level."

"Yeah. It's easy enough to check on the fundraiser, but I vote for the senator's daughter first."

"I'm with you."

They walked toward the car. Over Ben's mutter, Ed took the driver's side. "You know, something Tess said's been bothering me."

"What?"

"How you can pick up the phone and order anything. Do it all the time myself."

"Pizza or pornography?" Ben asked, but he was thinking too.

"Drywall. I had some delivered last month and had to give the guy my card number before he'd send it out. How many times have you given out your credit card number to somebody over the phone? All you need is the number and name, no plastic, no ID, no signature."

"Yeah." On a whoosh of breath, Ben took his seat. "I guess that narrows the field down to a couple hundred thousand."

Ed pulled away from the town house. "We can always hope the senator's daughter got stood up."

Chapter 10

MARY BETH MORRISON HAD been born to mother. By the time she was six, she'd possessed a collection of baby dolls that required regular feeding, changing, and pampering. Some had walked, some had talked, but her heart had been just as open to a button-eyed rag doll with a torn arm.

Unlike other children, she'd never balked at the domestic chores her parents had assigned to her. She'd loved the washing and the polishing. She'd had a pint-size ironing board, a miniature oven, and her own tea set. By her tenth birthday, she'd been a better hand at baking than her mother.

Her one true ambition had been to have a home and family of her own to care for. There had never been any vision of corporate boardrooms or briefcases in Mary Beth's dreams. She'd wanted a white picket fence and a baby carriage.

Mary Beth believed strongly that a person should do what he or she did best. Her sister had passed the bar and joined an upscale law firm in Chicago. Mary Beth was proud of her. She admired her sister's wardrobe, her forthright defense of the law, and the men who flowed in and out of her life. Mary Beth didn't have an envious bone in her body. She clipped coupons and baked brownies for the PTA bake sale and campaigned strongly for equal pay for equal work, though she'd never been a member of what society considered the workforce.

By nineteen, she'd married her childhood sweetheart, a boy she'd chosen when they'd attended elementary school together. He'd never had a chance. Mary Beth had been attentive, patient, understanding, and supportive. Not through guile, but with sincerity. She'd fallen in love with Harry Morrison the day two bullies had knocked him down on the playground and loosened his front tooth. After twenty-five years of friendship, twelve years of marriage, and four children, she still adored him.

Her world revolved around her home and her family to the point where even her outside interests circled back to them. There were many, her sister included, who felt that world was severely limited. Mary Beth just smiled and baked another cake. She was happy, and she was good, even excellent, at what she did. She had what to her was the greatest reward: the love of husband and children. She didn't need her sister's approval or anyone else's.

She kept herself in shape for her husband's pleasure as well as her own. As she approached her thirty-second birthday, she was a trim and lovely woman with unlined skin and soft brown eyes. Mary Beth understood and sympathized with women who felt themselves trapped in the role of housewife. She would have felt the same way in an office. When she found time, she worked with the PTA and the ASPCA. Other than family, her passion was animals. They too needed tending.

She was a nurturer and was considering the possibility of having one more child before calling it a day.

Her husband treasured her. Though she left most of the decisions in his hands, or seemed to, Mary Beth was no pushover. They had had their share of arguments during their marriage, and if the issue was important enough, she took it between her teeth and fretted at it until she got her way. The issue of Fantasy, Incorporated had been important enough.

Harry was a good provider, but there had been times when Mary Beth had taken on part-time jobs to supplement or enhance his income. She'd applied for and received a license for day-care. With the extra money she'd made, the family had been able to take a ten-day vacation to Florida and Disney World. Photos from that excursion were neatly filed in a blue album with the label OUR FAMILY VACATION.

At one time, she'd sold magazines over the phone. Though her soothing voice had helped her move inventory, she hadn't been satisfied. As a woman who had grown up knowing how to budget both time and money, she'd found the financial rewards less than worthy of the time involved.

She wanted another child, and she wanted to provide a college fund for the four children she'd already been blessed with. Her husband's salary from his position as foreman for a construction firm was adequate, but it didn't lend itself to many extras. She'd stumbled across Fantasy in the back of one of her husband's magazines. The idea of being paid just to talk fascinated her.

It had taken her three weeks, but she'd talked Harry down from adamantly opposed to skeptical. Another week had changed skepticism to grudging acceptance. Mary Beth had a way with words. Now she was turning that talent into dollars.

She and Harry had agreed to give Fantasy one year. In that time, it was Mary Beth's goal to make ten thousand dollars. Enough for a small college nest egg and maybe, if luck was with them, one more obstetrician's fee.

Mary Beth was starting her fourth month as an

operator for Fantasy and was nearly halfway to her projected goal. She was a very popular lady.

She didn't mind talking sex. After all, as she'd explained to her husband, it was hard to be a prude after twelve years of marriage and four children. Harry had come around to the point of being amused by her new job. Occasionally, he phoned her himself, on their personal line, to give her the chance to practice. He called himself Stud Brewster and made her giggle.

Perhaps because of her maternal instinct or her genuine understanding of men and their problems, most of her calls dealt less with sex than with sympathy. Clients who called her on a regular basis found they could talk to her about job frustrations or the grind of family life and receive an easy concern. She never sounded bored, as their wives and lovers often did, she never criticized, and when the occasion called for it, Mary Beth could issue the kind of commonsense advice they might have received if they'd written to Dear Abby—with the bonus of a sexual kick.

She was sister, mother, or lover, whatever the client required. Her clients were satisfied, and Mary Beth began thinking seriously about tossing away her little packet of birth control pills and taking that last turn at bat.

She was a strong-willed, uncomplicated woman who believed most problems could be worked through with time, good intentions, and a plate of fudge brownies. But she'd never encountered anyone like Jerald.

And he was listening. Night after night he waited to hear her voice. There was something gentle and calming about it. He was on the edge of being in love with her, and almost as obsessed with her as he'd been with Desiree. Roxanne was forgotten. Roxanne had been little more to him than a laboratory rat. But there was a goodness in Mary Beth's voice, an old-fashioned solidity to her name, which she'd kept because she was too comfortable with it to play games. A man could believe what a woman like Mary Beth told him. The promises she made would be kept.

Mary Beth was a different style altogether.

Jerald believed her. He wanted to meet her. He wanted to show her how grateful he was to her.

Early in the evening, late into the night, he listened. And planned.

GRACE WAS TIRED OF hitting dead ends and being patient. More than a week had passed since the second murder, and if there was any progress in the investigation, Ed wasn't sharing it with her. She thought she understood him. He was a generous man, and a compassionate one. But he was also a cop who lived by the department's rules, and his own. She could respect his discipline while being frustrated with his discretion. The time she spent with him had a way of calming her, while the time she spent alone left her with nothing to do but think. So she too began to plan.

She set up appointments. Her brief meetings with Kathleen's attorney and the detective she'd hired shed no light. They couldn't tell her anything she didn't already know. She'd hoped, somehow, that she'd be able to dig up information that would point to Jonathan. In her heart, she still wanted him to be guilty, though in her own words, she knew it didn't play. It was a hard belief to give up. In the end, she had to accept that however much Jonathan had been responsible for the state of Kathleen's mind in the last days of her life, he hadn't been responsible for ending it.

But Kathleen was still dead, and there were other avenues to explore.

The straightest, and most easily navigated, led her to Fantasy, Incorporated.

Grace found Eileen in her usual position behind her desk. When she entered, Eileen closed the checkbook she'd been balancing and smiled. A cigarette burned in an ashtray at her elbow. Over the last few days, Eileen had given up even the pretense of quitting.

"Good afternoon. Can I help you?"

"I'm Grace McCabe."

It took Eileen a moment to place the name. Grace was dressed in a baggy red sweater, skinny black pants, and a pair of snakeskin boots. She no longer looked like the grieving sister in the newspaper photo. "Yes, Miss McCabe. We're all very sorry about Kathleen."

"Thank you." She could see by the tensing of Eileen's fingers that she was bracing for an attack. Perhaps it would be best to keep the woman nervous and on guard. Grace had no qualms about stirring the guilt. "It seems your company was the catalyst for the attack on my sister."

"Miss McCabe." Eileen picked up her cigarette and took a quick, jittery puff. "I feel badly, very badly about what happened to Kathleen. But I don't feel responsible."

"Don't you?" Grace smiled and took a seat. "Then I don't suppose you feel responsible for Mary Grice either. Do you have any coffee?"

"Yes, yes, of course."

Eileen rose and went into the broom closet–size storeroom behind the desk. She was feeling far from well and wished now she'd taken her husband up on that quick vacation in Bermuda. "I'm sure you know we're cooperating with the police in any way we can. Everyone wants this man stopped."

"Yes, but you see, I also want him to pay. No cream," she added and waited for Eileen to bring out an oversize stoneware mug. "You understand that I feel a bit closer to all of this than you, or the police. I need the answers to some questions."

"I don't know what I can tell you." Eileen went behind her desk again. The minute she landed she reached for the cigarette. "I've told the police absolutely everything I could.

I didn't know your sister well, you see. I only met her when she came in that first time to interview. Everything else was done by phone."

No, Eileen hadn't known Kathleen well, Grace thought. Perhaps no one had. "The phone," Grace repeated as she sat back. "I guess we could say the phone's the core of it all. I know how your business works. Kathleen explained it to me, so there's no need to get into all of that. Tell me, do any of the men who call ever come by here?"

"No." Eileen rubbed at a headache just above her eyes. She hadn't been able to get rid of it completely since she'd read about Mary Grice in the papers. "We don't give out our address to clients. Of course, it would be possible for someone to find us if they were determined, but there isn't any reason for it. Even potential employees are screened before they're given the address for the personal interview. We're very careful, Miss McCabe. I want you to understand that."

"Did anyone ever call asking questions about Kathy— about Desiree?"

"No. And if they had, they wouldn't have gotten any answers. Excuse me," she said quickly as the phone rang.

Grace sipped her coffee and listened with half an ear. Why had she come? She'd known that there would be very little, if anything, she could learn that the police hadn't. A few missing details, a few pieces; she was groping. Yet this was it. This tiny, unassuming office was the key. All she had to figure out was how to turn it.

"I'm sorry, Mr. Peterson, Jezebel isn't on call today. Would you like to talk with someone else?" As she spoke, Eileen punched a few buttons on her keyboard, then read off the monitor. "If you had something specific in mind . . . I sec. I think you'd enjoy speaking with Magda. Yes, she is. I'm sure she'll be glad to help you. I'll arrange it."

When she hung up, Eileen shot Grace a nervous

glance. "I'm sorry, this is going to take a few minutes. I wish I could help but—"

"It's all right. I'll wait until you're finished." Grace lifted her cup again. She had a new idea, and one she intended to move on right away. She smiled at Eileen when the business was completed. "Tell me, just how do you go about getting a job here?"

ED WASN'T IN THE best of moods when he pulled into his drive. He'd spent the better part of the day kicking his heels in court, waiting to testify in the appeal of a case he'd worked on two years earlier. Ed had never had any doubt about the guilt of the defendant. The evidence had been there, the motive and the opportunity. He and Ben had tied it up in a bow and handed it to the DA.

Though the press had made the most of it at the time, it had been a fairly simple investigation. The man had killed his wife, his older and wealthy wife, then had scrambled to make it look like robbery. The first jury had deliberated less than six hours and had come back with a guilty verdict. The law said the defendant was entitled to an appeal, and that justice could drag its heels. Now, two years later, the man who had willfully taken the life of the woman he'd promised to love, honor, and cherish was being portrayed as a victim of circumstance.

Ed knew the man had a good chance of getting off. It was on days like this he wondered why he bothered to pick up his shield every morning. He could take the mountains of paperwork with little complaint. He could put his life in jeopardy to protect society. He could spend hours in stakeouts in the dead of winter or the height of summer. That was all part of the job. But it was becoming harder every year to accept the twists he confronted in the courts of law.

He was going to spend the evening putting up drywall, measuring, cutting, and banging until he forgot that however hard he worked, he would lose every bit as often as he would win.

Clouds were coming in from the west, promising an evening rain. His plants needed it, here and in the little patch he'd cultivated in a community garden a couple of miles away. He hoped he'd have the time over the weekend to check on his zucchini. As he climbed out of the car, he heard the steady hum of a lawn mower. Glancing over, he watched Grace push a trail up and down the small yard in front of her sister's house.

She looked so pretty. Every time he saw her, he found himself content to simply watch. The little breeze that helped blow in the clouds caught at her hair so that it danced erratically around her face. She wore earphones attached to a portable stereo she'd hooked in the waist of her jeans.

He'd meant to take care of the lawn for her, but now he was glad he hadn't had the chance. It gave him the opportunity to watch her while she worked, while she was unaware of him. He could stand there and imagine what it would be like to come home every day and find her waiting.

The tight knot of anger he'd been carrying with him loosened. He walked toward her.

With vintage Chuck Berry blasting in her ears, Grace leapt when he touched her shoulder. Holding the lawn mower with one hand and her heart with the other, she smiled up at him. She watched his mouth move as "Maybelline" danced in her head. Her smile turned to a grin. She got such a kick out of looking at him, at the kind, even soft eyes in the strong face. He'd have made a perfect Mountain Man, Grace decided, living alone, living off the land. And the Indians would have trusted him because his eyes wouldn't lie.

Maybe she should try her hand at writing a historical,

a western—something with a posse and a hard-riding, straight-shooting sheriff with a red beard.

After a moment, Ed slipped the headphones off and let them dangle around her neck. Grace reached up to run a hand over his beard. "Hi. I didn't hear a word you said."

"I noticed. You know, you shouldn't play that thing so loud. It's bad for your ears."

"Rock's no good unless it's loud." She reached down to her hip and shut it off. "Are you home early?"

"No." Because they were both shouting over the roar of the mower, he pressed down the idle switch. "You're never going to be able to finish this before the rain."

"Rain?" Surprised, she looked up at the sky. "When did that happen?"

He laughed and the hours spent in court were forgotten. "Are you always oblivious to what's happening around you?"

"As often as possible." Grace checked the sky again, then the remainder of the lawn. "Well, I can hit the rest tomorrow."

"I can take care of it for you. I've got tomorrow off."

"Thanks, but you've got enough to do. I'd better put this thing around back."

"I'll give you a hand." Because he seemed to want to, Grace relinquished her hold on the mower to him.

"I met Ida today," she began as they walked the chugging machine to the rear of the house.

"Second house up?"

"I guess. She must have seen me around back; she came down. She smelled like a cat."

"I'm not surprised."

"Anyway, she wanted me to know that she'd had very good vibrations about me." Grace picked up a tarp when Ed stopped the mower at the corner of the house. "She wondered if I'd been at Shiloh—the battle of."

"And what did you say?"

"I didn't want to disappoint her." After draping the tarp over the mower, Grace flexed her shoulders. "I told her I'd caught a Yankee bullet in the leg. And that even today I occasionally walk with a limp. It satisfied her. Do you have any plans for tonight?"

He was learning to twist his thoughts with hers. "Drywall."

"Drywall? Oh, that ugly gray stuff, right? Can I give you a hand?"

"If you want."

"Have you got any real food over there?"

"I can probably dig up something."

Remembering the asparagus, Grace took him literally. "Hold on a minute." She dashed into the house just as the first drops of rain began to fall. She ran out again carrying a bag of potato chips. "Emergency rations. Race you." Before he could agree, she took off in a dead run, amusing him by agilely taking the fence with a one-handed leap. He caught up with her three yards from his back door and surprised them both by sweeping her up in his arms. Laughing, she kissed him hard and quick. "You're fast on your feet, Jackson."

"I practice chasing the bad guys." As the rain fell steadily, he pressed his mouth to hers again. It was sweet, and so much sweeter as he heard her murmured sigh. Her face was damp wherever his lips touched. Cool and damp. It seemed she weighed nothing at all, and he could have stood there for hours. Then she shivered so he drew her closer to him.

"Getting wet." He made a dash for the back door, then regretfully put her down beside him to draw out his keys. Grace walked inside and shook herself like the family dog.

"It's warm. I like warm rain." She dragged both hands through her hair. It sprang back in the wild disorder that suited her. "I know I'm going to spoil the mood, but I was hoping you might have something more to tell me."

It didn't spoil it, because it was expected. "It's moving slow, Grace. The only lead we had was a dead end."

"You're sure the congressman's kid's alibi holds up?"

"Like a rock." He put on the kettle for tea. "He was front row center at the Kennedy Center the night Kathleen was killed. He's got the ticket stubs, his girl's word, and another dozen witnesses who saw him there."

"He could have slipped away."

"Not enough time. There was an intermission at nine-fifteen. He was in the lobby sipping lemonade. I'm sorry."

She shook her head. Leaning against the counter, she drew out a cigarette. "You know the really terrible thing? I find myself wishing that this kid I've never seen is guilty. I keep hoping his alibi will fall apart and he'll be arrested. I don't even know him."

"It's human. You're just looking for it to be over."

"I don't know what I'm looking for." A sigh slipped out. She didn't like the plaintive, fragile sound of it. "I wanted it to be Jonathan, too, *because* I knew him, because he—it doesn't matter," she decided as she flicked on her lighter. "It wasn't either one of them."

"We will find him, Grace."

She studied Ed as steam began to shoot through the spout of the kettle. "I know. I don't think I could go on doing the ordinary things, thinking about what I'll do tomorrow, if I didn't know." She took a long, steadying drag. There was something else she was thinking about, something that couldn't be avoided. "He isn't finished, is he?"

Turning away, he measured out tea. "It's hard to say."

"No, it's not. Be straight with me, Ed. I don't like being shielded."

He wanted to shield, not simply because it was his vocation, but because it was her. And because it was her, it wasn't possible to shield. "I don't think he's finished."

She nodded, then gestured to the kettle. "You'd better fix that before the water boils away." While he took out mugs, she thought about what she'd done that day. She should tell him. The tug on her conscience was sharp and impatient. It wasn't easy to ignore. She would tell him, Grace reminded herself. As soon as it was too late for him to do anything about it.

She walked over to poke into his refrigerator. "I don't guess you have any hot dogs."

He shot her a look of such genuine concern she had to bite her lip. "You don't really eat those?"

"Nah." She shut the door and hoped for peanut butter.

They worked well together. Grace polished off most of the chips as she tried her hand with a hammer. She'd had to argue with Ed first. His idea of letting her help had been to sit her in a chair so she could watch. He'd finally relented, but kept an eagle eye on her. It wasn't so much that he was afraid she'd screw up, though that was part of it. It was more that he worried she'd hurt herself. It only took an hour for him to see that once she dug her heels into a project, she handled herself like a pro. She might have been a bit sloppy with the joint compound, but he figured it would sand down. The extra time that took him didn't matter. It might have been silly, but just having her there made the work go faster.

"This is going to be a great room." Grace rubbed at an itch on her chin with the back of her hand. "I really like the way you're shaping it like a little L. Every civilized bedroom should have a sitting room."

He'd wanted her to like it. In his mind he could already see it finished, down to the curtains on the window. Priscillas in blue, tied back so the sun would stream in. It was easy for him to see it, just as it was easy for him to see her there.

"I'm thinking about putting in a couple of skylights."

"Really?" Grace walked over to the bed, sat down, and craned her neck. "You could lie here and watch the stars.

Or on a night like this, the rain." That would be nice, she thought as she looked up at the unfinished ceiling. It would be lovely to sleep, or make love, or just daydream under the glass. "If you ever decided to take your trade to New York, you could make a fortune remodeling lofts."

"Do you miss it?" Rather than look at her, Ed busied himself taping a seam.

"New York? Sometimes." Less, she realized, than she'd expected to. "You know what you need over there? A window seat." From her perch on the bed, she pointed to the west window. "When I was a little girl I always thought how wonderful it would be to have a window seat where you could curl up and dream." She rose and flexed her arms. It was funny how quickly unused muscles got sore. "I spent most of my time hiding out in the attic and dreaming."

"Did you always want to write?"

Grace dipped into the bucket of compound again. "I liked to lie." She laughed and smeared the mudlike mixture over a nailhead. "Not big ones, just clever ones. I could get out of trouble by making up stories, and adults were usually amused enough to let me off lightly. It always infuriated Kathleen." She was silent for a minute. She didn't want to remember the bad times. "What's that song?"

"It's Patsy Cline."

Grace listened a moment. It wasn't the kind of music she would have chosen, but it had an edge she liked. "Didn't they make a movie about her? Sure they did. She was killed in a plane crash in the sixties." She listened again. The song sounded so alive, so vital. Grace wasn't sure if it made her want to smile or weep. "I guess that's another reason I wanted to write. To leave something behind. A story's like a song. It lasts. I guess I've been thinking more about that lately. Do you ever think about that, about leaving something behind?"

"Sure." More lately as well, he thought, but for different reasons. "Great-grandchildren."

That made her laugh. Compound slopped onto the cuff of her sweater, but she didn't bother to wipe it off. "That's nice. I guess you'd think that way, coming from a big family."

"How do you know I have a big family?"

"Your mother mentioned it. Two brothers and a sister. Both your brothers are married, even though Tom and . . ." —she had to think back a moment—"Scott are younger than you. You have, let's see, I think it's three nephews. Made me think of Huey, Dewey, and Louie—no offense."

He could only shake his head. "Don't you ever forget anything?"

"Nope. Your mother's holding out for a granddaughter, but no one's cooperating. She's still hoping you'll give up crime and join your uncle's construction firm."

Uncomfortable, he picked up a piece of corner bead and began hammering it in. "Apparently you two had quite a conversation."

"She was auditioning me, remember?" He was blushing, just a little, but enough to make her want to hug him. "Anyway, people are always telling me intimate details of their lives. I've never known why."

"Because you listen."

She smiled, considering that one of the greatest compliments. "So why aren't you building condos with your uncle? You like to build."

"It relaxes me." Just as the Merle Haggard number playing on the radio now relaxed him. "If I did it all day every day, I'd be bored."

She caught her tongue between her teeth as she slopped compound down a seam. "You're talking to someone who knows just how boring police work can be."

"It's a puzzle. You ever do jigsaws when you were a kid? The big twenty-five-thousand-piece jobs?"

"Sure. After a couple of hours, I'd cheat. It would drive everyone crazy when they found out I'd torn off the end of a piece to make it fit."

"I could spend days on one and never lose interest. Always working from the outside to the core. The more pieces you put in, the more detail; the more detail, the closer you are to the whole picture."

She stopped a moment, because she understood. "Didn't you ever want to go right for the heart of it and the hell with the details?"

"No. If you do that, you're always searching for the loose ends, that one elusive piece that ties it all up and makes it right." After tacking in the last nail, he stepped back to be sure he'd done the job right. "There's a tremendous satisfaction when you put in the last piece and see the full picture. This guy we're after now—we just don't have all the pieces yet. But we will. Once we do, we'll shuffle them around until everything fits."

"Do they always?"

He looked down at her then. She had the damn compound smeared on her face, and her expression was so earnest. Ed rubbed his thumb over her cheek to remove the worst of it. "Sooner or later." Setting down his tool, he framed her face in his hands. "Trust me."

"I do." Kind eyes, strong hands. She leaned closer. She wanted more than comfort, needed more. "Ed—" The banging on the door downstairs made her shut her eyes in frustration. "Sounds like we've got company."

"Yeah. With luck I can get rid of them in five minutes."

Her brows arched. There was an edge to his voice that pleased and flattered her. "Detective, this could be your lucky day." She took his hand so that they walked downstairs together. The minute Ed opened the door, Ben pulled Tess inside.

"Christ, Ed, don't you know people could drown out here? What were you—" He caught sight of Grace. "Oh. Hi."

"Hi. Relax. We were playing with drywall. Hello, Tess. I'm glad to see you. I never had a chance to thank you."

"You're welcome." Tess rose on her toes and pulled Ed down for a kiss. "I'm sorry, Ed. I told Ben we should call first."

"No problem. Sit down."

"Sure, pull up a crate." Ben eased his wife down on a packing box, then held up a bottle of wine. "You've got glasses, don't you?"

Ed took the bottle, then lifted both brows. "What's the occasion? You usually bring over a six-pack of Moosehead or sponge off me."

"That's gratitude for you, especially now when we're making you a godfather." Ben took Tess's hand and held it in both of his. "In seven months, one week, and three days. More or less."

"A baby? You guys are having a baby?" Ed swung an arm around Ben and squeezed. "Nice going, partner." He took Tess's free hand almost as if he were going to monitor her pulse. "Are you okay?"

"I'm fine. Ben nearly collapsed, but I'm fine."

"I didn't nearly collapse. Maybe I babbled for a couple of minutes, but I didn't collapse. I'll get glasses. Make sure she stays sitting down, will you?" he said to Ed.

"I'll give you a hand." Grace took the wine from Ed and followed Ben to the kitchen. "You must be on top of the world."

"I don't think I've taken it in yet. A family." He started to rummage through cupboards while Grace found a corkscrew. "I never thought about having a family. Then all of a sudden there was Tess. Everything changed."

Grace stared at the bottle as she began to draw out the cork. "It's funny how family can keep everything focused."

"Yeah." After setting out glasses, Ben laid a hand on her shoulder. "How are you holding up?"

"Better, most of the time better. The hardest thing is believing she's gone and that I won't ever see her again."

"I know how you feel. I do," he said when he felt her instant withdrawal. "I lost my brother."

After drawing the cork out, she made herself look at him. There was kindness there too, in the eyes. He was more intense than Ed, more restless and wired, but the kindness was there. "How did you handle it?"

"Badly. He had everything going for him, and I was crazy about him. We didn't see eye to eye on everything, but we were tight. He got shipped to Nam right out of high school."

"I'm sorry. It must be horrible to lose someone you love in a war."

"He didn't die in Nam, only the best parts of him did." Ben picked up the bottle and began to pour. It was funny; even after all the years, he remembered too well. "He came back a different person, withdrawn, bitter, lost. He turned to drugs to wipe it out, fog it up, but it didn't help." He saw she was thinking of her sister, and the bottles that had been stashed throughout the house. "It's tough not to blame them for choosing an easy way."

"Yes, yes, it is. What happened to him?"

"In the end, he couldn't take it anymore. So he opted out."

"I'm sorry. I'm really sorry." The tears started again, the ones she'd been able to hold off for days. "I don't want to do this."

"No." He understood that as well. "But sometimes it's better after you do."

"Everyone says they understand, but they don't."
When he put his arms around her, she held on. "You don't
know what it is to lose a part of yourself until it happens.
There's nothing you can do to prepare for it, you know?
And nothing you can do afterward, after you've handled all
the details. That's the worst part, not being able to do anything. How long—how long did it take you to put it behind you?"

"I'll let you know when it happens."

She nodded, letting her head rest against his shoulder
for another minute. "All you can do is go on?"

"That's right. After a while you don't think about it
every day. Then something happens in your life like Tess
did to mine. You can go on. You don't forget, but you can
go on."

She drew back to wipe the tears from her cheeks with
both hands. "Thanks."

"You going to be okay?"

"Sooner or later." She sniffled once, then managed a
smile. "Sooner, I think. Let's take this back in. We're going
to celebrate life tonight."

Chapter 11

MARY BETH MORRISON HUNCHED over her monthly budget and listened to her two oldest squabble over a board game. The natives were restless, she thought, and tried to figure out where she'd overextended in the grocery department.

"Jonas, if you're going to get that upset when Lori takes over your country, you shouldn't play the game."

"She cheats," Jonas complained. "She always cheats."

"Do not."

"Do too."

If Mary Beth hadn't been trying to find how to cut back an extra hundred a month, she might have let the argument run its course. "Maybe you'd be better off if you put the game away and went to your rooms." The mild comment had the desired effect. Both children calmed down enough to make their accusations in whispers.

The baby of the family, Prissy Pat as the other children liked to call her, wandered over to demand that her mother fix the bow in her hair. At five, Patricia was all girl. Mary Beth set aside her accounts long enough to fuss with the lace ribbon. Her six-year-old son was doing his best to instigate another battle between his older brother and sister as they vied to take over the world. After a time, both Jonas and Lori turned on him. The television blared and the newest kitten was busy hissing at Binky, their middle-aged cocker spaniel. All in all, it was a typical Friday night at the Morrisons'.

"I think I fixed the Chevy. Needed timing, that's all." Harry came into the family room wiping his hands on a dish towel. Mary Beth thought briefly of how often she'd told him not to spread the kitchen linens around the house, then lifted her face for his kiss. The scent of the aftershave she'd given him for his birthday lingered on his cheeks.

"My hero. I hated the idea of breaking down on the way to the bake sale on Sunday."

"It's humming right along now. Pipe down, Jonas." Without breaking rhythm, he lifted Pat into his arms for a snuggle. "Why don't we take her for a test drive?"

Mary Beth pushed back from the desk. It was tempting, just the idea of getting out of the house for an hour, maybe stopping off for ice cream or indulging the kids in a round of miniature golf. Then she looked back down at her accounts.

"I've got to get this straightened out so I can make a deposit in the automatic teller tomorrow morning."

"You look tired." Harry planted a kiss on Pat's cheek, then set her down again.

"Just a little."

He eyed the bills and numbers. "I could give you a hand."

Mary Beth tallied figures without looking up. "Thanks, but the last time you helped me, it took me six months to get us back on track."

"Insults." He ruffled her hair. "I'd take offense if it wasn't true. Jonas, you're pressing your luck."

"He takes his games too seriously," Mary Beth murmured. "Just like his father."

"Games are serious." He bent down again to whisper in her ear. "Wanna play?"

She laughed. This was a man she'd known for over twenty years, and he still made her pulse flutter. "At this rate I should be done by midnight."

"Would it help if I cleared the kids out for a while?"

She smiled up at him. "You read my mind. If I had an hour of uninterrupted silence, I might figure out how to squeeze out the money for those new tires."

"Say no more." He leaned over and kissed her. From his position on the floor, Jonas rolled his eyes. His parents were always kissing each other. "Do yourself a favor and take those contacts out. You've had them in too long again."

"You're probably right. Thanks, Harry, you may be saving my sanity."

"I like you crazy." He kissed her again, then held up his hands. "Anyone in the mood for a drive and hot fudge sundaes meet in the garage in two minutes."

The scrambling started instantly. Game pieces scattered, shoes were hunted up. Binky went off on a tangent of barking until the kitten chased him out of the room. Mary Beth unearthed Pat's little pink sweater with the rhinestones and reminded Jonas to comb his hair. He didn't, but it was the thought that counted.

Inside of ten minutes, the house was empty. Hugging the silence to her for a moment, Mary Beth sat at the desk again. There would be a family cleanup the next day, but right now she wasn't even going to look at the mess the kids had left behind.

She had everything she wanted: a loving husband, kids that made her laugh, a house filled with character, and, hopefully, a Chevy that didn't misfire. Bending back over her account book, she began to work.

Half an hour later, she remembered Harry's advice about her contacts. They had been her one true personal indulgence. She hated glasses, had hated them since she'd put on her first pair at the age of eight. She'd been wearing Coke-bottle lenses by high school and had embarrassed herself time after time by walking blindly down the halls because she refused to put her glasses on. Always one to know what she wanted and how to get it, she'd taken a summer job in her junior year and spent every dime on contact lenses. Since that moment, she'd gotten into the habit of popping them in almost from her first waking moment and leaving them in place until she climbed into bed.

Because reading or bookwork made her eyes ache after a few hours, she often took them out, then with her nose against the page finished the job. With a little grumble of complaint, she got up and went upstairs to take them out for the night.

As in all things, Mary Beth was conscientious. She cleaned her lenses, put them in new solution, and left them to soak. Because Pat liked to poke in the vanity drawers for lipstick, Mary Beth put the case on the top shelf of the medicine cabinet. Leaning close to the bathroom mirror, she considered touching up her makeup. She and Harry hadn't managed to find time to make love in days. But tonight, if they could tuck all the kids into bed . . .

With a smile, Mary Beth reached for her lipstick. When the dog began to bark, she ignored him. If he had to go out, he'd just have to hold his bladder a minute.

Jerald pushed open the door that led from the garage to the kitchen. He hadn't felt this good in days. It was this edgy, one-foot-over-the-cliff feeling that really made life worthwhile. He should have realized it before. It was like being a demigod, one of the Greek myths with an immortal father and mortal mother. Heroic, ruthless, and blessed. That's really what he was. His father was so powerful, so all-seeing, so untouchable. His mother was beautiful . . . and flawed. That's why, as their son, he could feel such power and know such fear. The combination was incredible. And because of all that he could feel such pity and such disdain for ordinary mortals. They walked blindly through life, never realizing how closely they marched with death, or how easily he could quicken death's pace.

He was becoming more like his father every day, Jerald thought. More all-seeing, more all-knowing. Soon he wouldn't need the computer to show him the way. He would simply know.

Wetting his lips, he peered through the crack of the door. He hadn't counted on a dog. He could see it, backed into a corner of the kitchen and snarling. He'd have to kill it of course. His teeth gleamed in the darkness a minute as he considered it. He thought it was a pity he wouldn't be able to take his time about it, to experiment. He opened the door a bit wider and started to step out when he heard her.

"Oh, for heaven's sake, Binky, that's enough. You'll have Mr. Carlyse complaining again." Moving by memory more than sight, Mary Beth walked to the back door without bothering with the lights. "Come on, out you go."

From his corner, Binky continued to watch the garage door and snarl.

"Look, I don't have time for this. I want to finish things up." She walked over and took the dog by the collar. "Out, Binky. I can't believe you're worked up over a silly kitten. You'll get used to her." She pulled the dog to the door and gave him a none-too-gentle shove. The indulgent laugh caught in her throat when she turned.

She was everything Jerald had known she would be. Soft, warm, understanding. She'd been waiting for him, of course. She'd even put the dog outside so they wouldn't be disturbed. She was so pretty with her big frightened eyes and her high rounded breasts. She smelled like honeysuckle. He remembered how she talked of making long, slow love in a meadow. As he looked at her, he could almost see the clover.

He wanted to hold her, to let her do all the sweet, gentle things she'd promised. Then he wanted to give her the best. The ultimate.

"What do you want?" She could see little more than a shadow, but it was enough to have her heart pounding in her throat.

"Everything you promised, Mary Beth."

"I don't know you." Stay calm, she ordered herself. If he'd come to rob the house, he could take whatever he wanted. She'd personally hand over her grandmother's crystal goblets. Thank God the children weren't home. Thank God they were safe. The Feldspars had been robbed last year, and it had taken months to straighten out the insurance. How long had Harry been gone? Her thoughts tumbled one into the next as she tried to hold on.

"Yes, you do. You've talked to me, really only to me all these nights. You always understood. Now we can finally be together." He was walking toward her. She backed up until her hips hit the counter. "I'm going to give you more than you can imagine. I know how."

"My husband's coming right back."

He just continued to smile, his eyes blank, his lips curved. "I want you to undress me the way you promised." He gathered her hair in his hand. Not to hurt her, just to be firm. Women liked men to be firm, especially delicate women with gentle voices. "Now, Mary Beth. Take your clothes off, slowly. Then I want you to touch me, everywhere. Do all those sweet things to me, Mary Beth. All those sweet, gentle things you promised."

He was just a child. Wasn't he? She tried to focus on his face, but the room was dark and her vision fuzzy. "I can't. You don't want to do this. Just go and I'll—" The words were cut off as he jerked her hair. She cringed back as his free hand covered her throat.

"You want to be persuaded. That's all right." He talked quietly, but his excitement was building, spreading, banding tight around his heart, pushing hard into his lungs. "Desiree wanted to be persuaded too. I didn't mind. I loved her. She was perfect. I think you are too, but I need to be sure. I'll undress you. I'll touch you." When he moved his hand from her throat to her breast she drew in her breath to scream. "Don't." His fingers dug in cruelly. His voice changed again. There was a whine in it now that was much more frightening than when he gave orders. "I don't want you to scream. That's not what I want and I'll hurt you if you do. I liked hearing Roxanne scream, but not you. She was a slut, do you understand?"

"Yes." She would have told him anything he wanted to hear. "Yes, I understand."

"But you're not a slut. You and Desiree are different. I could tell the minute I heard you." He was calming again, calming, though he was hard as a rock and wanted to be free of his jeans. "Now, I want you to talk to me while I do this. Talk to me, like you did before."

"I don't know what you mean." Bile rose up as he pressed against her. God, he couldn't be doing this. It couldn't be happening. She wanted Harry. She wanted her babies. She wanted it to be over. "I don't know you. You're making a mistake."

He brought his hand between her legs. He enjoyed the way she jerked and whimpered. She was ready for him all right, sweet and ready. "It's going to be different this time. This time, we won't hurry. I want you to show me things, do things, then when I'm finished it'll be even better than the others. Touch me, Mary Beth. The others didn't touch me."

She was crying now and hating herself for it. This was her house, her home, and she wouldn't be violated this way. She made herself reach for him, and waited until she heard him groan. Going with desperation, she rammed her elbow into his stomach and ran. He caught her hair with a vicious jerk as her hand closed over the doorknob. The moment he did, she knew he was going to kill her.

"You lied. You're a liar and a whore just like the others. So I'll treat you like the others." Near tears himself, he brought the back of his hand hard against her face. Her lip split. It was the taste of her own blood that galvanized her.

She was not going to die like this, in her own kitchen. She was not going to leave her husband and children alone. Screaming, she clawed at his face and when he yelped, managed to yank open the door. She'd intended to run for her life, but Binky wanted to be a hero.

The small dog had sharp teeth. He used them viciously on Jerald's calf. Howling with rage, he managed to kick the dog aside, only to turn and find himself faced with the business end of a butcher knife.

"Get out of my house." Mary Beth held the handle with both hands. She was too dazed to be surprised that she had every intention of using it if he took another step toward her.

Binky managed to get to his feet. As soon as he'd shaken his head clear, he began to growl again.

"Bitch," Jerald hissed at her as he edged toward the door. None of them had ever hurt him before. His face was aching, and his leg—he could feel the warm, wet blood seep through his jeans. He'd make her pay. He'd make all of them pay. "Lying whores, all of you. I only wanted to give you what you wanted. I was going to be good to you." There was a whine in his voice again that made her shudder. He sounded like a small, evil boy who'd broken his favorite toy. "I was going to give you the best. Next time you're all going to suffer."

When Harry brought the kids home twenty minutes later, Mary Beth was sitting at the kitchen table, still holding the butcher knife and watching the back door.

◆ ◆ ◆

*W*INE ALL AROUND, EXCEPT for the expectant mother." Grace passed out glasses as Ben poured. "You get some kind of juice, Tess. God knows what it is, you can never tell with Ed."

"Papaya," Ed muttered as Tess sniffed dubiously at her glass.

"A toast then." Grace lifted her glass in salute. "To new beginnings and continuity."

Glasses clinked.

"So when are you going to get some furniture in here?" Ben sat on the edge of the crate beside Tess. "You can't live in a construction zone forever."

"It's a matter of priorities. I'm finishing the drywall in the bedroom over the weekend." Ed sipped as he considered his partner. "What are you doing tomorrow?"

"Busy," Ben said immediately. "I've got to—ah, clean out the vegetable bin in the fridge. Can't have Tess slaving over housework in her condition."

"I'll remember that." Tess took another tentative sip of the juice. "Anyway, I've got to run into the clinic for a couple of hours tomorrow. I could drop you off."

Ben gave her a sour look. "Thanks. Ed, don't you think Tess should cut back, take some time off? Put her feet up?"

"Actually . . ." Ed leaned back comfortably against a sawhorse. "An active mind and body make for healthier mother and baby. Studies initiated by obstetricians over the last ten years indicate that—"

"Shit," Ben interrupted. "Ask a simple question. What about you, Grace? As a woman, don't you believe an expectant mother should pamper herself?"

Unmindful of sawdust, Grace lowered herself to the floor, Indian style. "It depends."

"On?"

"On whether she'd die of boredom. I would. Now, if

she were considering the Boston Marathon, it might require discussion. Are you thinking of that, Tess?"

"I was thinking of starting with something local first."

"Sensible," Grace decided. "This is a sensible woman. You, on the other hand," she said to Ben, "are typical."

"Typical what?"

"A typical male. And that makes you, under the circumstances, an overprotective worrywart. Which is okay. It's cute. And I'm sure that Tess, being a woman, and one with psychiatric training, will be able to satisfactorily exploit that over the next seven months, one week, and three days." Lifting the bottle of wine, she tipped more into Ben's glass.

"Thanks. I think."

Grace smiled at him over the rim of her own glass. "I like you, Detective Paris."

He grinned and, leaning over, touched his glass to hers. "I like you too, Gracie." He glanced up when Ed's phone rang. "While you're answering that, see if you've got anything to eat in the kitchen that isn't green."

"Amen," Grace murmured into her glass. After glancing over her shoulder, Grace spoke again. "You won't believe what I ate over here the other night. Artichoke bottoms."

"Please." Ben shuddered. "Not while I'm breathing."

"Actually, they weren't nearly as bad as I thought they'd be. Has he always been this way? Eating roots and things?"

"That man hasn't had a hamburger in years. It's scary."

"But sweet," Grace added and smiled into her glass in a way that had Tess speculating.

"Sorry," Ed began as he walked back in. "We've got a call."

"Christ, can't a man even celebrate childbirth?" But Ben automatically set his drink aside.

"It's in Montgomery County."

"Over the line? What do they want us for?"

Ed glanced at Grace. "Attempted rape. Looks like our man."

"Oh God." Grace jolted to her feet so that wine sloshed over her hand.

Tess rose with her husband. "Ed—the victim?"

"Shaken, but okay. Got her hands on a butcher knife. Between that and the family dog, she held him off."

"Let me have the address. I'll drop Tess off and meet you there."

"I'm going with you." Before Ben could object, Tess laid a hand on his arm. "I can help, not only you, but the victim. I know how to handle this, and it's almost certain she'll be more comfortable talking to a woman."

"Tess is right." Ed walked to the closet off the hall to get his gun. It was the first time Grace had seen him with it. She tried to equate the man who so easily strapped it on with the one who'd carried her through the rain. "This is the first woman we know of that he's made contact with who's still alive. Tess might make it easier for her to talk." He pulled a jacket over his shoulder holster. Grace's long, speculative look at him, and at his weapon, hadn't gone unnoticed. "I'm sorry, Grace, I don't have any idea how long we'll be."

"I want to go. I want to talk to her."

"It's not possible. It's not," he repeated, taking her shoulders as she started to move past him. "It won't help you, and it would only make it harder on her. Grace . . ." She had a stubborn chin. Ed cupped a hand under it until her gaze met his. "She's been badly frightened. Think about it. She doesn't need more people around, especially one who would remind her of what might have happened. Even if I bent the rules, going there wouldn't help."

She knew he was right. She hated knowing he was right. "I'm not going home until you get back and tell me everything. I want to know what he looks like. I want a picture in my head."

He didn't like the way she made the last statement. Revenge almost always bit the one who held it the tightest. "I'll let you know what I can. It could take a while."

"I'll wait." She folded her arms across her chest. "Right here."

He kissed her, lingering over it a moment. "Lock the door."

$\mathcal{M}$ARY BETH DIDN'T WANT a tranquilizer. She'd always had a morbid fear of pills that had prevented her from taking anything stronger than aspirin. She was, however, holding on to a snifter of the brandy she and Harry saved for special guests.

The children had been sent to a neighbor's as soon as Harry had gotten a grip on what had happened. Now, he was sitting as close to his wife as he could manage, his arm around her waist and his hand stroking wherever he could reach. He'd always known he loved her, but until tonight he hadn't known she was the beginning and the end of his world.

"We've already talked to the police," he said when Ed showed his identification. "How many times does she have to answer the same questions? Hasn't she been through enough already?"

"I'm sorry, Mr. Morrison. We'll do everything we can to make this easier."

"The only thing you have to do is get the bastard. That's what cops are for. That's what you get paid for."

"Harry, please."

"I'm sorry, baby." His tone changed instantly as he turned to his wife. It was more difficult for him to look at the bruise on her face than to think about what might have been. The bruise was tangible, the might-have-been a nightmare, unreal. "You don't have to talk anymore if you don't want to."

"We just have a few questions." Ben eased down in a chair, hoping that seated he'd be less intimidating. "Believe me, Mr. Morrison, we want to get him. We need your help."

"How the hell would you feel if it was your wife?" Harry demanded. "If I knew where to start I'd be after him myself."

"This is my wife." Ben spoke quietly as he gestured to Tess. "And I know exactly how you feel."

"Mrs. Morrison." Instead of sitting, Tess crouched down beside the sofa. "Maybe you'd be more comfortable talking to me. I'm a doctor."

"I don't need a doctor." Mary Beth glanced down at the brandy as if surprised to find it in her hand. "He didn't—he was going to, but he didn't."

"He didn't rape you," Tess said gently. "But that doesn't mean you weren't violated, and frightened. Holding in the anger, the fear, the shame—" She saw the last word hit home and waited just a moment. "Holding it all in only hurts more. There are places you can go, people you can talk to who have gone through the same ordeal. They know what you're feeling, and what your husband is feeling now."

"It was in my home." Mary Beth began to cry for the first time. The tears that squeezed out of her eyes and ran down her face were thin and hot. "It seemed so much worse that it was in my home. I kept thinking, what will I do if my children come in. What will he do to my babies. And then . . ." Tess eased the snifter from her as her hands began to shake. "I kept praying that it was all a dream, that it wasn't really happening. He said he knew me, and he called me by name. But I didn't know who he was and he was going to rape me. He—he touched me. Harry." She turned her head into his shoulder and sobbed.

"Oh baby, he won't hurt you again." His hands were gentle on her hair, but there was a look in his eyes that said murder, plain and simple. "You're safe. Nobody's going to hurt you. Damn you, can't you see what this is doing to her?"

"Mr. Morrison." Ed wasn't sure how to begin. The anger was justified. He felt some of it himself but knew, as a cop, he could never let it blind him to procedure. Still, he understood, and he decided to play it straight. "We have reason to believe your wife was very lucky tonight. This man has attacked twice before, and the other women weren't so lucky."

"He's done this before?" The tears were still flowing but Mary Beth turned to Ed. "Are you sure?"

"We'll be sure, after you answer some questions."

She was breathing very fast, but he saw that she was fighting to steady herself. "All right, but I've already told the other officers what happened. I don't want to go through it all again."

"You won't have to," Ben assured her. "Will you work with a police artist on a composite drawing?"

"I didn't see him very well." Grateful, she accepted the snifter back from Tess. "It was dark in the kitchen, and I'd taken out my contacts. I have very bad vision. He wasn't much more than a blur."

"You'll be surprised how much you saw when you start piecing it together." Ed took out his notebook. He wanted to treat her gently. With her cozy little house and pretty face, she reminded him of his sister. "Mrs. Morrison, you said he called you by name."

"Yes, he called me Mary Beth several times. It was so strange to hear him say it. He told me, he said something about how I'd promised him things. That he wanted . . ." Even with her blurred vision, she couldn't look at Ed. Swallowing, she looked down at Tess. "He said he wanted me to do things to him, sweet, gentle things. I remember because I was so scared and it seemed so crazy to hear that."

Ben waited while she sipped the brandy. "Mrs.

Morrison, do you know anything about a company called Fantasy, Incorporated?"

When she blushed, the bruise on her face stood out. But she would no more lie than cut out her tongue. "Yes."

"That's none of your business," Harry began.

"The other two victims were both employees of Fantasy," Ed said flatly.

"Oh God." Mary Beth squeezed her eyes shut. There were no tears now, just a dull, dry fear. "Oh my God."

"I should never have let you do that." Harry rubbed his hand over his face. "I must have been crazy."

"His voice, Mrs. Morrison," Ben prompted. "Did you recognize it? Have you talked to him before?"

"No, no, I'm sure I haven't. He was only a child. We don't take calls from minors."

"Why do you say he was a child?" Ed spoke quickly, while they had the edge.

"Because he was. Seventeen or eighteen at best. Yes." The flush faded into pallor as she thought back. "I'm not sure how, but I know he was young. Not tall, only a few inches taller than me. I'm five-five. And he wasn't, well, filled out. I just kept thinking he was a kid and it couldn't be real. I know I've never heard his voice before. I couldn't have forgotten it." Even now, with her husband's arm around her, she could hear it. "And he said—" Without thinking, she reached out for Tess's hand. "Oh God, I remember he said it was going to be different this time. He wasn't going to rush. He kept talking about someone named Desiree and how he loved her. He mentioned her a few times. He said something about a Roxanne and that she was a slut. Does that make sense?"

"Yes, ma'am." Ed noted it down. One more piece, he thought. One more piece to the puzzle.

"Mrs. Morrison." Tess touched her hand again. "Did he seem to confuse you with Desiree?"

"No," Mary Beth decided after a minute. "No, it was more like a comparison. Whenever he said that name, it was almost with a kind of reverence. That sounds stupid."

"No." Tess turned until her gaze met Ben's. "No, it doesn't."

"He seemed, well, almost friendly in a horrible way. I don't know how to explain it. It was as if he expected me to be pleased to see him. He only got angry when I resisted. Then he was furious—like a child is when you take something away. There were tears in his voice. He called me a whore—no, he said we were all whores, all lying whores and that the next time he'd make all of us suffer."

The fat cocker spaniel waddled in and sniffed at Tess.

"That's Binky," Mary Beth said with a few fresh tears. "If it hadn't been for him—"

"He's eating steak for the rest of his life." Harry brought her hand to his lips as she managed a watery laugh.

"I'd dragged the poor dog outside thinking he was barking at the cat, and all the time . . ." She trailed off again and shook her head. "I know this is going to get in the papers, but I'd appreciate it if you could minimize it. The children." She looked toward Tess again, feeling a woman would understand. "I don't want them to have to face all of this. And the business about Fantasy, well, it's not that I'm ashamed of it, really. It seemed like such a handy way to start college funds, but I'm not sure the other mothers would like the Brownie troop leader involved in that sort of thing."

"We'll do what we can," Ed promised. "If I could give you some advice, I'd say to turn in your resignation there."

"Already done," Harry said.

"It would also be best if you weren't alone for the next few days."

Mary Beth paled again. This time her skin seemed

translucent. Whatever courage she'd managed to work up trembled on the edge. "You think he'll be back?"

"There's no way to be sure." Ed hated to frighten her, but he wanted to save her life. "This is a very dangerous man, Mrs. Morrison. We don't want you to take any unnecessary chances. We're going to arrange for protection. In the meantime, we'd like you to come down to the station and look at mug shots, and work with the police artist."

"I'll do whatever I can. I want you to catch him soon. Very soon."

"You may just have helped us do that." Ben rose. "We appreciate your cooperation."

"I—I never offered you coffee." Mary Beth found herself suddenly and terribly afraid to let them go. She wanted to be surrounded and safe. They were policemen, and police knew what to do. "I don't know what I could have been thinking of."

"That's all right." Tess squeezed her hand so that they rose together. "You should rest now. Let your husband take you upstairs. He'll stay with you. When you go down to the station tomorrow, they can give you numbers to call, organizations that can help you deal with this. Or you can just call and talk to me."

"I'm not used to being scared." In Tess's eyes she saw compassion, female compassion. And she needed it, she discovered, more than she needed the police. "In my own kitchen. I'm afraid to go in my own kitchen."

"Why don't you let me take you upstairs?" Tess murmured as she slipped an arm around Mary Beth's waist. "You can lie down." Tess led her from the room. Frustrated, helpless, her husband looked after her.

"If I'd stayed home—"

"He'd have waited," Ed interrupted. "We're dealing with a very dangerous, very determined man, Mr. Morrison."

"Mary Beth never hurt anyone in her life. She's the most generous woman I've ever known. He had no right to do this to her, to put that look on her face." Harry picked up Mary Beth's brandy and downed it in two swallows. "Maybe he's a dangerous man, but if I find him first, he's going to be a eunuch."

Chapter 12

SHE'D LEFT A LIGHT burning for him. Ed was glad Grace had gone home to bed because she would ask questions. And he would have to answer them. Still, it touched him, foolishly, that she'd left the light burning.

He was tired, dead tired, but too wound up to sleep. In the kitchen, he reached for the juice and drank straight from the pitcher. She'd put the wine away and washed the glasses. When a man had spent so many years doing for himself, such little things were overwhelming.

He was already in love with her. The first romantic fantasies he'd indulged in had cemented. The trouble was, he didn't know quite what to do about it. He'd been infatuated before, and had never had a problem taking those feelings to their logical conclusion. But love was a different ball game.

He'd always been a traditional man. Women were to be treasured and appreciated and protected. The woman you loved was to be treated gently, respected, and above all, cherished. He wanted to put her on a pedestal, but he was already aware that Grace would squirm until she toppled off.

He could be patient. That was one of the best qualities in a cop and one he'd been lucky enough to be born with. So the logical step was to give her time and space until he could successfully maneuver her exactly where he wanted her to be. With him.

Ed left enough juice for breakfast, then started upstairs. On the top landing he began to strip out of his jacket. He'd meant to leave both that and his weapon in the closet downstairs but was too tired to go back. Rubbing the tension at the nape of his neck, he pushed open the bedroom door with his foot, then hit the lights.

"Oh God, is it morning already?"

His hand was on the butt of his weapon instantly, then his fingers went quietly numb. Grace was stretched out over his bed. Shifting, she shielded her eyes with one hand and yawned. It took him a minute to realize that she was wearing one of his shirts and nothing else.

"Hi." She blinked and managed a smile as she squinted at him. "What time is it?"

"Late."

"Yeah." After pushing herself up, she stretched her shoulders. "I was just going to lie down a minute. This body isn't used to manual labor. I had a shower. I hope that's okay."

"Sure." He thought it might help if he looked at her face, just her face. But it didn't. His mouth was bone-dry again.

"I closed up that gunk you put on the walls and cleaned off the tools. After that I twiddled my thumbs." She was awake now, her eyes adjusted. Tilting her head, she studied him. He looked as though someone had just planted a sledgehammer in the region of his solar plexus. "You all right?"

"Yeah. I didn't know you were still here."

"I couldn't go until you got back. Can you tell me what happened?"

After peeling off his shoulder holster, he hooked it over a rickety ladder-back chair he planned to refinish. "The lady was lucky. She fought him off, then her dog got to him."

"I hope the dog hadn't had his shots. Was it the same man, Ed? I need to know."

"You want the official response or mine?"

"Yours."

"It was the same guy. He's pissed now, Grace." Rubbing his hands over his face, Ed sat on the edge of the bed. "Tess thinks this is only going to make him more volatile, more unpredictable. He's been threatened now, and his pattern destroyed. She thinks he'll lick his wounds, and when he's ready, he's going to go hunting."

She nodded. Now wasn't the time to tell him the chance she was taking herself. "The woman—she saw him?"

"It was dark. Apparently she can't see two feet in front of her face anyway." He would have sworn if he'd thought it would do any good. A decent description and they'd have him, prince or pauper, off the streets and into a cage. "She got impressions. We'll see what we can do with them."

"More of your pieces?"

He moved his shoulders, but the tension stayed lodged. "We'll do some cross-checking on Fantasy's client list, talk to neighbors. Sometimes you get lucky."

"You're tied up about this," she murmured. Because he seemed to need it, she shifted to rub his shoulders. "I didn't realize that before. I guess I thought you just took it all as it came. Routine."

He glanced over his shoulder. His eyes were cooler than she'd seen them before, and harder. "It's never routine."

No, it wouldn't be, not with a man like this. He would care too much. Despite her effort to prevent it, her gaze drifted over to rest on his weapon. He didn't change when he took it off. That was something she'd have to remember. "How do you get through it? How do you manage to see what you see and do what you do and get through the next day?"

"Some drink. A lot of us drink." He gave a half laugh. The tension was easing out of his shoulders and moving elsewhere. She had great hands. He wanted to tell her how much he wanted to put himself in them. "It's escape. Everybody looks for their own."

"What's yours?"

"I work with my hands, I read books." He shrugged. "I drink."

Grace rested her chin on his shoulder. It was a strong one, a broad one. She felt at home there. "Ever since Kathleen was killed I've been feeling sorry for myself. I kept thinking it wasn't fair, what did I do to deserve it? It's been hard to get beyond losing my sister to look at the overall picture." She shut her eyes a moment. He smelled good. Homey, secure, like a quiet fire in the evening. "For the last couple of days I've really been trying to do that. When I pull it off, I realize how much you've helped me. I don't know if I'd have been able to get through the last two weeks or so without you. You've been a good friend, Ed."

"Glad I could help."

She smiled a little. "I've been wondering if you've given any thought to being more. I got the impression, correct me if I'm wrong, that before we were interrupted tonight we were about to move on to the next stage."

He caught her hand in his. If she kept touching him, he wouldn't be able to give her that time and space he was so sure she needed. "Why don't you let me walk you home?"

She wasn't a woman to give up easily. Nor was she one to keep banging her head against a stone wall. On a long breath, she sat back on her heels. "You know what, Jackson, if I didn't know better I'd swear you were afraid of me."

"I'm terrified of you."

Surprise came first, then a slow, easy smile. "Really? Tell you what . . ." She began to unbutton his shirt. "I'll be gentle."

"Grace." Still cautious, he covered her hands with his. "Once isn't going to be enough."

She curled her fingers into his. She didn't make commitments easily, but when she did, she meant it. "Okay. Why don't you let me finish seducing you?"

This time he smiled. He released her hands to brush his own up her arms. "You did that the day I looked up and saw you in the window."

With his hand on her cheek he leaned to kiss her gently, softly. This was a taste he wanted to remember. It was richer, sweeter than he allowed himself. He felt her arms slip around his neck. He felt her give. Generosity. Wasn't that really what every man wanted from a woman? Grace would never be miserly with her emotions and now, just now, he needed all she could spare. With care, he lowered her back against the mattress.

The light was bright and the room smelled of dust. He'd imagined it so much differently. Candles, music, the glint of wine in glasses. He'd wanted to give her all those pretty, romantic trappings. But she was exactly what he'd imagined. She was exactly what he'd wanted.

Her murmur against his mouth sent his pulse scrambling. As she unbuttoned his shirt he felt the cool brush of her fingers against his chest. Her lips curved against his, then parted. Her sigh filled his mouth with warmth.

He didn't want to rush her. He was almost afraid to touch, knowing once he did his control might snap. But she moved against him and he was lost.

She'd never known any man to be so gentle, so sweet, so concerned. That in itself became an arousal. No one had ever treated her as if she were fragile—perhaps because she wasn't. But now, with him taking such care, with him showing such tenderness, she felt fragile.

Her skin seemed softer. Her heart beat faster. Her hands, as she ran them over him, shook slightly. She'd known she'd wanted this, wanted him, but she hadn't known it would be so important.

This wasn't just the next stage, she realized, but something altogether different from anything she'd experienced. For a moment she thought she understood what he'd meant when he'd said he was terrified.

She lifted her mouth to his again and felt the need tangle with nerves, then nerves twine with an ache. Her fingers were trembling when she reached for the snap of his jeans. Again, his hand covered hers.

"I want you," she murmured. "I didn't know how much."

He ran kisses over her face as emotion swelled in him. He never wanted to forget how she looked just now, with her eyes like smoke and her skin flushed with passion. "We have time. We have plenty of time."

With his eyes on hers, he unbuttoned her shirt, then spread it open so he could look at her. "You're so pretty."

The ache faded a bit, so she smiled. "So are you." Reaching up, she slipped his shirt from his shoulders. He was powerfully built, almost ferocious to look at, but she felt nothing like fear this time. She reached up again and brought him down to her.

Flesh warmed flesh, then heated. Though the gentleness remained in his hands, there was steel beneath it. Time spun out. He touched. She stroked. He tasted. She savored. There were degrees to intimacy. She'd thought she'd known them. Until now, she hadn't fully comprehended how intense it could be. She shuddered when his beard brushed over her breasts. This was a primitive feeling, like the flash heat of a tree struck by lightning. As she took her hands over his back to test the muscles that bunched and flexed, she felt both the strength and the control.

His lips coursed down, hot against her dampening skin. Not lightning now, but a low, smoldering fire. She arched against him, trust absolute, desire overpowering. When he took her over the first peak, he groaned with her.

She struggled to fill her lungs with air. She wanted to say his name, to tell him—anything. But she could only shudder and reach for him.

Her pulse was galloping and the knot that had lodged in his chest was spreading. She was pulling at the rest of his clothes now, suddenly strong, desperately determined. She rolled on top of him, covering his flesh with frantic kisses, then laughing with delight as his clothes were finally peeled away.

He had a warrior's body—and so he was. The strength, the discipline, and the scars were there. So there were true heroes, Grace thought as she touched him. They were flesh and blood and very, very rare.

He would have waited, or would have tried to. He would have pulled the strings of passion still tauter. But she was sliding down on him, taking him into her, filling herself with him. He could only grasp her hips and let her ride.

Grace threw her head back and peaked so fast she nearly crumpled forward. Then their hands clasped hard, fingers linking. The need built again, incredibly, until she was driving him as furiously as she drove herself.

She heard his long, desperate moan. Then her own body arched as pleasure arrowed into it. Her mind emptied as she slid bonelessly down to him.

He'd PULLED THE SPREAD over them, but he hadn't turned off the light. Grace was cuddled against his chest, dozing, he thought. Ed didn't think he'd ever need to sleep again. He liked the way she tossed one leg over his, the way she'd wrapped herself around him as if she wanted to stay. He was stroking her hair because he couldn't bring himself to stop touching her.

"You know what?" Her voice was throaty as she snuggled a little closer.

"What?"

"I feel like I've just climbed a mountain. Something on the scale of Everest. Then I parachuted down through all that cold, thin air. Nothing has ever felt so wonderful." She turned her head so that she could smile up at him. "And you were right, once would never be enough." She laughed and snuggled into his neck. "You smell so good. You know, when I put your shirt on before, I finally hit on it. Ed Jackson, tough cop, former linebacker—"

"Defensive tackle," he corrected.

"Whatever. Detective Jackson uses baby powder. Johnson & Johnson. Right?"

"It works."

"I can attest to that." Like a puppy, she sniffed along his neck and shoulders. "The only trouble is, I have a feeling every time I smell a baby I'm going to get turned on."

"I'm thinking about having that shirt bronzed."

She nipped at his ear. "Is that what finally turned the trick?"

"No, but it didn't hurt. I've always been a sucker for legs."

"Oh yeah." Smiling, she rubbed hers against his. "And what else?"

"You. Right from the start." He caught her hair in his hand so that he could look at her. So much for timing and caution and well-laid plans. "Grace, I want you to marry me."

She couldn't stop her mouth from dropping open, or prevent the gasp that was one part surprise, one part alarm. She tried to speak, but her mind, for once, was completely blank. She could only stare, and as she did, she saw his words hadn't been spoken on impulse; he'd thought them through very carefully.

"Wow."

"I love you, Grace." He saw her eyes change at that, soften. But they were still shadowed by something like fear. "You're everything I've ever wanted. I want to spend my life with you, take care of you. I know it's not easy being married to a cop, but I can promise to do everything I can to make it work."

She drew away slowly. "I'll say this, once you get going, you move fast."

"I didn't know what I was waiting for, but I knew I'd recognize it. I recognized you, Grace."

"God." She pressed a hand to her heart. If she wasn't careful, she was going to hyperventilate. "I'm not often taken so completely by surprise. Ed, we've only known each other for a few weeks, and . . ." She trailed off as he continued to look at her. "You're serious."

"I never asked anyone to marry me before, because I didn't want to make a mistake. This isn't a mistake."

"You—you don't really know me. I'm not really a nice person. I'm cranky when things aren't going my way. And God knows, I'm moody. I have a temper even my closest friends live in fear of, and—this isn't getting through."

"I love you."

"Oh Ed." She took both of his hands. "I don't know what to say to you."

She wasn't going to say what he wanted to hear. He was already dealing with that. "Tell me how you feel."

"I don't know. I haven't worked it out. Tonight—I can tell you truthfully that I've never felt closer to anyone. I've never felt stronger about anyone. But marriage. Ed, I've never even thought about marriage for myself in general, much less to a specific person. I don't know how to be a wife."

He brought her hand to his lips. "Are you telling me no?"

She opened her mouth, then closed it again. "I can't seem to. I can't say yes either. It's a hell of a spot to be in."

"Why don't you just tell me you'll think about it."

"I'll think about it," she said quickly. "Christ, you made my head spin."

"That's a start." He pulled her to him again. "Why don't I finish the job?"

"Ed." She put her hand to his cheek before he could kiss her. "Thanks for asking."

"You're welcome."

"Ed." She held him off a second time, but now her eyes were laughing. "Are you sure you don't just want my body?"

"Could be. Why don't I check it out again, to be sure?"

It WOULD HAVE BEEN nice to spend Saturday lazing around, or helping Ed give the drywall a second coat. Still, Grace was grateful he had to spend most of his day off at the station. She had a lot to think about, and she did that best alone. It also gave her the opportunity to have the extra phone line hooked up without having to explain herself. That would have to happen soon enough.

She was setting herself up as bait. That meant going to work for Fantasy. For as long as it took, or until they caught her sister's killer some other way, Grace was going to be spending her evenings on the phone talking to strangers. One of them, sooner or later, would put in a personal appearance.

Ed would work his puzzle his way, but she would go straight to the heart and make the pieces fit.

She hadn't liked buying the gun. In Manhattan, she'd never felt the need for one. She knew the city was dangerous, but to others, to those who didn't know where and when to walk. Somehow, she'd always felt safe there, in the crowds, on the streets that were so familiar. But now, living in this quiet suburban neighborhood, she felt the need.

It was a .32, small and snub-nosed. It looked like it meant business. She'd handled guns before. Research. She'd even spent time on the firing range so she would understand what it felt like when you pulled the trigger. She'd been told she had an excellent eye. Even when she bought it, Grace had serious doubts about whether she could fire one of those neat little bullets into a living thing.

She tucked it into her nightstand and tried to forget it.

The morning passed while she served the man from the phone company coffee and kept an eye on the window. She didn't want Ed to get back before it was a *fait accompli*. He couldn't do anything to stop her, of course. It helped to repeat that a few times. Still, Grace watched the window as she sipped coffee and listened to the installer talk about his son's Little League prowess.

As she'd told Ed, people always talked to her. Usually within minutes of an acquaintance they were telling her things reserved for family or the closest of friends. It was something she'd always taken in stride, but now, just now, she thought it would be wise to analyze it.

Did she have that kind of face? Absently Grace ran a hand over her cheek. That might be part of it, she decided, but it probably had more to do with her being a good listener, as Ed had suggested. She often listened with half an ear while she worked out a plot complication or characterization. But because she listened well, half was apparently enough.

People trusted her. She was going to exploit that now. She was going to harden herself and make Kathleen's killer trust her. When he trusted her enough, he'd come to her. She moistened her lips and smiled as the installer told her about his son's phenomenal play at second in his last game.

When he came to her, she was going to be ready. She wasn't going to be taken by surprise like Kathleen and the others.

She knew exactly what she was doing. Hadn't she spent most of her life structuring plots? This was the most vital story she'd ever manipulated. She wouldn't make a mistake.

She and the installer were on a first-name basis by the time she led him downstairs and through the front door. She wished him luck on his son's game that afternoon and said she expected to see Junior in the majors in a few years. Alone, she thought of the shiny new phone sitting on the little desk in the corner of her bedroom. In a matter of hours it would ring for the first time. She had a great deal to do before that.

Making the call to Tess helped. Perhaps the approval hadn't been without reservations, but Grace had more ammunition now. Satisfied, she picked up her sister's keys and held them tight in her hand. It was right; she was sure of it. All she had to do was convince everyone else.

She wasn't shaking when she drove to the station this time. Her strength was back and with it a determination to finish what she'd started at Fantasy. Out of habit, she turned the radio up loud and let Madonna's latest pouty number blast through her head. It felt good. She felt good. For the first time in weeks she could really appreciate the full-fledged spring that had burst on Washington.

The azaleas were in their glory. Yards had violet and scarlet and coral bushes bunched together. Daffodils were beginning to fade as tulips usurped them. Lawns were green and receiving their Saturday trim. She saw young boys in T-shirts and old men in baseball caps pushing mowers. Baby's breath and Dogwood added fragile white.

Life renewed. It wasn't really corny, she thought. She needed badly to hang on to that. Life had to do more than go on, it had to improve. It had to justify itself year after year. If weapons were being tested somewhere in a desert, here the birds were singing and people could worry about the important things: a Little League game, a family barbecue, a spring wedding; those were important things. If Kathleen's death had brought her grief, it had also brought her the belief that the everyday was what really mattered. Once she had justice, she could accept the ordinary again.

Pretty suburbs gave way to concrete and testy traffic. Grace swerved around other cars with a natural competitiveness. It didn't matter that she rarely found herself behind the wheel. Once she was there, she drove with a breezy kind of negligence that had other drivers gritting their teeth and swearing. She made two wrong turns because her mind was elsewhere, then pulled into the parking lot beside the station.

If she had any luck, Ed wouldn't be in. Then she could explain herself to the stern-faced Captain Harris.

She saw Ed the moment she walked into Homicide. The little flutter in her stomach wasn't anxiety, she discovered. It was pleasure. For a moment she simply watched him and absorbed. He was sitting behind a desk typing with a steady, two-finger style.

His hands were so big. Then she remembered how gently, how devastatingly he'd used them the night before. This was the man who loved her, she thought. This was the man who was willing to make promises to her. And this was a man who would keep them. Because the urge to go to him, to put her arms around him came so strong, she crossed the room and did just that.

He stopped typing to close his hand over hers on his shoulder. As soon as she'd touched him, he'd known. There was her scent, and her feel. Several cops smirked in his direction as she leaned over his shoulder to kiss him. If he'd noticed, he might have been embarrassed. But he only noticed her.

"Hi." He kept her hand in his as he drew her around. "I didn't expect to see you here today."

"And I'm interrupting. I hate it when people interrupt me when I'm working."

"I'm nearly finished."

"Ed, I really need to see your captain."

He caught it, the trace of apology in her voice. "Why?"

"I'd rather go through it all just once. Is he available?"

Thoughtful, he studied her. By this time he knew her well enough to understand she would say nothing until she was ready. "I don't know if he's still here. Take a seat and I'll check."

"Thanks." She held his hand a moment longer. Around them phones rang steadily and typewriters clacked. "Ed, when I tell you what I have to say, be a cop. Please."

He didn't like the way she looked at him when she asked. As she did, something curled into his stomach and lodged there, but he nodded. "I'll see if I can find Harris."

Grace took his seat when he left. In his typewriter was the report on Mary Beth Morrison. Grace tried to read it with the same kind of detachment with which Ed had written it.

"Come on, Lowenstein, just let me look at it."

At the sound of Ben's voice, Grace turned and watched him troop into the room on the tail of a slim brunette.

"Go find something to do, Ben," Lowenstein suggested. She carried a cardboard box tied with string. "I've only got fifteen minutes to get out of here and make that mother-daughter lunch."

"Lowenstein, be a pal. Do you know the last time I had any homemade pie?" He leaned closer to the box until her forefinger jammed into his stomach. "It's cherry, isn't it? Just let me look at it."

"You'll only suffer more." She set the box on her desk, then shielded it with her body. "It's beautiful. Work of art."

"Does it have that fancy braided crust?" When she only smiled, he looked over her shoulder. It could have been sympathy cravings, he told himself. Hadn't he felt queasy this morning? If he was going to have Tess's morning sickness, then at least he was entitled to her cravings. "Come on, just a peek."

"I'll send you a Polaroid." She put a hand on his chest, then spotted Grace across the room. "Who's the knockout sitting at Ed's desk? I'd kill for a jacket like that."

Ben glanced over and grinned at Grace. "Give me the pie. I'll see if I can make a trade."

"Knock it off, Paris. Is that Ed's new lady?"

"You want gossip, you gotta pay for it." When Lowenstein stared at him, he relented. "That's her. Grace McCabe. Writes first-class murder mysteries."

"Really?" Lowenstein's bottom lip jutted out as she considered. "Looks more like a rock star. I can't remember the last time I sat down with a book. I can't remember when I had time to read a cereal box." Her eyes narrowed as she took in the funky and very expensive sneakers. Funky and expensive. The two words seemed to suit the woman, but Lowenstein wondered how Ed fit in. "She's not going to break Ed's heart, is she?"

"I wish I knew. He's nuts about her."

"Seriously nuts?"

"Dead seriously nuts."

Anticipating Ben, she laid a hand on top of the box. "Here he comes now. Christ, you can almost hear the violins."

"Getting cynical, Lowenstein?"

"I threw rice at your wedding, didn't I?" And the truth was she had a soft spot for romance. "I guess if you can talk a class act into marrying you, Ed can carve hearts with Greenwich Village." She nodded toward Ed. "Looks like you're being summoned."

"Yeah. Lowenstein, five bucks for the pie."

"Don't insult me."

"Ten."

"It's yours." She held out her palm, then counted the

singles Ben put into it. Already planning on eating half for lunch, Ben slipped the box into the bottom drawer of his desk before he followed Ed into Harris's office.

"What's up?"

"Miss McCabe requested a meeting," Harris began. He was already half an hour behind schedule and anxious to be gone.

"I appreciate you giving me the time." Grace smiled at Harris and almost managed to charm him. "I won't waste any of it, so I'll get right to the point. We're all aware that Fantasy is the link between the three attacks that have already taken place. And I'm sure we're all aware there'll be others—"

"The investigation's in full swing, Miss McCabe," Harris interrupted. "I can assure you we have our best people working on it."

"You don't have to assure me of that." She sent Ed a last look, hoping he'd understand. "I've thought about this a great deal, first because of my sister, and second because murder has always interested me. If I were plotting this out, there would be only one logical step to take at this time. I think it's the right one."

"We appreciate your interest, Miss McCabe." When she smiled at him again, Harris felt almost fatherly. But she still didn't know diddly about real police work. "But my people are much more experienced with the reality of investigation."

"I understand that. Would you be interested if I told you I think I've found a way to trap this man? I've already taken the steps, Captain, I simply want to apprise you of them, then you can do whatever you think necessary."

"Grace, this isn't a book or a television show." Ed interrupted her because he had a feeling, a very bad feeling, that he knew where she was heading.

The glance she gave him was apologetic and worried him even more. "I know that. You don't know how much I wish it were." She took a deep breath and faced Harris again. "I went to see Eileen Cawfield."

"Miss McCabe—"

"Please, hear me out." She lifted her hand a moment, not so much in a plea as in a gesture of determination. "I know that every lead you've had has been a dead end. Except Fantasy. Have you been able to shut down the company?"

Harris scowled and shuffled papers. "That sort of thing takes time. Without cooperation, a great deal of time."

"And every one of the women who work for Fantasy is a potential victim. Do we agree?"

"In theory," Harris answered.

"And in theory, is it possible for you to put guards on all of them? No," she answered before Harris could. "It can't be. But you could put guards on one person. On a person who understands what's going on, on a person who's willing to take the chance, and more, already has a link with the killer."

"Are you out of your mind?" Ed said it quietly, too quietly. That more than anything warned Grace that he was ready to explode.

"It makes sense." To calm herself, she dug in her bag for a cigarette. "It was Kathleen's voice that first drew him. When we were growing up, we were always mistaken for each other over the phone. If I'm Desiree, he'll want to find me again. We know he can."

"It's too loose, too risky, and it's just plain stupid." Ed bit off the last words as he looked to his partner for support.

"I don't like it either." Ben said it, but he saw the merit of Grace's plan. "Solid police work is always better than the big play. You've got no guarantee he'll fall for it, less that you can anticipate his actions if he does. In any case, Mrs.

Morrison's on her way in to work with the police artist. Any luck and we'll have a composite by the end of the day."

"Fine. Then maybe you'll pick him up before any of this becomes necessary." Grace lifted her hands, palms out, then dropped them. "I'm not going to bank on it when we're talking about a nearsighted, terrified woman in a dark room." She blew out a stream of smoke and prepared to drop the next bomb. "I spoke with Tess this morning, and I asked her what she thought about the chances of this man being pulled in by the same voice, the same name, even the same address." She looked at Ben because it was easier than looking at Ed. "She told me he'd find it next to impossible to resist. It was Desiree who started him. It's going to be Desiree who finishes him."

"I trust Dr. Court's opinion," Harris put in, holding up a hand to block Ed's protest. "I also believe, after three attacks, it's time we tried something more aggressive."

"The task force," Ed began.

"Will still go into operation." Harris tapped the top folder on a pile. "The press conference Monday morning will go as scheduled. The bottom line is we don't want another fatality. I'm willing to give this a shot." He turned back to Grace. "If we move on this theory, we'll need your cooperation at every step, Miss McCabe. We'll assign a policewoman to take the calls from your house. You can be put up at a hotel until and if it works."

"It's my voice," Grace said flatly. And her sister. She wasn't about to forget it had been her sister. "You can set up all the policewomen you like, but I've already made arrangements. I'm working for Fantasy, and I start tonight."

"The hell you do." Ed rose and, grabbing her arm, pulled her from the room.

"Wait a minute."

"Shut up." Lowenstein, on her way to the coffee

machine, backed up and let Ed pass. "I thought you had a head on your shoulders, then you come up with this."

"I've got a head, but I won't have an arm if you yank it out of its socket." He was through the door and into the parking lot with Grace scrambling and puffing behind him. She began to wonder if it was time to give up smoking.

"Get in your car and go home. I'll tell Cawfield you've changed your mind."

"I've told you about orders before, Ed." It wasn't easy to catch her breath and hold on to her temper, but she did her best. "I'm sorry you're upset."

"Upset?" He took her by the forearms. He was very close to lifting her up and tossing her bodily into the car. "Is that what you call this?"

"All right, I'm sorry you're a madman. Why don't you count to ten and listen to me?"

"There's nothing you can say that'll convince me you haven't gone crazy. If you've got any sense left, if what I feel means anything to you, you'll get in your car, go home, and wait."

"Do you think that's fair? Do you think it's right for you to put this on that level?" Her voice had risen. She lifted a fist and thumped it against his chest. "I know people think I'm eccentric, I know they think I haven't got everything screwed on too tight, but I didn't expect that attitude from you. Yes, I care how you feel. I'm crazy about you. Hell, let's take the big leap. I'm in love with you. Now leave me alone."

Instead, he caught her face in his hands. His lips weren't so gentle now and they weren't so patient either. As if he sensed she would have pulled away, he tightened his hold until they both relaxed. "Go home, Gracie," he murmured.

She closed her eyes a moment, then turned away until she thought herself strong enough to refuse him. "All right. Then I have something to ask of you." When she turned back, her eyes were very dark and very determined. "I want you to go back in and give your shield and your gun to your captain. I want you to join your uncle's firm."

"What the hell does that have to do with anything?"

"It's something I want you to do, something I need you to do so I won't worry about you anymore." She watched his face, the struggle, the answer. "You'd do it, wouldn't you?" she said quietly. "Because I said I needed you to. You'd do it for me, and you'd be miserable. You'd do it, but you'd never completely forgive me for asking. Sooner or later, you'd hate me for making you give up something that important. If I do this for you, I'll wonder my whole life if I could have done this one last thing for my sister."

"Grace, this isn't something you have to prove."

"I want to explain something to you. Maybe it'll help." She dragged both hands through her hair before she pushed herself up on the hood of the car. Now that the shouting was over, a pigeon settled back on the asphalt to peck hopefully at a discarded wrapper. "It isn't easy to say all of this out loud. I've told you Kathy and I weren't close. What it really comes down to is she was never the person I wanted her to be. I pretended, and I covered for her when I could. The truth is she resented me, even hated me from time to time. She didn't want to, she couldn't help it."

"Grace, don't drag all this up."

"I have to. If I don't I'll never be able to bury it, or her. I detested Jonathan. It hurt so much less to blame everything on him. I don't like problems, you know." In a gesture she used only when she was very tired or very tense, she began to knead her brow. "I avoid them or ignore them. I decided I'd make it his fault that Kathleen didn't bother to answer my letters, or that she was never warm whenever I convinced her to let me visit. I told myself he'd turned her into a snob, that if she was busy climbing the social ladder, it was for him. When they divorced I blamed that on him, totally. I'm not good with middle ground."

She stopped here because the rest was harder. After folding her hands in her lap, she continued. "I blamed her drug problem on him, even her death. Ed, I can't tell you how much I wanted to believe he'd killed her." When she looked at him again her eyes were dry, but vulnerable, so achingly vulnerable. "At the funeral, he let me have it. He told me things I already knew in my heart but had never been able to accept about Kathleen. I hated him for it. I hated him for stripping away the illusion I'd allowed myself. In the past few weeks I've had to accept who Kathleen was, what she was, and even why."

He touched her cheek. "You couldn't have been another person, Grace."

So he understood, so easily. If it already hadn't happened, she'd have fallen in love with him then. "No, I couldn't. I can't. The guilt's eased considerably. But you see, she was still my sister. I can still love her. And I know if I can do this one last thing, I can let go. If I took the easy road now, I don't think I could live with it."

"Grace, there are other ways."

"Not for me. Not this time." She took his hand and cupped it between the two of hers. "You don't know me as well as you think. For years I've turned over all the dirty work to someone else, for ten percent. If there was something unpleasant to be dealt with, I'd toss it to my agent, or my business manager, or my lawyer. That way I could just go along without too many distractions and write. If it was something I had to handle myself, I'd pick the easiest route or ignore it completely. Don't ask me, please don't ask me to turn this over to you and do nothing. Because I might."

He pushed a hand through his hair. "What the hell do you want me to do?"

"Understand," she murmured. "It's important to me for you to understand. I'll have to do it even if you don't, but I'd be happier if you could. I'm sorry."

"It's not that I don't understand, it's that I think it's a mistake. Call it instinct."

"If it's a mistake, it's one I have to make. I can't pick up my life, not really pick it up again, until I do this."

There were a dozen valid, sensible arguments he could make. But there was only one that mattered. "I couldn't take it if anything happened to you."

She managed to smile. "Me either. Look, I'm not really stupid. I can swear to you I won't do something idiotic like the heroine in a B movie. You know, the kind who knows there's a homicidal maniac on the loose and hears a noise?"

"Instead of locking the doors, she goes outside to see what it is."

"Yeah." Now she grinned at him. "It drives me crazy. I hate a contrived plot device."

"You can't forget this isn't a plot. You don't have a screenplay, Grace."

"I intend to be very careful. And I'm counting on the department's finest."

"If we agree, you'll do exactly as you're told?"

"Absolutely."

"Even if you don't like it."

"I hate blanket promises, but okay."

He lifted her down from the car. "We'll talk about it."

Chapter 13

CHARLTON P. HAYDEN HAD had a very successful trip north. In Detroit he'd drummed up solid support from the unions. Blue-collar workers were lined up behind him, drawn in by his America for Americans campaign. Fords and Chevys were decorated with HAYDEN'S AMERICA— SOLID, SECURE, SUCCESSFUL bumper stickers. He spoke in simple terms, everyman's terms, in orations two speech writers collaborated on and he edited. His ride to the White House was more than a decade in the making. Hayden might have preferred a Mercedes, but he made certain his staff had rented a Lincoln.

His appearance at Tiger Stadium had been as solidly cheered as the two-hit shutout. His picture, in a fielder's cap with his arm around the winning pitcher, had made the front page of the *Free Press*. The crowds in Michigan and Ohio had been vocal, his promises believed, his speeches applauded.

Already in the works was a trip to America's heartland. Kansas, Nebraska, Iowa. He wanted the farmer behind him. As fate would have it, he could fall back on his great-grandfather who had tilled the land. That made him America's son, the salt of the earth, despite the fact that he was the third generation of Haydens to graduate from Princeton.

When he won the election—Hayden never thought in terms of if's—he would implement his plans to strengthen the backbone of the country. Hayden believed in America, so that his vigorous speeches and impassioned pleas rang with sincerity. Destinies—his own and his country's—were innate beliefs, but Hayden knew both games and war had to be played to achieve them. He was a man with a single purpose: to rule, and rule well. Some would suffer, some would sacrifice, some would weep. Hayden was a firm believer in the needs of the many outweighing the needs of the few. Even when the few were his own family.

He loved his wife. The fact was he could never have fallen in love with anyone unsuitable. His ambition was too much a part of what made him. Claire suited him—her looks, her background, and her manner. She was a Merriville and, like the Vanderbilts and Kennedys, had grown up in the comfortable surroundings of inherited wealth and position sweated for by immigrant forefathers. Claire was a bright woman who understood that in their circle the planning of a menu could be as important as the passage of a bill.

She had married Hayden knowing that ninety percent of his energy would always be earmarked for his work. He was a vigorous, dedicated man and considered ten percent more than enough for his family. If anyone had accused him of neglecting them, he would have been more amused than annoyed.

He loved them. Naturally he expected top performances from the members of his family, but that was a matter of pride as well as ambition. It pleased him to see his wife dressed beautifully. It pleased him to see his son in the top ten percent of his class. Hayden wasn't a man to give praise for what he expected. If Jerald's grades had dipped, it would have been a different matter altogether. Hayden wanted the best for his son, and wanted the best out of him.

He was seeing that Jerald had the best education, and was proud of what his son seemed to be doing with it. Already Hayden was making plans for his son's political career. Though he had no intention of passing on his power for a few decades, when he did, he would damn well pass it on to his own.

He expected Jerald to be ready and willing.

Jerald was well mannered, bright, sensible. If he spent too much time by himself, Hayden usually dismissed it as adolescent intensity. The boy was almost emotionally attached to his computer. Girls hadn't entered the picture, and Hayden could only be relieved. Studies and ambition always took second place to females with an impressionable young man. Of course, the boy wasn't particularly good-looking. A late bloomer, Hayden had often told himself. Jerald had always been a plain, thin boy who tended to slouch if he wasn't reminded to hold himself straight. He was on the dean's list consistently, always polite and attentive at dinner parties, and at eighteen had a firm handle on politics and the party line.

He rarely gave his father a moment's worry.

Until lately.

"The boy's sulking, Claire."

"Now, Charlton." Claire held up her pearl drops and her diamond studs to see which best suited her evening dress. "He has to be allowed his little moods."

"What about this business about having a headache and not attending tonight's dinner?" Charlton fussed with his monogrammed cuffs. The laundry had overstarched again. He'd have to speak with his secretary.

While his gaze was fixed elsewhere, Claire shot her husband a quick, worried look. "I think he's been studying too hard. He does it to please you." She decided on the pearls. "You know how much he looks up to you."

"He's a bright boy." Hayden relented a bit as he checked his jacket for creases. "No need for him to make himself sick."

"It's just a headache," she murmured. Tonight's dinner was important. They all were, with the election coming up. Whatever worries she had about their son, she didn't want to bring them up tonight. Her husband was a good man, an honest man, but he had a low tolerance for weaknesses. "Don't push him just now, Charlton. I think he's going through some kind of phase."

"You're thinking about those scratches on his face." Satisfied with his jacket, Hayden checked the shine on his shoes. Image. Image was so important. "Do you believe he ran his bike into some rosebushes?"

"Why shouldn't I?" She fumbled over the clasp of her necklace. It was ridiculous, but her fingers were damp. "Jerald doesn't lie."

"Never known him to be awkward either. Claire, to tell you the truth, he hasn't been himself since we got back from up north. He seems nervous, edgy."

"He's concerned over the election, that's all. He wants you to win, Charlton. To Jerald, you already are the president. Do this for me, darling. I'm all thumbs tonight."

Obliging, Hayden crossed over to hook the chain. "Nervous?"

"I can't deny I'll be glad when the election's over. I know how much pressure you're under, all of us are under. Charlton . . ." She reached over her shoulder to take his hand. It had to be said. Perhaps it would be best to say it now and gauge her husband's reaction. "Do you think, well, have you ever considered, that Jerald might be—experimenting?"

"With what?"

"Drugs?"

It wasn't often he was thrown a curve that rocked him. For ten seconds, Hayden could only stare. "That's absurd. Why, Jerald was one of the first to join the antidrug campaign at his school. He even wrote a paper on the dangers and the long-term effects."

"I know, I know. I'm being ridiculous." But she couldn't quite let it go. "It's just that he's seemed so erratic lately, particularly in the last few weeks. He's either closed up in his room or spending the evening at the library. Charlton, the boy doesn't have any friends. No one ever calls here for him. He never has anyone come over. Just last week he snapped at Janet for putting his laundry away."

"You know how he feels about his privacy. We've always respected that."

"I wonder if we've respected it too much."

"Would you like me to talk to him?"

"No." Shutting her eyes, she shook her head. "I'm being silly. It's the pressure, that's all. You know how closed up Jerald becomes when you lecture."

"For Christ's sake, Claire, I'm not a monster."

"No." She took his hands then and squeezed. "Just the opposite, dear. Sometimes it's hard for the rest of us to be as strong, or as good as you. Let's leave him be for a while. Things will be better when he graduates."

JERALD WAITED UNTIL HE heard them leave. He'd been half-afraid his father would come in and insist that he join them for the evening. Some stupid rubber-chicken-and-asparagus dinner. Everyone would talk politics and tout their favored causes while watching out of the corners of their eyes for which coattail to grab on to.

Most would be grasping on to his father's. People were brownnosing him already. It made Jerald sick. Most of them were just out for what they could get. Like the reporters Jerald had spotted outside the house. Looking to dig up dirt on Charlton P. Hayden. They wouldn't find any because his father was perfect. His father was the best. And when he was elected in November, the shit would hit the fan. His father didn't need anyone. He'd kick out all those pussies in their soft jobs and run the government the correct way. And Jerald would be right there beside him, soaking up the power. Laughing. Busting his gut laughing at all the idiots.

The women would come begging, pleading for the son of the president of the United States to pay attention to them. Mary Beth would be sorry, so sorry she'd rejected him. Almost lovingly, he ran his fingers over the scratches on his face. She'd fall on her knees and beg him to forgive her. But he wouldn't forgive. True power didn't forgive. It punished. He'd punish Mary Beth and all the other sluts who'd made promises they didn't intend to keep.

And no one could touch him because he'd gone beyond their pitiful scope of understanding. He could still feel pain. Even now the gashes in his leg throbbed. Soon there wouldn't even be that. He knew the secret, and the secret was all in the mind. He'd been born for greatness. Just as his father had always told him. That's why none of the small-minded wimps who went to school with him ever came close to being his friends. The truly great, the truly powerful were never understood. But they were admired. They were revered. The time would come when he had the world in his two palms, like his father. He'd have the power to reshape it. Or to crush it.

He gave a quick giggle, then dug into his stash. Jerald never smoked at home. He knew the sweet smell of pot was easily detected and would be reported to his parents. When he had a yen for a joint, he took it outside. He eschewed cigarettes. Both of his parents were very active in nonsmokers' rights. Any trace of smoke, tobacco or otherwise, would besmirch the purity of Hayden air. Jerald giggled again as he pulled out a prime joint laced with flake. PCP. Angel dust. He smiled as he ran his fingers down it. A few tokes of this and you could feel like an angel. Or Satan himself.

His parents would be gone for hours. The servants were all tucked away in their wing of the house. He needed a lift. No, not needed, he corrected. Needs were for ordinary people. He wanted a lift. He wanted to fly sky-high while he listened for the next one. Because the next one was going to suffer. Jerald took out his father's service revolver, the one Captain Charlton P. Hayden had shot so many geeks with in good old Nam. His father had won medals for shooting strangers. There was something glorious about that.

Jerald didn't want any medals, he just wanted a kick. The big kick. The teenager in him opened the window before he lit the joint. The madman booted up the computer to search.

GRACE SPENT HER FIRST night on call torn between amusement and amazement. She was glad that she could still be surprised. Working in the arts and living in New York didn't mean she'd seen and heard everything. Not by a long shot. She took calls from whiners, from dreamers, from the bizarre and the mundane. For a woman who considered herself sophisticated and sexually savvy, she found herself stumbling more than once. One man calling from rural West Virginia recognized her as a novice.

"Don't worry, honey," he'd told her. "I'll talk you through it."

She worked three hours, a light load, and had to fight back giggles, simple shock, and the lingering discomfort that Ed was waiting downstairs.

At eleven, she took her last call. Tucking away her notes—you never knew what you could use—she walked downstairs. She spotted Ed first, then his partner.

"Hello, Ben. I didn't know you were here."

"You get the whole team." As he checked his watch he noted they were well past the latest time their man had struck. Still, he'd give it another half hour. "So how'd it go?"

Grace settled on the arm of a chair. She shot Ed a look, then shrugged. "It's different. You ever get turned on listening to a woman sneeze? Never mind."

As she spoke, Ed watched her. He'd have sworn she looked embarrassed. "Anyone make you uneasy, suspicious?"

"Uh-uh. For the most part you've got guys who are looking for a little companionship, some sympathy, and I guess in an odd sense a way to be faithful to their wives. Talking on the phone's a lot safer, and less drastic, than paying for a prostitute." But it wasn't anything to get on a soapbox about either, she reminded herself. "You're getting it all on tape anyway, right?"

"That's right." Ed lifted a brow. "Is that what's bothering you?"

"Maybe." She fiddled with the hem of her sleeve. "It feels odd knowing the boys at the station are going to be playing back what I said." Always resilient, she shook it off. "I can't believe what I said myself. I had this one guy who does bonsai trees, you know those little Japanese things? He spent most of the call telling me how much he loves them."

"Takes all kinds." Ben passed her a cigarette. "Did any of them ask to meet you?"

"I got some hints, nothing hard-line. Anyway, in my orientation session this afternoon I got some tips on how to handle that, and a lot of other things." She was relaxed again, even amused. "I spent the afternoon with Jezebel. She's been doing this for five years. After listening to her take calls for a few hours, I got the drift. Then there's this." She lifted a blue binder from the coffee table. "My training manual."

"No shit?" Delighted, Ben took it from her.

"It lists sexual penchants, the usual and a few I've never heard of."

"Me either," Ben murmured as he flipped a page.

"It also gives you different ways to say the same things. Like a thesaurus." She blew out smoke, then chuckled. "Do you know how many ways there are to say . . ." She trailed off when she looked at Ed. It only took her a moment to decide he wouldn't care for a rundown. "Well, it's handy. Let me tell you, it's a lot easier to have sex than to talk about it. Anybody want some stale chocolate-chip cookies?"

Ed shook his head, but all she got from Ben was a grunt as he leafed through the manual. "You'll grow hair on your palms," Ed said mildly when Grace left the room.

"Could be worth it." With a grin, Ben glanced up. "You wouldn't believe some of this. How come we're not working Vice?"

"Your wife's a shrink," Ed reminded him. "Nothing you could come up with in there's going to surprise her."

"Yeah. You're right." Ben set the manual aside. "Sounds to me like Grace handled herself all right."

"Looks like."

"Give her a break, Ed. She needs to do this. And she might just help bust things open."

"When they bust, they could fall all over her."

"We're here to see that doesn't happen." He paused a moment. He knew what it was to want to kick something, but not to have anything around big enough. "Do you remember how I felt when Tess was involved last winter?"

"I remember."

"I'm on your side, buddy. I always am."

Ed stopped pacing to just look at the room. It was funny how quickly it had become Grace's. Kathleen was gone; perhaps Grace didn't realize it yet, but she'd nudged her sister out with opened magazines and discarded shoes. There were wilting flowers in an old jar and dust on the furniture. In days, without even intending to, she'd made a home.

"I want her to marry me."

Ben stared at his partner a minute, then slowly sat back. "I'll be damned. Looks like Doc hit the bull's-eye again. Did you ask her?"

"Yeah, I asked her."

"And?"

"She needs some time."

Ben only nodded. He understood perfectly. She needed time. Ed didn't. "Want some advice?"

"Why not?"

"Don't let her think too long. She might find out what an asshole you are." When Ed grinned, Ben rose and reached for his jacket. "Wouldn't hurt to look over that training manual either. Page six looks like a winner."

"You leaving?" Grace walked back in with a tray of cookies and three beers.

"Jackson should be able to handle the night shift." Ben picked up a cookie and bit in. "These are terrible."

"I know." She laughed when he picked up another. "Got time for a beer?"

"I'll take it with me." Ben slipped the bottle into his pocket. "You did good, sugar." Because she looked like she could use it, Ben leaned over the tray to kiss her. "See you."

"Thanks." Grace waited until she heard the front door shut before she set down the tray. "He's quite a guy."

"The best."

And as long as he'd been there, they hadn't had to talk too directly to each other. Taking the end of the sofa, Grace began to nibble on a cookie. "I guess you've known him a long time."

"Long enough. Ben's got the best instincts in the department."

"Yours don't seem too shabby."

Ed watched her as he picked up his beer. "Mine tell me to shove you on the shuttle back to New York."

Grace lifted a brow. Apparently they were finished circling each other. "Are you still upset with me?"

"Worried about you."

"I don't want you to be." Then she smiled and held out a hand. "Yes, I do." When his fingers linked with hers, she brought them to her lips. "I have a feeling you're the best thing that ever happened to me. I'm sorry I can't make things easier."

"You screwed up my plans, Grace."

There was a half smile on her face as she tilted her head. "I did?"

"Come here."

Obliging, she wriggled along the sofa until she was cuddled against him. "When I bought the place next door, I had it all worked out. I was going to fix it up, just right, just the way I'd always imagined a house should be. When it was done, I was going to find the right woman. I didn't know what she'd look like, but that wasn't so important. She'd be sweet and patient and want me to take care of her. She'd never have to work the way my mother did. She'd stay home and take care of the house, the garden, the kids. She'd like to cook, and iron my shirts."

Grace wrinkled her nose. "She'd have to like doing that?"

"She'd love doing that."

"Sounds like you'd have to find some nice Nebraskan farm girl who'd been out of touch the last ten years."

"This is my fantasy, remember?"

Her lips curved again. "Sorry. Go on."

"Every night when I got home, she'd be waiting. We'd sit down, put our feet up, and talk. Not about my work. I wouldn't want that to touch her. She'd be too fragile. When it was time for me to retire, we'd just putter around the house together." He stroked a hand down her hair, then cupped it under her chin. As the seconds passed he simply studied her, the strong bones, the big eyes and flyaway hair. "You're not that woman, Grace."

She felt one very strong, very sharp moment of regret. "No, I'm not."

"But you're the only one I want." He touched his lips to hers in the soft, gentle way that made her pulse flutter. "You see, you screwed up my plans. I've got to thank you."

She wrapped her arms around him and settled in.

GRACE AWOKE IN ED'S arms at dawn. The sheets were up to her nose and her head was nestled against his chest. The first thing she heard was the slow, steady beat of his heart. It made her smile. Soft and hazy, the light trickled in the windows, sweetened by the first birdcalls of morning. Her legs were tangled with his so that the warmth and security reached all the way to her toes.

Turning her head, she pressed a kiss to his chest. She wondered if there were a woman in the world who wouldn't want to wake this way, content and secure in her lover's arms.

He stirred and drew her a bit closer. His body was so hard, the power so controlled. Where her flesh rested against his it was hot and damp and sensitized. Before the last mists of sleep had cleared, she was aroused.

On a sigh, she ran her hands over him, exploring, testing, enjoying. Still lazy, she let her lips skim over his flesh. When she felt his heartbeat accelerate, she murmured in satisfaction. With a half smile, she turned her head to look at him.

His eyes were intense, dark, then everything blurred when he pulled her up to cover her mouth with his. No gentleness this time; only demand and desperation. The strength was as raw as the need. Grace was swept away on a wave of panicky excitement.

The control he had always relied upon was gone. He was a man who moved carefully, all too aware of his own size and strength. But not now. They rolled over the bed as if chained together and he took exactly what he wanted.

She was trembling, but not weak. With each second that passed, her passion grew, so that she met demand with demand. He'd shown her tenderness and a deep-seated respect she could only marvel at. Now he showed her the dark and dangerous side of his love.

With his arms braced on either side of her head, he drove himself into her. Her fingers, slick with sweat, slipped down him, then found purchase and dug in. In the end they found more than release. They found deliverance.

She was still gasping when he lowered himself to her. His head nestled between her breasts, her hands tangled in his hair. "I think I found the substitute for coffee," she managed to say, then began to laugh.

"Nothing funny about caffeine," he muttered. "It'll kill you."

"No, I was just thinking if this keeps up I could write my own training manual." Stretching her arms over her head, she yawned. "I wonder if my agent could market it."

He lifted his head so that the tip of his beard tickled her skin. "Stick to mysteries." He started to say something else, when the radio beside the bed went on with a blast of rock. "Christ, how can you wake up to that?"

"No one gets the blood moving like Tina Turner."

Ed picked her up, turned her around, and laid her against the pillows. "Why don't you get some more sleep? I've got to get ready for work."

She kept her arms around his neck. He was so cute when he tried to pamper. "I'd rather take a shower with you."

Ed switched Tina off in midhowl, then carried Grace into the bath.

◆ ◆ ◆

A HALF HOUR LATER, she was sitting at the kitchen table going through yesterday's mail while Ed made oatmeal. "Sure I can't talk you into a moldy Danish?"

"Not a chance. I threw them out."

Grace glanced up. "They only had green stuff on one corner." With a shrug, she went back to the mail. "Ah, looks like royalties. It's that time of the year again." She slit open the envelope, set the check aside, and studied the forms. "Thank God old G. B.'s still pulling through. How about some cookies?"

"Grace, one of these days we're going to have a serious talk about your diet."

"I have no diet."

"Exactly."

She watched as he spooned oatmeal into the bowl he'd set in front of her. "You're too good to me."

"I know." Grinning, he switched to his own bowl. As he began to scoop oatmeal from the pan, his gaze landed on the check Grace had set aside. Oatmeal landed with a plop on the table.

"Missed," she said lightly and tasted.

"You, ah, get many of these?"

"Of what? Oh, royalty checks? Twice a year, God bless them every one." She was hungrier than she'd thought and took a real spoonful. If she didn't watch herself, Grace mused, she might get to like this stuff. "Plus the advances, of course. You know, this wouldn't be half bad with some sugar." She started to reach for the bowl when she noticed his expression. "Something wrong?"

"What? No." After setting the pan aside, he got a rag to wipe up the spill. "I guess I didn't realize how much money you could make writing."

"It's a crap shoot. Sometimes you get lucky." She was on her first cup of coffee, but still she noticed he was concentrating very hard on wiping up one blob of oatmeal. "Is it a problem?"

He thought of the house next door, the one he'd saved for. She could have bought it with loose change. "I don't know. I guess it shouldn't be."

She hadn't expected this. Not from him. The truth was Grace was careless with money, not negligent in the way of the truly rich, but careless, thoughtless. She'd been the same when she'd been poor.

"No, it shouldn't. Over the last few years writing's made me rich. That's not why I started writing. That's not why I'm still writing. I'd hate to think that would be the reason you'd change your mind about me."

"Mostly I feel like an idiot thinking you'd be happy here, in a place like this, with me."

Her eyes narrowed as she frowned up at him. "That's probably the first really stupid thing I've heard you say. I may not know what's right yet, for either of us, but when I do, the place won't mean a damn. Now why don't you shut up? Your feet are too big to fit comfortably in your mouth." After shoving the mail aside, she picked up the paper. The first thing she saw when she unfolded it was the composite drawing of Kathleen's killer.

"You guys work fast," she said softly.

"We wanted to get it out. They'll flash it on TV today off and on. It gives us something solid to take to the press conference."

"He could be almost anyone."

"Mrs. Morrison wasn't able to pull in many details." He didn't like the way Grace was studying the drawing, as if she was memorizing every line and curve. "She thinks she got the shape of the face and the eyes."

"He's just a kid. If you combed the high schools in the area you could find a couple hundred kids who come close to this description." Because her stomach was churning, she rose to pour some water. But Ed had been right. She'd memorized the face. With or without the sketch, she wouldn't forget it. "A kid," she repeated. "I can't believe some teenager did that to Kathleen."

"Not all teenagers go to proms and pizza parlors, Grace."

"I'm not a fool." Abruptly furious, she whirled on him. "I know what's out there, dammit. Maybe I don't like to live my life checking dark alleys and dirty corners, but I know. I put it on paper every day, and if I'm naive it's by choice. First I have to accept the fact that my sister was murdered, now I have to accept that she was murdered— raped, beaten, *and* murdered—by some juvenile delinquent."

"Psychotic," Ed corrected very quietly. "Insanity isn't picky about age-groups."

Setting her jaw, she walked back to the paper. She'd said she wanted a picture; now she had one, however vague. She would study it. She would cut the goddamn thing out and stick it on her bedroom wall. When she was done, she'd know that face as well as her own.

"I can tell you one thing, I didn't talk to any teenagers last night. I listened to every voice over that phone, every nuance, every tone. I'd have recognized someone this young."

"Voices change by the time a kid hits twelve or thirteen." When she reached for a cigarette, he nearly winced. She couldn't keep living off tobacco and coffee.

"It's not just the depth of the voice, it's the rap, it's the phrasing. Dialogue's one of my specialties." Struggling to calm herself, she ran her hands over her face. "I'd have recognized a kid."

"Maybe. Maybe you would have. You pick up details and log them in. I've noticed."

"Tools of the trade," she muttered. She forgot the cigarette as she studied the picture. There were details missing there. If she looked hard enough, long enough, she might be able to flesh them out, just as she did a character conceived in her own mind. "His hair's short. Military, conservative. Doesn't look like a street kid."

He'd thought the same thing, but a haircut wasn't going to narrow the field. "Back off a little, Grace."

"I'm involved."

"That doesn't mean you can be objective about all of this." He turned the paper facedown. "Or that I can be. Dammit, this is my job and you're playing hell with it."

"How?"

"How?" He pinched his nose between his thumb and forefinger and nearly laughed. "Maybe it has something to do with the fact that I'm crazy about you. While I'm still working my feet out of my mouth, I might as well say it all. I don't like thinking about you talking to those men."

She ran her tongue over her teeth. "I see."

"The fact is, I hate it. I can understand why you're doing it, and from a cop's standpoint, I can see the advantage. But—"

"You're jealous."

"Like hell."

"Yes, you are." She patted his hand. "Thanks. Tell you what, if any of them gets me excited, I'll come looking for you."

"It's not a joke."

"Christ, Ed, it has to be. Because I'll drive myself crazy otherwise. I don't know if I can make you understand, but it was weird listening to them, knowing someone else was listening too. I sat there concentrating on every voice that came over the phone and wondering what the others, the ones who were listening in, taping the evidence, were thinking." She let out a breath, and her honesty. "I guess I wondered what you'd have thought if you'd been listening too. Because of that I concentrated harder." Deliberately she turned the paper over again and looked down at the composite. "I have to look at the ridiculous side of it, and at the same time remember why. You see, I'll know if I hear him. I can promise you that."

But Ed was just looking at her. Something she'd said had started a new train of thought. It made sense. Maybe the best sense. He was itching to go when he heard the knock on the front door. "That should be my relief. You going to be okay?"

"Sure. I'm going to try to work. I figure I'll do better if I get back to my routine."

"You can call me if you need to. If I'm not in, the desk knows how to reach me."

"I'll be fine, really."

He tilted her chin up. "Call me anyway."

"Okay. Get out of here before the bad guys get away."

Chapter 14

BEN WAS ALREADY HIP-DEEP in phone calls and paperwork when Ed came into the station. Spotting his partner, Ben swallowed the better part of a powdered doughnut. "I know," he began as he put a hand over the receiver. "Your alarm didn't go off. You had a flat tire. The dog ate your shield."

"I stopped by Tess's office," Ed said.

The tone, even more than the statement, had Ben straightening at his desk. "I'll get back to you," he said into the receiver, then hung up. "Why?"

"Something Grace said this morning." After a quick scan of the messages and files on his desk, Ed decided they could wait. "I wanted to run the idea by Tess, see if she thought it fit into the psychiatric profile."

"And?"

"Bingo. Remember Billings? Used to work Robbery?"

"Sure, pain in the ass. He went private a couple years ago. Surveillance specialist."

"Let's pay him a visit."

♦ ♦ ♦

"Looks like bugs pay," Ben observed as he glanced around Billings's office. The walls were covered in ivory silk and the pewter-colored carpet flowed right up to the ankles. There were a couple of paintings on the walls Ben thought Tess would like. French and muted. Outside the wide, tinted windows was a classy view of the Potomac.

"The private sector, my man." Billings pushed a button on his desk and sent a panel sliding back to reveal a range of television monitors. "The world's my oyster. Anytime you want to ditch public service, give me a call. Always willing to give a couple of bright boys a break."

As Ben had said, Billings always had been a pain in the ass. Disregarding it, Ed settled on the corner of his desk. "Nice setup."

The only thing Billings liked better than playing high-tech "I Spy" was to brag. "This ain't the half of it. I've got five offices on this floor and I'm thinking about opening another branch. Politics, friends and neighbors." Billings gestured with his long, narrow hands. "In this town someone's always willing to shell out to get the edge on the next guy."

"Dirty business, Billings."

He only grinned at Ben. He'd had two thousand dollars' worth of bridgework done recently and his teeth marched as straight as a Marine band. "Yeah, ain't it just? So what are two of the department's finest doing here? Want me to find out who's playing with the commissioner when his wife's out of town?"

"Maybe some other time," Ed told him.

"Professional discount for you, Jackson."

"I'll keep it in mind. Meanwhile, I'd like to tell you a little story."

"Shoot."

"Say we've got a snooper, he's smart but wired wrong. He likes to listen. You know about that."

"Sure." Billings leaned back in his custom-made chair.

"He likes to listen to women," Ben continued. "He likes to listen to them talk sex, but he doesn't talk back. He hits a gold mine when he locks into fantasy calls. Now he can just sit there and listen, pick out the voice that turns him on, and he listens for hours while she talks to other men. Can he do that, Billings, without the other guy or the woman knowing about it?"

"If he's got the right equipment, he can tap into any conversation he wants. I've got some stuff in stock that could plug you in from here to the West Coast, but it costs." He was interested. Anything that had to do with snooping interested him. Billings would have gone into espionage if he could have found a government to trust him. "What are you guys working on?"

"Let's just take the story a step further." Ben picked up a crystal pyramid from Billings's desk and examined the facets. "If this snooper wanted to find one of the women— he doesn't know her name or where she lives or what she looks like, but he wants a face-to-face and all he's got is the voice and the tap—can he get to her?"

"Does he have brains?"

"You tell me."

"If he's got brains and a good PC the world's his cupcake. Give me your phone number, Paris." Billings swung around to his workstation and tapped in the number Ben rattled off. The machine clicked and hummed as Billings programmed it. "Unlisted," he muttered. "Only makes it more of a challenge."

Ben lit a cigarette. Before it was smoked halfway to the filter, his address came up on the screen.

"Look familiar?" Billings asked him.

"Can anybody do that?" Ben asked him.

"Any decent hacker. Let me tell you something, with this baby and a little imagination, I can find out anything. Give me another minute." Using Ben's name and address, he began to work again. "Checking account balance is a little low, Paris. I wouldn't write anything over fifty-five dollars." He pushed away from the monitor again. "A really good snooper needs skill and patience as well as the right equipment. A couple of hours on this thing and I could tell you your mother's shoe size."

Ben tapped out his cigarette. "If we wired you into the bait, could you get me a fix on the snooper?"

Billings grinned. He knew he'd been smart to be expansive. "For an old buddy—and a reasonable fee—I'll tell you what he ate for breakfast."

$\mathcal{I}$'M TERRIBLY SORRY TO disturb you, Senator, but Mrs. Hayden's on the phone. She says it's important."

Hayden continued to read the revised speech he would give that afternoon at the League of Women Voters' luncheon. "What line, Susan?"

"Three."

Hayden pushed the button while keeping the phone cradled on his shoulder. "Yes, Claire. I'm a bit pressed for time."

"Charlton, it's Jerald."

After twenty years of marriage, Hayden knew his wife well enough to recognize true alarm. "What?"

"I've just gotten a call from school. He was in a brawl."

"A brawl? Jerald?" With a half laugh, Hayden picked up his speech again. "Don't be ridiculous."

"Charlton, Dean Wight himself called me. Jerald was in a fistfight with another student."

"Claire, not only is that difficult to believe given Jerald's temperament, it's quite annoying to be called just because Jerald and some other boy had a tiff of some kind. We'll discuss it when I get home."

"Charlton." It was the sharp edge to her voice that prevented him from hanging up. "According to Wight this was not a little tiff. The other boy—he's been taken to the hospital."

"Ridiculous." But Hayden was no longer looking at his speech. "It sounds to me like a few cuts and bruises are being blown out of proportion."

"Charlton." Claire felt her stomach flutter. "They're saying Jerald tried to strangle him."

Twenty minutes later Hayden was sitting, ramrod straight, in Dean Wight's office. In the chair beside him, Jerald sat with his eyes downcast and his mouth set. His white linen shirt was creased and smudged, but he'd taken the time to straighten his tie. The scratches on his face had been joined by darkening bruises. The knuckles of both hands were swollen.

A look at him had affirmed Hayden's opinion that the incident had been nothing more than a rough-and-tumble. Jerald would be called to task, certainly. A lecture, a reduction of privileges for a time. Still, Hayden was already working out his position should the matter leak to the press.

"I hope we can clear this matter up shortly."

Wight nearly sighed. He was two years away from retirement and his pension. In his twenty years at St. James's he'd taught, lectured, and disciplined the sons of the rich and the privileged. Many of his former students had gone on to become public figures in their own right. If he understood one solid fact about those who sent their offspring to him, it was that they didn't care for criticism.

"I know your schedule must be hectic, Senator Hayden. I wouldn't have requested this meeting unless I felt it was for the best."

"I'm aware you know your job, Dean Wight. Otherwise Jerald wouldn't be here. However, I'm forced to say that this entire scenario is being blown out of proportion. Naturally, I will not condone my son participating in fisticuffs." This was said directly to the top of Jerald's head.

"And I can assure you this matter will be taken up at home, and dealt with."

Wight adjusted his glasses. It was a gesture both Hayden and Jerald recognized as the product of nervousness. Hayden sat patiently while Jerald gloated. "I appreciate that, Senator. However, as dean, I have a responsibility to St. James's, and to the student body. I have no choice but to suspend Jerald."

Hayden's mouth firmed. Jerald saw it out of the corner of his eye. Now that fat-faced dean was in for it, he thought.

"I find that rather extreme. I went to a preparatory school myself. Skirmishes were frowned on, certainly, but they didn't result in suspension."

"This was hardly a skirmish, Senator." He'd seen the look in Jerald's eyes when he'd had his hands around young Lithgow's throat. It had frightened him, frightened him badly. Even now, studying the boy's downcast face, he felt uneasy. Randolf Lithgow had suffered severe facial injuries. When Mr. Burns had attempted to break up the fight, Jerald had attacked him with a ferocity that had sent the older man to the ground. He had then tried to choke the nearly unconscious Lithgow until several members of the student body managed to restrain him.

Wight coughed into his hands. He knew the power and wealth of the man he was speaking with. In all probability, Hayden would be the next president. To have had the son of a president graduate from St. James's would be a tremendous coup. It was that, and only that, that prevented Wight from expelling Jerald.

"In the four years Jerald has been with us, we have never had a problem of any kind in his conduct or his studies."

Naturally, Hayden had expected no less. "In that case, it appears Jerald must have been extremely provoked."

"Perhaps." Wight coughed into his hand again.

"Though the severity of the attack can't be condoned, we are willing to hear Jerald's side of the story before we take disciplinary action. I assure you, Senator, we do not suspend students out of hand."

"Well then?"

"Jerald has refused to explain."

Hayden bit off a sigh. He was paying several thousand dollars a year to have Jerald seen to properly, and this man didn't have the capability to draw an explanation out of a high school senior. "If you'd give us a few moments alone, Dean Wight?"

"Of course." He rose, only too glad to distance himself from the silent, cool-eyed stare of the senator's son.

"Dean—" Hayden's authoritative voice stopped him at the door. "I'm sure I can rely on your discretion in this matter."

Wight was very aware of the generous contributions the Haydens had made to St. James's over the last four years. He was also aware of how easily a candidate's personal life could destroy his political one. "School problems remain in the school, Senator."

Hayden rose as soon as Wight left the room. It was an automatic gesture, even an ingrained one. Standing simply emphasized his authority. "All right, Jerald. I'm ready to hear your explanation."

Jerald, his hands resting lightly on his thighs as he'd been taught, looked up at his father. He saw more than a tall, vigorously handsome man. He saw a king, with blood on his sword and justice on his shoulders. "Why didn't you tell him to fuck off?" Jerald asked mildly.

Hayden stared. If his son had risen and slapped his face he would have been no less shocked. "I beg your pardon?"

"It's none of his business what we do," Jerald continued in the same reasonable tone. "He's only a fat little weasel who sits behind a desk and pretends to be important. He doesn't know anything about the way things really are. He's insignificant."

Jerald's tone was so polite, his smile so genuine, that Hayden found himself staring again. "Dean Wight is the head of this institution and, as long as you're enrolled in St. James's, deserves your respect."

As long as he was enrolled. One more month. If his father wanted to wait a few weeks before fixing Wight's ass, Jerald could be patient. "Yes, sir."

Relieved, Hayden nodded. The boy was obviously quite upset, perhaps even suffering from a touch of shock. Hayden hated to press him, but answers were necessary. "Tell me about your run-in with Lithgow."

"He was bugging me."

"Apparently." Hayden felt on more solid ground here. Young boys had an excess of energy and often took it out on each other. "I take it he initiated the incident?"

"He kept riding me. He was an idiot." Impatient, Jerald started to squirm, then caught himself. Control. His father demanded control. "I warned him to get off my back; it was only fair to warn him." Jerald smiled at his father. For a reason he couldn't name, Hayden felt his blood chill. "He said if I didn't have a date for the Graduation Ball he had a cousin with a clubfoot. I wanted to kill him right then; I wanted to smash his pretty face in."

Hayden wanted to believe it was a young boy's anger, a young boy's words, but he couldn't. Not quite. "Jerald, raising your fists isn't always the answer. We have a system, we have to work within it."

"We run the system!" Jerald flung his head up. His eyes. Even his father saw that his eyes were wild, rabid. Then the shutters came down again. Hayden could convince himself, had to convince himself he'd imagined it. "I told him, I told him I didn't want to go to any prissy school dance to drink punch and cop a few feels. He laughed. He shouldn't have laughed at me. He said maybe I didn't like girls." On a low chuckle, Jerald wiped the spittle from his lips. "And I knew I was going to kill him. I told him I didn't like girls. I liked women. Real women. Then I hit him so that blood spurted out of his nose all over his pretty face. And I kept hitting him." Jerald continued to smile as his father's face whitened. "I didn't blame him for being jealous, but he shouldn't have laughed at me. You'd have been proud of the way I punished him for laughing."

"Jerald . . ."

"I could have killed them all," Jerald continued. "I could have, but I didn't. It wouldn't have been worth it, would it?"

For one trembling moment, Hayden thought he was in the room with a stranger. But it was his son, his well-bred, well-educated son. The excitement, Hayden assured himself. It was only the strain of the afternoon. "Jerald, I don't condone losing your temper, but it happens to all of us. I also understand that when we're provoked we say things, do things that are uncharacteristic."

Jerald's lips curved almost sweetly. He loved his father's rich orator's voice. "Yes, sir."

"Wight said you tried to strangle the other boy."

"Did I?" Jerald's eyes were blank for a moment, then cleared with his shrug. "Well, that's the best way."

Hayden discovered he was sweating; his armpits were dripping. Was he afraid? That was ridiculous, he was the boy's father. He had no reason to be afraid. Sweat ran in a jagged line down his back. "I'll take you home." Just a small breakdown, Hayden told himself as he led Jerald from the room. The boy had been working too hard. He just needed to rest.

GRACE SIGHED WHEN THE phone rang. She'd been able to work for the first time that day. Really work. For hours she'd enveloped herself in her own imagination and had produced something that had pleased her.

She'd harbored a deep, secret fear that she wouldn't be able to write again. Not about murders and victims. But it had come back, rough at first, then with the old flow. The story, the act of writing, the world she created had nothing to do with Kathleen and everything to do with her. Another hour, maybe two, and she'd have enough to send to New York and ease her editor's nervous twitch. But the phone rang and brought her back to reality. And reality had everything to do with Kathleen.

Grace answered, then noted the number. After drawing out a cigarette, she dialed. "Collect call, from Desiree." She waited until the call had been accepted and the operator clicked off. "Hello, Mike, what can I do for you?"

A hell of a way to spend the evening, she thought some minutes later. Ed was downstairs playing gin with Ben and she was pretending she was a peasant to Sir Michael's black knight.

Harmless. Most of the men who called were just that. They were lonely, looking for companionship. They were cautious and looking for safe, electronic sex. They were tense, pressured by family and profession, and had decided a phone call was cheaper than paying for a prostitute or a psychiatrist. That was the simple way to look at it.

But Grace knew, better than most, that it wasn't really that simple.

The newspaper reproduction of the police artist's sketch was on her nightstand. How many times had she studied it? How many times had she looked at it and tried to see . . . something? Murderers, rapists should look different from other men in society. Yet they looked the same— normal, unmarked. That was so frightening. You could pass them on the street, stand with them in an elevator, shake their hands at a cocktail party and never know.

Would she know him when she heard him? His voice

would be as normal, and as harmless, as Sir Michael's. Yet somehow she thought she would know. She held the sketch in her hand and studied it. The voice would fit, and she'd put it together with the sketch of his face.

Outside, Ben crossed the street to an unmarked van. Ed had already taken him for twelve-fifty at gin, and he thought it was time to check on Billings. He pulled open the side door. Billings glanced up, then saluted.

"Amazing stuff." Billings cackled to himself. "Yes, sir, it's capital A amazing. Want to listen in?"

"You're a sick man, Billings."

Billings only grinned and cracked a peanut. "The lady gives great phone, old buddy. I have to thank you for letting me make her acquaintance. I'm tempted to give her a ring myself."

"Why don't you do that? I'd love to see Ed rip off your arms and stuff them up your nose." But it was precisely to avoid that possibility that Ben had come out to do the checking. "You doing anything with the taxpayers' money in here besides jerking off?"

"Don't get hyper, Paris. Remember, you came to me." He swallowed the peanut. "Oh yeah, she's really got this one going. He's about to—" Billings broke off. "Hold it." With one hand pressed against his headphones he began to fiddle with dials on the equipment lined up in front of him. "Sounds like somebody wants a free ride."

Ben moved forward until he was leaning over Billings's shoulder. "Have you got him?"

"Maybe, just maybe. A little click, a little surge. Watch the needle. Yeah, yeah, he's on there." Billings flipped switches and cackled. "Got ourself a ménage à trois."

"Can you trace it?"

"Does the pope wear a beanie? Shit, he's clever. A clever sonofabitch. Got himself a scrambler. Goddamn."

"What?"

"She hung up. I guess the guy's three minutes were up."

"Did you trace it, Billings?"

"I need more than thirty seconds, for Christ's sake. We'll wait and see if he comes back." Billings dug into the peanuts again. "You know, Paris, if this guy's doing what you think he's doing, he's not stupid. No, baby, he's sharp, real sharp. Chances are he's got himself some top of the line equipment and he knows how to use it. He's going to cover his trail."

"Are you telling me you're not going to be able to nail him?"

"No, I'm telling you he's good. Real good. But I'm better. There's the phone."

JERALD COULDN'T BELIEVE IT. His palms were sweating. It was a miracle, and he'd made it happen. He'd never stopped thinking about her, wanting her. Now she'd come back, just for him. Desiree was back. And she was waiting for him.

Giddy, he put his headphones on again and tuned back in.

That voice. Desiree's voice. Just hearing it made him edgy, sweaty, desperate. She was the only one who could really do it for him. Take him to the brink. The power was in her just the way it was in him. Closing his eyes, he let it flow over him. He let it take him up and over. She was back. She'd come back for him because he was the best.

God, it was all coming together. He'd been right to drop the mask and show those pussies at school what he was made of. Desiree was back. She wanted him, wanted him inside her, wanted him to give her that ultimate thrill.

He could almost feel her under him, bucking and screaming, begging him to do it. She'd come back to show him he not only had the power over life, but the power over death. He'd brought her back. When he went to her this time, it would be even better. The best.

The others had only been a test. He understood that now. The others had only happened to show him how much he and Desiree belonged together. Now she was talking to him, promising herself to him, eternally.

He'd have to go to her, but not tonight. He had to prepare first.

*H*E PULLED OFF." BILLINGS swore and punched buttons. "The little bastard pulled off. Come on back, come back, I've almost got you."

"Give me what you've got, Billings."

Still swearing, Billings pulled out a map. Keeping his headphones in place, he drew four lines, connecting them into a rectangle over six blocks. "He's in there. Until I get him back that's the best I can do. Jesus, no wonder he pulled out, this other guy's bawling like a baby."

"Just keep at it." Ben tucked the map into his pocket and jumped out of the van. It wasn't enough, but it was more than they'd had an hour before. He knocked on the front door, then strode in when Ed opened it. "We've got it down to a quadrant of about six square blocks." After glancing upstairs, Ben walked into the living room to spread the map on the coffee table.

Keeping on the edge of the couch, Ed leaned over it. "Upscale neighborhood."

"Yeah. Tess's grandfather lives here." Ben tapped a forefinger on the map just outside the quadrant. "And Congressman Morgan's Washington address is here." His finger moved inside the red lines.

"Maybe it wasn't just a coincidence that Morgan's credit card was used for the flowers," Ed murmured. "Maybe our boy knows him, or his kids."

"Morgan's son's the right age." Ben picked up a watered-down glass of Pepsi.

"His alibi's solid, and the description's off."

"Yeah, but I wonder what he'd have to say if we had him take a good hard look at the sketch."

"That school the Morgan kid goes to. St James's, right?"

"Prep school. Upper-crust and conservative."

Ed remembered the haircut in the sketch. He took out his notebook as he rose. "I'll call."

Ben paced to the window. Through it he could see the van. Inside, Billings was gnawing peanuts and maybe, just maybe, narrowing down the possibilities. There wasn't much time. He could feel it. Something was going to break, and soon. If things didn't go right, Grace was going to be squeezed from both sides.

He glanced over his shoulder at Ed talking on the phone. He knew how it felt, how frustrating, how just plain scary it was to have the woman you loved in the middle of something you couldn't control. You tried to be a cop, a good one, but holding on to your objectivity was like trying to cling to a wet rope. You kept losing your grip.

"Morgan's mother died this morning," Ed said as he hung up. "The family'll be out of town for a couple of days." In Ben's eyes Ed saw what he felt in his gut. They didn't have a couple of days. "I want to pull her off."

"I know."

"Goddamn it, she's got no business exposing herself this way. She doesn't even belong here. She should be back in her penthouse in New York. The longer she stays—"

"The harder it's going to be to watch her leave," Ben finished. "Maybe she isn't going to leave, Ed."

A man didn't evade his partner. "I love her enough that it would be easier to know she was there, safe, than here with me."

Ben sat on the arm of the couch and pulled out a

cigarette. The eighteenth of the day. Damn Ed for getting him into the habit of counting. "You know one thing I've always admired about you—besides your arm-wrestling skills, that is—you're a hell of a judge of character, Ed. You usually put your finger on a person after ten minutes. So I figure you already know Grace isn't going to budge."

"Maybe she hasn't been shoved hard enough." Ed pushed his big hands into his pockets.

"A few months ago I gave serious thought to slipping the cuffs on Tess and shipping her off. Anywhere, as long as it was away from here." Ben studied the end of his cigarette. "Looking back, I can see a bit clearer. It wouldn't have worked. What made her the person she is made her determined to do what she was doing. It scared the shit out of me, and I took a lot of it out on her."

"Maybe if you'd pushed harder, you wouldn't have almost lost her." Ed spit it out, then immediately detested himself. "Out of line. I'm sorry."

If it had been anyone else, Ben would have released his temper in whatever way seemed the handiest. Because it was Ed, he bit it back. "It's nothing I haven't asked myself a few hundred times. I don't forget what it felt like when I knew he had her. I'll never forget it." After crushing out his cigarette, he rose to pace again. "You want to keep Grace out of this part of your life completely, totally separated from it. You want her untouched and unsullied by all the shit you wade through day after day. The gang hits, the domestic explosions, the prossies and the pimps. Let me tell you, it ain't never going to work because no matter what you do, you bring pieces of it home with you."

"What you bring home doesn't have to put her in firing range."

"No, but she's in this one." Ben dragged a hand through his hair. "Christ, I know what you're going through and I hate it. Not just for you, but for me, because it brings it right back to the bone. But the fact that keeps slapping us in the face is that she's reeling him in. No matter how much you might wish it otherwise, she's the one who's going to nail him."

"That's what I'm counting on," Grace said from the doorway. Both men turned toward her, but she looked only at Ed. "I'm sorry, by the time I realized this was a private conversation I'd already heard too much. I'm going for some coffee, but before I do, I'd like to add my two cents. I finish what I start. Always."

Ben picked up his jacket as Grace walked away. "Look, I'll go on out and wrap things up with Billings for the night."

"Yeah. Thanks."

"Catch you in the morning." He headed for the door, then paused. "I'd tell you to ease up, but I won't. If I had it to do over again, I'd do the same thing."

Grace heard the door close. Minutes later, she listened to Ed's footsteps come toward the kitchen. Immediately she began to fool with the coffeepot she'd simply been staring at.

"I don't know why in the hell Kathy didn't get a microwave. Every time I go to cook something I feel like I'm on Plymouth Rock. I'm thinking about frozen pizza. Are you hungry?"

"No."

"Coffee probably tastes like mud by now." She clanged cups in the cabinet. "There's probably some juice or something in the fridge."

"I'm fine. Why don't you sit down and let me do that?"

"Stop it!" She spun around, shattering the cup in the sink. "Dammit! Just stop trying to tuck me in and pat me on the head. I'm not a child. I've been taking care of myself for years and doing a hell of a good job of it. I don't want you to fix my coffee or anything else."

"All right." She wanted a fight. Fine. He was more

than ready for one himself. "Just what the hell *do* you want?"

"I want you to back off, back way off. I want you to stop watching me as though I were going to fall on my face every time I take a step."

"That'd be easy if you'd watch where you were going."

"I know what I'm doing and I don't need you or anyone else standing around waiting to catch me. I'm a capable, reasonably intelligent woman."

"Maybe you are, when you're not wearing blinders. You're looking straight ahead, Grace, but you don't know what the hell's happening on either side or behind you. Nobody's backing off, especially me, until this thing's over."

"Then stop making me feel guilty for doing the only thing I can do."

"What do you want me to do, stop worrying about you, stop caring what happens to you? Do you think I can turn my feelings off and on like a faucet?"

"You're a cop," she shot back. "You're supposed to be objective. You're supposed to want him no matter what."

"I want him." She saw his expression cool again. It was that look which made her realize how far he'd go when pushed.

"Then you know what I'm doing could drop him in your lap. Think about it for a minute, Ed. Maybe some woman is alive tonight because he's tuned in to me."

He believed it, but the problem was he couldn't get around her. "It'd be a hell of a lot easier for me if I didn't love you."

"Then love me enough to understand."

He wanted to be reasonable. He wanted to pull back and be the logical, mild-tempered man he knew himself to be. But he wasn't reasonable. If it wasn't over soon he might never be that same man again. Tired suddenly, he pressed his fingers to his eyes. Six square blocks and a vague sketch. It had to be enough. He'd end it. He'd find a way to end it or by the following night he'd find a way to put Grace on a plane to New York. He dropped his hands.

"You're boiling your coffee."

Biting off an oath, she turned and switched off the flame. She grabbed for the handle, missed, and burned the tips of three fingers. "Don't," she said instantly when Ed stepped forward. "I burned myself, I'll fix it." Glaring at him, she stuck her hand under cold water from the tap. "See? I can take care of it. I don't need you to kiss it and make it better."

With a furious turn of her wrist, she shut off the tap, then stood staring at her dripping fingers. "I'm sorry. Oh Christ, I'm sorry. I hate myself when I'm ugly."

"You going to kick at me if I ask you to sit down?"

Shaking her head, she walked to the table. "I guess I was on edge in the first place, then when I came down and heard you talking to Ben it set me off." She picked up a dishcloth and began to twist it. "I don't know how to handle your feelings and my own. As far as I know, no one's ever felt about me the way you do."

"Good."

That brought a halfhearted laugh and made it easier for her to look at him. "It's only fair to take that a step further and tell you I've never felt about anyone the way I feel about you."

He waited a beat. "But?"

"If I were plotting this out, I could figure how to work it. The thing is, I want to tell you how I feel, but I'm afraid it'll just make things harder for both of us."

"Give it a shot."

"I'm scared." She shut her eyes but didn't object when his hand reached for hers. "I'm so scared. When I was upstairs on that damn phone, I wanted to hang up and say screw it. But I couldn't. I'm not even sure anymore that what I'm doing's right. I don't even have that, but I have to go on with it. It's worse, a lot worse because you're pulling me the other way and I don't want to hurt you."

"You want my support, you want me to tell you what you're doing is the right thing. I don't know if I can."

"Then just don't tell me it's the wrong thing, because if you do enough times, I'll believe you."

He studied their joined hands. Hers were small, even delicate, the nails short and unpainted. There was a chunk of gold and diamonds on her pinky. "Have you ever been camping?"

"In a tent?" A little baffled, she shook her head. "No. I've never understood why people get off sleeping in the dirt."

"I know a place in West Virginia. There's a river, lots of rock. Wildflowers. I'd like to take you there."

She smiled. It was his way of offering peace. "In a tent?"

"Yeah."

"I guess that leaves out room service."

"I might bring a cup of tea to your sleeping bag."

"Okay. Ed?" She turned her hand over in offering. "Why don't you kiss my fingers and make them better?"

Chapter 15

"TESS, HOW WONDERFUL YOU look." Claire Hayden brushed her cheek over Tess's, then settled into the corner table at the Mayflower. "I really appreciate you meeting me like this at the end of one of your busy days."

"It's always nice to see you, Claire." Tess smiled though her feet were aching and she was already dreaming of a hot bath. "And you made it sound important."

"I'm probably overreacting." Claire adjusted the jacket of her shell-pink suit. "I'll have a dry vermouth," she told the waiter before glancing back at Tess. "Two?"

"No, I'll just have a Perrier." Tess watched Claire twist the thick band of her wedding ring around and around on her finger. "How is Charlton, Claire? It's been months since I've seen either of you except on the evening news. This must be a very exciting time for all of you."

"You know Charlton, he takes all of it in stride. For myself, I'm trying to gear up for the madness this summer. Smiles and speeches and smoldering podiums. The press already has the house under siege." She moved her small shoulders as if to shrug the inconvenience away. "That's all part of it. You know, Charlton always says the issues are more important than the candidate, but I wonder. If he slams a door, twenty reporters are ready to print that he threw a tantrum."

"Public life is never easy. Being the wife of the party's favored son can be a strain."

"Oh, it's not that. I've accepted that." She paused while their drinks were served. She would only have one, no matter how much she was tempted to order a second. It wouldn't do to have anyone report that the candidate's wife sucked the bottle. "I can admit to you that there are times I wish we could bundle off to some little farm somewhere." She sipped. "Of course, I'd hate that quickly enough. I love Washington. I love being a Washington wife. And I have no doubt I'll love being First Lady."

"If my grandfather's on the mark, you'll find out very soon."

"Dear Jonathan." Claire smiled again, but Tess saw the strain that still shadowed her eyes. "How is he?"

"As ever. He'll be pleased when I tell him we got together."

"I'm afraid this isn't social, and it's not something I want you to discuss with your grandfather. Or anyone."

"All right, Claire. Why don't you tell me what's bothering you?"

"Tess, I've always respected your professional credentials, and I know I can rely on your discretion."

"If you're asking me to consider anything you say to me here as privileged, I understand."

"Yes, I knew you would." Claire paused again, to sip, then to simply run her finger down the stem of her glass. "As I said, it's probably nothing. Charlton wouldn't be pleased that I'm making anything out of it, but I can't ignore it any longer."

"Then Charlton doesn't know you're here."

"No." Claire looked up again. Her eyes were more

than shadowed now, Tess saw. They were frantic. "I don't want him to know, not yet. You have to understand the enormous pressure he's under to be, well, ideal. In today's climate no one wants imperfection in their leaders. Once a flaw is dug out, as the press is hell-bent to do, it's maximized and twisted until it becomes a bigger issue than a man's record. Tess, you know what smears on a candidate's family life, his personal relationships, can do to his campaign."

"But you didn't ask me here to talk about Charlton's campaign."

"No." Claire hesitated. Once it was said, it couldn't be taken back. Twenty years of her life, and five more of her husband's, could hang in the balance of this one decision. "It's about Jerald. My son. I'm afraid he's, well, I don't think Jerald's been himself lately."

"In what way?"

"He's always been a quiet boy, a loner. You probably don't even remember him, though he's often attended receptions and other functions with us."

Tess had a recollection of a thin young boy who faded into corners. "I'm afraid I don't remember him well."

"People don't." Claire's smile flared and faded. With her hands in her lap she began to pleat the tablecloth. "He's very unobtrusive. Bright. Jerald's a terribly bright young man. He's in the top ten percent of his graduating class. He's been on the dean's list consistently through prep school. Several excellent private colleges have accepted him, though he'll follow tradition and attend Princeton." She began to talk quickly, too quickly, as though she were now on the down side of a roller coaster ride and frightened that she'd run out of breath. "I'm afraid he spends more time with his computer than with people. I can't understand the things myself, but Jerald's just a whiz with machines. I can honestly say I've never had a moment's trouble from him. He's never been rebellious or impolite. When friends would tell me how frustrated they were with their teenagers, I would just marvel that Jerald was always such a quiet, agreeable boy. Perhaps not overly affectionate, but good-natured."

"The ideal son?" Tess murmured. She knew how deceptive "perfection" could be, how many jagged flaws it could conceal.

"Yes, yes, exactly. He simply worships Charlton. Almost too much, you understand. At times I would be a bit uneasy about it, but it's so gratifying for a boy to look up to his father. In any case, we've never had to be concerned with the problems so many parents seem to face today. Drugs, promiscuity, defiance. Then lately—"

"Take your time, Claire."

"Thank you." After reaching for her glass, Claire sipped to moisten her dry throat. "In the last few months, Jerald's been spending more and more time on his own. He's locked himself in his room every night. I know how hard he studies and I've even tried to persuade him to slow down a bit. He looks so worn-out some mornings. His moods seem to swing. I know I've been tied up with the election and campaign, so I excused those swings. I've been a bit moody myself."

"Have you talked with him?"

"I've tried. Perhaps not hard enough. I didn't realize how difficult it could be to deal with. He came home from the library one night recently, and he was—Tess, he was a mess. His clothes were disheveled, his face was scratched up. It was obvious he'd been in a fight of some kind, but he would only say he'd fallen off his bike. I let it drop. I regret that now. I even let his father believe it, though I know Jerald had taken the car that night. I told myself he was entitled to his privacy and that, being a well-brought-up boy, he wouldn't get in over his head. But there's been something, something in his eyes lately."

"Claire, do you suspect Jerald is experimenting with drugs?"

"I don't know." For a moment she allowed herself the luxury of covering her face with her hands. "I don't know, but I do know we have to do something before it gets worse. Just yesterday Jerald was in a dreadful fight at school. He's been suspended. Tess, they're claiming he tried to kill the other boy . . . with his bare hands." She looked down at her own. Her wedding ring glinted up at her. "He's never been in trouble before."

Tess felt chilled to the bone. She swallowed hard, then asked in a carefully managed, neutral tone, "What does Jerald say about the fight?"

"Nothing, not to me. I know he spoke with Charlton, but neither of them will discuss it. Charlton's worried." Her gaze darted to Tess's, then shifted back to the tablecloth. "Charlton is trying to pretend he's not, but I can see it. I know how damaging this could be if it leaks to the press and I'm terrified about what it might do to his campaign. He keeps insisting that all Jerald needs is a few days to rest his mind and calm down. I wish I could believe it."

"Would you like me to talk to Jerald?"

"Yes." Claire reached over to take her hand. "Very much. I don't know what else to do. I've been a better wife, a better partner than a mother. Jerald seems to have slipped out of my hands. I'm really worried about him. He seems distant, and smug somehow, as though he knows something no one else does. I'm hoping that if he talks to someone outside the family, yet someone who's still one of us, he'll open up."

"I'll do what I can, Claire."

"I know you will."

$\mathcal{R}$ANDOLF LITHGOW HATED THE hospital. He hated Jerald Hayden for putting him there. It had been the humiliation more than the pain. How could he go back and face the other guys after he'd been beaten to a pulp by the class freak?

Little creep thought he was big shit on campus because his father was running for president. Lithgow hoped Charlton P. Hayden lost the election without pulling one state. He hoped he lost so bad he'd have to crawl out of Washington in the dead of night, dragging his crazy son with him.

Lithgow shifted in bed and wished, too, that it was time for visiting hours. He sipped through a straw and managed to swallow though his throat still burned like hell. He was going to make that pasty-faced nerd pay when he got back on his feet again.

Bored, restless, and feeling sorry for himself, Lithgow began to switch the television channels with his remote. He wasn't in the mood for the six o'clock news. He could get all that crap in Current Events when he went back to school. He flipped again and landed on a rerun of a situation comedy. He knew the damn dialogue in that old horse by heart. Swearing, he switched channels. More news. Just when Lithgow was about to give up and read a book, they flashed the sketch of Mary Beth Morrison's assailant on the screen.

He might have passed it by, but for the eyes. The eyes made him narrow his own. They were the same ones he'd seen as he was losing consciousness and Jerald's hands had squeezed the air out of him. Concentrating, he struggled to fill in the details the artist had missed. Before he was sure, absolutely sure, the image was replaced by a reporter. Excited, no longer restless, Randolf switched to the next network. He might see it again.

If he did, he had a pretty good idea what to do about it.

WE'RE GOING TO HAVE cruisers sweeping that area all night." Ben flipped the file closed. Ed was still staring at the map as though he were waiting for something to jump out at him. "He comes out, odds are they'll spot him."

"I don't like the odds." He glanced toward the hall. Upstairs, Grace was completing her third night as bait. "How many times do you figure we went through that quadrant today, in wheels and on foot?"

"Lost count. Listen, I still figure the school's a good shot. Wight might not have recognized the sketch, but he was nervous."

"People get nervous when cops come around."

"Yeah, but I've got a feeling something's going to click when Lowenstein finishes passing out the sketch to the students."

"Maybe. But that gives him tonight, and too many hours tomorrow."

"Look, there're two of us in the house. Billings is outside and we've got pass-bys every fifteen minutes. She's safer here than if we had her in lockup."

"I've been thinking about the psychiatric profile Tess worked up. Wondering why I can't seem to think like him."

"Could be because you've got both oars in the water."

"That's not it. You know how it gets when you're close to one of these. No matter how wacko, no matter how sick the perp is, you start to think like him, anticipate him."

"We are. That's why we're going to get him."

"We're not on the money." Ed ran his fingers over his eyes. They'd started aching by midafternoon. "And we're not on the money because he's a kid. The more I think about it, the more I'm sure of it. Not just because of Morrison's ID. Kids don't think the same way adults do. I always figured that's why they send kids to war, because they haven't faced their own mortality yet. It doesn't hit until a person's in his twenties."

It made Ben think of his brother. "Some kids are grown up by the time they hit sixteen."

"Not this one. Everything Tess has here leads not just to a psychotic but an immature one."

"So we think like a kid."

"He's probably done some pouting since he botched Morrison." Trying to ride with it, Ed began to pace the room. "It's just like she said, he was whining like a kid who busted his favorite toy. What does a real snot-nosed little brat do when he breaks his toy?"

"He breaks someone else's."

"Bull's-eye." Ed turned to him. "You're going to make a hell of a father."

"Thanks. Look, the rapes and attempteds that've come in since Morrison don't fit."

"I know." Hadn't he read every report word by word, hoping for a link? "Maybe he hasn't hit on another woman, that doesn't mean he hasn't hit. You know, when a rapist is prevented from following through, he only gets more frustrated and angry. And he's a kid. He has to take it out on someone."

"So you figure he was ready for a fight, looking to mix it up with some other kid?"

"I figure he'd go after someone weaker, someone he thought was weaker anyway. It'd make him feel better if it was someone he knew."

"So we can check the arrest reports for assaults over the last couple of days."

"And the hospitals. I don't think he'd settle for a little pushy-shovey."

"You're starting to think like Tess." Ben grinned at him. "That's why I love you. That's probably her now," he said as the phone rang. "I told her to give me a call when she got home."

"Tell her to push calcium." Ed picked up the file again. The tone of Ben's voice had him ignoring it.

"When? You got an address? You and Renockie cover us here and we'll take it. Look, Lowenstein, I don't give a shit who—*Who?* Christ." Ben ran a hand over his face and tried to think. "Get Judge Meiter, he's a Republican. No, I'm not kidding. I want the warrant in my hands in an hour or we go without it."

He hung up. If he could have risked it, he'd have taken a nice clean shot of vodka. "Got an identification on the sketch. A kid in Georgetown Hospital fingered a school buddy who tried to smother his windpipe. He's a senior at St. James's. The captain's sending someone down to get a written statement."

"Do we have a name?"

"Caller ID'd our boy as Jerald Hayden, address is smack dab in the middle of Billings's little square."

"Then let's move."

"We've got to go through channels on this one, partner."

"Fuck channels."

Ben didn't bother to point out that Ed was the one who always touched the system. "The kid's the son of Charlton P. Hayden, the people's choice."

Ed stared at him for several long seconds. "I'm going up to get Grace."

Ben barely nodded before the phone rang again. "Paris."

"Ben, I'm sorry to interrupt."

"Look, Doc, I can't tie up this phone."

"I'll be quick. I think it may be important."

With a check of his watch Ben figured Lowenstein still had fifty-eight minutes to come through. "Shoot."

"I'm skirting very close to patient confidentiality here." And that had worried her all during her soul-searching. "I talked with a woman today, a woman I know. She's concerned about her son. He was in an apparently serious fight at school yesterday. He nearly strangled another boy. Ben, a great deal of what she told me mirrors the profile on your serial killer."

"He broke someone else's toy," Ben murmured. "Give me a name, Doc." When he was met with silence, he pictured her, sitting at her desk wrestling with her oath and her conscience. "Play it this way. Tell me if this name sounds familiar. Jerald Hayden."

"Oh God."

"Tess, I need clout. We're already working on the warrant. A call from you would speed it up."

"Ben, I agreed to take this boy on as a patient."

There was no use swearing at her, he thought. She couldn't help herself. "Then you can consider it in his best interest for us to bring him in quick. And alive. Get in touch with Harris, Tess. Tell him what you told me."

"Be careful. He's much more dangerous now."

"You and Junior wait up for me. I'm crazy about you."

Ben put down the receiver as Ed led Grace into the room. "Ed says you know who he is."

"Yeah. You ready to retire as a phone mistress?"

"More than. How much longer before you have him?"

"We're getting a warrant. You're a little pale, Grace. Want a brandy?"

"No. Thanks."

"That was Tess." Ben took out a cigarette, lit it, and handed it to Grace. "Washington's a small town. She talked with Jerald Hayden's mother today. The lady thinks her kid needs a shrink."

"It's funny." Grace blew out a stream of smoke as she waited for it to sink in. "I thought when it happened it would be sort of climactic. Instead, it's a phone call and a piece of paper."

"Police work's mostly paperwork," Ed told her.

"Yeah." She tried to smile. "I've got the same problem with my job. I want to see him." She took another drag. "I still want to see him, Ed."

"Why don't we wait on that until we tie up loose ends?" He touched her cheek so that she turned her head to look at him. "You did what you needed to do, Grace. You have to let go of Kathleen now."

"Once it's done, and I can call my parents and . . . and Jonathan, I think I can."

IT TOOK LOWENSTEIN LESS than forty minutes to deliver the warrant. She slapped it into Ben's hand. "Hayden's blood type was on file at Georgetown Hospital. It's a match. Take him down. We'll cover the house until you call in."

"Stay." Ed put his hands on Grace's shoulders.

"I'm not going anywhere. Listen, I know the world needs heroes, but I figure I need you more. So be a good cop, Jackson, and watch yourself." Taking his shirtfront, she pulled him down for a kiss. "See you."

"Take care of his lady, Renockie," Ben said as they swung out the door. "I'd hate to see Ed drop-kick you."

Grace let out a long breath and turned to her new guards. "Anybody want some lousy coffee?"

CLAIRE HEARD THE DOORBELL ring and nearly swore with annoyance. If they didn't leave in five minutes they were going to be late. After signaling back the housekeeper, she smoothed down her hair and answered herself.

"Detectives Jackson and Paris." The badges Claire saw set off a slow, dull alarm within her. "We'd like to speak with Jerald Hayden."

"Jerald?" Years of training had her lips curving automatically. "What's this about?" The Lithgow boy, she thought. His parents were going to press charges.

"We have a search warrant, ma'am." Ben passed it to her. "Jerald Hayden is wanted for questioning in connection with the murders of Kathleen Breezewood and Mary Grice and the attempted rape of Mary Beth Morrison."

"No." She was a strong woman. She'd never fainted in her life. Now, she dug her nails into her palm until her vision cleared. "There's a mistake."

"Is there a holdup, Claire? We've pushed right to the time limit." Hayden strode to the door. The friendly impatience on his face changed only slightly when he saw the identification. "Officers, is there a problem?"

"It's Jerald." Claire dug her fingers into his arms. "They want Jerald. Oh God, Charlton. They're talking about murder."

"That's absurd."

"Your wife has the papers, Senator." Ed's usual compassion had dried up on the drive over. "We've been authorized to take your son down for questioning."

"Call Stuart, Claire." It was a time for lawyers, he thought. Though he didn't believe it, couldn't believe it, Hayden saw the years of building a strong, careful platform disintegrating. "I'm sure we can clear this up quickly. I'll send for Jerald."

"We'd prefer to go along," Ed said.

"Very well." Turning, Hayden started for the stairs. With every step he felt his life, his ambitions, his beliefs slip away. He could see clearly, painfully clearly, the look in Jerald's eyes as they'd sat in the dean's office. He held himself straight, as a courageous man would facing a firing squad, and knocked on Jerald's door.

"Excuse me, Senator." Ben reached around to push the door open. The light was burning, the radio playing quietly. And the room was empty.

"He must be downstairs." Cold sweat ran a line down Hayden's back.

"I'll go with you."

With a barely perceptible nod to Ben, Ed stepped inside Jerald's room.

It took under ten minutes to determine that Jerald

Hayden was no longer in the house. When Ben returned to the bedroom, the senator and his wife were with him.

"He's got quite a cache." Ed indicated the open desk drawer. "Please, don't touch anything," he warned Hayden as the senator stepped forward. "We'll have someone come down and log this. Looks like about forty grams of coke, maybe an eighth of a kilo of grass." He touched the lid of a jar with the tip of a pencil. "Some flake."

"It's a mistake." Hysteria began to bubble in Claire's voice. "Jerald doesn't take drugs. He's an honor student."

"I'm sorry." Ben looked from Claire to the computer which took up most of the desk, then to Ed. As Billings had said, the equipment was state-of-the-art. "He's not in the house."

𝒲HILE HIS MOTHER WAS sobbing in his bedroom, Jerald was climbing the fence between Ed's property and the Breezewood house. He'd never felt better in his life. His blood was pumping, his heart was hammering. Desiree was waiting for him, to take him beyond the mortal into forever.

Renockie drank coffee in the living room while Grace played with hers and watched the clock. Where was Ed? Why didn't he call?

"I guess you could say I'm a big fan of yours, Miss McCabe."

"I appreciate that, Detective."

"I waited to tell you until Lowenstein was out with Billings that I'm an amateur writer myself."

Who wasn't? she thought, then forced a smile. It wasn't like her to be unkind. "Oh, really? Are you writing detective novels?"

"Just short stories." His wide, pleasant face flushed with the admission. "You spend a lot of time in the car and just sitting and waiting in my business. Gives you a lot of time to think."

"Maybe you could show me something you've done."

"I wouldn't want to impose."

"I'd like to see it. Why don't you . . ." She trailed off when the expression on his face changed. She'd heard it too, a shuffling, the opening of a door.

"Why don't you go upstairs? Lock the door." He drew his weapon out as he took her arm. "Just in case."

She moved quickly and without argument. Renockie held his weapon in both hands, pointing up, as he moved.

In the bedroom, Grace stood with her back to the door, waiting, listening. It was probably nothing. How could it be anything? Ed had him by now. The phone would ring any minute and he'd tell her it was all over.

Then she heard a board creak and she jumped. Sweat was pouring down her forehead, into her eyes. Calling herself a fool, Grace wiped it away. It was just the aspiring writer coming to tell her all was clear.

"Desiree?"

The whisper dried every drop of sweat on her body. She tasted fear. It filled her mouth, but she couldn't swallow it. As she watched, the doorknob turned to the left, then to the right.

"Desiree."

Trapped. Trapped. The word ran through her mind over and over. She was alone, somehow alone with the man who'd come to kill her. Grace muffled the scream with both hands before it could burst out. She'd known he would come. She'd known yet still she was trapped. But she wasn't helpless. She scrambled to the drawer that held the gun and fumbled for it just as the door broke in.

He's a child, she thought as she stared at him. How could it be that this young boy with an alligator stitched on his shirt and a smattering of pimples on his chin had killed her sister? Then she looked into his eyes, and his eyes told the story.

"Desiree, you knew I'd come back."

"I'm not Desiree." He had a gun as well. Her heart nearly stopped when she saw it and the smear of blood on his wrist. He carried flowers in his other hand. A bouquet of pink carnations.

"It doesn't matter what you call yourself. You came back. You called me back."

"Don't." She lifted the gun as he took a step toward her. "Don't come near me. I don't want to hurt you."

"You can't." He laughed as though delighted with her. He'd never wanted anything more than he wanted her. Never wanted anything more than he wanted to please her. "We both know you can't hurt me. We're beyond that now, you and I. Remember what it was like? Remember, Desiree? Your life flowed out into my hands while mine flowed into you."

"You killed my sister. I know it. The police know it. They're coming."

"I love you." He stepped closer as he spoke, nearly hypnotizing her with those eyes. "It's only been you. Together we can do anything, be anything. You'll keep coming back to me. And I'll keep listening, and waiting. It'll be just like before. Time after time." He held out the flowers.

They heard the sound at the same time. Grace saw Renockie, the blood flowing down his face from where the butt of Jerald's gun had struck him. He was propped against the door, struggling to steady himself.

Jerald turned, his lips drawn back in a snarl. As he raised his gun, Grace fired.

WHAT THE HELL'S GOING on?" Ben and Ed raced up the walk just as Lowenstein managed to kick the front door in.

"I went to get doughnuts for Billings and tell him to wrap it up. When I came back, the door was locked." Weapons came out and the three of them entered and separated. Ed saw the blood. His gaze followed the trail upstairs. He'd already sprung forward when they heard the shot.

His heart stopped. He felt it wink out as he raced up. He heard Grace's name shouted, roared, but wasn't aware it came from him. Leaping over Renockie, he planted himself. He was ready, and more than willing to kill.

She'd slid to the floor so that her back rested against the bed. She still had the gun in her hand. Her face was colorless, her eyes dark and dazed. But she was breathing. Ed crushed carnations underfoot as he went to her.

"Grace?" He touched her, her shoulders, face, hair. "Grace, I want you to tell me if he hurt you. Look at me, Gracie. Talk to me." As he spoke, he eased the gun out of her hand.

"He was so young. I couldn't believe how young. He brought me flowers." Her eyes focused on Ed when he shifted between her and the body sprawled a few feet away. "He said he loved me." When she began to gasp, he tried to gather her to him, but she held him off. "No, I'm all right. I'm okay."

Lowenstein picked up the phone behind her. "According to Renockie, you saved his life. You handled yourself like a pro."

"Yeah." Grace rested her head on her hand a moment. "Ed, I'm okay, really. But I don't think I can stand up without some help."

"Lean on me," he murmured. "Just a little."

With her head resting against his shoulder, she nodded. "Okay."

"You're not going to make it, kid." Ben leaned over Jerald. He'd already examined the wound, and though Lowenstein was calling an ambulance, it wouldn't do any good. "If there's anything you want to get off your chest, now's the time."

"I'm not afraid to die." He didn't feel any pain. That made it all the sweeter. "It's the ultimate experience. Desiree knows. She already knows."

"Did you off Desiree and Roxanne, Jerald?"

"I gave them the best." Looking up, he saw Desiree's face floating above his. "Desiree."

Though Ed tried to draw her aside, Grace stood where she was and stared down at Jerald. She'd wanted a picture, and now she would carry it with her the rest of her life. She'd wanted justice, but at this moment she couldn't be sure just what that meant.

"I'll be back," he told her. "I'll be waiting. Remember." His lips curved before he died.

"Come downstairs, Grace." Ed pulled her from the room.

"Do you think we'll ever know why? Really why?"

"You learn to be satisfied with whatever answers you find. Sit down, I'll get you a brandy."

"I won't argue with that." She sat, elbows on knees and her face in her hands. "I told him I didn't want to hurt him. And thank God, I meant it. Once I saw him, saw how it was, I didn't hate him quite so much."

"Here, drink."

"Thanks." She managed one shaky sip, then a second stronger one. "So . . ." After a sniffle, she rubbed the back of her hand under her nose. "How was your day?"

He studied her a moment. Her color was coming back and her hands were steady. Tough lady, he thought. She was one tough lady. Crouching in front of her, he took the snifter from her hands. She opened her arms, and he gathered her to him.

"Oh Ed, I never want to be that scared again, ever."

"Me either."

She turned her head so that she could press her lips to his throat. "You're shaking."

"That's you."

On a half laugh, she held tighter. "Whatever."

Ben hesitated in the doorway, then cleared his throat. "Kiss off, Paris."

"In a minute," he promised his partner. "Look, we've got Renockie's statement, so there's no hurry for yours, Grace. We'll have our people in and out of here as soon as we can and leave you the hell alone."

"Thanks." Grace drew away from Ed far enough to hold out a hand. "You're a pal, Ben."

"I wish we'd been quicker." He took the offered hand and squeezed. "You've had a rough time, Gracie. Tess would want me to tell you that if you need to talk it through, she'll be there."

"I know. Tell her I'm glad to give her back her husband in the evenings."

Ben laid a hand on Ed's shoulder. "In the morning."

"Yeah." When Ben slipped out, Ed handed Grace the snifter again. "Try a little more."

"I could use the bottle." She heard the steps and voices on the stairs and knew what they meant. This time she didn't rise to watch. "Ed, would you mind? I don't want to stay here, I want to go home."

He touched her cheek before he rose. It wasn't possible to stay close to her when he was losing. "I'm sorry, Grace, it wouldn't be possible for you to go back to New York tonight. In a couple of days, after we've got the paperwork wrapped up."

"New York?" Grace set the brandy aside. She didn't need it after all. "I said I wanted to go home, Ed. That's next door." When he turned to stare down at her, she tried a half smile. "That is, if the offer still holds."

"It holds." He slipped his arms around her. "It's not much of a home yet, Grace. It needs a lot of work."

"My evenings are free." Content, she snuggled against him. "I never told you that when I first came I picked your house out as the one I'd most like to live in. Let's go home, Ed."

"Sure." He helped her to her feet.

"One thing." She dragged the heels of her hands over her face until she was sure it was dry. "I'm not going to iron your shirts."

ABOUT THE AUTHOR

Nora Roberts was the first writer to be inducted into the Romance Writers of America Hall of Fame. The *New York Times* bestselling author of such novels as *Montana Sky, Born in Ice, True Betrayals,* and *Divine Evil,* she has become one of today's most successful and best-loved writers. Nora Roberts lives in Maryland.

Read on for a taste of

Hot Ice

Available now from Buntam Books

$\mathcal{T}$RAFFIC WAS LIGHT ON the Long Island Expressway as Whitney headed into town. Her flight from Paris had landed at Kennedy an hour behind schedule. The back seat and trunk of her little Mercedes were crammed with luggage. The radio was turned up high so that the gritty strains of Springsteen's latest hit could ricochet through the car and out the open window. The two-week trip to France had been a gift to herself for finally working up the courage to break off her engagement to Tad Carlyse IV.

No matter how pleased her parents had been, she just couldn't marry a man who color-coordinated his socks and ties.

Whitney began to sing harmony with Springsteen as she tooled around a slower-moving compact. She was twenty-eight, attractive, moderately successful in her own career while having enough family money to back her up if things got really tough. She was accustomed to affluence and deference. She'd never had to demand either one, only expect them. She enjoyed being able to slip into one of

New York's posher clubs late at night and find it filled with people she knew.

She didn't mind if the paparazzi snapped her or if the gossip columns speculated on what her latest outrage would be. She'd often explained to her frustrated father that she wasn't outrageous by design, but by nature.

She liked fast cars, old movies, and Italian boots.

At the moment, she was wondering if she should go home or drop in at Elaine's and see who'd been up to what in the past two weeks. She didn't feel jet lag, but a trace of boredom. More than a trace, she admitted. She was nearly smothered with it. The question was what to do about it.

Whitney was the product of new money, big money. She'd grown up with the world at her fingertips, but she hadn't always found it interesting enough to reach for. Where was the challenge? she wondered. Where was the— she hated to use the word—purpose? Her circle of friends was wide, and from the outside appeared to be diverse. But once you got in, once you really saw beneath the silk dresses or chinos, there was a sameness to these young, urbane, wealthy, pampered people. Where was the thrill? That was better, she thought. Thrill was an easier word to deal with than purpose. It wasn't a thrill to jet to Aruba if you only had to pick up the phone to arrange it.

Her two weeks in Paris had been quiet and soothing— and uneventful. Uneventful. Maybe that was the crux. She wanted something—something more than she could pay for with a check or credit card. She wanted action. Whitney also understood herself well enough to know she could be dangerous in this kind of mood.

But she wasn't in the mood to go home, alone, and un- pack. Then again, she wasn't feeling much like a club crowded with familiar faces. She wanted something new, something different. She could try one of the new clubs that were always popping up. If she liked, she could have a couple of drinks and make conversation. Then, if the club interested her enough, she could drop a few words in the right places and make it the newest hot spot in Manhattan. The fact that she had the power to do so didn't astonish her, or even particularly please her. It simply was.

Whitney squealed to a halt at a red light to give herself time to make up her mind. It seemed like nothing was happening in her life lately. There wasn't any excitement, any, well, zing.

She was more surprised than alarmed when her passenger door was yanked open. One look at the black zippered jacket and wraparound glasses of the hitchhiker had her shaking her head. "You aren't keeping up with fashion trends," she told him.

Doug shot a look over his shoulder. The street was clear, but it wouldn't be for long. He jumped in and slammed the door. "Drive."

"Forget it. I don't drive around with guys who wear last year's clothes. Take a walk."

Doug stuck his hand in his pocket, using his forefinger to simulate the barrel of a gun. "Drive," he repeated.

She looked at his pocket, then back at his face. On the radio the disk jockey announced a full hour of blasts from the past. Vintage Stones began to pour out. "If there's a gun in there, I want to see it. Otherwise, take off."

Of all the cars he could've picked . . . Why the hell wasn't she shaking and pleading like any normal person would've done? "Dammit, I don't want to have to use this, but if you don't throw this thing in gear and get moving, I'm going to have to put a hole in you."

Whitney stared at her own reflection in his glasses. Mick Jagger was demanding that someone give him shelter. "Bullshit," she said, her diction exquisite.

Doug gave a moment's consideration to knocking her cold, dumping her out, and taking the car. Another glance over his shoulder showed him there wasn't much time to waste.

"Look, lady, if you don't get moving, there're three men in that Lincoln coming up behind us that'll do a lot of damage to your toy here."

She looked in the rearview mirror and saw the big, black car slowing down as it approached. "My father had a car like that once," she commented. "I always called it his funeral car."

"Yeah—get it in gear or it's going to be my funeral."

Whitney frowned, watching the Lincoln in her rearview mirror, then impulsively decided to see what would happen next. She threw the car into first and zipped across the intersection. The Lincoln immediately picked up the pace. "They're following."

"Of course they're following," Doug spat out. "And if you don't step on it, they're going to crawl into the back seat and shake hands."

Mostly out of curiosity, Whitney punched the gas and turned down Fifty-seventh. The Lincoln stayed with her. "They're really following," she said again, but with a grin of excitement.

"Can't this thing go any faster?"

She turned the grin on him. "Are you kidding?" Before he could respond, she gunned the engine and was off like a shot. This was definitely the most interesting way to spend the evening she could imagine. "Think I can lose them?" Whitney looked behind her, craning her neck to see if the Lincoln was still following. "Ever see Bullitt? Of course, we don't have any of those nifty hills, but—"

"Hey, watch it!"

Whitney turned back around and, whipping the wheel, skimmed around a slower-moving sedan.

"Look." Doug gritted his teeth. "The whole purpose of this is to stay alive. You watch the road, I'll watch the Lincoln."

"Don't be so snotty." Whitney careened around the next corner. "I know what I'm doing."

"Look where you're going!" Doug grabbed the wheel, yanking it so that the fender missed a car parked at the curb. "Damn idiot woman."

Whitney lifted her chin. "If you're going to be insulting, you'll just have to get out." Slowing down, she swung toward the curb.

"For God's sake don't stop."

"I don't tolerate insults. Now—"

"Down!" Doug hauled her sideways and pulled her down to the seat just before the windshield exploded into spiderweb cracks.

"My car!" She struggled to sit up, but only managed to twist her head to survey the damage. "Goddamn it, it didn't have a scratch on it. I've only had it for two months."

"It's going to have a lot more than a scratch if you don't step on the gas and keep going." From his crouched position, Doug twisted the wheel toward the street and peered cautiously over the dash. "Now!"

Infuriated, Whitney stepped hard on the accelerator, moving blindly into the street while Doug held on to the wheel with one hand and held her down with the other.

"I can't drive this way."

"You can't drive with a bullet in your head either."

"A bullet?" Her voice didn't crack with fear, but vibrated with annoyance. "They're shooting at us?"

"They ain't throwing rocks." Tightening his grip, he spun the wheel so that the car bumped into the curb and around the next corner. Frustrated that he couldn't take the controls himself, he took a cautious look behind. The Lincoln was still there, but they'd gained a few seconds. "Okay, sit up, but keep low. And for Chrissake keep moving."

"How'm I supposed to explain this to the insurance company?" Whitney poked up her head and tried to find a clear spot in the broken windshield. "They're never going to believe someone was shooting at me and I've already got a filthy record. Do you know what my rates are?"

"The way you drive, I can imagine."

"Well, I've had enough." Setting her jaw, Whitney turned left.

"This is a one-way street." He looked around helplessly. "Didn't you see the sign?"

"I know it's a one-way street," she muttered and pressed harder on the gas. "It's also the quickest way across town."

"Oh, Jesus." Doug watched the headlights bearing down on them. Automatically he gripped the door handle and braced for the impact. If he was going to die, he thought fatalistically, he'd rather be shot, nice and clean through the heart, than be spread all over a street in Manhattan.

Ignoring the screams of horns, Whitney jerked the car to the right, then to the left. Fools and small animals, Doug thought as they breezed between two oncoming cars. God looked out for fools and small animals. He could only be grateful he was with a fool.

"They're still coming." Doug turned in the seat to watch the progress of the Lincoln. Somehow it was easier if he didn't watch where he was going. They bounced from side to side as she maneuvered between cars, then with a force that threw him against the door, she turned another corner. Doug swore and grabbed for the wound on his arm. Pain began again with a low, insistent thud. "Stop trying to kill us, will you? They don't need any help."

"Always complaining," Whitney tossed back. "Let me tell you something, you're not a real fun guy."

"I tend to get moody when somebody's trying to kill me."

"Well, try to lighten up a bit," Whitney suggested. She barreled around the next corner, skimming the curb. "You're making me nervous."

Doug flopped back in his seat and wondered why, with all the possibilities, it had to end this way—smashed into unrecognizable pulp in some crazy woman's Mercedes. He could've gone quietly with Remo and had Dimitri murder him with some ritual. There'd have been more justice in that.

They were on Fifth again, moving south at what Doug saw was better than ninety. As they went through a puddle, water slushed up as far as the window. Even now, the Lincoln was less than a half block behind. "Dammit. They just won't shake lose."

"Oh yeah?" Whitney set her teeth and gave the mirror a quick check. She'd never been a gracious loser. "Watch this." Before Doug could draw a breath, she whipped the Mercedes around in a tight U-turn and headed dead-on for the Lincoln.

He watched with a kind of fascinated dread. "Oh my God."

Remo, in the passenger seat of the Lincoln, echoed the sentiment just before his driver lost courage and steered toward the curb. The speed took them over it, across the sidewalk, and with an impressive flourish, through the plate-glass window of Godiva Chocolatiers. Without slackening pace, Whitney spun the Mercedes around again and cruised down Fifth.

Dropping back in his seat, Doug let out a series of long, deep breaths. "Lady," he managed to say, "you got more guts than brains."

"And you owe me three hundred bucks for the windshield." Rather sedately, she pulled into the underground parking of a high rise.

"Yeah." Absently, he patted his chest and torso to see if he was all in one piece. "I'll send you a check."

"Cash." After pulling into her space, Whitney turned off the ignition and hopped out. "Now, you can carry my luggage up." She popped the trunk before she strolled toward the elevator. Maybe her knees were shaking, but she'd be damned if she'd admit it. "I want a drink."

Doug looked back toward the entrance of the garage and calculated his chances on the street. Maybe an hour or so inside would give him the chance to outline the best plan. And, he supposed, he owed her. He started to haul out the luggage.

"There's more in the back."

"I'll get it later." He slung a garment bag over his shoulder and hoisted two cases. Gucci, he noted with a smirk. And she was bitching about a lousy three hundred.

Doug walked into the elevator and dumped the two cases unceremoniously on the floor. "Been on a trip?"

Whitney punched the button for the forty-second floor. "A couple of weeks in Paris."

"Couple of weeks." Doug glanced at the three bags. And she'd said there were more. "Travel light, do you?"

"I travel," Whitney said rather grandly, "as I please. Ever been to Europe?"

He grinned, and though the sunglasses hid his eyes, she found the smile appealing. He had a well-shaped mouth and teeth that weren't quite straight. "Few times."

They measured each other in silence. It was the first opportunity Doug had had to really look at her. She was taller than he'd expected—though he wasn't altogether sure just what he'd expected. Her hair was almost completely hidden under an angled white fedora, but what he could see was as pale as the punker's he'd stopped on the street, though a richer shade. The brim of the hat shaded her face, but he could see a flawless ivory complexion over elegant bones. Her eyes were round, the color of the whiskey he'd downed earlier. Her mouth was naked and unsmiling. She smelled like something soft and silky you wanted to touch in a dark room.

She was what he'd have termed a stunner, though she didn't appear to have any obvious curves beneath the simple sable jacket and silk slacks. Doug had always preferred the obvious in women. Perhaps the flamboyant. Still, he didn't find it any real hardship to look at her.

Casually, Whitney reached in her snakeskin bag and drew out her keys. "Those glasses are ridiculous."

"Yeah. Well they served their purpose." He took them off.

His eyes surprised her. They were very light, very clear, and green. Somehow they were at odds with his face and his coloring—until you noticed how direct they were, and how carefully they watched, as if he were a man who measured everything and everyone.

He hadn't worried her before. The glasses had made him appear silly and harmless. Now, Whitney had her first stirrings of discomfort. Who the hell was he, and why were men shooting at him?

When the doors slid open, Doug bent to pick up the suitcases. Whitney glanced down and noticed the thin stream of red dripping down his wrist. "You're bleeding."

Doug looked down dispassionately. "Yeah. Which way?"

She hesitated only a moment. She could be just as cavalier as he. "To the right. And don't bleed on those cases." Breezing past him, she turned the key in the lock.

Through annoyance and pain, Doug noticed she had quite a walk. Slow and loose with an elegant sort of swing. It made him conclude that she was a woman accustomed to being followed by men. Deliberately he came up alongside her. Whitney spared him a glance before she pushed open the door. Then, flicking on the lights, she walked inside and went directly to the bar. She chose a bottle of Remy Martin and poured generous amounts into two glasses.

Impressive, Doug thought as he took stock of her apartment. The carpet was so thick and soft he could be happy sleeping on it. He knew enough to recognize the French influence in her furnishings, but not enough to pin down the period. She'd used deep sapphire blue and mustard yellow to offset the stunning white of the carpet. He could spot an antique when he saw one, and he spotted quite a few in this room. Her romantic taste was as obvious to him as the Monet seascape on the wall. A damn good copy, he decided. If he just had the time to hock it, he could be on his way. It didn't take more than a cursory glance to make him realize he could fill his zippered pockets with handfuls of her fancy French whatnots to pawn for a first-class ticket that would get him far away from this burg. Trouble was, he didn't dare deal in any pawnshop in the city. Not now that Dimitri had his tentacles out.

Because the furnishings weren't of any use to him, he wasn't sure why they appealed. Normally he would have found them too feminine and formal. Perhaps after an evening of running, he needed the comfort of silk pillows and lace. Whitney sipped her cognac as she carried the glasses across the room.

"You can bring this into the bathroom," she told him as she handed him his drink. Negligently she tossed the fur over the back of the sofa. "I'll take a look at that arm."

Doug frowned while he watched her walk away. Women were supposed to ask questions, dozens of them. Maybe this one just didn't have the brains to think of them. Reluctantly he followed her, and the trail of her scent. But she was classy, he admitted. There was no denying it.

"Take off that jacket and sit down," she ordered, running water over a monogrammed washcloth.

Doug stripped off the jacket, gritting his teeth as he peeled it from his left arm. After carefully folding it and laying it on the lip of the tub, he sat on a ladder-back chair anyone else would have had in their living room. He looked down and saw the sleeve of his shirt was caked with blood. Swearing, he ripped it off and exposed the wound. "I can do it myself," he muttered and reached for the cloth.

"Be still." Whitney began to wipe away the dried

blood with the soapy warm cloth. "I can't very well see how much damage was done until I clean it up."

He sat back because the warm water was soothing and her touch was gentle. But while he sat back, he watched her. Just what kind of woman was she? he wondered. She drove like a nerveless maniac, dressed like Harper's Bazaar, and drank—he'd noticed she'd already knocked back her cognac—like a sailor. He'd have been more comfortable if she'd shown just a touch of the hysteria he'd expected.

"Don't you want to know how I got this?"

"Hmmm." Whitney pressed a clean cloth to the wound to slow the new bleeding. Because he wanted her to ask, she was determined not to.

"A bullet," Doug said with relish.

"Really?" Interested, Whitney removed the cloth to get a closer look. "I've never seen a bullet wound before."

"Terrific." He swallowed more cognac. "How do you like it?"

She shrugged before she slid back the mirrored door of the medicine cabinet. "It's not terribly impressive."

Frowning, he looked down at the wound himself. True, the bullet had only nicked him, but he had been shot. It wasn't every day a man got shot. "It hurts."

"Aw, well we'll bandage it all up. Scratches don't hurt nearly so much if you can't see them."

He watched her root through jars of face cream and bath oils. "You've got a smart mouth, lady."

"Whitney," she corrected. "Whitney MacAllister." Turning she offered her hand formally.

His lips curved. "Lord, Doug Lord."

"Hello, Doug. Now, after I fix this up, we'll have to discuss the damage to my car and the payment." She went back to the medicine cabinet. "Three hundred dollars."

He took another swallow of cognac. "How come you know it's three hundred?"

"I'm giving you the low end of the scale. You can't fix a spark plug in a Mercedes for less than three hundred."

"I'll have to owe you. I spent my last two hundred on the jacket."

"That jacket?" Amazed, Whitney twisted her head and stared at him. "You look smarter."

"I needed it," Doug tossed back. "Besides, it's leather."

This time she laughed. "As in genuine imitation."

"What d'you mean, imitation?"

"That zippered monstrosity didn't come off any cow. Ah, here it is. I knew I had some." With a satisfied nod, she took a bottle from the cabinet.

"That little sonofabitch," Doug mumbled. He hadn't had the time or the opportunity to look too closely at his purchase before. Now, in the bright bathroom light, he saw it was nothing more than cheap vinyl. Two hundred dollars' worth. The sudden fire in his arm had him jerking. "Goddamn it! What're you doing?"

"Iodine," Whitney told him, smearing it on generously.

He settled down, scowling. "It stings."

"Don't be a baby." Briskly, she wrapped gauze around his upper arm until the wound was covered. She snipped off tape, secured it, then gave it a final pat. "There," she said, rather pleased with herself. "Good as new." Still bent over, she turned her head and smiled at him. Their faces were close, hers full of laughter, his full of annoyance. "Now about my car—"

"I could be a murderer, a rapist, a psychopath for all you know." He said it softly, dangerously. She felt a tremor move up her back and straightened.

"I don't think so." But she picked up her empty glass and went back into the living room. "Another drink?"

Damn, she did have guts. Doug grabbed the jacket and followed her. "Don't you want to know why they were after me?"

"The bad guys?"

"The—the bad guys?" he repeated on an astonished laugh.

"Good guys don't shoot at innocent bystanders." She poured herself another drink, then sat on the sofa. "So, by process of elimination I figure you're the good guy."

He laughed again and dropped down beside her. "A lot of people might disagree with you."

Whitney studied him again over the rim of her glass. No, perhaps good was too concise a word. He looked more complicated than that. "Well, why don't you tell me why those three men wanted to kill you."

"Just doing their job." Doug drank again. "They work for a man named Dimitri. He wants something I've got."

"Which is?"

"The route to a pot of gold," he said absently. Rising, he began to pace. Less than twenty dollars in cash nestled with an expired credit card in his pocket. Neither could buy his way out of the country. What he had carefully folded in a manila envelope was worth a fortune, but he had to buy himself a ticket before he could cash it in. He could lift a wallet at the airport. Better, he could try rushing on the plane, flashing his fake ID, and play the hard-bitten, impatient FBI agent. It had worked in Miami. But it didn't feel right this time. He knew enough to go with his instincts.

"I need a stake," he muttered. "A few hundred—maybe a thousand." Thoughtfully, he turned back and looked at Whitney.

"Forget it," she said simply. "You already owe me three hundred dollars."

"You'll get it," he snapped. "Dammit, in six months I'll buy you a whole car. Look at it as an investment."

"My broker takes care of that." She sipped again and smiled. He was very attractive in this mood, restless, anxious to move. His exposed arm rippled with muscle that was subtle and lean. His eyes were lit with enthusiasm.

"Look, Whitney." He came back and sat on the arm of the sofa beside her. "A thousand. That's nothing after what we've been through together."

"It's seven hundred dollars more than what you already owe me," she corrected him.

"I'll pay you back double within six months. I need to buy a plane ticket, some supplies..." He looked down at himself, then back at her with that quick, appealing grin. "A new shirt."

An operator, she thought, intrigued. Just what did a pot of gold mean to him? "I'd have to know a lot more before I put my money down."

He'd charmed women out of more than money. So, confidently, he took her hand between his, rubbing his thumb over her knuckles. His voice was soft, compelling. "Treasure. The kind you only read about in fairy stories. I'll bring you back diamonds for your hair. Big, glittery diamonds. They'll make you look like a princess." He skimmed a finger up her cheek. It was soft, cool. For a moment, only a moment, he lost the thread of his pitch. "Something else out of a fairy story."

Slowly, he removed her hat, then watched in astonished admiration as her hair tumbled down, over her shoulders, over her arms. Pale as winter sunlight, soft as silk. "Diamonds," he repeated, tangling his fingers through it. "Hair like this should have diamonds in it."

She was caught up in him. Part of her would have believed anything he said, done anything he asked, as long as he continued to touch her in just that way. But it was the other part, the survivor, who managed to take control. "I like diamonds. But I also know a lot of people who pay for them, and end up with pretty glass. Guarantees, Douglas." To distract herself, she drank more cognac. "I always want to see the guarantee—the certificate of value."

Frustrated, he rose. She might look like a pushover, but she was as tough as they came. "Look, nothing's stopping me from just taking it." He snatched her purse off the sofa and held it out to her. "I can walk out of here with this or we can make a deal."

Standing, she plucked it out of his hands. "I don't make deals until I know all the terms. You've got a hell of a nerve threatening me after I saved your life."

"Saved my life?" Doug exploded. "You damn near killed me twenty times."

Her chin lifted. Her voice became regal and haughty. "If I hadn't outwitted those men, getting my car damaged in the process, you'd be floating in the East River."

The image was entirely too close to the truth. "You've been watching too many Cagney movies," he tossed back.

"I want to know what you have and where you intend to go."

"A puzzle. I've got pieces to a puzzle and I'm going to Madagascar."

"Madagascar?" Intrigued, she turned it over in her mind. Hot, sultry nights, exotic birds, adventure. "What kind of puzzle? What kind of treasure?"

"My business." Favoring his arm, he slipped on the jacket again.

"I want to see it."

"You can't see it. It's in Madagascar." He took out a cigarette as he calculated. He could give her enough, just enough to interest her and not enough to cause trouble. Blowing out smoke, he glanced around the room. "Looks like you know something about France."

Her eyes narrowed. "Enough to order escargots and Dom Pérignon."

"Yeah, I bet." He lifted a pearl-crusted snuffbox from the top of a curio cabinet. "Let's just say the goodies I'm after have a French accent. An old French accent."

She caught her bottom lip between her teeth. He'd hit a button. The little snuffbox he was tossing from hand to hand was two hundred years old and part of an extensive collection. "How old?"

"Couple centuries. Look, sugar, you could back me." He set the box down and walked to her again. "Think of it as a cultural investment. I take the cash, and I bring you back a few trinkets."

Two hundred years meant the French Revolution. Marie and Louis. Opulence, decadence, and intrigue. A smile began to form as she thought it through. History had always fascinated her, French history in particular with its royalty and court politics, philosophers and artists. If he really had something —and the look in his eyes convinced her he did—why shouldn't she have a share? A treasure hunt was bound to be more fun than an afternoon at Sotheby's.

"Say I was interested," she began as she worked out her terms. "What kind of a stake would be needed?"

He grinned. He hadn't thought she'd take the bait so easily. "Couple thousand."

"I don't mean money." Whitney dismissed it as only the wealthy could. "I mean how do we go about getting it?"

"We?" He wasn't grinning now. "There's no we."

She examined her nails. "No we, no money." She sat back, stretching her arms on the top of the sofa. "I've never been to Madagascar."

"Then call your travel agent, sugar. I work alone."

"Too bad." She tossed her hair and smiled. "Well, it's been nice. Now if you'll pay me for the damages..."

"Look, I haven't got time to—" He broke off at the quiet sound behind him. Spinning around, Doug saw the door handle turn slowly—right, then left. He held up a hand, signaling silence. "Get behind the couch," he whispered while he scanned the room for the handiest weapon. "Stay there and don't make a sound."

Whitney started to object, then heard the quiet rattle

of the knob. She watched Doug pick up a heavy porcelain vase.

"Get down," he hissed again as he switched off the lights. Deciding to take his advice, Whitney crouched behind the sofa and waited.

Doug stood behind the door, watching as it opened slowly, silently. He gripped the vase in both hands and wished he knew how many of them he had to go through. He waited until the first shadow was completely inside, then lifting the vase over his head, brought it down hard. There was a crash, a grunt, then a thud. Whitney heard all three before the chaos began.

There was a shuffle of feet, another splinter of glass—her Meissen tea set if the direction of the sound meant anything—then a man cursed. A muffled pop was followed by another tinkle of glass. A silenced bullet, she decided. She'd heard the sound on enough late-night movies to recognize it. And the glass—twisting her head she saw the hole in the picture window behind her.

The super wasn't going to like it, she reflected. Not one bit. And she was already on his list since the last party she'd given had gotten slightly out of hand. Dammit, Douglas Lord was bringing her a great deal of trouble. The treasure—she drew her brows together—the treasure better be worth it.